In the Name of Honor

Book One of the Vows & Valor Trilogy

"A classic fantasy told in a modern voice. With vibrant characters, a compelling evil, and a well-crafted world, *In the Name of Honor* delivers something for every fantasy reader. You will root for the good guys, boo the bad, and when the story winds to the end, you'll want more."

—Kaitlin Corvus, author of the *Sorrow's Forest* Duology

"*In the Name of Honor* is a refreshing debut for traditional fantasy lovers and will excite anyone eager to be lost to another time and place. Between characters readers will grow to steadfastly declare their favorite, the delicacies of families both lost and found, and the conclusion focused on a tough and detailed battle, readers of great fantasies will find themselves unable to put *In the Name of Honor* down. The sweeping landscapes, hollowed woods, and heartfelt friendships of *In the Name of Honor* take readers from their earthly existence into that which the Collinses created. The Collinses present a promising start to a trilogy sure to bring both tears and hearts filled with joy."

—Erica Rose Eberhart, author of *The Elder Tree* Trilogy

"A fresh breath of air for epic fantasy lovers, Courtney and Clarke Collins' debut is an action-packed, heart-wrenching, romantic, and modern spin on *The Lord of the Rings*. With explorations of grief, friendship, betrayal, loss, and fantastical creatures both familiar and new, *In the Name of Honor* will gallop into and wedge itself right into readers' hearts."

—C.W. Rose, author of *Oceansong*

"This author duo achieved something special with *In the Name of Honor*. Somehow, the Collinses captured the fantastical world I grew

up yearning to experience, inserted a dynamic and lovable cast of characters, and left me craving another chapter to fill the hollow ache it left when I finished. I laughed out loud, swallowed back tears, and fell in love with a glorious cheese thief. What's more, when I thought it couldn't get any better, the Collinses whispered a delicious promise to me: there is more to come, and the core four are just getting started."
—Kassidy Coursey, author of *The Sins of the Maker* Trilogy

"Courtney and Clarke Collins have managed to create a world that is both familiar and unique in this touching adventure story. *In the Name of Honor* reads like a love letter to every little girl who grew up reading Tolkien. The characters come to life so vividly, they feel like old friends—and the raw, honest inclusivity of the cast is so natural and earnest, it's like a breath of fresh air."
—Katie Abdou, author of *A Prince Among Pirates*

"Perfect for fans of Kristen Britain and Susan Dennard, *In the Name of Honor* is an adventure fantasy novel worthy of every shelf. It sucked me in from page one and never let up!"
—Claire M. Andrews, author of the *Daughter of Sparta* Trilogy

IN THE NAME OF HONOR

VOWS & VALOR BOOK I

COURTNEY & CLARKE
COLLINS

In the Name of Honor

Book One of the Vows & Valor Trilogy

Map by: Tiffany Munro

Cover design by: David Gardias

Corruptor cover art by: Black Meadow VT

To my parents, who always told me I should write:
my father, who is my first and best storyteller,
and my mother—I miss you every day.
—Courtney

To all those seeking friends in unexpected places,
honor to guide a path forward,
and love to shine in the shadows.
—Clarke

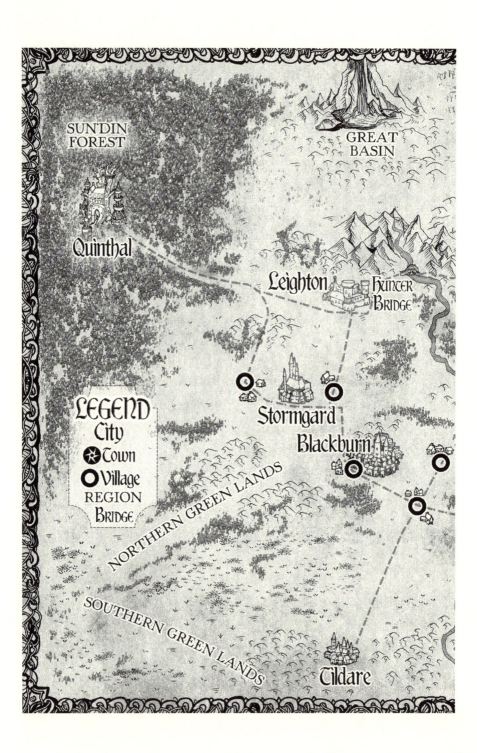

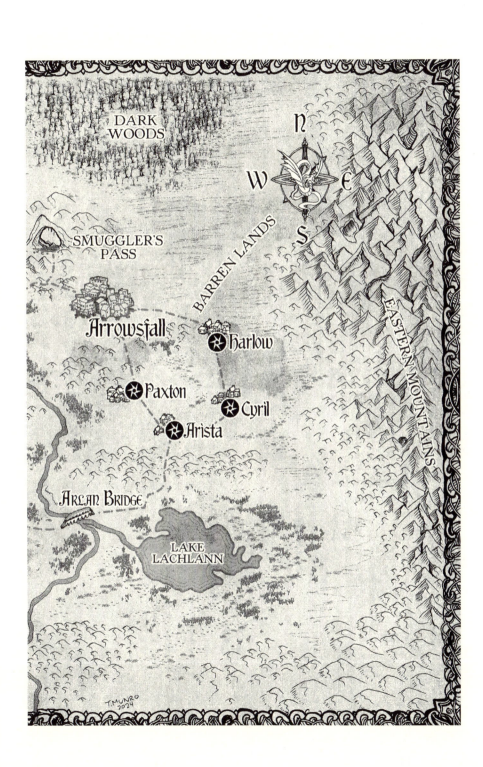

IN THE NAME OF HONOR

Courtney and Clarke Collins

SHADOW SPARK PUBLISHING

PART ONE

1

DIMITAR

Dimitar raced along the road, carrying the worst message possible. He urged his horse a step faster, muscles trembling with fatigue. He rode himself and Deepshade too hard and expected his stallion to falter well before they reached Blackburn. The news he carried gave him little choice.

A tinge of light chased the nighttime hours away, catching up with Dimitar as he rode up and down the worn hillside paths. In the distance, early morning fog parted over towering slabs of weathered stone that comprised the castle's outer wall. Saying a silent prayer of gratitude to the gods, he lifted himself in the saddle and clucked for whatever speed Deepshade had left.

Almost home.

Blackburn's city stretched out below the castle, a vast mosaic of stores and houses lining the cobble-paved streets. Additional thick stone ramparts a story high ran around the entire town, broken twice by wide, ironclad gates, securing the people within. Dimitar aimed for one of the gates, preparing himself to meet with the king.

For the hundredth time, he grasped the satchel at his waist. Hefting it, Dimitar shifted the gold signet's weight, relieved the hard ride hadn't knocked the precious ring loose. Its presence reminded him of the grave message circling in his mind. Reaching further back along the saddlebag, he unfastened a banner with three entwined, silver circles resting on a deep-blue field, hoisting the pole end into the crook of the saddle flap.

3

Blackburn's banner uncurled with a whip, tossed by urgency, and the gatemaster set about opening the portcullis as fast as one man could. Dimitar streaked through the half-opened entrance and tore his way down the main street.

"What burr snuck up your arse?" the gate master yelled after him as he began the arduous task of closing the door.

Dimitar came to a halt at the castle's stables. Ignoring the stable hand's shocked expression as he glanced over the horse's condition, he dismounted and hurried into the castle, toward the throne room. A lone guard stood watch at the door, his halberd recently polished given the smell of oil surrounding him, done most likely out of boredom in the early morning hours.

"'Lo there, Dimitar. What news from the north?"

Dimitar winced, and the guard's welcoming grin disappeared under a concerned frown. Dimitar's raven hair, normally well-kept, fell around his face, limp and disheveled. He pushed the strands back, wavering on saddle-weary legs. This relentless fatigue aged him past his twenty-four years. Of all the times he'd come and gone bearing word from other kingdoms over the years, never had he exhausted himself to this extent.

Never had a message been so urgent.

"Is he in there? I need to see him. Now."

The guard straightened to attention, gaze sharpening. "Wait here. I'll announce your arrival."

Dimitar leaned against the doorframe, willing his legs to keep standing as he collected himself. His appearance was beyond help, so instead he focused on replaying the message one last time in his mind. The words came to him without fail, seared into his mind from sharp memorization. On reflex, his hand touched the satchel again. His breath drew tight; he'd soon repeat these words to his king, the man who gave his heart a purpose and his hand a sword when he needed it most.

And I'm about to destroy his world.

The door opened, and the guard's voice issued forth. "The king will see you now."

Dimitar half-heartedly tapped his fist against his chest, returning salute to the guard as he gathered the last of his strength, trying to find confidence in his step.

King Kahled, known as an early riser, sat on the throne with his chamberlain before him. A sudden burst of color illuminated the throne, the sun coming forth from behind the lifting mist and casting its light through one of the many stained-glass windows set high on the ceiling.

Dimitar had learned from tales passed around the Tankard Inn that the Blackburn throne room was once an empty, cold hall, as intimidating and powerful as its ruler, King Rayburn, a High Knight like Kahled. When Rayburn perished in the great Reclamation War, leaving no heritage, Kahled received the throne and steadily transformed the lengthy chamber.

Thick tapestries now buffered the stone walls, detailed designs interwoven in rich velvet. Tall suits of armor lined the walls, steel glimmering from careful polishing. Kahled replaced the harsh, stone thrones with ones fashioned from carved wood, featuring the intricate, circled knot work of Blackburn's insignia and padded with plush cushions. The room was still impressive, and no one who entered doubted Kahled as a powerful king, yet the overall impression was one of welcome over intimidation.

Little of that warmth reached him now as Dimitar approached his king, who raised a finger at him to indicate he needed a moment.

While King Kahled ran through the day's business with the chamberlain, Dimitar got a chance to take in the man he served. Kahled wasn't truly striking in any of his features: neither tall nor short, thin nor heavy, handsome nor hideous. The lines upon his face chronicled a lifetime of joy and sorrow, and he held himself with a strength that eclipsed his late middle-age years.

Dismissing the chamberlain, Kahled turned to him, reminding Dimitar why even the largest of men quivered under the weight of this man's gaze. He wagered Kahled's enemies would falter beneath the steel-gray depths, having been judged and found wanting.

Dimitar reached the throne base and took a knee, stifling a groan.

Kahled's rich baritone voice filled the room. "You're late."

It wasn't an accusation, but also not quite a question. Dimitar had the chance to either defend himself or take responsibility for his actions. Either way, Kahled wouldn't force his hand.

"I'm sorry, Your Majesty. I had no choice." Dimitar raised his head and caught astonishment shadowing his king's face. Oh gods, had he disappointed his king? He pushed himself back to his feet. "I traveled as fast as I could."

Kahled's raised hand cut his explanation short. "When did you last get sound rest?"

"I... I don't know. Two, maybe three days ago."

Kahled's face melted into empathy, any signs of consternation at Dimitar's late arrival erased in seconds. He clapped his hands twice, and right away a servant appeared from a side entrance. "Prepare a room and bath for Dimitar."

Without a blink of hesitation, the servant bowed and left the room.

"We'll speak when you've restored yourself."

"It can't wait." Dimitar willed the emotion out of his voice, digging for whatever strength he had left. "I must—"

"What you must do," Kahled spoke louder, rising from his seat to leave the chamber, "is rest. I've seen men in your state, and..."

Dimitar stood fast, refusing to follow, his determination driven by something he hoped the king wouldn't catch in his eyes: fear. He couldn't hold it in any longer.

"The Corrupted are back."

A slight tremble betrayed his voice. He'd somehow kept the message's meaning distant in his mind during the near week of travel, but speaking the words brought out the distress he'd tried to keep at bay. For a second, his own fear mirrored that in the great High Knight's eyes, gone as quickly as it emerged. Was it an illusion brought on by his exhaustion? The paleness of the scar that snaked its way down Kahled's cheek told otherwise.

As if to comfort Dimitar, or perhaps to support himself in the wake of this terrible news, Kahled wrapped his arm around Dimitar's shoulders and pulled him to sit together on the steps leading to the throne. Dimitar could only guess at the memories of death and feral shadow hordes unfolding behind the king's eyes, the war against the Corrupted creatures reawakened after a quarter century.

"Then it's as Conrad feared." Kahled heaved a sigh and clapped Dimitar's shoulder. "Continue with your message."

Dimitar's muscles bunched with tension at the touch. He didn't want to hurt this man. Bracing himself, Dimitar repeated the words he'd so painstakingly memorized. "'The Corrupted have returned. They ambushed us in the middle of the night and killed many of my men with little warning. Those who survived drove the creatures off, but this is a sign of more to come. Send word to King Kahled of Blackburn, fellow High Knight and friend. We need to vanquish this enemy now, lest they build again. Only he can stop this before it begins.'"

"Who gave this message to you? Did you not speak with King Conrad? You were instructed to meet with him personally."

"No, Your Majesty, a messenger bore the king's words." Dimitar looked to the floor. His throat ached from holding the next words back.

"Why didn't Conrad tell you, himself?"

Dimitar hesitated. For all his knighthood training thus far, for all the skills and maturity he'd achieved, he couldn't bring himself to tell Kahled the second part of the message.

Kahled's gaze sharpened. "You're not telling me everything."

Gods, give me courage. Dimitar opened his mouth but couldn't find the words, and shook his head, overwhelmed. Instead, he held out the leather satchel. Kahled raised an inquisitive eyebrow, untying the bindings and shaking out the contents into his hand. The signet ring landed with a soft sound, and Dimitar clenched his jaw. Daring a look into the great man's eyes, he found not anger nor fear, but profound grief.

"The courier told me King Conrad thought of you in his last breath, sire." Now the words came, breaking through his defenses, a relief at unburdening the message yet with heartache for its truth. "I'm late because I rode further past Stormgard than planned. I received word that King Conrad left to investigate claims of Corruptor sightings near the Barren Lands in the northeast, about a week before I arrived. I hurried to catch up and met a returning messenger from his company. He gave me this ring and showed me a letter addressed to Stormgard's royal council that King Conrad dictated after he was attacked and before he... passed away."

Kahled raised his eyes from the ring, and Dimitar answered his unspoken question. "I saw the seal on the letter. Would that I could say otherwise, but the seal's genuine."

"And the words?" Kahled rasped, clenching the ring with a shaking hand.

"Aye, sire."

When Dimitar had delivered his first message between the two kings years ago, Kahled made him memorize a series of elvish words that he and Conrad used to sign all of their correspondence. Dimitar was never told what the phrasing meant and wasn't versed in elvish anyway, but guessed the ritual came from their High Knight training within the elven Sun'Din Forest. As much as he wished the words were missing from the message, they'd been there as always, this time etched in the weakened print of a dying man.

Kahled squeezed his eyes shut as if willing away the sight of the ring in his palm and the truth of its significance. A long moment passed before he turned to Dimitar. "Go rest now. You've done well. Report back to me at sunset; I'll confer further with you then."

Dimitar nodded and pulled himself to a shaky stand. The last few days had passed in a blur, and just the thought of rest sapped any remaining strength. He saluted his king with a low bow, fist against his heart, and paused before turning to leave. "I'm sorry to bear the news of King Conrad's death."

"Aye, Dimitar." Kahled's voice scratched over the words, gruff with checked sorrow. He rose from the stairs and made his way back to the throne, dropping into it. "He was a brother on the field and the closest of friends. He'll be missed by many more than just those in his kingdom."

Dimitar bowed his head before exiting the room, leaving Kahled clutching the signet ring. His leaden feet were determined to keep him planted to the ground. A servant led him to the room Kahled ordered prepared, and only due to the warm bath and quarters ahead could he convince his body to keep moving. After closing the door, Dimitar let the emotions he'd kept at bay over the last several days breach. Slumping his back against the wood, he slid to the floor and lowered his head into hands that shook with a mix of dismay and sorrow.

2

DIMITAR

Dimitar eased into the hot, fragranced water, savoring the warmth bringing life back to his sore muscles. As the knots in his legs and lower back unwound, he grimaced with aches in places not felt since beginning knighthood training twelve years ago. Although his limbs complained of the motions, he set about scrubbing himself with the soft cloth and soap bar beside the copper tub. When his body bore some semblance of cleanliness, he leaned back and breathed in the lavender and bergamot in an attempt to further loosen his tired muscles. The soothing aromas worked wonders, and he relaxed.

Bits of familiar sounds floated through an open window: the scrape of clashing steel, the occasional holler and often an answering curse. He wasn't far from the training grounds. Drowsy, additional warmth seeped across his body from a deep-seated satisfaction of home.

The walls around the castle were a haven to him. Yet the very idea of home tied into a single person, someone he considered family. *The only family I have.* Dimitar shifted in the tub, draping a warm washcloth over his eyes. His best friend would be anxious to learn of his arrival, late as he'd been. He was the one person who knew Dimitar longer and better than any other, who'd grown by his side like a brother and who—

"Up ya go, ya lazy whelp."

The booming voice ruptured his calm, followed by a deluge of frigid water drenching his upper body. Dimitar bolted upright, sputtering and howling as ice-cold rivulets soaked his head and dripped without mercy down his chest. Glaring at the hearty laughter from one eye, he wiped hair out of his face and muttered a string of curses taught years ago, fittingly, by the man before him.

"You bastard." Dimitar flung the wet washcloth in Olaf's direction. "You know that's not funny."

Olaf dodged out of the way, the washcloth slopping to the floor. "Aye, it shouldn't be. But it's well worth the look on yer face."

Olaf retreated a few steps anyway, taking a seat. After weeks of instruction in the summer sun alongside Dimitar and the other guardsmen trainees, his creamy brown skin had darkened, radiating his smile. A smattering of freckles crossed the bridge of his nose to his cheeks, where a perpetual boyish grin undermined the enormity of his height and size. Olaf never let him forget that as the elder of the two at a full twenty-five years, his wisdom and worldly knowledge vastly outranked Dimitar's.

"The look on my face was from my heart nearly stopping." With a final shiver and scowl Dimitar scooped warmer bathwater over his shoulders. "You know, the same look you get when you wake up too late and miss breakfast."

"If you were half the man I am, you'd understand what it means to miss a meal. I'm still growin', don't ya know."

Dimitar gestured at his friend's sizable height and girth. "Olaf, I *am* half the man you are."

"And more's the pity, I say. Otherwise, ya might stand a chance against me in the fighters' circle."

"I don't need a chance," Dimitar shot back, pulling himself out of the water and wrapping the towel around his waist. Lobbing a pointed look at Olaf, he added, "I have skill."

"Not with keepin' a schedule." Olaf's grin faded as he eyed Dimitar's stiff movements.

Dimitar grabbed another towel to dry off his limbs and rake across his hair. He then reached for his clothes, noting they'd been taken away for cleaning. A new guard uniform identical to Olaf's lay on a bench, the deep blue tunic pressed and folded with the city's three-ring insignia embroidered on the back. Mindful of his aching muscles, Dimitar slipped on the clean underclothes and breeches, and tugged the tunic over his head.

Olaf let out a yawn. "So, what kept ya this time?"

Dimitar pulled on his boots and strapped the hand-and-a-half blade to his waist with practiced ease as he jerked his head toward the voices passing in the hallway. The castle staff's tempo picked up into full swing with morning chores, and in a matter of minutes they'd enter his suite to drain the bath and tidy up.

"This isn't the place to tell you. Let's go for a walk. Someplace more private."

Dimitar's legs complained, but he willed them forward through the castle halls. Olaf caught him up on all the city happenings while he was gone. Since the information came from Olaf, half the reports revolved around which tavern received the best ale shipment or which knights in training fell to his mighty axe during practice, but the news put Dimitar at ease. Something about life moving along at its normal pace despite the information he carried from up north put things into perspective.

They headed to the guard barracks. This late in the morning, the rest of the guards attended to various duties out and about the castle and city, lending extra privacy. A breeze swept through the common area thanks to open windows, easing the blended odors of sour sweat, leather, and steel-working oil. Once inside, Dimitar sat on a chair by the door and ran a hand through his damp hair.

Olaf appraised him with a deepening frown, dragging over a chair and flipping it around to sit opposite him. "What happened?"

Dimitar told Olaf about the last week and a half of travel, ending with Kahled's reaction. The message's weight dragged at him, tension reknitting the back of his neck, but Olaf wanted to hear every single detail.

Kahled had long ago permitted Dimitar to review his reports with Olaf. Not only was it difficult to keep a secret between the two, but Olaf was the best strategist among the knights in training. Belying his towering size and quick laugh, Olaf analyzed situations with a tactician's mind, and it wasn't long before his mentors realized his ability. Dimitar often wondered if Kahled secretly valued Olaf's advice almost as much as that of the knights who served on his council.

When he finished, Olaf crossed his arms, considering. "That's a big weight to carry, lad. How ya doin' with it?"

Dimitar shrugged but took comfort in the question. Olaf might be the biggest, most intimidating-looking man he knew, but he'd supported Dimitar since they were young boys. Dimitar's small fists were ablaze at even the most minor offenses when he'd first arrived at the orphanage, to the point where he didn't know why he threw the first punch. But Olaf did. Somehow, he knew just what Dimitar needed, much like now. Olaf could always read him like a damn book.

"It's just, when I told Kahled..." Dimitar trailed off and slumped in his seat, resting his forearms on his thighs. A knot lodged in his gut. "The way his face fell; I did that to him."

"Messenger's guilt."

"Aye, a whole lot of messenger's guilt."

"What about the man who brought the letter? What's he like?"

"Now that you say it, I've never dealt with him." To Olaf's raised eyebrow, Dimitar added, "I would've remembered him."

"What do ya mean by that?"

"He wasn't that talkative, and I don't mean how everyone in this world is compared to your big mouth. He had a bit of an accent; I couldn't place it, though. He wore a scarf around his head, maybe to catch the sweat from this bugger heat." Dimitar circled a hand around his forehead and ears.

"And this didn't strike ya as odd?"

"Hells, I don't know. He wore the right gear and knew the right names. And I checked and double-checked the message; the words he carried are true."

"Or forged."

"No, it couldn't have been. The elven words were there." Dimitar shook his head. "Only the High Knights know that greeting."

"Aye, you're right, lad. Somethin' ain't rubbin' me right, and I'm just pickin' on the messenger." With a sigh, he added, "I'll figure it out."

"You always do." Dimitar stretched his arms over his head, pulling out the kinks that had worked themselves into his back again.

"We better head down to South Gate." Olaf stood and clapped his hands together once. "I don't look forward to sweatin' m'balls off on the wall today, but that's where we're assigned, at least until they need us to help get the knights ready. If I know King Kahled, he's gonna meet with his council and prepare to leave."

"He might want to consult with Stormgard's delegation first, though. Maybe send a messenger ahead."

"King Conrad asked him to take up arms against the Corrupted. Not only is he asked by his friend but also a neighborin' king and High Knight. If Corruptors are comin', he can't waste time."

Dimitar let Olaf's words sink in. They stood on the brink of war against a foe of infamous legend. He'd grown up alongside tales of the evil creatures that almost took over the world as he knew it; stories of ravaged cities and victory led by High Knight warriors. A shiver ran up Dimitar's spine, and he shuddered.

"Exactly my thoughts, lad," Olaf said.

They headed out across town to the South Gate where ramparts gave them a full view of the main courtyard. A large group of Blackburn's knights gathered, dust kicked up underfoot, gritty and dry from summer's heat. Some wore their full uniform, while others had just arrived from home, armor and weaponry strapped to their horses. All of them harbored the same solemn expression as they conferred with one another.

As the afternoon passed and shadows grew long in the streets, their shift ended, and it came time to meet with Kahled again. Dimitar took his leave from Olaf, who made him swear they'd share a drink later.

He waited in the castle throne room, caught up studying a noticeably foreign suit of armor against the far wall. Darkened to a dull gray, the steel reflected his solemn expression as clearly as if from a mirror. He reached out a hand to touch the metal but snapped his arm back, no longer alone. Kahled waited behind him, arms crossed over his chest and an unexpected smile on his lips.

Dimitar dropped into a bow. "Your Majesty, I didn't hear you."

"You have a good eye for quality." Kahled lifted the arm of the armor. "This suit is the best in the room. Dwarven-hammered steel mined so deep within their mountains, none save the most daring have ventured there. Lighter than most steel yet so hard it's nigh impenetrable. 'Tis armor truly suited for a king."

"Where did you get it?"

"A gift, given to me for my feats in the Reclamation War. Conrad has its exact mirror in his court." With a chuckle, Kahled added, "Although I dare say his is taller than mine."

Kahled's grin disappeared, and pain clutched behind his eyes. He turned toward the thrones. "Come sit by me."

Dimitar's mind raced as he walked up the short steps and gingerly took one of the councilors' chairs next to Kahled's throne. This was it. He'd proved himself time and time again in training and was now ready to stand alongside Kahled and his knights. The call to join the gathering knights bestowed the honor he'd worked so hard for. *Surely, he'll ask Olaf to join us too. He's as ready as I am.*

"I have an important assignment for you. Something I trust no one else with."

Dimitar straightened with sharp interest. Of all the guardsmen he served alongside, what could he be worthy of over another? "I live only in your service, as you see best to honor me."

"You've served me well in recent years. Your abilities haven't gone unnoticed, and..." Kahled paused, as if regrouping his thoughts. "I see myself in you. You carry something in your heart that I share, which drives you to fight and protect. One day you'll be a great knight and warrior."

Heat flushed Dimitar's face. He trusted his own skills as a fighter, confident he'd someday be recognized with knighthood. Yet he never dreamed of being compared to the High Knight he'd grown up idolizing.

"I'm honored you think so"—Dimitar bowed his head—"but I have much training to do before I could even spar your shadow, I'm afraid."

Kahled raised his hand. "I didn't call you here to discuss your prowess with a sword. I summoned you because I need your help. I cannot have you accompany our troops tomorrow. King Conrad's death hit my daughter hard, more than I would wish. Kaleela is weighed down by grief but may soon fall to anger. I need someone to look after her, to guard her until I return. You must do this for me, Dimitar."

Kahled's words sunk in and struck him speechless. Being told outright not to join his king's troops as they marched north was one thing; being asked to stay behind and mind the princess was a different matter. Dimitar's confidence, which had soared to new heights a few moments ago, plummeted.

This is how my hard work in drill is rewarded? With more guard duty?

"Sire, of course I'll do whatever you ask, but couldn't I serve you better fighting alongside you?" Dimitar said, trying to hide the disappointment in his voice.

"You're not looking past your training," Kahled said, his tone patient. "Honor isn't always won with a swinging blade. For every soldier who kills an enemy, a warrior protected him while he attacked. I survived the Reclamation because of those around me, not by my skills alone. I need you, Dimitar, to stay here, as the battlefront extends far beyond the front lines. Kaleela is the true heart of my kingdom, and you will be her guardian."

Dimitar's frustration abated as he listened to the sincerity in Kahled's words. Placed in his safekeeping was the one joy remaining in the High Knight's life, the one person treasured above all else. Kahled wouldn't leave Blackburn unless Kaleela was well-looked after, and he honored Dimitar with that distinction.

Pride worked its way back as he bowed to Kahled. "It would be my honor."

"The gratitude is mine. I'll meet with my council and let them know your duties."

"She'll be safe in my care, sire." He bowed low once more, and Kahled dismissed him.

Dimitar left the castle in search of Olaf, both eager for and apprehensive of his friend's reaction to Kahled's decree. Evening fires sprung up in several makeshift fire pits as guardsmen and knights continued into the night to gather necessary supplies for early morning departure. As Dimitar weaved a path around the goings-on, stopping here and there to inquire about Olaf's last known whereabouts, his thoughts drifted to Kahled's daughter. All other distractions unconsciously faded as he recalled her image.

3

KALEELA

Kaleela stared down the shaft's length as her hand settled into the anchor point against the corner of her mouth. Focusing on the target, the heat in her arm, and the angle of the bow's draw, numbed away her broken parts. She lingered in the blessed stillness, until the moment she aligned her entire body just-so, a knowledge born of her training and innate from her blood. The arrow sliced through the air and hit the target in the middle of a bullseye cloth secured over a bale. Without stopping to admire her aim, she grabbed another bolt and this time pulled back the string, aimed, and shot in between a single breath. The second shot landed less than an arrow's tip from the first, grazing the innermost circle.

It had been too long since her last practice.

The late-morning sun warmed her back, but a light summer breeze kept the heat from becoming uncomfortable. She ran a gloved hand down her doe-brown surcoat layered over a lightweight, cream underdress. She should don the traditional mourning outfit, grays and veils to reflect the light of a life now gone. Why wasn't she mourning yet?

Instead, Kaleela had cleared the training arena from almost all guards and servants, gathering as much seclusion as permitted to a royal family member. On any other occasion, the weather was perfect for one of her escapes into the forest surrounding the kingdom. There, she'd find peace from the daily demands within the castle, and her elven senses would sharpen to the pleasant hum of the trees.

But not today. The comforting retreat within the trees would loosen more heartache than she was willing to bear. Father understood her need for this connection within the woods, but Conrad always argued about her coming and going unescorted. Fighting the brief tremor in her chin, Kaleela drew another arrow. Wetting her thumb against her lips, she stroked back the feathers as she aimed and released. She noted its equal accuracy before signaling a servant boy to retrieve the arrows.

Kaleela closed her eyes, running her bare thumb and gloved forefinger over her eyelids. Her body thrummed from the exertion, yet her eyes felt heavy, tired. Images had plagued her dreams over the course of the night, Corruptors' claws shredding Conrad's body, the horrible beings feasting on his remains. She tried to fight them in these nightmares, to save the man whom she loved like a second father. Yet some force held her powerless, every arrow she let loose flying wide, and she wept in agony from the futility, waking in tears.

Her mind was leaden, a dull roar in her ears removing her from the past day's overwhelming sorrow. She welcomed this barrier and practiced her weapon for the past hour with unrelenting determination. As such, her senses were somewhat muddled. With instinct rather than conscious thought, she notched an arrow against her bow's string and turned to challenge the man in the shadows of a nearby tree.

"Good morning, Your Highness."

Kaleela recognized his face as he stepped into the sunlight, and relaxed her aim. She spun back toward the target, drawing quick and sure, releasing another perfect shot as if requiring no effort whatsoever. Only the slight heaving of her breath betrayed the weariness.

He's come for me. I don't need this. The unfairness of her situation sat upon her chest, a dull ache. She remained focused on the target, and her voice revealed nothing. "You should be more careful, Dimitar. I could've put this arrow in your heart."

Another arrow, a short *whip*, and a bullseye hit.

With cautious steps, Dimitar walked over to her, stopping at a respectful distance. Taking in the pierced target, he said, "I believe you could, my lady. I just didn't want to disturb your practice."

"That would take more"—Kaleela wetted her thumb and sighted down another shaft—"than you standing beside me," she finished, and let go. This shot landed so close to the last arrow that it sheared off one of the feathers. *Much better.*

Dimitar shook his head as he looked over the cluster in the bullseye. "Then I'll stand here if it doesn't bother you, my lady."

Kaleela waved at her servant to collect arrows and glanced at Dimitar. His dark hair was half-tied back save a few pieces that escaped onto his forehead, tanned from the summer sun. At least she didn't have to look too far up at him; she didn't like when men towered over her. He carried a seriousness about him, from their situation or his regular demeanor she wasn't yet sure. His hand rested casually against the sword pommel, but his thumb tapped a steady, nervous beat.

"Why do you attend my practice?"

"I'm here to guard you, my lady. While your father—"

"While my father is away, I know." *Gone seeking the revenge I should be a part of.* Kaleela tugged at the well-worn leather arm guard and resumed her shooting. "What I'm wondering, is why you found it necessary to guard me while I practice with a weapon that I'm more than able to defend myself with."

Dimitar hesitated. "I thought it best to make sure you were safe."

"And have I satisfied your concern?" Although she meant the words in jest, her voice came out husky with the weight of checked grief, and she avoided his gaze, reluctant to reveal what she held behind the surface.

Dimitar glanced aside with a small frown, as if debating what to do next. He then took a few strides toward her, closing the distance, and his voice pitched low with earnestness. "I'm sorry about the loss of King Conrad. I know he was important to you and your father."

Kaleela let loose her next shot as he searched her face. Her bolt drove into the target's edge, nicking the side of the bale. Dimitar glanced at her missed shot, then back at her, and this time she turned to him. As their gazes locked, a wave of deep grief pummeled her, and she blinked back the stinging sorrow. Wordless empathy flickered across Dimitar's eyes, as blue as the summer sky.

Kaleela wrestled with his compassion, undermining her carefully veiled emotions. She'd never felt indignant toward her father before, stung by his assigning a protector to mind her like a child. She knew Dimitar from receiving the messages he retrieved and delivered on her father's behalf throughout the northern Green Lands. On the occasions she presented in court beside her father, Dimitar always acknowledged her with a respectful smile along with his obeisance. She could think of worse people to guard her, although she resented her father overprotecting her in the first place.

Silence followed as Kaleela turned back to the target, Conrad's name an echo. With a small bow, Dimitar began to retreat, and for the first time that morning, she relaxed her hold on the string. As her defenses tumbled, she yearned to hear Conrad's name again, as if doing so would bring him closer to her once more.

"Wait, Dimitar." She stopped him. "You're welcome to stay a while."

"I apologize if I spoke out of turn, my lady."

"You have nothing to apologize for." She called forward the servant to readjust the target to a farther distance. Surprising herself as much as him, she said, "Did you know him well?"

"Do you mean King Conrad?" Dimitar asked, and she nodded slowly. "Not as well as I would've wished. I delivered quite a few messages to him from your father. I can expect a nice bed and meal at any other castle your father sends me to, but in Stormgard, they give me a knightly welcome." With a grin, he added, "And oftentimes a knightly share of their ale, I'm afraid to say."

"That doesn't surprise me." She cracked a fleeting smile and considered Dimitar, leaning on her bow. "Did you know Conrad's friendship with my father began with a duel to the death?"

"No, not at all." Dimitar blinked in surprise. "I thought they were like brothers."

"'Tis true, they're very much connected, perhaps more so than most people realize. But not at first." Kaleela hesitated, debating whether or not to share further. "Would you like to hear about it?"

"Absolutely." He broke into a curious grin, and Kaleela gestured to a nearby bench.

The morning breeze teased out tendrils of sunlit hair around her face, and she brushed them aside before removing the protective archer gloves, working them off her three middle fingers. She took a drink from a water skin, the cool sweetness a balm.

"Father and Conrad were among a hundred men selected for the High Knight training in the Sun'Din Forest. The elven king offered the honor of wearing my mother's colors to the knight of greatest skill and wisdom for inspiration. That got the men all riled up, as Conrad tells it: boasting, exaggerating, and trying to win her attention. And in the end, she chose Father."

As Kaleela settled into the familiar family story, a lightness returned to her shoulders. "Conrad didn't take the rejection well and wouldn't let it go. The day came when he dropped his gauntlet at my father's feet in challenge. Father didn't wish a fight, but his honor was in question. They dueled before the elven royalty and other High Knight men well into an hour. Here, Father would tell you Conrad made a mistake; Conrad would say he just got tired of looking at my father's face."

Dimitar laughed aloud, and Kaleela's eyes crinkled as she continued. "At any rate, Conrad slipped up, and Father had him by the blade point, pinned to the ground."

"Your father didn't kill him though."

"No, he did Conrad one better: he offered him a hand up. Conrad took his hand but remained on one knee, asking forgiveness. Father wouldn't accept until Conrad got to his feet. He forgave Conrad for the challenge, but did so on equal ground. Conrad said he enjoyed Father immensely from that moment on."

Dimitar laughed again and, despite the weight of her sorrow, Kaleela laughed too.

"And Conrad helped raised you, here in Blackburn?"

Kaleela nodded, growing serious once more. "Conrad waited alongside my father for the day I was born, in the Sun'Din Forest. My father was... overwhelmed when my mother died. And then the Reclamation War happened, and they were granted kingships afterwards. Father lost himself for a long while. Conrad came here often, and I had my entire childhood with him. We were a family."

She cut off her next words, a salty pang rising in the back of her throat as the pain of Conrad's loss returned. This time, something else brewed inside her, a spark that kindled a new emotion.

"Conrad was a far greater man... No man deserved his fate." Kaleela hid behind her façade as she slid her gloves back on. She picked up her bow and plucked an arrow from the ground-mounted quiver. "Thank you for listening, but I must ask you to leave me." She raised a hand before he could protest. "I'll be safe here. I just want to be alone right now."

She met his gaze, helpless to hide the haunted grief shadowing her, and was once again struck by the understanding in Dimitar's face.

"Your Highness." He bowed and turned back toward the castle.

Kaleela dropped her bow to her side, contemplating his retreating form until well out of sight.

4

KALEELA

Kaleela winced as she adjusted the chest guard armor straps. A long time had passed since she last put on the sun-hardened leather by herself. Her window of opportunity faded along with the dimming candlelight in her room. Stretching her fingers and calming her rising frustration, she started over with the fastenings. This time she whispered the instructions to herself, recalling the steps Conrad had taught her, newly of age, a dozen years before. He'd made her repeat them until satisfied. The memories made her resolution that much stronger.

Pulling the last buckle tight, she checked her suite to make sure she hadn't forgotten anything. She blew out the candle and headed for the door, grabbing the knapsack she'd packed earlier that evening. The corridor remained clear and silent, as expected. Kaleela increased her pace as she headed toward the stable grounds.

Since childhood, Kaleela had mastered the art of escaping the castle walls undetected. At times, she yearned to break away from constant guard and sought comfort in the nearby forests. The trees quieted her mind and played a soft melody in her heart that she guessed rooted itself in her elven blood. The guards at the castle, in turn, became very good at keeping her escorted both in and outside the kingdom's walls; yet she was even better at finding holes in their routines.

The leather soles of her knee-high boots beat a soft, steady rhythm on the stone floor. As she approached the next corridor, Kaleela froze. Her sensitive ears picked up the hushed tones of someone approaching, and within mere seconds their paths would intersect. Rising onto her tiptoes, she spun across the hall with silent steps into a niche concealed by ornamental armor. A moment later, two maids emerged around the corner, passing with their heads put together as they gossiped with muted giggles.

Her heart pounded against her ribcage, and only after she'd taken several breaths without detecting further footsteps did Kaleela step out from the shadows and continue out the nearest door. The price for being out of her room at this hour, unescorted, was steep indeed. Her father's absence wouldn't lessen the confinement placed upon her should she be caught, for the kingdom's advisors were well aware of the level of protection both Kahled and Conrad demanded she receive.

Focusing on the need for success, Kaleela entered the stable, warm hay smells curling in her nose. She dug into one of the piles and pulled out a saddlebag laden with supplies, including her bow and quiver. She looked over the horses with an appraising eye, settling on one of her favorites, a feisty mare.

At first displeased to be called to service this late at night, ears back and nostrils flared, the horse relaxed to Kaleela's gentle touch and accepted the heavy saddlebags and gear. Leading her out the stable doors, Kaleela flinched at the sudden creak from the hinge as she secured the bolt. Moving deeper into the shadows as clouds rolled over the moon, she pulled herself into the saddle and situated herself comfortably. In her mind, Kaleela traced the path she needed to take out of Blackburn's walls.

She would leave to join her father and his troops as they marched to attend the council called for in Conrad's last breath. When Kahled had come to her suite and told her the course of action decided upon, her grief silenced her, still too raw. She sat rigid on her chaise, subdued by numbness, as he kissed her head and told her to remain safe and in charge within the castle until his return. Time since then had allowed his departure to set in, and the day's archery practice helped clear her mind. Now, the consequence of Conrad's death, of his *murder*, settled in her, senses igniting with anger, growing in each passing moment.

I refuse to be left out of his retribution.

With the dark night welcoming her ride, Kaleela started to dig in her heels but stopped as a shadow stirred and came to stand before her.

Kaleela cursed silently, her impulse to spur the horse forward, but the cloaked figure blocked her path. She instead addressed the man in a stern tone. "Who stands in my way? Show yourself, and step aside, by my command."

"No."

Kaleela sat back in her saddle, startled. Who she assumed was one of the castle guards or stable hands would never speak to her this way. She urged her horse forward a few steps, hoping to intimidate the man to yield, but instead, he drew closer.

"Stand back..." she began, then the man lowered his hood.

Dimitar glanced at her and pressed a finger to his lips. Kaleela was about to ask him the meaning of his behavior when she caught low footsteps in the distance. She froze, tilting her head as the night watch guard's steps passed across the courtyard.

Kaleela looked back at Dimitar, his gaze piercing her as unspoken intentions warred between them. Dark hair swept his shoulders, tousled by the gentle night air. A lightweight cloak, clasped against his upper chest, hung over the swell of his shoulders.

"Dimitar." Kaleela exhaled and lifted her chin, willing good sense to return to her.

"Forgive me, Your Highness, for startling you," he said in a low voice and with a bow of his head, "but you must return to the castle."

"I'm out for a night ride." She tried to keep the soft tone of her voice carefree. "The summer days are too hot, and I often go out at nighttime to stretch my mare's legs in cooler temperatures."

A poor excuse, but she trusted he wouldn't question her authority. Dimitar looked over the overloaded saddlebags and weaponry strapped to her back, before putting his hand on the reins. "I'm afraid I cannot allow this, my lady."

Kaleela shot him a pointed look. "Allow it? And who, pray tell, says I need your permission?"

"Your father."

A flicker of doubt made her hesitate. Before she could mount an argument, he continued. "I'm not happy to be here either, Your Highness. I'd rather be with my king, sword at hand. But he ordered me to watch over you."

"I don't need you for that," Kaleela retorted, her voice gaining heat. She yanked the reins, but Dimitar's grip held strong.

"Apparently you do, my lady." Her gaze scorched the night air as he spoke with insistence. "Because you're heading into certain death if you leave to join your father. He goes to face Corruptors, not passing marauders. I've seen your skills with that weapon, but you're no match for a Corruptor. None of us here are."

"That doesn't matter." A hitch scratched its way into her voice. She swallowed to clear her throat and tasted an edge of salty tears close to surfacing. Angry with herself at this sign of fatigue, she pressed on.

"I was trained by High Knights," Kaleela said, pride infusing her words, "and I'll do what I must to avenge Conrad's death. If that means riding into the midst of those ungodly creatures to destroy each and every one of them, then so help me, I will."

Another yank at the reins proved futile.

"I don't doubt you would. But leaving in the middle of the night, without your guards and secretive like a thief, isn't the way to honor him. What would your father say if he received word that you're missing?"

That lump in her throat would never leave. "Conrad was a father, too."

The grounds fell silent, not a word, night bird, or choking cry echoing inside her mind to break the sudden stillness.

She gazed at Dimitar, her chest aching but no longer holding the wild, unchecked pace of her grief. It would be easier to resist if he was arrogant or demanding, instead of this disarming compassion she didn't ask for or want.

She lessened her grip on the reins. "Father has an eager streak that I inherited. I fear I don't have enough elven blood to hold back. I'll stay... but not for long."

"It may not have to be, Your Highness. Before your father rode off, he told me he'd send a message of how things fared. He spoke of returning something only you could identify, so we'd know it came from him. Will you wait until then? For your father."

She bit her lower lip and looked away, tucking a loose wave of hair behind her delicate, pointed ear. *Why didn't Father tell me about this message?* But she knew the answer to that. She didn't have the patience to wait for it.

Kaleela looked past Dimitar into the night, as if seeking some guidance from the dark, before turning back to him. "Until then, but no longer. I *will* see Conrad avenged."

"And hopefully I'll be there to help you," he replied.

She looked at him anew. *He's not just offering false reassurance. He's serious.*

Before she could think more upon his words, he raised a hand to help her off the horse, who pawed the ground in apparent restlessness. Kaleela considered his offered hand, still reluctant to give up her intentions, then swung her leg over the side. She was unprepared when he lifted her down with firm hands upon her waist, her feet touching the ground with unexpected lightness. *Oh... he's quite strong.* With a quick blush to her cheeks, she took the reins once more and led the horse back into the stables.

Dimitar followed, untying the saddlebags' belts and hefting them off the mare with a grunt. He chuckled, unsuccessfully muffling the sound.

"What's so amusing?" she asked, her brow furrowed.

"You've never packed one of these, have you?" Dimitar set the bags on the ground with a thump.

"Of course I have," she said with a jut of her chin. Dimitar bowed his head in acknowledgement, but his smile didn't waver. She held back a scowl and shifted her weight on her feet a few times. Finally, she could stand it no longer. "Out of curiosity, why do you ask?"

Dimitar's tone was neutral, although his eyes danced as he crouched next to the bags. "With this much weight, you'd barely make it out of the kingdom without breaking your horse's back. You'd need half this load if you hoped to catch up with your father."

"There's nothing I wouldn't need," Kaleela protested as he untied one of the laces.

Reaching inside, he pulled out a handful of unlit candles. He raised an eyebrow, holding the thin pillars up.

"In case I needed to see at night." Warmth touched her cheeks once more. *Except a campfire would serve as both heat and light.* Her self-consciousness heightened as he pulled out another leather satchel, laden with gold coins embossed with Blackburn's currency mark.

"I couldn't very well leave without any coin, could I?" She snatched the bag from him.

"Perhaps, although these days a single gold coin in any local marketplace buys you an entire month's supplies, and then some."

Her utter astonishment broke out his laughter, a rich, joyful sound that could easily catch others up in his mirth. Given she was most certainly its cause, however, Kaleela crossed her arms, impervious. "All right, how would you pack the bags?"

Dimitar looked at her with an easy smile, erasing her irritation in a heartbeat. A good-natured kindness radiated from the man kneeling before her. "Well, Your Highness, the first thing—"

She interrupted him in a quiet voice. "Kaleela."

"Pardon, my lady?"

"Call me Kaleela." She dropped her gaze, intent on her erroneous saddlebags, trying to ignore the weight of his stare.

"As you wish... Kaleela," Dimitar managed, his smile widening.

He emptied her entire saddlebag and showed her in detail how to pack for quick travel: tying the laces in knots that withheld the constant fall of hooves, rolling clothes into tight bundles to take up less space, and packing foods that would spoil on top to ensure they were eaten first. He instructed with patience, and more than once Kaleela caught herself listening to his voice more than what he said.

The first tinge of morning's glow peeped over the horizon. Now, with morning coming on, she had to get back to her room. "Thank you, Dimitar."

He secured the last of her belongings, meeting her gaze.

"'To share the weight of another's grief binds two people together,'" Dimitar quoted, his hand lingering on hers as he passed her the bag. "My best friend told me that once."

Vulnerability welled within her, and she hugged the knapsack in front of her.

"Rest now, my lady. I'll guard your door to make sure you're uninterrupted."

"I don't need you for that," she replied in a soft voice.

"Apparently you do." He echoed his earlier words with a grin. "Sleep well, with pleasant dreams. May any nightmares hold visions of over-packed saddlebags and not Corruptors."

The idea kept a small smile on her face as she made her way to her chambers, undressed, and climbed into bed, exhausted. Yet not until she swayed on the edge of sleep, did she consider how Dimitar could have known about and understood her nightmares.

5

DIMITAR

Everywhere Kaleela went around the castle grounds, Dimitar accompanied her. He attended her councils, shadowing her chair and ignoring the odd looks he received from the elder advisors with measured patience. Kaleela's ladies-in-waiting grew bolder in their interest and whispered incessantly to one another, giggling whenever he made eye contact. Sparring against another guard with sword and shield gave him no pause, but soft-spoken words from the ladies of the court cut through his defenses and mortified him.

Nevertheless, his attention remained reserved for one person alone. Despite the curiosity his presence stirred among the castle staff, Dimitar stayed by Kaleela's side, trying not to present as more intrusive than required.

Over the next week, several duties arose within the kingdom that called Kaleela's attention: a land dispute between two farming families, a trade deal with the dwarven miners, and ongoing correspondence with a representative from Stormgard regarding Conrad's funeral plans. While Kahled's top advisors continued to provide their council, she now sat in charge of Blackburn's subjects and kingdom until his return.

After several days of activity, mild unrest fell once more upon the castle, most apparent in Kaleela herself.

"I need to be outside these walls." The yearning sat plain on her face. She selected a worn book from her shelves. "Would you care to join me in the courtyard?"

Dimitar bowed as she preceded him, noting with a reluctant grin that she offered for him to escort her as if he would give her a choice in the matter. Kahled had asked him to watch his daughter, and Dimitar would see the Corrupted themselves upon him before he'd leave her side.

The Blackburn castle gardens stretched the length of the wall, with small paths winding through flourishing groupings of trees, wildflowers, and thick, soft grass warmed in the summer sun. If not for the stone walls touching each side, the yard would appear a lush vale in the wild. Although some monarchs would clear such an expanse for tournaments, Kahled left it open and untouched save for groundskeepers maintaining the paths and tending the flowers. The courtyard served as a retreat from the busy castle life for all, from scullery maid to First Knight Talin himself.

Dimitar leaned against a tree along the path, hands idly loosening the leather sword straps hardened by mud and rain in his race to return to the castle. They shared an unspoken truce, but Kaleela was still thwarted from her revenge, and he wanted to respect her need for space. He adjusted the belt, and Kaleela moved from one seat in the courtyard to another in more shade beneath a tree.

Stretching as he crossed to her, Dimitar peered over her shoulder to figure out what she was reading. For the most part, the orphanage children were untaught, and not until knighthood training did he learn to read and write. Although he picked up the common letters with ease, he couldn't make out a single word on the page.

"If I may ask..." Dimitar was taken aback, as always, when she looked up.

Blonde braids encircled her head, elegantly arranged with hair jewels sparkling in the sun. An exquisiteness softened her features, eyes like emeralds and a small yet noticeable tip to her ears, all born from her half-elven blood. To say she was beautiful would be to call a field of wildflowers colorless or the stars faded, yet an aura of sadness hovered around her.

Dimitar cleared his throat. "What are you reading?"

"'Tis a book of legends, written in elvish." She closed the book to show the artistry stamped into the leather cover. An armor-clad man raised a sword in one hand and palmed fire in the other, light rays surrounding him.

"Who's this?"

"His name was Ruarc, one of the original Mage Warriors."

"Ah, the Mage Warriors," Dimitar echoed with fondness. He and the other orphaned boys had spent many an afternoon playing "Warriors and Corruptors," envisioning a time when the greatest human fighters combined physical strength with magic to defeat the shadow forces. The Age of Blood destroyed the Mage Warrior bloodline centuries earlier and in doing so, almost defeated the ethereal forces. Yet, the legends held limitless enactments for young boys, and Dimitar smiled at the memories.

"None matched Ruarc's strength of arms or mind," Kaleela said. "He took on legions of enemies at a time and never suffered a wound. At least, that's how the fairytale is spun."

"If you believe the tales in the barracks," Dimitar said in mock seriousness, "none of the knights serving Blackburn ever suffered a scratch either."

A brief smile hinted at the full blossom of beauty within her features. "This book was always one of my father's favorites. He used to have me read it to him and Conrad as they acted out the scenes. The best was when we'd go to the western forest grove, just outside of town. We played around those trees like a stage as we became the characters."

She ran her hand over the intricate designs on the book cover, lost in memory. "Conrad always played the evil villain and my father the victor. We usually didn't finish the tale because we'd end up laughing so hard. Then we'd all switch, and Conrad would take over with the reading with Father and I acting out the tales. Today I read it again, all the way through. The stories Conrad told aren't even in the book. He must've made them up, pretending to understand the elven letters."

Kaleela looked up from the book in her lap. Dimitar expected tears, but instead her quiet anger startled him.

"And now I'll never hear his stories again," she said.

"Of course you will." To her questioning glance, he said, "They're in your heart where they'll stay forever. I remember the sayings of my mother and village elders, and still hear them if I think about it long enough."

The intensity in Kaleela's eyes eased any remaining resentment at not joining his king. Her grief was real and tangible. He'd navigated this burden in life before and would not have its weight settle on her. "King Conrad will always be with you."

A bell interrupted him, signaling the afternoon guard training. Dimitar turned toward the sound with a hint of longing. He'd neglected his own training since being assigned as Kaleela's guard. As Kahled instructed, Dimitar stayed by her side but in doing so sacrificed his daily exercises and practices.

Kaleela caught his expression as the nearby guardsmen headed to the training grounds. "You wish to go practice with them."

Heat rose to his face as her words hit square on the truth of the matter. "No, my lady, I merely wish..." Dimitar sighed and tried again. "I asked you to wait within the city until we receive word from your father. At times, I wish I could go against my king's own orders."

"Waiting is difficult in a time when action feels necessary." Kaleela afforded him one of her brilliant smiles, and a burst of flutters danced across his stomach. "But I'll not have you misleading me to argue for your counsel as if staying here was my idea."

A servant interrupted Dimitar's chuckle. She curtseyed before Kaleela. "Your Highness, the Stormgard representative wishes to discuss the High Knight verses to be read at King Conrad's burial. He awaits your counsel in the north wing meeting room."

Kaleela dismissed the servant, a slight tension in her chin as her eyes shadowed once more with unvoiced sorrow.

"Go with the men," she said, returning to their conversation. "Conduct your training exercises. I'll be safe within these walls. We can reconvene in a few hours."

Her thoughtfulness shook him off guard. It'd be foolish to argue otherwise. His muscles ached to heft a practice sword in mock combat, and he and Olaf were well-matched against one another. Dimitar nodded his assent.

Those couple hours passed quicker than he hoped for, and when Dimitar came back inside at last, satisfyingly worn out with a few new bruises to prove it, he didn't expect to find Kaleela missing.

6

Dimitar

S he's gone, Olaf." Dimitar cursed for the hundredth time since searching the castle and meeting with staff who were all told Kaleela was with him. The muscles in his back and shoulders, loosened and stretched in practice, now bunched and tightened in anxiety once more. A strange sense of loss struck him, not merely Kaleela's physical absence but something that tugged at his chest. He trusted her at last and moreover, thought she'd grown to share a measure of trust with him as well.

"Slow down, lad," Olaf said, but his face remained worried. "How can ya be sure she's taken off outside the city somewhere?"

"We were talking about leaving; no, I mean about staying and how hard it is to wait." Dimitar ran his hand through his hair, the dark locks still damp with sweat. "I should've known she'd want to leave again." He called a nearby pageboy over. "Lad, go run and check the stables to ask if anyone has word of the princess. Make your feet swift."

The boy scampered off as Dimitar paced the training grounds, his thoughts dark and full of worry. Wooden sparring weapons lined several racks against the back wall of the barracks. Worn dirt patches scarred the ground, still soft from last night's rainfall. The knights' training area, usually bustling with men in practice armor, was unsettlingly empty.

Olaf grabbed him by the arm and held him still. "Think, Dim—just stop and think for a moment. Where was she before ya left her?"

"She went to speak with the Stormgard representative... I don't recall the man's name."

"That's not important. Did anyone ask him if he actually met with the princess?"

"Yes, of course I asked him."

"And what did he say?" Olaf gave his arm a little shake.

Dimitar let out a breath in a huff. "Yes, he met with her for some time, discussing King Conrad's burial passages. When I spoke with him, Kaleela had dismissed him within the half-hour at most."

"So at this point, she'd be gone less than an hour, right? That's not much time to gather supplies, pack, and find a way to leave the castle unannounced." He clapped Dimitar on the shoulder. "I'm askin' myself at this point, where could she go on such short notice?"

The young page came running back to Dimitar's side, who motioned for him to speak.

"The stable master says her ladyship took a horse and told him she was being escorted out for a bit." The young lad panted as if out of breath, more from the effect of carrying a seemingly important message. "She—the Lady Princess, that is—said she was seeing to plans for the dead king."

The two men exchanged a look. This time, Dimitar grabbed Olaf's arm and led him away from young ears. Something Kaleela told him earlier skirted his memory's edge, yet he had to remember. Olaf dismissed the pageboy, and Dimitar focused on the young boy's retreating form, willing the thought to crystallize. As if to sidetrack his intentions, suddenly Dimitar recalled when he and Olaf were both that tender age, newly met at Blackburn's orphanage. How he'd resisted Olaf's continual presence in his desire for isolation, his grief still tangible.

And now seeing to plans for the dead king.

The thought clicked into place.

Turning past Olaf, Dimitar set a quick pace to the stables. Olaf hurried to his side with a questioning look.

"We need to go get her, else there's hells to pay."

"Ya can't get in trouble for being misled—"

"No, not me," Dimitar cut off his friend. "It's Kaleela who's in trouble if she's caught."

As if marking his words, a clatter of hooves caught the men's attention. Out of the stables and headed by Sir Talin, First Knight of

Blackburn, three senior guardsmen rushed away, heading for the city streets.

"We have to get to her before they do." Dimitar entered the stable side door and reached for the nearest saddled horse. "It looks like they're going through town first, and I know a quicker way. We may not be too late."

"Where are we going?"

"Just hurry, Olaf. I know where to find her."

7

KALEELA

Kaleela knelt and leaned to kiss the trunk of the old oak tree. She lifted the wildflowers collected on her way, multi-colors bursting forth as if in vivid reflection of her sorrow's strength, and arranged them against the base. She gazed up at the whole of the tree, its branches wide and firm, bark warm and darkened in contrast to leaves illuminated by the sunlight filtering down. Its strength resonated from within, thrumming with an unseen power Kaleela always sensed among the forests, supporting her.

Strong, tall, steadfast—like him. She placed a palm on the trunk. *You taught me how to climb this tree once, when I was a skinny girl and you, larger than life itself.*

Years ago, in one of the brief moments Kahled ever spoke of her late mother, he'd described the elven mourning tradition. At the time of birth, a tree is planted in the Sun'Din Forest for each elf. Upon death, their remains are returned to the tree's soil, forever entwined among the roots to flourish as part of the tree forevermore. Her mother, said Kahled, had a beautiful, unblemished birch tree where her remains now lay. Kahled had visited her mother's memorial tree just once; Kaleela never even set foot inside the Sun'Din forest since infanthood. Yet, it felt right to honor Conrad with a memorial tree. Since the human way of passing differed, she chose this tree to carry his legacy, in his memory. Here, too, she wished to keep the connection with Conrad's spirit each time she ventured into this part of the forest.

She dug inside a pouch and brought out a vial of purified cleansing water, drawn from the Great Basin itself and blessed by the realm's healers. With a steady hand, Kaleela sprinkled its drops along the tree roots before replacing the crystal stopper.

"You hold his memory now and with it, a piece of my heart," she whispered to the gods, willing the ache in her chest to recede enough to finish her prayers. "Guide his spirit true, and let him one day recognize my own."

Bowing her head toward the rough, warm bark, she murmured halting sentences in elvish, her language broken by tears that constricted her throat. "*Hahl'lay mis tua, Fah'lel, und sol'ath tua nuen.*"

May the gods take you, Father, and keep you close always.

Oh, it hurt to shed these hot tears, welling from a source within her that reached so deep. It pained her to say goodbye when the last thing Kaleela wanted to do was let go of the man who served as a second, beloved father.

Her intentions were lost in the next moment when a hoof beat pattern against the forest floor grew nearer. She roused from her thoughts and emotions, swimming to rise above them with weights around her feet. Her sorrow had drowned out the world around her. *Oh no. I've been gone too long.*

Dimitar and a tall, heavyset man dismounted at the edge of the clearing. Tossing his reins to the man, Dimitar rushed over. He drew up short before her, brow creasing as his gaze searched her face.

A tear clung to her chin, a drop of innocence falling away. "How did you find me here?"

Dimitar shot a look over his shoulder, then held out his hands in a placating gesture. "I need you to trust me."

"What?" As her mind whirled to process his words, additional horsemen approached upon the forest path.

"Just trust me."

She rose and turned toward the arriving city guardsmen led by Sir Talin as they veered off the weathered path and reined in. Their deep-blue tunics stood out among the forest greens and browns, and Sir Talin's ranking three silver chains across his shoulder flashed glints of sunlight. With Kahled having led away a good number of knights, Sir Talin remained in charge of the kingdom's remaining defenses.

"My Lady Kaleela," he said with a perfunctory bow of his head, salt and pepper hair cropped short. His anger was tangible. With a practiced eye, Sir Talin took a quick measure of the two guardsmen before addressing her. "Your absence wasn't cleared by the castle guards, ladies-in-waiting, or stable master. Your father expects you to remain within the city walls, as do I."

Kaleela brushed the tears off her cheek with her palm and met Talin's gaze. Her face contorted in pain for a second as she struggled to put in place the cool, collected composure of her defense.

"Leave me alone," she said, low enough to mask the slight quaver. "I'm not to be disturbed."

"Your Highness, my orders from the king are to bring you—"

"Leave me alone!" she cried out and turned away, buying time to collect herself as she placed a steadying hand against the tree. This fragility within herself spiraled, yet she'd be damned if these guardsmen judged her as a mere weeping woman.

Yet Sir Talin wasn't a cruel man, nor oblivious to her tears or their source. As First Knight of Blackburn, Sir Talin lived his life as a warrior foremost and therefore understood grief in its many forms. The lines across his face and gray throughout his beard were tribute not just to his age, but to battles he'd survived when others did not. Kaleela had grown up under his watch, once a little girl dodging across the training grounds underfoot while the men practiced. Perhaps that's why he softened his next words.

"I would not intrude upon you at this time unless ordered to. Your father was specific in the commands he left, however, and adamant. Please, Your Highness, I insist we return. Now."

Kaleela clenched her fist, too frustrated to voice her thoughts. In the courtyard earlier that day, she'd shared with Dimitar about this private grove she used to play in. Solitude called to her in the face of her immediate grief and brought her here to this special place where she'd always escape; sometimes with eventual capture, other times evading the guards, and often returning before anyone was the wiser. The sympathy from Sir Talin and the guards hung over her, yet they always shadowed her when she most wanted—needed—solitude.

Kaleela dropped her hand from the tree and turned back to the group, too exhausted to defy Talin any longer. He was justified, too, in that he obeyed her father first and foremost, and Kaleela risked leaving the castle alone in this perilous time. Any moment now, Talin would step down to place her upon a horse and bring her back to the castle.

But she couldn't fight the pain in her heart nor the guards and their duty.

"Sir Talin, if I may bring to light." Dimitar stepped forward. "With respect, sir, you presume the princess traveled out of the city alone. We accompanied the lady on her short trip and were getting ready to return."

Kaleela's eyes widened at this lie, but Dimitar kept his own gaze fixed upon the First Knight. Talin turned in the saddle to face Dimitar as he approached, and looked him up and down with a somewhat critical eye that one's elders are entitled to.

"No one informed me of any permission for her to leave the castle this afternoon," Talin said, a crease deepening upon his brow, "and your duties do not include—"

Dimitar cut in with smooth competence. "My duties are also from King Kahled and expressly commit my presence at the princess's side. Her safety is paramount to the kingdom, that I'm well aware of."

"Then you've noticed these present times are strained at best," Talin said, his displeasure unmitigated. "The princess is best served within the safety of the city walls and not wandering throughout the lands, despite any usual inclination for such." Turning from Dimitar, he addressed Kaleela. "Come, Your Highness; your ladies are waiting to attend to you."

"Naturally, sir." The large guardsman next to Dimitar jumped into the conversation with an easy-going tone. "And far from m'self or my companion to ever presume to fill such dainty shoes."

A few guards chuckled before catching Sir Talin's glare and falling silent once more.

"I'll escort the princess back, as intended this entire time," Dimitar said.

A pregnant pause hung in the clearing.

"King Kahled appointed you for a reason, so I'll trust you to do your duty here—as well as to report to me at once upon return." With a tug of the reins, Talin pointed his steed toward the city. "My lady, I am still responsible for you. I'll have you inside the castle wall within the hour."

With that parting command, Talin dug his heels into the horse's sides, and the retinue followed suit down the pathway.

Only when a nearby bird trilled a quiet song did a small sob escape Kaleela's lips, which she silenced with the back of her hand. Grief welled within her, and she might choke on its waves crashing over her, inescapable and suffocating.

She didn't raise her head when Dimitar approached her.

"I'm so sorry for surprising you here, like this." With slow movements, he dabbed the last of her tears away with his fingertips. "'Tis natural for a kingdom to worry about their king and his daughter. They're concerned for you at all times, even more so with your father away."

Kaleela looked at him then, her composure growing and her eyes wide with gratitude. He'd tried to spare her from Sir Talin, yet the way Dimitar spoke, calm and sincere, grounded her once more. Her chest tightened with their shared intimacy.

"I'm concerned for you too," he added.

A twinge of guilt swept through her; she'd tested his trust in her. She lowered her lashes, self-conscious again.

"We were both worried for ya, Princess." The other man stepped forward with a flourishing bow. "Olaf, guardsman and knight in training, at yer service."

An intentional stubble along his jaw couldn't quite cover the merry flush higher up on his tawny cheeks. His sun-kissed brown hair was short and tousled, as if he'd just woken up, yet suited him nevertheless. Kaleela couldn't help but like him instantly.

"Don't worry yourselves for me." She glanced at the wildflowers. "I've finished what I came here to do. There's no more I can say."

"It needn't end here," Olaf said. "King Conrad's always with ya, not only in this grove. He'll hear yer words no matter when ya want to speak to him."

Kaleela placed her hand on the tree trunk once more, a goodbye and unspoken promise. A curl of warm breeze swept through the clearing, chasing out the last clouds lingering among them.

"Come then, Princess." Olaf bent toward Kaleela and gave her a quick hug and gentle thump on the back, his easy-going affection an unexpected comfort. "Let's bring ya home, else Sir Talin will have me and the lad muckin' the stables all tomorrow. And I don't feel like bein' knee-deep in shit."

"Gods, Olaf." Dimitar turned beet red. "In front of the princess, just like that?"

"If ya pardon my language, Princess."

"Call me Kaleela." A grin tugged the corner of her mouth. "And there's no curse that Conrad didn't say on the daily."

As the trio rode back to the castle, Dimitar and Olaf bantered back and forth, not just for her benefit but from apparent years of comradeship. The burden of bereavement lessened from her shoulders, and Kaleela welcomed the lift in mood. After reaching the stables, Dimitar helped her dismount, then bowed his leave to speak with Sir Talin as promised.

Olaf offered Kaleela his arm, which she was pleased to accept. She caught Olaf's meaningful glance with Dimitar as he headed to the castle. She could almost read their thoughts; Olaf now covered Dimitar's duty of accompanying her. The two men risked themselves for her, and she hoped Sir Talin wouldn't be too hard on Dimitar. Still, it intrigued her that two people knew each other's intentions so well.

"Call yer ladies if ya wish, Princess," Olaf said, unaware she'd caught his unspoken signal to Dimitar. "Let's take a wee stroll around the grounds, so all the staff can see ya alive and well."

A walk was just the thing to shake off the afternoon's events. "Tell me Olaf, how did you and Dimitar meet?"

"Ach, now that's a tale." Olaf patted her hand, his own big enough to engulf hers. "When I first met wee Dimitar, he was as cute and wide-eyed as a puppy, and twice as disobedient..."

8

KALEELA

Partway through Olaf's reminiscing, Dimitar rejoined them, now seated upon the worn benches inside the great hall, and suggested they find a meal for dinnertime. Kaleela shyly caught his eye. What did he and Talin talk about?

"Is Sir Talin gonna flay ya alive?" Olaf asked, half-joking.

"Not this time." Dimitar's boyish grin lit his face. "It took several 'yes, sirs' to calm him down, but in the end, we agreed that we share the same goal."

His gaze flicked to hers, and a weight lifted off her shoulders. *He lied point-blank to the First Knight. He's not just guarding me; he's protecting me.*

"That's a relief, lad," Olaf said. "I'd be mighty disappointed if m'dinner got ruined by yer public execution."

Olaf's love of storytelling could only be interrupted for a few select reasons, food topping the list. Kaleela began to summon a servant with orders for dinner, but Olaf spoke up. "Well, 'tis midweek, and we sup at one place every midweek: the Tankard Inn."

The local pub and inn was a popular spot for many of Blackburn's guardsmen and knights, and traveling folk sought out the decent fare. However, Kaleela protested at once, having suffered the embarrassment of being tracked to the forest grove earlier.

"Ach, nonsense." Olaf snorted. "You're bein' accompanied, and where else is half of Blackburn's army found if not at the Tankard Inn?"

"Please Olaf, no, I cannot leave the castle walls, not after today," Kaleela said, somewhat panicked when he showed no intention of listening. "You go without me."

"With respect, my lady, Sir Talin did say your father's orders are to remain within the city's walls, and the Tankard Inn is a few streets over from the castle gate," Dimitar said.

Kaleela shot an incensed look his way. Despite her objections, Dimitar nabbed a servant to request a light, hooded cloak to throw over her shoulders, then led the way toward the castle doors. Kaleela continued to plead silently toward Dimitar whenever he glanced her way, expecting him to see the folly of this suggestion.

What are you aiming for? An actual beating after our encounter in the forest?

The command to stop them touched her lips, but then a thought crossed her mind. Perhaps Dimitar and Olaf weren't so much reckless as willing to show her that she wasn't a prisoner within her own kingdom. The experience earlier with Sir Talin and his guards had unsettled her, but she'd been unprepared and vulnerable. Now, she remained in charge and could do as she pleased within the boundaries of protection. As she thought it over, Kaleela welcomed the idea of trying the local bar of myth and legend. Any distraction at this point would soothe her impatience for her father's message to arrive. Swallowing the last of her objections, she let Dimitar and Olaf lead the way into town, tucking the cloak's hood closer to hide her features.

Olaf's commentary about his and Dimitar's most egregious exploits rolled forth without apparent restraint as they made their way down Blackburn's main street. "Did ya know, Old Man Murray had me pegged for the blacksmiths until Dim here came along."

Olaf gestured at the main forge as they passed by, the air filled with ringing metal and belching smoke even this late in the day.

"The smiths sure dodged that one, didn't they." Dimitar grinned as he sidestepped a follow-up jab, and a slow smile crept onto Kaleela's face.

They could've joined any guild, yet they wanted to serve my father.

Blackburn's foundations rested on different guilds, from blacksmithing to culinary, alchemy to arts, and beyond. The city's central location in the Green Lands served as a natural destination point, in this case for all seeking education and skills refinement.

Blackburn remained split into districts, each section with a main headquarters and halls for apprentices to call home.

The Tankard Inn stood near the foot of the castle, among the oldest of Blackburn's buildings. Surrounded by merchant tents selling the guilds' wares, the inn's high-reaching gables stretched three stories high. Olaf explained the top two floors offered simple, clean rooms, welcoming travelers to spend the night for a few coppers or a few more for a pint and stew along with the bed. With the marketplace seldom quiet, vacancies were rare, and the price of copper sometimes became silver as travelers competed for a place to stay. The Tankard Inn was also one of the few places in the Northern Kingdoms that acquired shipments of dwarven ale and elven wines. The proprietor, a largish, courteous man named Brand, rarely had trouble making ends meet.

Dimitar, Kaleela, and Olaf entered through the wide door next to a planter filled with basil, the local shops still open and taking the majority of the crowds that would hit later. Round, well-used tables spread across the generous room, encircled with simple seating. Soot darkened the considerable, unlit stone fireplace in the rear. In a little time yet, a barmaid would make rounds to light the candle pillars in the table centers. The bar itself stretched half the length of the left-hand side of the room, polished a deep mahogany. Warm aromas issued from the kitchen, its narrow double doors swinging as dinner orders came in. Cozy, like a home away from home.

Brand swept up to them from behind the bar with practiced ease, and Kaleela braced for a scene.

"Good evening, lads. My lady." He extended his arm in service. "Looking for your usual seats?"

If he recognized Kaleela as the princess, then he also respected her wish to remain concealed within the plain cloak, and she relaxed. He led them toward the back nearest an open window, the setting sun masking the cooling air. Brand took their orders, then ducked behind the bar. A barmaid served hot plates of honeyed ham with gravy, and the trio dug in with hearty appetites. In between mopping up gravy with thick, fresh baked bread, Olaf continued with highlights of his and Dimitar's time in the orphanage.

"I'm thinkin' what finally sent Old Man Murray to toss us into knighthood training was that year at Winterfest, remember?" Olaf cuffed Dimitar on his upper arm, and the two chuckled at the memory. "We got a hold of his horse saddle and loosened it a wee bit. Somebody... and I'm sure I'm not knowin' who *at all*... aimed a well-timed snowball to its flank. The horse reared, and off slid the saddle, dumpin' Old Man Murray straight into mud and slush before a crowd of hundreds."

Olaf illustrated the poor headmaster's drenched reaction, and Kaleela burst out laughing, the release a relief in her body. *By the gods, this fellow can tell a story.* Olaf joined in, motioning for a barmaid to bring over the next round. Dimitar took a sip of his ale, a troubled smile on his face.

"Whatsa' matter, m'boy? Ya seem a wee put out."

Dimitar gave a small head shake and lowered his voice. "Something feels out of place, as if a guardian of the Dark Woods just brushed across my grave marker. Can you feel it?"

As if the forces themselves responded, the tavern door swung wide. Many patrons had filled the bar over the past few hours, folks coming and going about their business as usual, unremarkable and blending into the ambiance. Yet this particular entrance rang out to catch Kaleela's attention, cutting through the crowds and conversations. A caress ran up her spine, a call for connection.

Craning her neck around a group of patrons, she caught sight of a shrouded man entering, wrapped head to toe in a cloak. Dimitar followed her gaze, tilting back his chair onto two legs as he assessed this man. The hooded stranger searched the tavern and unmistakably locked on their table.

The cloak hid what strength he possessed and obscured his face. No matter which way the stranger looked, light couldn't penetrate the darkness cast by his hood. Only a hint of eyes gleamed when touched by candlelight. He seemed more shadow than man, and indeed the rest of the bar patrons and staff paid no heed to his presence.

The man made his way straight to their table. Dimitar and Olaf stood and stepped in front of him as one, a solid wall between her and the man, who halted in his tracks. With careful, non-threatening movements, he reached into a deep fold of his cloak and withdrew a small satchel, tossing it onto the table. The stranger held out his hand, dark olive-toned and with slim fingers, indicating Kaleela should open it. She glanced at him, seeking a face she could not see, then undid the leather bindings.

Her eyes filled with understanding. "Let him through."

Dimitar and Olaf didn't budge.

"What's in the satchel?" Dimitar said.

"This is our sign. Only my father could've sent this."

"Are ya sure about that?"

"'Tis a lock of my mother's hair." She withdrew a small braid of silken blonde hair as if taken from her own head, tied at both ends with a faded ribbon. "My father carries this with him whenever he travels. It looks as if our messenger has arrived, Dimitar. We must let this man speak."

Dimitar and Olaf returned to their seats; Olaf pulled up an extra chair for their visitor, who sat and stretched his legs. Kaleela searched again for the man's face but still couldn't perceive more than a glimpse of eyes and the mere hint of features. Dimitar did the same, openly staring, and he shifted his gaze across the hooded face. The material, so dark that at first it appeared black, upon closer look reflected the deepest red.

"Why are you in a magicked cloak?" Dimitar said, distrust lacing his words, but Kaleela cut him off.

"Please, tell me about my father."

The cloaked man motioned with his hands. Dimitar and Olaf both seemed to understand, and Olaf caught her questioning glance.

"He's usin' silent language," he explained. "Somethin' King Kahled wanted us to know 'cause he learned it from the elves. This way, you can talk with yer allies in the heat o' things without sayin' a word. It's not normally part of knight trainin', but with yer father the High Knight in charge, he wanted us all instructed."

Kaleela sighed. "Aye, I know about this. Father and Conrad signed around me when I was a child, and they didn't want me to know what they discussed. Terrible parents," she added under her breath, and Dimitar choked on his drink. She shot him a wry grin, then turned back to Olaf. "Can you help me understand?"

"Aye, Princess. The man's name is Ral, and he was indeed sent by your father."

Ral nodded at Olaf's words, and the tale unraveled as Olaf translated his hand gestures.

'There's no getting around this, so I'll just say it: I belong to the Thieves' Guild,' Ral signed. 'Picking off traveling groups is fairly easy, especially at night, so I made my move then. The king... well, I don't know how he did it, but he caught me as I went for a piece in his tent. I swear he was deep asleep.'

"He's a High Knight." Dimitar scoffed. "Of course you'd get caught."

Ral's hooded face tilted just so to the side, as if he wanted to argue the point, but instead continued. 'He said I deserved justice, but that could wait until morning. They trussed me up and set a guard.'

"Any other company woulda' had yer hands for tryin' to steal from a king, so there's that," Olaf interjected.

Ral lifted his palms up to concede the point. 'That very night we were ambushed. Corruptors swarmed out of the darkness, surrounding us. I really picked the wrong company on the wrong night. Right after the attack started, Kahled broke my bonds so I could fight.'

"You mean to say you stayed to fight, when you could've escaped?" Dimitar interrupted.

Ral nodded and motioned as if to refute Dimitar's ungenerous question. 'Their numbers were too great, and they killed many of the knights then and there. They took the king prisoner, along with me and the other captured knights, and forced us into the Eastern Mountains.'

Ral stopped, inhaling long and slow, somehow retreating even further into the hood's darkness.

Kaleela waited, eyes wide, the *thud thud thud* of her heart drowning out the noise from the tavern. Her father, taken by Corruptors. Oh gods, would this man tell her Father was dead, just like Conrad? She couldn't breathe, willing with every fiber in her body for his next words to be anything else, anything but that.

Ral took a drink of ale and set the glass down with slow precision before raising his hands once more. This time, Dimitar translated for her, his eyes flitting between the man's hands and her face, gauging her reaction. 'They separated the king from the rest of us, shoved him into a cell down a passageway. Corruptor bindings are much easier to escape, and I set to freeing the knights. But they stopped me.'

"Stopped you?" Dimitar echoed, breaking off the translation.

'They told me to save the king, to free him first.'

Here, Dimitar exchanged glances with Olaf. "Our knights would see to King Kahled's safety first and foremost," he said, and Olaf nodded.

Ral paused his gestures, as if reluctant to reveal what came next. 'Your father spared my life when others wouldn't because of my thieving. I owe him reciprocation. I backtracked to his cell, and when I found him... he was stripped of his armor, beaten. I went to pick the lock, but some substance, black, oily, and pulsing, covered the surface. It reeked of evil, whatever it was, something that leads to death—or worse.'

"You couldn't free him?" Kaleela asked, her voice small yet with growing hope; her father still lived. She knew the answer even as Ral shook his head.

'He removed this satchel hidden under a rock and lifted it out to me through the barred door window. He told me to take it to you, here in Blackburn. We didn't have much time; the Corruptors were coming back, and one of the knights... started screaming. They were doing something to him; I think they wanted Kahled to hear. He only had time to tell me this, a message for you: 'Search out Gar'Ret in the Sun'Din Forest. He'll know what to do. Tell him what this man has told you. Times are dangerous. Take refuge in the trees of your elven ancestors.' Kahled said I must hurry; time is not with us.'

Ral finished motioning and leaned back in his chair.

"How did you find us?" Dimitar asked, arms crossed.

Ral lifted one shoulder in a shrug. 'You're not that hard to track.'

Dimitar bristled at this, and Kaleela placed a hand on his arm to cut off any retort. Gathering herself, she took two measured breaths in and out. She held Dimitar's stare, not with grief but with pure determination. Olaf shared a similar look. Dimitar glanced between the two, and his expression darkened.

"No." Dimitar emphasized his point to both of them. "Absolutely not. We're not disobeying this order. *No.*"

Kaleela's eyes flashed a warning. Finally, the single reason for her to act, and act she must. Dimitar had been so eager to fight beside her father. Now he balked at the thought of fighting for him, bound to her safety first. *He thinks there's a choice when there is none.*

Kaleela gave voice to their silent struggle but on her own terms. "I have no time for this Gar'Ret. I'm going to rescue my father."

9

DIMITAR

"W ith all respect, Kaleela, that's out of the question, and you know it." Growing alarm deepened the pit in Dimitar's stomach as stormy determination settled into her features.

"The time for action has come. We talked about this, and our waiting is done."

"No, we didn't discuss anything of the sort. Your father gave us a specific order, one intended for your safety, and he entrusted this to me. I swore to him, Kaleela. You cannot make me break this oath."

Dimitar stopped, emotions tugging too close at the surface. The chosen men accompanying Kahled to the council, ambushed with little warning, now lay strewn in some field to be worked over by carrion. His mind flashed across the faces of men he'd trained under, unwilling to settle on one as the knight in the mountainside whose fate led to such horror. And above all else, Dimitar recalled the lines on Kahled's face when they discussed Kaleela's safety, traces of a smile and hope lighting the eyes of the aging king amidst all his cares and grief.

"Dimitar." Kaleela's voice was quiet but no less firm. Patrons now filled the tavern, busy in conversation and drink, and the men leaned in to hear her next words. "I do not ask you to break the promise made to my father. Listen to this man's message. Father thinks of all others first, this I know better than anyone else. But he's out of time, and I must do something."

Olaf knocked back the rest of his pint and set the mug down with a thunk. "And just what are ya suggestin', Princess? Our king is in desperate need, that's the fact, but that's for us remainin' soldiers to set out and see to. Sorry, m'boy"—Olaf looked at Dimitar—"you and the lady are stayin' put."

"Don't you see?" Kaleela said. "I have a better chance at getting in and out of a mountainside undetected. If you've forgotten I can handle a weapon or two, I'll gladly give you a demonstration. I can take care of myself."

Olaf looked thoughtful, considering her words, but Dimitar frowned.

"So, you suggest a single person—yourself—has a better chance at rescuing Kahled than Blackburn's knights?" said Dimitar. "What about Stormgard, for that matter? They'll willingly send additional forces to storm the mountains. We need only send a messenger tonight, and they'll respond with aid."

"And how long would that take?" Kaleela shook her head. "Neither of you are listening to what Ral told us. The entire army accompanying my father is now dead or captured. Do you believe another troop will fare any better? We need to take a different approach. Stealth and haste are the strategy now."

"Ya can't be goin' all by yerself," Olaf said. Dimitar turned in his seat, shooting daggers, but he continued. "I'm not leavin' her to do all the work alone."

"She's not going in the first place," Dimitar said. "If Kahled says bringing Kaleela to the elves is the best hope, then that's where we travel."

"More delay, more politics, all to arrange a rescue that will come too late and meet the same fate. Ral said my father's guards were slaughtered. The rest of our army and any others that join in will be butchered if they attempt to go after him. This is my father and our soldiers we speak of." Kaleela paused to hold Dimitar's and then Olaf's gaze, her own face pleading for their understanding. "You've both trained for years, and waiting is not an exercise on the practice grounds. Hear this: I won't wait here again. I am my father's daughter, and I will see him home."

With a great sigh, Olaf snagged a fresh pint off a passing barmaid's tray, tossing it down in gulps. "I still don't think this is a good idea," he grumbled into the emptied mug.

"You know strategy, Olaf," Kaleela said. "What would the elves do with this message?"

Olaf appeared taken aback by the question but answered right away. "I wager they'd form a small rescue team. Big enough to kick some arse but small enough to sneak..." His words trailed off as he realized what he was saying.

"That's right, they'd come to the same conclusion. But by the time we traveled out there and they held a council to debate the so-called honor of rescuing a human, who knows how much time would pass. You know as well as I do that Blackburn's advisors would take just as long." She placed a hand over her heart, emphasizing her next words. "I won't allow this atrocity to continue. Ral said time was of the essence. I'm going to save my father."

Dimitar checked his exasperation. She wasn't wrong, but there had to be more consideration than just action. The message he delivered to Kahled had been a trap, and damned if he'd make the same mistake twice.

"We're all desperate for our king's return," he said. "But I don't see how we can do it ourselves without the kingdom's aid. What would happen to Blackburn when tomorrow they discover not only their king imprisoned, but also their princess gone as well? The council will panic if you up and disappear."

Dimitar expected her to lash out with her unceasing bravado or worse, grief-stricken tears. Instead, she considered him as her lips pursed in thought.

"Perhaps we'll need to inform them, and the advantage would still be ours." Kaleela pronounced her next words with the authority of a kingdom's ruler. "I'll summon the council tonight and inform them of my father's kidnapping and his directives. They only need to know he's in enemy hands and that I plan to go to the Sun'Din Forest as bidden with you"—she nodded to the men—"as my accompaniment. With so few of our army's knights remaining, Talin's main duty is to protect the kingdom. He'll have to request assistance from Stormgard and other allied kingdoms, and these councils will take time, which gives us more."

At first, no one responded to her declaration. Olaf looked uneasy at the fact her plan had merit and he seemed out of arguments. Ral's expression, if any, hid behind the hood's shadows. Only now did Dimitar acknowledge the full depth of Kaleela's determination. Her cheeks flamed with color, and passion commanded her words. But he also noted hidden deep within her eyes, fear threatening to emerge. Although her resolve was unbending, it rested upon a very real, raw terror for her father. *I'd feel the same if Kahled was my father.*

What she proposed invited unimaginable dangers, but her logic held true. Once more, Dimitar recalled the many knights who rode off with Kahled in the courtyard. He'd be lying to himself if he didn't recognize the overwhelming urge to rescue them as soon as possible. He inwardly winced at his forming decision. He'd only leave the kingdom if Kaleela was safe. And the only way to guarantee her safety was to remain by her side.

This is my fault, and I'll see it made right.

Clearing his throat, Dimitar bowed his head. "As you wish, Kaleela. I'll be ready to part with you at dawn and make speed to your father."

"I'll protect the lot of ya." To emphasize the point, Olaf placed his hand upon the axe handle. "Me and Lucky says we're goin'."

"Thank you," Kaleela said, a tremble upon her voice. "I'm grateful for your help."

Around the Tankard Inn, customers swayed and clapped as a fellow took up a fiddle, the crowd oblivious to the tragedy they would wake up to the next morning once the kingdom revealed word of Kahled's capture. Silence hung in the air between the four of them until Ral knocked on the tabletop. He made a few passes with his hands, and Olaf translated, but the message was clear without his interpretation.

"He's goin' too. Says we need him 'cause he knows the way into Kahled's cell and how to get out. He'll also go for his honor's sake."

"My father trusted you." Kaleela clasped the man's hand in an unexpected gesture of warmth. "And I trust you too."

Dimitar held back a grimace; he had no choice. That they needed the thief—a common criminal—for this mission rankled Dimitar. But they'd be lost without him as a guide, both getting to the right part of the mountains and inside.

Trying to hide his suspicion, he turned to Ral. "Are you handy with a weapon, stranger?"

Show me what you're capable of.

Ral turned toward Dimitar, who felt himself looked up and down within the hood in return.

'Yes. Are you?' came the derisive gesture.

Dimitar stiffened, and Kaleela once again placed her hand on his arm, her touch soothing and electric at the same time. "Ral has been in and out of a Corruptor lair. He can handle himself."

She gave a tired sigh. Dimitar bit back his response and shifted his attention to her, mindful of the fresh distress she now carried.

"We've had a long day," Kaleela said, "and I suggest we all go home to prepare and get what rest we can. Ral, I'll arrange for you to take a room above the bar."

Ral gave a nod of confirmation and thanks.

"We'll leave early tomorrow, and I still have to meet with the councilors. Shall we meet at the city gates at first light then?"

Everyone agreed, pushing back their chairs. Arrangements were made, and Ral headed upstairs as the trio made their way out, Dimitar holding the door open for Kaleela to pass. As they exited the Tankard Inn, a tingling grasped the base of his spine and worked its way up his back: the distinct feeling of being watched. Almost without conscious thought, Dimitar turned and glanced back at the Inn. In a second-floor window, Ral's shadowy figure observed their retreat.

10

KAHLED

Kahled refused to acknowledge the grate of the wooden door on stone as it opened, his eyes closed and his mind relaxed within a meditative state. He'd lost track of the number of days held captive in the mountainside, the crude, thick walls masking any chance of counting sunrises and sunsets. Meal delivery served as the one sign of passing time, a small cup of water and hardened bread slab sometimes paired with a dubious meat chunk shoved into his cell. These portions were brought to him irregularly during the days, if at all, a ploy Kahled was certain they used to make him further lost within the mountain.

A clatter of clay bowls echoed in his small cell, followed by the rasping breath of an ancient evil. A surrounding reek of decay slithered into the small space, poisoning Kahled's meditation. A Corruptor lingered at the entrance, as if hoping for some response, but Kahled remained seated, legs crossed and eyes shut, hands resting at his sides in the small pool of chains that bound him. The Corruptor took two clicking steps toward him.

Kahled opened his eyes.

Thorny protrusions pocked the Corruptor's skin, and Kahled choked back a gag as the rotten stench hit him anew. Eyes, an ever-turbulent inky pool, darted around like a hawk searching for prey. Even after fighting thousands during the Reclamation, Kahled reacted with instinctive repulsion, and the hairs on the back of his neck stood. His stare, however, did not waver.

The Corruptor raised its upper lip in a hiss, needle teeth bared, before it turned and slunk out, the low clang of the lock falling into place. Corruptors clamored their way down the tunnel, and Kahled unfolded his legs with a grimace. The small chamber was cramped enough that he crouched when standing, no longer able to stretch his legs and test their strength. He'd be damned, though, if he gave them the pleasure of seeing him crawl. He hunched over to the bowls, chains dragging behind him and pulling taut just as his fingers brushed over the bowls.

Mold splotches bloomed on the bread in the shallow light provided by a torch somewhere outside his cell. Yet another meal he'd have to skip. Kahled licked his chapped lips and appraised the small bowl, the water stale at best, tepid and gritty at worst. He could live days without the bread, but water he couldn't afford to pass up.

Saying a silent prayer, he took a tentative sip. The liquid had a sweetness of water drawn from a fresh spring, cool and refreshing. His body's desire could not be stayed, and with one swift tilt, Kahled drained the bowl. Coolness ran down his throat, its effect spreading to his limbs, erasing some of the exhaustion that robbed his will to fight.

That's when the pain hit him.

Crooked nails jumped from his stomach back up his throat, their barbed grip ripping tender flesh. Tears sprung from Kahled's eyes unbidden, and the strength in his legs disappeared, his body springing into a fetal position. Convulsions wracked his frame, and he banged his head on the stone floor. His vision faded to gray, tunneling on the excruciating, inescapable pain igniting every nerve. He screamed against this torture, more intense with each passing second as his fists clenched hard enough to draw blood with his fingernails, smearing his palms with crimson wetness. Just when he'd surely die from the agony, it stopped all at once.

Oppressive silence in the cell hung around his head as his vision cleared, punctuated by harsh gasps for air. Bracing against the aches that would strike him, Kahled unfolded his shaking body. Instead, he discovered a throbbing heat of power radiating in his center. His trembling came to an end, and the spasms that gripped his lower back disappeared. Even some injuries that had plagued him for years were now restored to a health not felt since his youth. Coming to his feet, he groaned in relief.

On a whim not entirely his own, Kahled wrapped one of the chains tethering him to the wall twice around his forearm. In one quick whipping motion, the base ripped from the wall and clanged to the floor before the chain snapped. His grimace grew as he gathered the other chain. Once unfettered, he'd tear the cell door clear off its hinges. Almost as compelling as his desire for freedom came the urge to use his newfound strength. His fingers itched to hold a stone, a sword, anything he could use to break and smash his surroundings.

Just as he tensed to jerk the second chain from the wall, a new blast of pain soared through him. This time it wasn't his body under assault, but his mind.

A thousand screeching hisses cried out in his head, igniting a primitive urge raw enough to unleash a howl deep from his chest. The thirst for power surged through every limb, fingers hooking into claws and lips peeling back with a guttural growl. Visions of rending men into gory pieces grew so acute that coppery blood saturated his mouth. To his own revolted horror, the taste excited him on a primal level he never even knew existed.

Appalled at the bombardment of Corruptor urges and his own sick temptation, he renewed his efforts to fight the mental penetration. Grabbing his head and yelling, he tried to block out the carnage from the Corrupted in his mind. Their every thought, every vile impulse pressed into his head with a force he could not long resist. An outraged cry escaped him as his will was overpowered by the Corrupted collective consciousness. His mind's last barrier gave way with a frightening crash.

Yooooou are now usssss.

A splinter of ice shattered into his head, ripping recollections from his past and discarding them just as quickly, as if the Corruptors searched for something of importance. The gears of his thoughts slipped as the Corrupted consciousness plundered his mind, shoving their own terrifying images in place of his own memories. Nothing was sacred; Kahled's mind lay exposed and violated as the Corrupted mindset sorted his thoughts with driven predation. Amidst visions of arms ripped from torsos and teeth rending flesh off bodies, something was pulled from his heart, robbing him of his very center of self.

He clutched at this thought as he would an object of infinite worth, one he'd give his own life to protect, but it slipped from his grasp and solidified even clearer. There, in the middle of the intrusions whipping around his mind, an image of his darling girl appeared. Helplessly whispering her name aloud, he staggered toward the back wall. As if saying the name gave the vision a focus, Kaleela became the sole picture before him.

In despair, Kahled now understood what was happening. Using the last of his free will, he punched the stone with all his newfound strength, pain flashing up his arm. Kaleela's image wavered, his focus shifting to his throbbing hand. Punching out again, he split his knuckles on the rock, blood streaking across the stone. The pain dropped him to his knees but also withdrew the probing collected consciousness. With his mind now centered on his bloodied hand, he pulled his will away from the Corrupted just long enough to act. Taking his good hand, he shoved two fingers deep into his mouth. His throat flexed once and then again before his stomach retched up its contents. A flow of black liquid deeper than any midnight and thriving with living energy flung from his mouth, spilling into a small pool at his feet. The water had diluted its potency just enough for him to evade a full transformation.

At once, the growls and hisses quieted in his mind, and his thoughts returned to his own. Scrambling on all fours, Kahled pushed himself to the other side of the cell as far away from the Corrupted taint as he could in tight quarters, the substance leaching into the dirt. The pain in his hand became solely his own, and he cradled his bleeding, wounded fist as tears trickled from his eyes. The Reclamation War horrors were not so far buried in his mind that he could ever forget the monstrous effects on soldiers infected with Corrupted essence. Gods, he'd been moments from turning.

"An acquired taste, to be sure," came a new voice outside the cell, jerking Kahled's head to weary attention. The words sounded as though the owner had swallowed gravel and spoke through the congestion. "You soon learn to control their minds, and with that comes great power."

The lock on his cell released, and the door swung open with the complaint of wood on stone. A figure stood in the doorway, his frame engulfing any light that came from the hall. Through his watery sight, Kahled made out no more than an outline. He faced a man, or at the very least, something that used to be one.

"Who are you?" Kahled winced at the scratchiness of his voice; it revealed, against his will, the all-too-effective Corrupted intrusion.

"Come now, Kahled. Such a simple-minded question. Asking something you should know the answer to. I expected more from you." The man crouched into the room and picked up the chain's remnants. "Amazing, is it not? I remember my first taste of this strength, although my target was much more alive than this steel."

Wrapping the chain around his hand, he shattered the links like eggs. "To answer your feeble question, I am Overlord of these beasts and ruler in these mountains, living in shadow but growing with a power you can only imagine." With sudden and terrible quickness, the man loomed over Kahled. "But that isn't what you need to know, is it, High Knight? Try again."

Kahled's newly despoiled mind reeled, trying to grasp what this Overlord would pry from him. He knew Kahled was a High Knight, which meant Kahled and Conrad were targeted. And judging this Overlord's strength and clawed hands, it stood to reason he'd killed the missing third High Knight, Rippold, years ago. But why was he after the last of the High Knights?

"Why am I being kept alive when you killed the others?"

A pregnant pause followed, then the Overlord laughed, deeply and with malice. "Much better, Kahled. You showed some thought. But I'm afraid I cannot answer you this time. Far too many assumptions and plans yet to unfold." The Overlord leaned closer, a shadowed mass trapping the light behind him and further obscuring Kahled's view. "You can trust I'll answer you in time."

In the recess of Kahled's chest, hot rage simmered. This man was responsible for murdering Conrad and his knights. He willed himself to recapture the remarkable strength that had been his mere minutes ago, so he could use his bare hands to kill the Overlord, but he was spent. He swallowed convulsively, unable to escape the pain in his throat and throughout his wracked body.

He's taken everything from me.

Oblivious to Kahled's spark of growing rage, the Overlord crouched over to the door. He turned to look over his shoulder at Kahled. The Overlord's profile struck a chord, just out of reach. Try as he could to better trace the shadowed outline, any familiarity was destroyed by what the Overlord said next.

"By the way, who is she?"

Kahled's stomach sank. His vision of Kaleela came back to him with startling clarity. Finding the last hidden strength in his legs, he flung himself at the Overlord. His hand grazed the creature's back before the other chain still attached to his wrist stopped him with a snap. Agony wrenched across his shoulder, and he stumbled against the wall with a gasp. Tears welled once more, not only from pain, but sheer fury and helplessness.

The Overlord cocked his head as if sorting over the information gained from the Corrupted consciousness before his laughter rang, louder this time and with more malevolence. "Ahhh. She must be your lovely daughter. Kaleela, wasn't it? She looks just like her mother."

Kahled tried to reply, tried to understand how this creature could know such things, but his body gave out. He pushed all his resistance into a single word, even as his legs crumpled, bringing him to his knees. "No."

The Overlord's voice trailed over the noise of the prison door slamming and locking shut, his footsteps receding into the distant corridor. "She'll do nicely."

Horror filled Kahled as his hoarse cries went unanswered.

11

DIMITAR

D imitar didn't think things would go so wrong, so soon after
leaving Blackburn.

After all, they'd left without issue, having conveyed Kahled's
message to Blackburn's council the night before. Kaleela encouraged
his plan; indeed, Blackburn dispatched a messenger to Stormgard at
first light to request aid. In front of the council, Kaleela put on a brave
face, stating that Kahled wanted her to travel to the Sun'Din Forest
for the first time in her life. Dimitar requested fellow guardsman Olaf
for additional protection, and Kaleela declined any further troops or
ladies-in-waiting, citing the need for discreet travels. The messenger
had been unable to stay to address the council, Kaleela explained, and
she used the token lock of her mother's hair as proof of the message.

Using half-truths to cover their actual plan made lying easier
yet did nothing to lessen Dimitar's guilt. The three rode out the
next morning under Sir Talin's watchful eye, the rosy blush of dawn
warming into a golden day. The men wore guardsmen's uniforms and
light armor, a mix of authority and protection. Kaleela now donned
a long leather jerkin split at the sides for riding, with a light blouse
and pants protected by leather bracers and high boots. Talin himself
strapped her bow and quiver to her horse, but his parting words were
for Dimitar.

"I trust you with this task." His next words had a chilling effect. "Do
not let me down."

They met up with Ral just past the city gates at the crossing
roads. Rolling lands gave way to level fields heavy with crops this time

of year as they veered toward the Arlan Bridge south of the city. If significantly fewer travelers shared their path as they grew closer to the crossing point later the next evening, Dimitar dismissed their absence for inconsequential reasons.

Now, however, he surveyed the unchecked river, its connecting bridge destroyed. The regular flow of travelers was literally cut off.

"Ah, hells. Of all the ruttin' ass luck!" Olaf swore with great gusto, his voice carrying downstream. "For the love of the gods, what happened here?"

The group faced the open river, startlingly expansive without the bridge to diminish its considerable distance from bank to bank. The Tempest River lived up to its name, with currents flowing to near-rapids. Water pounded on the larger planks caught against the rocks along the riverside.

"I thought you said you went over this on the way back!" Kaleela shouted over the crash of the rapids, her voice strained in distress.

Ral knelt and picked at the edge of what was once the largest bridge humans ever built. Somehow, over the course of a few days, it had been chopped asunder. He stood and motioned.

"Says he did cross this bridge," Olaf translated. "It could've been torn down as soon as last night. The cuts are still fresh."

"But why? And by whom?" Dimitar dismounted and knelt to inspect the wood in the waning sunlight. "Did any of the Corrupted follow you?"

'This isn't Corruptor work. It's not in their strength.' Ral shook his head, still shrouded by the cloak's hood, and motioned again with a hand gesturing high above him.

Dimitar tensed. *Goblins.* Large, lumbering giants with no thought in their skulls but violence. As mountain dwellers, their presence along this branch of the Tempest River made no sense.

"Are ya sure?" Olaf asked after Ral finished. "I didn't think they came this far out. How would ya know?"

Kaleela cleared her throat, impatient puzzlement upon her face.

"Oh, sorry 'bout that, Princess. Ral's sayin' goblins chopped down this bridge."

"I didn't think they ventured this far west either," she said. "Why does he think goblins did it?"

Olaf shot Ral a look as if to say, 'I told you so,' before responding. "This bridge was a big'un. Ral thinks t'would take a goblin's strength to cut it down. And the chops in these planks are uneven, unskilled. I think that's hasty work, but Ral says 'twas clumsy goblin hands. Maybe both. And so few travelers hereabouts... if goblins came through, folks would've scattered in a hurry all right—or been captured."

"Whatever got this bridge down doesn't help us crossing the river, does it?" Kaleela said, edging back into the conversation. "I don't care the reason it's gone, only that we're stuck on this side. We can try to ford it."

Olaf raised his eyebrows and assessed the turbulent river. "I don't think so, Princess. The current's pretty strong."

"Our horses are stronger."

"That water reaches well o'er your head 'bout twice a dozen paces out. Our horses won't make it that distance without bein' pulled under by our equipment, much less ourselves. 'Tis far too risky."

"The Hunter Bridge is straight north of here," Dimitar pointed out. "I crossed it from Stormgard when I intercepted the messenger..." *With the news of Conrad's death.* He caught himself before voicing this thought aloud, not wanting to cause Kaleela further grief.

"Aye. 'Tis a four-, five-day ride or so from the north side of Blackburn's lands, if memory serves me." Olaf chewed his bottom lip in thought. "We'd hafta' make our path through part of the Barren Lands once we cross t'other side, but aye, that's our next quickest route."

"So we're retracing our steps? Adding more time to our travels?" Kaleela asked, frowning.

"There's no other choice given the bridge is out, but we can make up some time by leaving now, tonight," Dimitar said. "The roads are open, and we know them."

Across the river, off in the distance, the dark tops of the Eastern Mountain range lifted the day's last light, fading fast.

"Kaleela." Dimitar pulled her searching gaze to his own. Her urgency compelled him, but not as much as the desire to soothe her wild edges. "We will get there, to your father. We'll see this through with you."

The rising moon peeked in and out of lingering clouds, silver light falling in wavering patches on the ground as they headed back north. The river churned off to their right, neither current or breadth lessening. Another hour passed of careful riding before the heady scent of burning wood brought them to a halt. In a small patch of trees next to the road ahead rose a sliver of smoke.

The fire's presence struck Dimitar with uneasiness. Plenty of villages dotted the area, as he'd taken care to steer the group along the outskirts during the day. In all likelihood, the small dance of flames ahead warmed a couple of travelers sleeping under the stars. Having come across not a soul since reaching the felled Arlan Bridge, Dimitar couldn't shake the feeling that something sinister lay ahead.

Dimitar wasn't the only one with a gut instinct; Olaf had already unfastened Lucky from its baldric. With a jerk of his head at Olaf, Dimitar dismounted and pulled out his blade in one slow, silent motion. The path along the riverside was naturally swept clear, but several more paces back from the road lay dense underbrush among the uneven woods. Forging a path through thick growth was tedious, and the noise alone from snapping branches would alert whoever waited before them. With quick motions, the four decided to split up. Dimitar and Olaf would go in the middle while Ral and Kaleela waited. If the men found anything amiss, they'd decide how to get around.

Dimitar and Olaf crept toward the edge of the trees. As they got closer, deep grumblings issued forth, voices that resembled rocks rolling down a mountainside: voices definitely *not* human. Dimitar flexed his fingers on the pommel of his sword, the back of his neck alight with nerves, pricking his skin. Lowering themselves into a walking crouch, they crossed the remaining few yards to the clearing. As his eyes adjusted to the silhouettes against the light of the flames, the coldness of pure fear descended upon him.

Two goblins sat around a rising fire, their immensity perched on fallen tree trunks. Deep-green skin speckled with splotches dotted across their faces. Large tusks protruded underneath their bottom lips and curved toward their cheekbones, indicating this pair had been away from the goblin lairs for some time. Goblins' tusks would break or snap in half during the daily struggles to gain leadership over the goblin tribes.

They feasted upon some carcass, which Dimitar prayed wasn't human. Meat grease dripped in rivulets off their tusks and stained the leather hides that served as their protection. Their roughened skin glistened in the firelight, blood from the meal still drying.

Closing his eyes a moment, Dimitar forced back his fear and turned to Olaf.

"There's not a chance for us," Olaf whispered, having assessed the situation. "Fightin' isn't an option; it's reckless at best. Our best hope is findin' a path far 'round them. The last thing we want is to be spotted."

Dimitar cocked his head at a crack of leaves and twigs. The sounds intensified as an enormous creature plodded from the underbrush shadows. Dimitar turned around where, not even twenty paces away, a third goblin came back from the hunt, a large deer slung over its shoulder. With a growl, the goblin bared its tusked teeth as the deer slipped to the ground with a sickening thud.

Dimitar braced himself. "Well. We've been spotted."

12

DIMITAR

Cursing himself for not watching their backs, Dimitar took a split second to decide he'd need some light to fight by. Forcing his feet to move, he ran into the clearing and brought his sword up. Olaf, with less agility, came bounding forward with the same conclusion. Dimitar charged straight at the nearest goblin, using his only advantage: surprise. The goblin in front of the fire shared one more throaty laugh with its companion before turning its startled attention on the two men.

Their leather armor was crudely fashioned, tattered edges held together with strained cords, and the gaps provided a target. Dimitar ducked under the goblin's attempt to swat him and swung his blade in a slicing arc, dragging the edge along the goblin's ribs. Pivoting into a defensive posture, Dimitar dipped his sword; the burst of triumph that went with his perfect strike evaporated. Where there should've been a gaping wound came nothing; no scratch, no blood, not even a mark. He'd managed to cut some strings holding the leather together, nothing more. The goblin chuckled, a deep, menacing sound, at Dimitar's growing confusion and shook its arms a few times to dislodge the now loose armor.

A loud clang startled Dimitar's attention to Olaf locked in a push with the other goblin in the clearing, their axes caught together. Olaf's face turned red as he strained with every muscle against the creature, his head up to the goblin's chest. Even as Olaf matched the goblin's unblinking, menacing glare, his locked legs scraped backwards in the dirt. In a sudden move used many times in sparring, Olaf buckled his knees and arms and ducked to his right. The abrupt loss of resistance sent the goblin sprawling forward, its back exposed to Olaf, who raised Lucky.

Before the attack landed, Dimitar refocused on his own fight. Stretching, the goblin pulled itself to full height, towering close to eight feet tall, and dragged a scarred axe off the ground. As the axe came down, Dimitar stepped to the side and brought his blade across the goblin's arm. The goblin's skin absorbed the blow, its pebbled hide natural armor. Dimitar shoved his sword forward to pierce the goblin's middle, but it knocked his blade aside. In the same motion, the goblin brought the axe down with its other hand. Dimitar flung himself into a backwards roll, letting go of his sword to avoid harming himself.

The third goblin entered the clearing, and Dimitar scrambled forward in an attempt to gain his footing, just avoiding the fire blazing in its pit. Weaponless, he darted his gaze between the two goblins who leered, grotesque grins spread all the wider by their tusks. A thunderous roar to his right meant Olaf still fought the third goblin, and given the pain laced with the howl, his friend at least caused the creature some harm.

Dimitar took short steps backward to gain enough time and ground to react if the goblins charged. His sword lay out of reach, just past the approaching goblins. Training for years with Olaf, he knew the advantage speed had against stronger yet slower opponents. Right now, his quickness was the only thing keeping him alive until he reached his blade.

The goblins stepped toward Dimitar at the same time, axe and club coming down in unison. Dimitar didn't have time to marvel at the surprising strategy the creatures displayed and dove below the attack. Although he avoided the brunt of the strikes, the axe tip caught his calf in passing, rushing heat slamming through his leg. Grimacing against the pain, he spun into a purposeful roll that brought himself next to his sword, and grabbed the familiar hilt. His leg almost buckled underneath him as he squared himself off.

Saying a silent prayer, Dimitar loosened his shoulders and braced himself into a fighter's stance. His prayer was answered a moment later when a blur of red cloth flung upon the goblin to his right, a well-aimed kick knocking the axe to the ground. Ral latched onto the goblin's back, much to its fury and annoyance. In a flash, Ral brought out a dagger and swung it into the goblin's shoulder. It roared and spun in swift, tight circles, and Ral had to grip with both hands to keep from flinging off.

The other goblin slowed its approach toward Dimitar, gaping at the ensuing tussle until a new movement caught its eye. Kaleela stood in the clearing, bow in hand and uncertainty on her face, until she was forced to duck out of the way as the goblin whirled by with Ral on its back. The goblin facing Dimitar turned with a low growl as it raised the club and stomped toward Kaleela.

"No! Over here!" Dimitar startled himself with the force of his voice. As the goblin turned to him, he shouted to Kaleela, "Get back! Stay out of the way."

Any other direction failed on his lips as the goblin charged Dimitar with its own roar. Dimitar leapt aside as the air whooshed by him, the goblin's club smashing where he'd stood seconds before. Dimitar winced as fresh blood seeped down his injured leg, and thrust his sword out. The goblin twisted away, but not before the tip punctured its side.

The goblin's sloping brow furrowed into murderous rage. Dimitar backed up as the goblin raised its club once more, but his leg gave out, and he crumpled to the ground. He grabbed his calf to stem the shooting pain, blood wetting his palm. Steeling himself to rise, Dimitar flinched as a *hiss* of air cut above his head an instant before an arrow dug into the goblin's left shoulder. The creature howled, its cry rising in outrage as two more arrows shot through the night air and hit its legs.

Still, the goblin trudged forward, club poised over its head. As Dimitar brought his sword up in defense, knowing full well the blade would do little to deflect the goblin's massive club, another arrow took out the goblin's knee. Finally, the creature stumbled and came crashing down. At the last instant, Dimitar pushed himself forward and drove his sword hilt into the ground. By its own momentum, the goblin impaled itself on the blade, the tip driving straight through. The goblin twitched before its movements ceased, and Dimitar shoved it over to wrestle his sword free.

Dimitar came to his feet, gritting his teeth as blood trickled down his leg, and turned toward the source of the attack. *Smart of you.*

Kaleela had assumed a vantage point on a branch just above goblin reach. There, she could choose a target. She met his glance, eyes wide and face pale, before pulling another arrow from her quiver and fitting it into the notch with a lick of her thumb.

Dimitar drew his attention back to the clearing. Sweat and blood dampened Olaf's shirt, most of it the goblin's blackish-green blood. Still, Olaf seemed too tired. His arms hung limp, out of strength to even raise his axe.

The goblin, also laboring for breath, flung its axe forward. An arrow shot from the tree and into the goblin's lower back, breaking the charge for the briefest moment. Olaf took full advantage and swung his axe with a speed Dimitar hadn't seen before from his friend, burying the blade deep in the center of the creature's chest. Olaf had feigned his tiredness, just like in so many training matches before—a move that seemed to fool everyone, including Dimitar.

The goblin stood with its axe over its head, gasping for air that wouldn't come and eyes wide in shock. Olaf pulled his axe out of the goblin's chest in one swift motion, and the creature collapsed to the ground. It lay dying, panting in ragged breaths that dribbled viscous blood from its mouth. Olaf stood over it, glancing up as Kaleela whimpered.

"Oh, let it end... gods of mercy, let it end." She sat with her back against the tree trunk, her bow forgotten in a loose grasp. She cupped her free hand over her mouth, her eyes mirroring the horror before them as the monstrous creature writhed, its blood spilling across the ground. Dimitar caught Olaf's face, calm and blank as he turned to deliver death, hefting his axe with ease. With one swift, strong movement he swung his axe against the goblin's neck, silencing it.

The grunting in the clearing belonged to the third remaining goblin with Ral still squared upon its back. As if to add insult, the final goblin now ignored Ral, tired of spinning in circles to no avail. In a sudden move, the goblin turned and threw its shoulder against the tree where Kaleela perched. The unexpected collision jarred the tree enough to knock her loose. She dropped her bow to clamp her arms around the tree branch, kicking her legs for purchase a few feet above them.

When the goblin lifted its mass off the tree and turned, Ral clung tighter, refusing to let go as sure as his hood refused to fall from his face. The goblin swiped at Kaleela and then slammed against the tree trunk. She cried out as the branch shuddered, and her grip slipped. She fell hard to the ground at the goblin's feet, the wind knocked out of her.

"Kaleela!" Dimitar cried, starting toward her but faltering with a wordless shout when his leg buckled, driving him to the ground.

A sadistic growl issued forth as the goblin grabbed for her, but in the next moment, Ral was no longer weaponless. From within his cloak, he unsheathed a knife the length of his forearm, plunging it into the goblin's neck. A plume of blood shot into the night as the goblin arched back, wailing in mortal pain.

In one motion, Ral swung his weight to the other shoulder and reached around the front of the goblin. Grabbing the knife hilt with both hands, Ral worked the blade through the goblin's neck with a vicious strength Dimitar didn't know the smaller man possessed. He leaned back for leverage, and a rending sound followed as the blade ripped through the hide. With the blade more than halfway, Ral jerked the knife across the rest of the goblin's neck. The goblin fell to its knees, blood gurgling from the wound and its lips, splashing against its tusks. Ral stood free, panting, as the goblin fell face-first to the ground, the body hitting the clearing hard enough that the landing reverberated in the soles of Dimitar's boots.

"Well, if that ain't the damnedest—" Olaf drew up short as Ral grabbed another knife from his belt, spun the blade in his hand, and came down onto the goblin's back, burying the blade to the hilt. He pulled the blade out and brought it down again and again. On the next upswing, Ral hesitated, his bloodied, raised fist clenching the knife hilt, trembling.

Olaf took a cautious step. "It's dead, lad. Let it be." He put his hand on Ral's shoulder.

Ral swung around with a whip of cloth and stopped the dagger just before slicing Olaf's chest. His hand still shook as thick blood dripped from the blade tip, his hood infallibly hiding his face and the expression he wore.

Dimitar and Kaleela stared in bewilderment as he threw down the dagger in revulsion, shoulders heaving. Turning from Olaf, still frozen with his arm extended, Ral stumbled across the clearing and headed to the river. Water splashed as he presumably washed the blood from his hands and clothing.

"Hells was that all about?" Olaf asked, finding his voice.

"I don't know, and don't think that..."

Dimitar trailed off at the unexpected movement behind his friend. A goblin stood up, thick green blood oozing from its middle, and its face contorted with pain and rage. It lumbered faster than Dimitar expected, its club raised.

"Olaf, move, move!" Dimitar grabbed him, trying to pull him aside. He stumbled against Olaf, pain spiking up his damn calf, tangling as they grappled for their weapons, too late.

Without warning, a spear shot between them, piercing the goblin's throat with a burst of fresh blood. It lurched two more steps before collapsing to the ground, dead.

Dimitar, Olaf, and Kaleela turned as one, and a willowy figure emerged from the shadows.

13

KALEELA

Kaleela's jaw dropped as the dying firelight played against the burnt sienna skin of a Lachan woman. She shook back her textured curls, still damp and dripping, tapered along the side of her head. River water sluiced off her form-fitting clothing, a hint of fish-scale leather reflecting the flames. Stately in the quiet elegance of power, wisdom filled her features.

She pursed her full lips and peered at the goblins. "They're all dead now, yes?"

"Aye... yes," Kaleela stammered as the Lachan woman blinked, a milky white film sweeping across her eyes. Her heartbeat slowed; the lake kinfolk kept to themselves and were known for their peaceful nature. "How long have you been standing there?"

"Long enough to see you take on three at once." She gestured to the goblin bodies bleeding out. "It was well done but foolish."

"It wasn't quite what we planned." Dimitar wiped and sheathed his sword as he nodded at the spear in the goblin's neck. "Thank you for that."

"My pleasure," the Lachan woman replied. "But I do have questions for the other one."

The woman put two fingers in her mouth and issued a brief, high-pitched whistle. From the clearing shadows, two Lachan men appeared, their tanned bodies dripping from the river. The men's heads were shaved into a fade, traditional among the lake men who swam in waters almost as unencumbered as fish. Similar in appearance, the two men each adorned sheath-like clothing in muted yet varied colors, and held sharpened rattan spears with an ease that came from years of proficiency.

Ral stood between them at spearpoint.

"You three fought for your lives." The Lachan woman pointed at Ral. "But this one fought for another reason. I would know why."

Everyone turned to face Ral, recalling the brutal frenzy with which he killed the goblin. Ral's hooded face turned to each of them, and he made a sign even Kaleela understood.

'No.'

Ral had intervened the instant the goblin reached for her, stunned on the ground. He acted to save her; but his actions after he killed the goblin surpassed that. Kaleela worried, not about him but for him.

The Lachan woman assessed Ral, then said something in a low voice to her companions in their own language.

"We came upon these three on our own travels, by accident. If there are more, they're not at this site," Kaleela said, diverting the attention off Ral.

With a mumbled word from the woman and a gentle tap against her chest with her first two fingers, the two men searched the clearing. They dropped to one knee at times to examine some markings, trying to make any sense of tracking under the moonlight.

The Lachan woman turned back to Kaleela. "Feorn is my given name."

She placed her palm out straight, facing Kaleela who stared a moment before understanding her greeting. She placed her own palm against Feorn's then turned to the rest of the group to exchange introductions.

"I will speak further with you and your company, but our words risk discord on this ground, which has been injured tonight," Feorn said. "Let us make camp away from here where we can speak freely."

Kaleela was thankful to leave the meaty goblin carcasses behind, equal relief crossing Dimitar's and Olaf's faces. Dimitar's leg buckled as he turned, pant leg darkened with blood.

Olaf hooked an arm under his. "Steady there, m'boy."

Feorn clicked her tongue at Dimitar's grimace and motioned for him to sit and roll up his pant leg. She called for water while one of the Lachan men foraged at the base of the trees around the clearing. Reaching into a hole in the trunk of a large, bleached tree, he pulled out a small pile of moss cupped by fingers webbed past the first joint, picking at the plant as he brought it over to Feorn.

Opening a waxed leather pouch at her side, she removed a palmful of dried brown leaf. She worked efficiently yet in no haste to strike up further conversation with the others. She crushed the leaf and pinch of moss into a cup of water handed to her, using her finger to stir the thickening contents before applying the poultice. Kaleela watched Dimitar's face, but he didn't flinch; the salve must have a numbing agent. Feorn then adjusted a bandage cloth around his calf.

"Where are you hurt?" Dimitar faced Kaleela, seated next to him, catching her off guard with the frustration in his tone—not toward her but at what had happened.

"I'm not... I'm unharmed," she replied, startled into sudden shyness by his attention.

"I saw you fall out of the tree," he persisted, shifting to get a better look at her, his trained eyes searching for injury.

She studied his face as he looked her over, the light blue of his eyes under dark lashes and full lips pulled into a solemn line that then uplifted when he met her gaze. *He's quite handsome but acts like he doesn't know it. He's only focused on me.* Any anger furrowing his brow dissipated into connection as they studied one another.

"I'm all right." She touched his arm, noting the muscles under her fingertips, and blushed again. "Thank you."

Leaning across Dimitar, Feorn turned Kaleela's hands over, appraising the cuts on her palms. Feorn must've noticed her hands, scraped raw from clinging to the branch, when they touched palms. She cleaned and applied a clear balm to the minor cuts.

Kaleela murmured thanks when Feorn finished, cupping her hands as the balm soothed the pain and formed a protective seal over the cuts.

With help from the Lachans, the group gathered their tethered horses after rinsing the goblin blood and dirt off their clothes in the river. Kaleela caught sight of Ral offering Olaf a dampened cloth, miming for him to touch the side of his face. Olaf wiped at his temple, blood smearing from a cut. Ral blotted it for him until the wound was clean, earning a clap on the back in thanks.

And perhaps forgiveness for earlier in the clearing.

While the others walked, Dimitar rode to favor his injured leg, and within the quarter hour, they found a suitable glade to make camp next to the riverside. Ral struck flint and stone to start a new campfire, and the group gathered close around the flames. In the new light, Olaf passed around his liquor flask; Kaleela declined, and the lake men coughed after a sip each and did not partake anymore.

"I thank you again, Feorn, Lady of the Waters," Dimitar said with formal respect. "What brings you so far from your southern home in Lake Lachlann?"

"We have a common foe." Feorn's voice resonated with a low and pleasing quality. For the first time since the encounter, the lake woman's face twisted into a trace of repulsion. "The goblins' numbers have grown in the open lands near our waters. We tracked this group to determine their purpose and stop them if they were to further stain our river."

"Then maybe you can tell us what felled the Arlan Bridge?" Kaleela asked.

One of the Lachans spat into the fire with a guttural comment. Feorn glanced at him bemusedly, but her eyes were worried. "Yes, goblins destroyed the great bridge. They set axe, club, and fist to it. We could do nothing but watch as they sundered wood, and the waters ran foul with their deed. The town on the far side wasn't prepared for the attack and could offer little resistance. The men sheltered their people, barricading themselves within Hamelton's walls, their best course of action. The sun hadn't moved far across the sky by the time the goblins finished. Some of them swept downstream," she added as an afterthought.

"What a terrible thing to watch. I'll send word to my father, so we can lend aid to Hamelton's people."

With a sharp intake of breath, Kaleela caught herself. Her father wasn't at home within Blackburn Castle. As reality came crashing back, she missed him terribly and wanted both him and Conrad to stand next to her with their immovable strength. This night dragged on so very long, and she'd brought death by her own hand for the first time, gruesome and frightening.

Feorn shook her head in refusal. "And yet, as fast as they swarmed the bridge, after the goblins destroyed the crossing, they charged back to their mountainside. They didn't even stay to plunder Hamelton's streets and people."

Ral stopped stoking the fire and passed a hand over his face, still masked within the shadows of his cloak.

Olaf huffed. "It's not makin' any sense."

"The goblins' movements have increased as of late," Feorn said. "I caution you on your journey. We don't know what drives these creatures further out from the mountains."

One of the Lachan men spoke at length to Feorn in their language, his words clipped and solemn in a way that reminded Kaleela of the flow of water in a choppy stream. Feorn turned to the group with an easy smile, but questions flashed in her eyes. "Where does your journey bring you, and to what purpose?"

Kaleela looked to Dimitar, who looked to Olaf, who turned to them at a loss. With all their careful planning, they hadn't discussed what they'd say if questioned by folk along the way.

Kaleela broke the silence with a small sigh. "Feorn, your assistance tonight has been invaluable, and I do feel a debt is owed. I'll share with you the truth of our matter, but you and your men must understand what I'm about to tell you is of utmost secrecy.

"My father is King Kahled of Blackburn." She gestured toward Ral, withdrawn even deeper into his cloak. "This man brought word he's been captured by Corruptors, held within the Eastern Mountains. Fear for his very life led me to seek his rescue, and I aim to do so within my power and with the strength of these guardsmen."

Silence followed her explanation, and Kaleela questioned if she was right to give up her cover to these strangers.

"Corruptors." Feorn turned the word over in her mouth. She leaned toward her guardsmen and spoke in a low, hushed tone.

"Please," Kaleela said, desperation welling in her throat. "I need to know if there's a safe passageway across the Tempest now that the Arlan Bridge is down."

One of the lake men spoke to Kaleela with a brief gesture. Feorn repeated what the man advised. "If it's true what you claim, and Corruptors leach their evil in this world once more, then you have one solution. You must seek out Master Karn in the northern cities."

At Karn's name, Ral straightened at once, alert to the conversation at hand. Kaleela regarded Feorn with a mixture of relief that the lake woman wasn't inclined to argue against their mission, and despair at being sidetracked from their journey's path. Her distress must have sat plain across her face, for Feorn patted Kaleela's hand in comfort.

"I would not send just anyone to speak with them. If what you say is without doubt, Master Karn must hear of the Corruptors' attack and the goblins' destruction. I'm sure of this as I am of Mother Moon and Sister Sun gracing our sky. You must seek their counsel, without delay. For your father's sake, as well our own."

Ral shifted into a crouch beside Olaf and motioned as he translated. 'Leighton is a few leagues from the Hunter Bridge, on the western side of Arrowsfall Kingdom. We can get a room and some good food at a tavern, and summon Master Karn there.'

"How do you know him?" Dimitar asked, his voice tight.

'Not him. Them. Have you heard of the Storm of Banishment and the ten magic-users who became one person—'

"Hold up." Olaf stopped translating, astonished. "You're talkin' about the magic-user who ended the rift?"

Ral held up ten fingers, then one, and nodded.

"The ten magic-users who became one is Karn?" Olaf repeated, doubt and awe in his voice.

"Master Karn," Feorn corrected. "Their wisdom is invaluable and may help you save your king."

Olaf clapped his hands together once and addressed the Lachans. "Ya did us a great service tonight, and I'm speakin' for all of us when I say our gratitude runs as deep as the waters in that lake of yours." Olaf paused, clearly pleased at himself for the use of analogy. "If meetin' with Karn won't bring us too far out of our path and might help us rescue King Kahled, then I say that's where we're goin' next."

Kaleela forced her sore hands to unclench. She didn't want this detour, but what other choice was there? "All right. If Leighton is closest to the Hunter Bridge, we can stop to speak with this person. My thanks to you as well."

"My pleasure. Perhaps we'll meet again someday. Rest you all the remainder of tonight, for our Old Mother has drifted well across the sky path. Then, please, make haste to Master Karn."

Feorn bid her goodbye, raising her hands to the sky as if in offering to the waning moon, then crossed them over her chest and bowed her head. Her two companions followed likewise, and with a soft splash, the Lachans departed into the water.

Dimitar and Ral laid out their bedrolls. Olaf took another sip from his flask and leaned Lucky against a tree as he settled into the first round of watch. Kaleela ran over the night's events in her mind. Untested though they were, their training had proved its worth, and three goblins felt the strength of it. Yet the night's violence unnerved her, and she tossed in her bedroll. She fell asleep to the memory of Dimitar calling her name, echoing in her dreams, his voice a shield.

14

DIMITAR

After a day of hard travel back north, the hills surrounding Blackburn rose before them. They traveled at least two or three hilltops away from the kingdom itself, still far too close. Kaleela snuck furtive glances, and Dimitar guessed the same thoughts crossed her mind: if they came across any patrols from the city, they didn't have an explanation for why their princess and her guard were still within the kingdom's borders. Not until nightfall did he breathe a sigh of relief.

"I'm takin' first watch again," Olaf said, as the group dismounted in a grassy clearing off the path.

As they set up camp, Ral signaled to Dimitar. The cloaked man pointed to the sky—no, to the moon—and put up four fingers. The meaning was clear: they would arrive in Leighton on the fourth night.

Taking his bedroll over to the campfire, Dimitar sat beside Kaleela, who searched for a spot on the ground absent of roots and hidden rocks. "Ral says we have four more days of travel to reach Leighton."

Kaleela glanced up at the mention of the distance, and her shoulders slumped. "I can't stand the thought of him in those mountains. Or help but think about what those creatures are doing to him. What they did to Conrad."

Wrapping her arms around herself, Kaleela shivered despite the warmth spreading from the fire. Dimitar enfolded her body in his wool blanket, rubbing his hands up and down her arms for warmth and comfort. Something shifted in his chest, taking care of her like this, a move from obligation to desire.

"Your father is strong, Kaleela, the strongest man I've ever known." A touch of humor laced his next words. "I'm more concerned about what he's doing to the Corruptors than what they're doing to him."

He was rewarded with a small chuckle. Her resiliency since leaving Blackburn Castle impressed him, as did her competency both in the saddle and enduring unsheltered nights. Most of all, he wanted to bring out her smile.

Ral came over and motioned with slow intention to Kaleela. She answered aloud while practicing the hand gestures. Dimitar joined the impromptu lesson, correcting her translations when needed. *She's learning faster than I did.*

He brought out his whetstone as she practiced the silent language, the rhythmic swiping calming. Several burrs from the goblin fight needed smoothing. When the sword caught the firelight in its mirrored edge, Dimitar sat back, satisfied.

Olaf returned with water and a small satchel of spices to start a stew. Meatless again, but at least the meal filled them up when sopped up with the bread from their packs. Dimitar checked the bandage around his calf, noting the herbal poultice hastened the healing time, the sealed wound well on its way to becoming a scar and memory.

By the time the light of the fourth day faded into sunset, a large number of lanterns appeared up ahead, swinging off stakes pegged to the ground and marking the city entrance. Passing through a large gateway, Dimitar noted a hand-carved and weather-worn sign stating they indeed crossed into Leighton.

The city wasn't nearly the size of Blackburn nor close to its grandeur. Compared to Blackburn's orderly construction of streets around the castle, Leighton was a maze. Buildings on either side of the dirt road rose three tilted stories tall. Side streets peeked between wooden structures, creating an uncountable number of alleyways hidden by the dark. Several shops, from bakeries to smithies, blended along the bottom floors of the wall-to-wall buildings. Unlike Blackburn's daytime business district, Leighton's night market was underway, and the streets filled with merchants, gamblers, and carousers.

On some of the top floors, women stretched out of windows in various degrees of dress. *Or rather, undress.* Several offered him a healthy glimpse of flesh for coin. Two such women, their hair in oiled curls and cleavage on prominent display, sent a deluge of catcalls in their direction. A shirtless man joined the two, leaning out the window to see what caught his colleagues' attention. Dimitar couldn't miss the dark path of hair trailing down the man's lower stomach into some low-hung, loose linen pants. Dimitar glanced over at Kaleela and blushed, which deepened as Olaf took it upon himself to yell back.

"I got some important business to take care of right now, but I'll be 'round 'fore the night's done for ya." Pointing at each in turn, he added with a bellow, "And then for ya. And then for yer friend."

The pleasure sellers screeched in laughter and hollered various offers that Dimitar hadn't even realized could be purchased. Looking over his shoulder, Olaf chuckled as Dimitar threw his head back in exasperation. Ral snapped his fingers to get their attention.

'I know where to look for Master Karn,' Ral signaled. 'Grant us some time with them. It'll be well worth it.'

Dimitar scowled. *Why is he so set on meeting with this person?*

Something about Ral bothered him, an intangible connection hovering on an instinctive level that made no sense. This man, a self-admitted thief after all, had little reason to help them as he claimed. Dimitar tried to release his tension. After all, Ral had returned Kahled's message when he could've fled across the Green Lands instead.

With a sigh, Dimitar flipped a piece of hair off his forehead with a shake of his head. "Where might this Karn be, then?"

Ral pointed a short distance ahead to a tavern engulfed among the taller buildings, its worn sign hanging askew. Truth be told, Dwyer's Pub wasn't much on the outside. The small tavern sat tucked in the intersection of two back streets, its outer walls covered in dusty grime, giving it a used appearance. The maroon queendom banner of Arrowsfall hung outside, frayed at the edges. Dimitar exchanged a doubtful glance with Olaf as they led the group to rickety stables behind the tavern, the path winding and intersecting with more back alleys.

As they dismounted, Ral caught their attention and signaled. 'We should carry anything we value with us to our rooms. If we leave them out here, might be the last time we see them.'

"Great part of town you've brought us to," Dimitar said under his breath as he shot a pointed look at Ral, but grabbed the knapsack from his saddlebag and threw in the few things he'd be sorely parted from.

Kaleela did the same; among the items she shifted over included the Mage Warrior book he'd found her reading in the castle's gardens. Olaf shouldered his bag and strode toward a sneering stableman lurking in the corner. Dimitar headed out to get rooms for the night, securing the coin purse in his pack. He held the stable door open for Kaleela when she called for him to wait up.

"Olaf's bickering with the stable hand over the cost," she said, "and I think Ral's hanging around for sheer amusement. He told us to go ahead."

The pathway from the stables to the inn was indistinct in the dimly-lit gloom, but not so shadowed that Dimitar didn't see a man stumble toward them from the inn's entrance, coming to rest in the middle of the path. The sight of the bar patron fumbling about his waist greeted him, followed by a long trickle as the man rested a hand against the wall. *You'd think we entered the damn southern lands.*

Kaleela turned away in disgust and headed for the other side of the building. An alleyway veered off before them, and Dimitar's footsteps became more cautious. He slowed his steps, taking Kaleela's arm to stop her alongside him.

"I think we've taken a wrong turn." He scanned the shadows. Something triggered his senses yet remained out of reach. He cursed the poor light, as the crescent moon couldn't penetrate the dark. The hum of people within the bar was muted, blocked behind walls thicker than they appeared. "Let's go back the other way."

Dimitar drew up short as this time a crooked-back man approached from the alley, clutching a tattered wrap around him. He held out a worn tin cup.

"Your spare coins, if you please," the man croaked.

Kaleela reached for her bag, but Dimitar held her hand.

"We've nothing to spare." He ignored Kaleela's wounded look as he pulled her past the man without another glance. Trouble swarmed in a town like Leighton, and that very trouble closed around them like netting.

Dimitar stopped short a second time when the man stepped before them, now not so old in body, and came to a complete stand.

"It wasn't a request," came a much steadier, although still raspy voice.

Even in the gloom, Dimitar caught the glint of metal; the man no longer held a tin cup. Dimitar didn't have to turn at the slight scuffles behind him to know they'd just been surrounded. A match strike hissed, and lantern light illuminated the alleyway.

The man shrugged off the ragged blanket, tall and lanky in stature and dressed in black leathers. He rested a crossbow on his shoulder, at ease but cocked and ready to fire at a moment's notice. A deep scar across the underside of his left cheekbone made his crooked smile all the more prominent.

Dimitar situated himself between Kaleela and Scarface, and assessed the three other men standing in a semicircle. They blended with the shadows in their black leather and cloaks. One man stood with a dagger brandished, and another held an uncoiled whip that he swung lazily on the ground. The third man set the lantern on a barrel and stood with his arms crossed, a smirk on his greasy face.

"What do you want?" Dimitar asked the man with the crossbow.

"What else would we want?" he said. "Give us your coins and whatever else of value, and we'll let you go."

Dimitar swore beneath his breath, anger rising within him and emptying into a single, heated name: Ral. *He set us up. The bastard completely set us up.*

"And if we refuse?" Kaleela's voice lilted clear and calm.

In response, Greasy Face advanced to their right, arms now unfolded and fists clenched. The apparent leader shifted his crossbow from one shoulder to the other and eyed her with a wicked grin.

"Hand them over, and we won't harm you," he said, looking as if he preferred she put up a struggle.

"Somehow I doubt that." Dimitar shifted his knapsack straps around both shoulders in a firm grip.

"No, we'd rather not lose a gold piece in a brawl nor damage our jewels. Why, you have a lovely jewel with you. Step forward, Lady, for a look here."

Kaleela stiffened behind Dimitar, her body tensing against his, and instantly his anger boiled over. He'd expected Ral's thieving—*he's nothing better than a criminal*—but this put Kaleela in harm's way. Unforgivable.

81

"Don't you even think to look at her," Dimitar snarled, but the men chortled as Scarface crooked his finger at Kaleela. The situation spiraled out of hand, and he wasn't sure he could take on all the men without risking Kaleela's safety.

To his surprise, she stepped around him.

"Raised by High Knights, remember?" she whispered to him with a gleam in her eye before turning to face the thieves.

"Ah, there's a charming sight, boys, such a sparkly jewel. And the lady's a looker too, eh?" The men snickered while the leader motioned one of the thieves closer. "Why don't you relieve the lady of the burden of wearing such a large necklace gem, as well as that knapsack? I'll bet she'll even give ya a kiss in return as thanks."

Greasy Face grinned a mouthful of crooked teeth as he reached for her necklace with two groping hands. Dimitar moved to intercept the thief but stopped, helpless, as their leader leveled the crossbow at his chest. Kaleela evenly watched the man approach. When the thief stood inches away and his stale breath soiled the air around them, Kaleela snapped her knee straight up. Greasy crumpled to the ground, a small wheeze of agonized pain escaping his lips as he clutched his groin.

Dimitar didn't waste the sudden pause and charged the man with the whip. Although ready to lash out from the man's side in a heartbeat, use of such a weapon required distance. The man scrambled back to snap the whip up, but Dimitar shot forward and grabbed the man's wrist, twisting into a joint lock. The man yelled in pain as he was forced to drop his whip, so when Dimitar's fist connected, a tooth went flying into the night. The man wobbled on his legs, landing in a slump next to Greasy on the ground.

Dimitar faced the man with the dagger, moving with care. A well-placed knife cut didn't take much to inflict mortal damage. He jumped back as the man swung his blade in wide arcs toward his midsection.

"Watch out!" Kaleela cried, moments before Toothless stood and rushed Dimitar from behind.

He was enveloped in a bear hug, arms pinned to his sides as the other thief closed in with a snarl on his face. He twisted and tried to toss the man off, but Toothless held on. Dimitar leaned into him and kicked out at the thief in front, his knife sent careening to the back of the alley. He then snapped his head back, breaking Toothless's nose. The man howled as blood seeped between his fingers.

Dimitar pushed away from Toothless just in time to receive a punch to the jaw from the thief who lost his knife. With a crack of knuckles, he took another blow to the chest and stumbled against the alley wall. He launched a strike of his own, coming up low with the full of his shoulder behind the blow. It connected with the man's midsection and sent him sprawling. Dimitar turned and dodged another blow, Toothless apparently intent on doing as much damage to Dimitar's face as he received. He swung at his opponent, his strike blocked, and swung again.

The men were well used to the harsh life of thievery, but Dimitar had once survived on the streets as well. Unfortunately for the thieves, they'd never faced Olaf as a sparring partner. Dimitar could take hits and brawl with the best of them.

"Enough!" Everyone froze at the command. Scarface leveled his crossbow at Kaleela, who took a step back, all too familiar with the power of a bow.

Dimitar glanced at the leader, wiping blood from a split lip and pausing a breath before lowering his fists. Two of the thieves stumbled up to him, each grabbing an arm and shoving him to his knees. The men held Dimitar as Greasy grappled with the bag on his back.

"Move so much a hair and you'll find my aim is worthier than my friends'. Now hand over your money or things get real ugly." Scarface shifted the crossbow on his shoulder, checking down the sight pins as he threatened to fire.

The mounted arrow was gone, the chamber empty.

Spinning around, the leader gasped as he came face to face with a hooded figure spinning the crossbow's arrow across his fingers.

"Ral!" he rasped, instant recognition lighting a smile on his scarred face. "Hells, you scared another life out of my soul."

He clapped his hand on Ral's shoulder in greeting, and Ral reciprocated, at ease among the men. Ral handed back the arrow but held up his other hand to hold the man's attention, gesturing toward Dimitar pinned on the ground. Most of the thieves seemed unable to understand his communication, judging by their blank stares, but Scarface paled as he watched Ral's hands. With a quick nod from the leader, the thieves surrounding Dimitar hauled him to his feet none too gently.

Dimitar craned his neck and caught enough of Ral's signing to get the gist.

'They travel with me. Let them go.'

Dimitar yanked himself free from the thieves and turned on Ral, fists balled. "You son of a bitch! You set us up. Just what are you playing at?"

He lunged, and Ral backed away as the others restrained him once more.

"Damn you, Ral! Who do you think you are to threaten us?" Dimitar twisted against his captors who, with cries of 'Whoa there, lad!' now chuckled at his furious outburst.

"It was a misunderstanding—" Scarface began.

"A 'misunderstanding'?" Dimitar shouted.

Scarface raised an eyebrow and sauntered to the end of the alleyway without a backward glance. "Sorry 'bout the interruption, Lady."

He bowed before disappearing into the night. With a few mumbled greetings to Ral and apologies to Kaleela, the thieves dispersed into the streets and alleyways like smoke whisked away on a breeze. Dimitar spun around, but before he caught sight of any one man they were gone, blending back into the inky shadows. He turned to the one remaining thief.

"You." Dimitar pointed a finger at Ral, but a voice cut him off.

"Ach, for the love of all things good, what are the three of ya doin' out here while m'dinner grows cold and m'beer warm?" Olaf sounded genuinely exasperated, but his expression sharpened at Dimitar's rumpled hair, bloodied lip, and heated stare.

"A group of thieves jumped us in the alleyway." Dimitar's eyes flashed toward Ral. "Who just happened to be waiting for us to pass by. And who also know our guide Ral here."

'I have nothing to do with them,' Ral motioned.

"Is that so?" Dimitar countered. "Drop that damn magicked hood, look me in the eyes, and tell me this wasn't your doing."

Ral hesitated, then took a step back, shaking his head.

"Ral stopped them from harming us," Kaleela said.

Dimitar turned to her in disbelief, his temper still unmitigated.

"Well, before you beat them all senseless," she added, but her brow creased as he rounded on Ral once more.

"Kaleela, you were there. You saw how Ral set them up to rob us. They wanted my pack, your necklace, and wouldn't give a second thought to taking our lives as well."

Ral motioned with emphasis, but Dimitar refused to look at him. He faced his closest friend, beseeching.

"Well," Olaf said, after a beat, "I'm hopin' ya did more damage to them than they did to yer pretty face, lad. Ral's sayin' he wasn't a part of this. And he was with me the whole time."

Dimitar touched his swollen lip gingerly and glared at Ral. "He put Kaleela and me in danger. I don't doubt he has other friends coming by to—"

Olaf caught Ral's next gestures and explained before Dimitar exploded at Ral once more. "The crossbow bolt is tipped with a fake head; it would've never penetrated ya if the man fired. 'Tis meant to scare folks, but thieves ain't the killin' kind, not like mercenaries. Let this be, little pup."

Dimitar didn't want to acknowledge his friend's logic, but the use of his childhood nickname made him pause.

Olaf met Dimitar's angry stare and held it steady with his own. "Did ya hear what I said? Ral was with me the entire time. He didn't have a hand in this fight. I'm thinkin' ya just went off and got lucky without me."

Dimitar rubbed the growing ache on his jaw, suddenly too tired to argue with Olaf's rationale. Ral stepped next to Kaleela to make sure she was all right, a hand on her lower back as he guided her to the entrance and held the door open for her. She gave him a reassuring smile, caressing the pendant and tracing the elven letters etched in silver around the gemstone. Dimitar stiffened once more, bracing for another retort at the scrawnier man for no reason other than a flash of jealousy. Olaf intercepted by clasping Dimitar around the shoulders in a brief shake of a hug as they headed up the short steps to the entrance.

"Besides, if ya think the alleys 'round here are rough, wait 'til ya see the inside of this place."

15

KAHLED

Kahled was losing strength with each passing day. Even so, he refused help from the two Corruptors leading him down the dank tunnels. The Overlord summoned him, for what purpose Kahled couldn't fathom. He'd only known isolation since looking into the eyes of the bastard who murdered his knights and best friend. For the first time since the Reclamation, consuming rage filled him.

At first, he was relieved to leave his cell and have the chance to stretch out his body. His apprehension grew as his eyes adjusted to the torch light. Jagged cuts formed the walls, deep crags breaking through at various points. They dripped with moisture, the passageway damp and clammy despite the torches lit every few yards. The unfinished carving left countless handholds and crevices for the Corruptors to grab as they slid and crawled along the walls and ceilings. The Corruptors' mind invasion echoed in Kahled's thoughts as he pictured them swarming his guards, killing them with brutal senselessness as the days ticked by in his cell.

Gods damn them. His anger grew, anticipating the confrontation as a large entryway loomed. He called upon his training: gathering strength from anger caused more harm than good, and he tried to extinguish some of his fury as he walked across the vast hall.

In the room's center piled a raised throne composed of rough-hewn obsidian. Fires climbed the walls from an unseen heat source, like waterfalls flowing in reverse, reflected in the throne's surface. The oppressive heat in the colossal room sucked away his strength, and

Kahled fought to stay standing on shaky legs. The Corruptors grabbed him, claws drawing fresh blood, and led him to the front of the throne.

What was once a man now embodied corruption in every sense of the word. The Overlord looked down at Kahled through slits in an iron battle helm. Ill-formed spikes broke through leathery skin, covered with armor blackened with soot, mud, and blood. The eyes behind the helm were tinged red with cruelty.

Summoning what dignity he had remaining, Kahled spoke first, not allowing the Overlord the pleasure of the initial word.

"What will you have of me," he said, showing no indication of his failing strength.

"*Tsk tsk*, Sir Kahled." The Overlord's voice rumbled, guttural, as if the phlegm couldn't clear from his throat. "Where's my greeting?"

Kahled responded by spitting at his feet.

"Rude, but I'll forgive you. You've been under a lot of strain, and a few of your normal courtesies might be... lacking." The Overlord rose to stand next to Kahled and put an arm around his shoulders.

Kahled tried to shake it off in repulsion, but the Overlord possessed far more strength, and the arm remained in place.

"I'll grant you the reason I've brought you before me. But first, respect is in order."

With the swiftness of a snake, the Overlord struck out a kick to the back of Kahled's legs. Kahled fell hard to the ground on his knees, gritting his teeth against a groan.

"There; much better. Look at me."

Kahled refused and stared at the ground instead, grimacing in pain and defiance.

Grabbing him by the chin, the Overlord yanked his head up with clawed fingers. "Ah, there's still a fight in you. Good. Now, you will listen. I've brought you here and let you live this long because I have a simple proposition." The Overlord bent closer so that a hand's width remained between their faces, locked in mutual hostility. "Will you join my army, High Knight Kahled?"

Kahled wrenched away from the Overlord's grasp and sat on his heels. His first reaction was to laugh. "This... this is why you've kept me? You should've killed me long ago and saved us both time." The last words were lost in more laughing at the preposterousness of the request.

"I see." The Overlord weighed his words. When his voice issued forth, it sounded different, taking on a decidedly human timbre. "This is the same answer Conrad gave me."

Kahled's laughter halted in his throat.

"I've gone easy on you so far, Kahled." The Overlord drew himself up to his full height above Kahled, who remained on his hands and knees as weakness stole over his body. "You don't know the strength I've gained. This will only get as hard as you make it."

And with that—the posturing, the threats, the display of dominance—Kahled knew who stood before him. Disbelief registered in his eyes as realization hit him. "You!"

To confirm his suspicion, the Overlord removed his helm. The shock was too much for Kahled's weakened state. His vision tunneled and spun, and he collapsed, unconscious.

16

DIMITAR

Dwyer's interior hammered Dimitar with a cacophony of upbeat music, shattering glass, and elevated voices. Worn mahogany tables reflected the lanterns lining the walls and cast a drab warmth all their own. The bar counter circled the center of the large room, bottles of various spirits lining the shelves behind the barkeeps. A wide staircase led to the second-floor sleeping quarters. A mix of folk crowded the tables, a blend of race, class, and chaos.

In one corner, three young dwarves—their beards not quite grown beyond their breastbones—sat drinking enormous ale flagons, foam pouring over the sides as they clattered their mugs together. Hollering out the open window, they invited those passing by to come in and drink with them. Their short legs kicked back and forth beneath the bench. Dimitar couldn't guess what the dwarves celebrated, but by the twinkle in their eyes and the redness of their bulbous noses, he figured the dwarves had been celebrating for some time.

Next to the dwarves conferred a pair of elven men in a rather foul mood. Tall, elegantly robed, and with tell-tale pointed ears like Kaleela's, they seemed less than impressed with the dwarves' behavior, shooting stern glances over to the neighboring table as they sipped wine. A large parchment draped over the table, one of the elves standing as his eyes roved over the paper. The elven men spoke to each other in hushed tones, pointing to various points on the parchment. One glanced up from the scroll, his gaze stopping on Dimitar's group. He nudged the elf next to him, who looked up. The elves' blatant assessment surprised Dimitar in a town where staring could be a fatal mistake.

Olaf tugged on his arm, snagging his attention and bellowing over the din. "C'mon, lad, a table just opened, and I need to rest these legs o' mine."

He pushed Dimitar toward a table in the back. The previous occupants had slumped off their chairs, a large array of empty mugs strewn on the tabletop. Dimitar glanced back at the elves' table, the pair once again in deep conversation.

No stranger to finding tables in pubs, Olaf hooked under the arms of the two passed out men and dragged them a few yards closer to the back door, leaning them against the wall. Kaleela and Ral soon followed and sat themselves while a barmaid swept in and loaded the empty glasses onto her tray with efficiency, ignoring the group as well as the unconscious men.

Olaf caught Dimitar's gaze and tipped his chin before making his way to the bar.

"Olaf and I will get us some drinks and food, and see if any rooms are available," Dimitar said to Kaleela. "That is, if you'd like to stay here tonight."

She gave a patient smile. "I don't think there's much choice, I'm afraid. Like it or not, this is our best bet."

Dimitar shared her smile before searching out Olaf, although his friend was hard to miss. His bellowing laugh reached above the noise of the pub.

Olaf introduced the lanky barkeep wiping the bar counter. "This here's Neale."

He sported a mustache that twirled at the ends and winked as Dimitar approached. Neale, not much older than them by his looks, glowed with a pride in his work that tended to be lacking in the tavern business.

"And what can I do for you fine gentlemen this evening?" Neale smiled, flirtatious, and flipped a bar rag over his shoulder. "We just received a barrel of ale from those dwarves in the front corner. Normally, I wouldn't spread that kind of word around, but you look like the type of traveler who appreciates dwarven fire water."

"By the gods!" Olaf roared with a shared laugh. "Ya can count on that. I'll hold m'first toast to you, and may ya be blessed with many fine ladies in yer lap tonight."

"Is his lap available?" Neale tilted his head at Dimitar, giving him a coy once over.

"Sorry m'boy, this one's m'personal favorite." Olaf slung an arm around Dimitar's shoulder as Neale exaggerated a pout.

Dimitar chuckled at their banter, and Olaf put in an order for ham roast, potatoes, and pints of the dwarven ale. While Neale left to fill their order, the sound of a fist smacking against flesh drew Dimitar's attention.

Two men dressed in crude, sun-cracked leathers pushed back from their table and faced each other, spitting curses. The patrons next to them hollered, encouraging the fighters and slamming their mugs on the table at an increasing tempo. The two men grabbed at each other's throats at the same time. The table erupted in cheers, but contrary to the lively attitude of the surrounding crowd, the two weren't playing. This was no game, and one of the men dropped his chokehold to claw at the fingers around his own throat. His attempts to free his airway grew feeble as his eyes rolled back in his head. The other man gave him one last vicious strangle before tossing him to the floor as coins were passed, bets settled.

Dimitar reached for his sword and pushed away from the bar. A firm hand on his shoulder stopped him.

"Look 'round the room, lad. What do ya see?"

Dimitar didn't like what Olaf hinted at, but his friend's grip grew tight enough to let him know Olaf wasn't letting go. Taking a breath, he followed Olaf's advice and did a quick check. Despite the brutal murder that had taken place not five yards from everyone, not a single soul looked in that direction as the fight winner kicked the dead body aside. A few minor skirmishes broke out nearby, as if spurred on by the violence that just occurred, and fists continued to fly among drunken men until others pulled them apart. The few women in the bar cackled in laughter at the men's antics before going back to the business on the lap they perched on.

"They're mercenaries, by the look of 'em," Olaf said in his ear. "And this is the kinda' town that gettin' in the business of mercs ain't good practice."

"We can't just stand here and let this happen."

"We're not in Blackburn anymore, Dim. We've no friends here."

Damn it, this isn't right.

Dimitar gritted his teeth but peeled his hand off his sword's grip and tried to slow the pounding of his heart. Neale returned with their order, which gave Dimitar a good distraction as he gathered as much as he could and headed back to their table. He set the dishes down harder than intended, some of the ale slopping over the side.

Kaleela peeked out from her hood to appraise Dimitar, then placed her hand over his. "Is everything all right?"

She couldn't have seen the fight on the other side of the bar, her concern solely for him.

"I don't want you to stay here." His words came out rough. This was no place for her.

Kaleela watched him, her face impassive and her air far more dignified than anyone in the tavern. The juxtaposition struck him, her calm grace a haven next to the rowdy commotion around them. Dimitar wanted to take her home, back to the Blackburn Kingdom's guaranteed safety.

And in that moment, *he* wanted to return to Blackburn, and guilt spilled into him, fueling his frustration.

Olaf returned and plopped down the remaining plates and pints. He speared a small potato in victory. "I got the rooms arranged and this fine banquet for two silvers, if ya can believe it."

Dimitar wasn't sure he was hungry anymore, until he took a bite of the first piece of oven-fresh bread since leaving Blackburn. The group ate in silence, savoring the spiced meat and exquisite rarity of true dwarven ale, a delicacy not often found in the northern lands.

After everyone satisfied their hunger enough to peck at their remains, Kaleela turned to Ral. "How do we go about finding this Karn?"

He didn't answer right away, considering his words before signing.

"He says no one really finds Karn." Olaf leaned back in his seat and rested his glass on his stomach. "He just sorta' comes to you, ya know?"

'They'll come to us,' Ral corrected.

"So, what do we do now?" Dimitar's exasperation grew once more. "Just sit and wait?"

Ral shrugged.

"We came to this town to find Karn on your insistence." Dimitar stood and pointed at Ral. His patience had finally worn out, and the target of his anger sat right in front of him. "Since then, we've been attacked by thieves, I watched a man killed for sport, and all while our king sits in a Corruptor cell. While we... what? Sit here and wait for a mysterious person to arrive who might or might not feel like talking to us?"

A tap on his shoulder interrupted him. Spinning with a curse on his tongue, Dimitar found himself face to stomach with the biggest person he'd ever seen. The giant stood at least two heads taller than Olaf, broad shoulders thick and solid like a tree trunk. Braided black hair hung just past their shoulder blades, tied back with a leather strap. On their right shoulder sat a predatory bird, too large to be a common hawk, with molten black feathers and wicked-sharp talons.

Dimitar backed up instinctively, jolted to a stop by the table. He could do no more than stare up in surprise at the behemoth, who appraised Dimitar with dichromatic eyes and a deep crease rising on their ebony forehead.

"I heard you say my name." The voice reverberated in the air, carrying an overwhelming timbre of power. The enormous magic-user looked over the group with a judgmental eye, resting on Ral. "Well, I'll be damned by the shadow forces."

Ral rose and placed a fist over his heart, bowing in respect as Dimitar slipped next to Kaleela.

"All right, you have my full attention, as long as your news remains worthy." Karn seated themself in Dimitar's chair. Placing both hands upon their massive thighs, they leaned forward to fix each of them with an unnerving stare, one eye blue, the other brown.

"Now, what's this about the Corrupted?"

17

KALEELA

A ye, you heard us correctly," Kaleela said. "What do you know about the Corrupted?"

Karn's gaze lingered over Ral, yet Kaleela couldn't help but feel the weight of their judgment still upon her. Ral twirled a knife across his fingers, lantern light catching the blade. Dimitar scraped over a nearby chair and rejoined the table, his face lit with apprehension. As Neale approached to refill their drinks, Karn gave the barkeep a glance that meant they weren't to be disturbed further. Neale's smile disappeared, but he managed a nod of confirmation and backed away, juggling the glasses with shaking hands.

Karn turned to Kaleela and studied her in silent calculation. To her credit, Kaleela didn't back down from the stronghold of their gaze. Conrad had taught her how to hold her own.

"You're King Kahled's daughter, are you not?" Their voice rumbled in low baritone without any of the lilting northern dialect; in fact, Karn's speech had but a trace of an accent, one she couldn't identify.

"How... how did you know that?"

"Don't be dense. What other half-breed do we have living in these parts?"

Olaf cautiously raised a finger and pointed to himself, but Kaleela understood Karn wasn't speaking about Olaf's blended appearance.

Heat rushed to her face. "Who are you to address me in such a—"

Karn crossed their arms. "Now, ask me properly."

Ral gripped her arm, and she forced herself to bite back a retort. She ignored Ral's subtle yet persistent motioning, her gaze locked in a furious, silent battle with Karn's. Olaf leaned over to whisper the message.

"This fellow needs to be addressed by their title." Olaf gulped before translating the last of Ral's words. "Ral's sayin' he strongly advises you to address them as they are, a master of the magic craft."

Demanding my respect while giving me none. For an instant, Kaleela wanted to greet the magic-user with a word more commonly heard from the mouths of the mercenaries in the corner. With visible effort, she locked her jaw and tried again. "What do you know about the Corrupted, *Master* Karn?"

"Better, child."

Kaleela burned with annoyance but remained quiet. *Father's life is at stake.*

Karn took out a long, slender pipe from a knapsack and filled it with an orange-tinged, crushed leaf. Without any discernible movement from Karn, the tobacco flared as if lit by flame. They took a deep inhale and blew out a large, blue-gray trail of smoke that encircled their table, muting the tavern noise around them in a veil of privacy.

"The Corrupted are an elder race, born from the despair of evil's creations. They first came to power a thousand years ago, following the destruction of the Mage Warrior bloodline. These years of war, famine, and death are known as the Age of Blood. Just when hopelessness peaked and the ethereal forces were nearly depleted, magic-users made a plan to open a rift.

"Ten of us combined our powers, and the force of the connection bound our knowledge and abilities into one body. We gave everything to rip the sky open. The inner power of the abyss drew the Corruptors in, swallowed into the void."

"Oh, aye! 'Twas the Storm of Banishment," Olaf jumped in, excited to join the conversation.

A single, withering glance from Karn, displeased at the interruption, crushed his enthusiasm. Without a word of acknowledgement, they continued. "The ethereal forces regained balance, at least until the Corrupted gained a foothold back into our lands. The elves, of course, stayed safe within their magicked borders of the Sun'Din Forest, but they feared Corruptor evil would border their lands. Elves aren't fond of humans, to be sure, but are even less fond of Corruptors."

Kaleela shifted in her seat at this, her face carefully neutral. *If elves aren't fond of humans, what would they think of me?*

"Fighting on behalf of humans was unacceptable to elven pride, yet trusting their future to them was too risky. They allied to unite the humans' passion with the elven forces' skill. The elven general selected the most trusted elite fighters to drill and prepare an army of the best human knights: High Knights.

"The elven general and his elite pushed the men to their limits while teaching the oldest and truest elven warrior techniques: to see without sight, to hear without listening, to talk without a sound, and to kill with efficiency and quickness. Their training was almost cruel, but most survived.

"That's when your father"—Karn flicked their gaze to Kaleela—"and the High Knights fought bravely and with victory in the Reclamation War. And that's the answer to your question."

Karn leaned back and closed their eyes, as if telling the story sapped them of energy.

"I'm well aware of the High Knights and their history." Kaleela checked her impatience through clenched teeth. The last thing she needed was someone lecturing her on her own fathers' experience, as if they hadn't told her the tales growing up. "And none of this explains what the Corrupted want now and with my father."

"I've explained everything, half-breed."

"You've explained nothing!"

"You summoned me here for this?" Karn drawled at Ral, dragging a hand down their face.

Her resignation shattered, and Kaleela stood fast enough to knock back her chair. She leaned across the table and slammed both palms against the wood, rattling the empty dinner plates. Olaf's eyes grew to saucers as he brought himself to a protective stance, thrusting his arm out in front of her.

"I'm tired of playing games, Master Karn!" Kaleela shouted, pushing against Olaf, who didn't budge. The strange hawk-like creature resting on Karn's shoulder bristled its feathers. "You know why they're here, don't you? And you know why this filth has my father, don't you? I want you to tell me. Right. Now."

Karn set down the pipe and, remarkably, their stony features broke out into a satisfied, crooked grin. "Now you're asking the right questions."

Kaleela stared into the giant's mismatched eyes, defiant and refusing to banter any further.

"But first, the question I ask of you is, do you really want to know the answers to everything you asked me? Are you up to the challenge they pose?"

She emphasized each word, a command. "Tell me."

"Then pull up your chair, and I'll begin a new story."

18

DIMITAR

Kaleela returned to her chair and waited for Karn to answer her questions, her knee bobbing against Dimitar's in an impatient beat under the table. Despite being seated, she still seemed poised to strike if Karn disgraced her or her company further. Dimitar now understood her drive to reach her father better than ever; it stemmed from this same protectiveness. The effect wasn't lost on Karn, who now addressed her by her proper title.

"I admire your persistence, Princess of Blackburn... for one so inexperienced." Karn readjusted their seat, perhaps more out of discomfort from complimenting her than their position on the chair. "Now, you wish to know why the Corrupted have your father. The answer is in front of you, if you gave your elvish blood enough time to ponder it. But you were raised by humans and may need prodding.

"Corruptors are cruel in battle and never take captives. For that matter, they rarely leave survivors, such are their numbers. The Reclamation was no exception, and if not for the valor of the High Knights, the battle would've been lost. The casualties were many; only three High Knights left the battlefield, and the lands rewarded them for their service. Sir Kahled, granted the kingdom of Blackburn; Sir Conrad, granted Stormgard's throne; and Sir Rippold, given the First Knight position in Tildare. Yet unbeknownst to everyone, the Corrupted were far from defeated."

Dimitar touched upon a memory: his first mission from Kahled. When Sir Rippold had gone missing several years ago, Kahled sent Dimitar among the messengers to search for news. Dimitar brought back the detail of a deep scratch along the throne chair, similar to the marks on Kahled's High Knight suit of armor in Blackburn's great hall. And now, one High Knight missing and presumed dead, another murdered, and the last held prisoner.

"Someone has it in for the last High Knights," Dimitar murmured to Olaf, who nodded in agreement.

Karn emphasized their next words by pointing the pipe at each of them. "A weapon was taken that day. Even the greatest strategists didn't foresee its taking and capability for evil. 'Tis a leverage with more potential than all the High Knights combined—the very pathway with which the Corrupted can retake the Green Lands."

Dimitar and Kaleela shared a glance of wide-eyed alarm.

"But what does this have to do with my father?"

"That part is the easiest of all to see," Karn said. Kaleela's jaw muscles tightened, and Karn frowned in annoyance. "If it must be told to you, I will oblige. Your father faced this weapon sought by the Corrupted and—"

The hawk-like creature on Karn's shoulder let out a series of harsh shrieks, startling the group. Dimitar winced at the noise; the bird's cry broke whatever spell encased their table in privacy. In an instant, the atmosphere changed, conversations and drinking coming to a halt, the bar folk alert and on edge.

Bending close to the creature's beak, Karn seemed to understand the strange squawking. They scowled as the bird finished its chirruping, focusing their attention on something beyond the pub walls. A restless, low drone traveled across the room as patrons turned to one another in shared, rising anxiety.

Karn snapped their gaze back to Kaleela. "You've been tracked." Incredibly, their eye colors shifted, darkening. "If you truly love your father, I advise you to leave."

"What... How...?" Kaleela said, near speechless.

"This isn't the time to question. Just leave... *now!*"

The urgency and unquestioned authority in Karn's voice left no time for discussion, only time to react. Karn stood and, with a few long strides, reached the front door. A still-unnamed panic swept across the room like wildfire, even touching the elves at the front of the bar, and patrons jumbled together, seeking exit. A strong clap on his shoulder brought Dimitar's attention back as Ral passed by him. Cursing under his breath, he swept up his knapsack and rushed to the back exit with the others.

He halted in his tracks at a sudden, violent tremor followed by a deafening screech. His mind locked at the sight outside the window, allowing him to process only glimpses: scales, darkness, glowing eyes, and muscled limbs.

The dragon crouched on all fours, muddy wings curling to its side as its massive head swung around, surveying its surroundings with a cold, calculating eye. Black smoke rose from its nostrils, and a guttural noise hung low in the back of its winding neck. A handful of Corruptors rode—no, clung to—the dragon's back, creatures of inky blackness radiating sheer cunning and evil. Dimitar couldn't shake his gaze as a Corruptor unhooked its razor-sharp grip from the dragon's side, trickles of blood leaking where its claws barbed beneath the dragon's scales.

How?

Dragons were creatures of legend and tales, not seen across the Green Lands since the Age of Blood. And the Corruptors—even with his knighthood training, Dimitar's legs grew numb as horror flooded through his body to witness these infamous creatures. A woman screamed, throaty and piercing, turning Dimitar from the window and spurring him and the others out the nearest exit as Dwyer's erupted in panic.

Once outside, he fought his shaking body from running back in, too exposed under the night sky. Screaming intensified in the streets out front as more of the city roused to the dragon. Dimitar turned to the stables; Ral, several steps ahead, led out their horses. The animals jerked at the reins as people fled by in sheer terror, and Dimitar mounted his steed with difficulty after Olaf all but tossed Kaleela atop her horse.

The group couldn't wait in the narrow space between the stables and the back of Dwyer's, so Dimitar made the hardest move of his life: he urged Deepshade through the alleyway out to the main street before the dragon. Their chance of survival depended on leaving the city before the dragon attacked, although he couldn't fathom where this beast of myth came from. All he could do at this moment was battle the utter coldness of fear descending over his body.

As they emerged from the alleyway, Karn stood in front of the pub with arms raised and the entirety of their enormous body glowing with energy. The dragon crouched before Karn, all the more horrible in its realness, serpentine yet massive enough to reach the second floors. The Corruptors slid off the dragon's back and slipped into the gloom of the shadowed streets. Dimitar had difficulty following their obscured forms, even more terrified at what now became the unknown. A small cry escaped from Kaleela, her face a mask of fear.

Her terror brought a sudden calm down upon Dimitar, detaching his emotions from the situation. All that mattered was leading Kaleela to safety, and his courage rose, for he gave himself no other choice. Olaf swore repeatedly, his voice shaking even as he raised his axe. Dimitar pulled his blade, ready to stand at Karn's side. Before he could dismount, Karn turned toward the small company with silver-tinged magic whipping down both arms.

"Go now! The survival of this world depends on it!"

From behind Dimitar, Kaleela shrieked, the sound of sudden, primal fear. A Corruptor grappled on Kaleela's back. Inky shadow flashed with long, pointed teeth as she twisted, trying to throw the beast off, but its grip held true. She cried out again, almost pulled off her mount in its writhing grasp. A sudden flash of steel lit the air, and the Corruptor fell to the ground, screeching in pain, a throwing knife embedded deep in its hide. Ral grabbed her reins to hold the horse still as she steadied herself.

People fled alongside them in wild panic, screaming and cowering at the sight of the great beast. The dragon itself seemed unconcerned at the pandemonium and swatted in apparent irritation at those within reach. One man was crushed beneath its massive claws with an agonized scream. Its tail whipped out haphazardly, catching two men from Dwyer's in its path. Dimitar jerked back as the men collapsed in a broken, bloody pile, the mercenary's face captured in anguished death.

Dimitar couldn't bring the horses to a gallop or risk trampling the people. They pushed forward, and the dragon let out an abrasive cry as it caught sight of the fleeing group on horseback.

Karn stepped closer in an attempt to regain the dragon's attention, their arms charged with magical power. Bending at the waist, Karn flung a bolt of energy from each arm straight toward the heart of the beast. The attack landed upon the dragon with a flash of light and crack against flesh, and it stumbled. Twisting and rising on its back legs, the dragon clawed at the magic traveling across its chest before it dissipated.

Dimitar's brief hope of escape vanished with a deafening roar as the dragon shook off the assault, its eyes filled with hate and lethal violence. Leaning further back on its haunches, the dragon coiled its neck, sucking in air. In one sudden motion, it threw itself down and blasted a stream of pitch-black fire, coating the street in darkness. Dimitar pulled Deepshade up to place himself between Kaleela and the flames that should have ensued, but nothing burned.

By the gods, no. The legends were true.

Tales from the Age of Blood spoke of dragons' ebon fire, and the exaggeration of lore became a sickening reality before Dimitar's eyes. Almost too low to detect, the houses groaned, wood twisting and churning on their foundations. The air hummed with a tangible energy trying to break loose. All at once, the street exploded with blackened flames, drawing the night into further darkness and chaos.

Now the four companions shielded their eyes against the twisted flames and burst of heat. Sturdy walls erupted, wood and scorched stone flung into the night sky. Before Karn could move out of the way, Dwyer's front door exploded outwards and slammed into them with enough force to send them sprawling. The dragon stretched its wings out, blocking Dimitar's view, and he couldn't see if Karn survived the impact.

The horses neighed in protest, the detonation pounding their ears and dulling the group's hearing to near-deafness. People stumbled about the street, disoriented and frightened into recklessness. The nightmare had just begun, however; the buildings weren't the only things hit by ebon flames. A score of people caught in the wave of darkness howled as one. They fell to their knees, clawing at their chests and limbs with the ferocity of trapped animals. Dimitar's mind tried to block the truth of the matter, but his eyes riveted on these people. Caught in the dragon's fire, they burned from the inside out.

Dimitar almost retched as he urged their horses forward in hopes of getting past the dragon. The area next to it narrowed, smoke billowing from tinder that cracked in a sudden explosion by the dark fire, burning in outbursts. With little warning, the dragon unleashed another spurt of ebon fire, and Dimitar threw up his arms to dodge the acrid flames that licked past. Coughing out the stench, he sucked in a breath as a tingling sensation struck close to his forearms. He slipped off Deepshade and tore at his bracers, the ebon fire's heat rising against his skin.

"Olaf, I can't get them off," Dimitar choked out in desperation, but his friend had already dismounted and was at his side.

Olaf pulled a dagger and grabbed Dimitar's right arm, grimly shoving the dagger underneath the bracer and ripping up the laces. Dimitar grunted as the blade cut his skin but welcomed the sting as long as the smoking bracer fell loose. Another swipe from Olaf's blade, and Dimitar's left bracer hit the ground, bursting into violent flames. The two men stumbled back, panting, and grabbed the horses' reins that Ral had the peace of mind to hold onto.

The fire underfoot left the horses all but unmanageable, and it took a few tries before both men remounted. With her horse spinning in place, Kaleela pointed with a wordless cry at the dragon, which took deliberate steps toward the group. Straining to control his own horse, Dimitar spotted a side street further to their right. Fire engulfed the buildings on either side, but the road was unscathed. Their last chance at escape diminished, and they needed to act now.

"C'mon!" Dimitar cried, motioning toward the road. The men turned their horses and spurred them to the entrance as the flames continued to spread. Dimitar looked to Kaleela, and his heart sank. She was no longer beside him.

Yanking Deepshade's reins, he spun back. Kaleela struggled with her horse. Disoriented by the fire and with the dragon looming, it fought her attempts to control it. With a squeal of terror, her horse reared, and she lost her grip. She fell to the ground, landing away from the fire and in part buffered by the knapsack on her back.

"Kaleela!" he shouted, but she couldn't hear him in the chaos, stumbling to her feet and coughing on the thickening smoke.

Dimitar spotted Corruptors running in her direction. One had a good lead over the others and soon closed half the distance to her. A shrieking woman ran straight in front of its path, unable or unwilling to see its smaller form within the chaos. With rabid swiftness, the Corruptor landed atop the woman's chest, bringing her to the ground in one fell swoop. Tearing with a blinding blur of claws and teeth, it slashed her face and throat apart with bestial ferocity.

Kaleela grabbed for the reins, but her steed bolted away. The Corruptor scuttled ever closer. The dragon screamed as if in triumph.

Dimitar pushed down a searing bolt of fear. He would not lose her now, not like this.

"Kaleela!" He bore down from the side street, and this time she heard, whipping around and locking eyes with him. Dimitar timed their stride, and Deepshade launched over a fallen cart beam, landing upon the nearest Corruptor and crushing it. Without slowing, he turned the steed toward Kaleela, bending with an outstretched arm. She reached for him and, in one fluid movement, grabbed his forearm and pulled herself up behind him, locking her arms around his chest.

With a cry, Dimitar urged Deepshade back down the side street. Seconds later the burning frames on either side of the street collapsed, shooting rivers of sparks into the sky. They caught up to Olaf and Ral at the other end and together tore through Leighton's streets. The horses' hooves hammered the land as they sped out the town gates. Dimitar didn't know which direction they were going, only that it would get them away from the dragon and Corruptors.

Behind them, a deafening thunderclap cracked, and a lightning bolt drew power across the four corners of the night sky. The dragon's screech followed them out of town, this time with pain in its cry. Looking up at the sky, his heart pounding and Kaleela's arms squeezing around him, Dimitar faced the stars, the night clear and flawless.

PART TWO

19

DIMITAR

During the few hours he caught some rest, Dimitar failed to stop the Corruptors from harming Kaleela in his nightmares. Corruptors caught them, separating him from the others in pitch darkness, tearing into his limbs with needle-like teeth while somewhere nearby Kaleela screamed and screamed.

A rough shake jolted him to consciousness. Olaf leaned over him, water flask in hand.

"Where's Kaleela?" Dimitar blurted, still sluggish from sleep. He sat upright and grabbed Olaf's shirt. "Where did they take her?"

"Whoa there, m'boy. The princess is standin' right pretty over there." Olaf pointed to Kaleela and Ral gathering the blankets from last night's encampment, securing them on the horses. "Shake it off. We're okay, aye?"

Even with her soft humming reaching his ears, Dimitar still had trouble loosening his grip. He'd lost her, in his dreams. The one thing Kahled asked of him—*look after her*—Dimitar failed to do. His frantic desperation spurred on not just by his defeat or his own mortality, but her life taken and its loss upon him. And by the gods, he'd fight for her.

"It seemed so real," he said. Taking Olaf's offered flask, Dimitar slugged back the water, trying to chase away the taste of illusory blood that filled his mouth.

"Just a dream, boy-o. And a bitter one at that, from the twists in your bedroll." Olaf offered his hand to Dimitar, pulling him up.

Kaleela joined them, dark circles under her eyes. Dimitar wasn't the only one who'd slept in nightmares last night.

"Morning," he said. The stunned weariness in her face troubled him. "Are you all right?"

Kaleela hesitated, then shook her head, lips pressed together. Any number of platitudes meant for reassurance came to Dimitar's mind, but they all sounded hollow. Nothing was all right, and they both knew it.

He touched her arm, a comforting caress. "Last night was... terrible. What can I do for you, my lady?"

She stood before him with a lost expression, so he did the one thing that felt right. He opened his arms, and when she didn't protest, wrapped her in a hug. Only then did she release the tension in her body.

She rested her chin against his shoulder. "I can't—I can't bear to think about those creatures and what they did to Conrad and Father. I wish I knew what Master Karn was about to say."

"Me too. I'm at a loss. I've never heard of such a powerful weapon. And I'm not counting those," Dimitar added, cutting off Olaf who half-heartedly began to point at his massive, flexed bicep.

"Let me show ya somethin' that might help," he offered them.

Dimitar reluctantly let her go, and they followed Olaf's lead after Dimitar grabbed his sheath, strapping on the blade as they walked. Dream or not, the weight at his hip offered some comfort. Ral waved them off when Olaf called him to join, instead strapping supplies onto his horse, packing up their hasty camp.

The sun breached the horizon, and the summer day promised warmth. What Dimitar had taken for a grove in the darkness of night now revealed itself in the sunlight as lush grounds with patches of tall grass and ancient oaks. Olaf led them away from camp to the crest of a small hill and pointed.

"Look at that, lad. Bet ya never thought you'd see the day."

The Sun'Din Forest loomed a few hundred yards away. Translated into the common tongue, the name meant 'Jeweled Flame.' The rising sun shimmered on the leaves, each one casting a subtle, different hue than the next. Light reflected off every branch, twig, and leaf, setting the entire forest ablaze with vivid, green shades. The path they'd followed last night curled toward the forest but faded and ended several yards back from the wood's edge.

"It's so beautiful." Kaleela's face lit with wonder as she took in the expansive forest. A certain serenity crossed over her face, and Dimitar swore the same jeweled fervor sparkled in her emerald eyes. "Sir Talin will be glad we didn't lie to him after all. We ventured to the Sun'Din whether we wished to or not."

Dimitar listened to the whisper of a breeze caressing the treetops, light dancing upon the leaves. "Now that I've seen it, I'm almost glad we sidetracked this far north."

"I wonder if Father will want to stop here on our return for rest," she said, her voice full of hope. "For now, it's time we—"

Thwock.

In the ground behind them, an arrow planted itself, followed by a second.

"Warning shots." Olaf cursed, flinching as another arrow shot past too close for comfort. "I'll bet a belly of ale the border scouts found us."

Dimitar and Olaf pulled their weapons, spinning as arrows set around them in a rapid, neat circle.

"Elves," Kaleela whispered, moments before the thicket to either side of the group separated, and elf after elf emerged from behind trees and bushes, each with a short bow trained on one of the three. Before long, the small troop was surrounded with expert precision, not only by multiple arrow shafts piercing the ground, but by more than a dozen armed elves completing an outside circle. Dimitar and Olaf stood back-to-back, trying to assess any means of escape.

"'Tis no scouting party," Olaf muttered under his breath to Dimitar. "Their numbers are too many... and look, their armor."

Dimitar frowned, taking in the tough leather chest plates, bracers, and greaves. Their clothing was a mixture of soft browns and greens, camouflaging them all too well with their surroundings. Besides the bows in hand, the elves carried a short blade or dagger strapped to their body. Scouts wouldn't travel with such armor, however. The weight would prevent them from hurrying messages on foot, as Dimitar well knew from his experience as a messenger.

The elves each wore unreadable expressions, objectively neutral if not for their drawn weapons. For the first time, Dimitar observed the elven features up close. The men had a delicacy about the jaw and eyes, and a point to the tips of their ears like Kaleela's. Their skin varied from pale to deep brown, and most had fair-colored hair, braided or pinned off their smooth faces. He didn't fail to notice the unmistakable strength in their limbs, sculpted by the muted clothing.

One of the elves, perhaps the elder among the group upon closer look, called out in elvish what Dimitar guessed was a greeting or a question. The comment, however, wasn't aimed at them; instead, another elf stepped out from behind a tree several paces back. Dimitar recognized this elf as one of a pair, tall and proud, and with the same piercing gaze as in Dwyer's Pub.

The elf nodded without hesitation, and the first elf's expression turned grim as he surveyed the group once more. He gave an order, and two guards moved toward the group. Dimitar's instincts flared, and he placed himself in front of Kaleela as Olaf took up her other side, tightening his grip on Lucky's handle.

"Lay your weapons down, please." Kaleela removed the dagger strapped to her side and made a show of placing it on the ground. "Now is not the time to foolishly fight for honor."

Dimitar and Olaf exchanged frustrated glances. An arrow found home inches from Olaf's foot, startling the large man, followed by another next to Dimitar's. The next arrows wouldn't miss—nor aim at their feet. The men dropped their weapons.

Where's Ral? Dimitar craned his neck; the thief had disappeared. *Left us. Of course he would.*

Kaleela turned to address the elves, and Dimitar caught her clasping her hands to hide their shaking. "We're passing through. Our apologies for stopping so close to your lands. We're on our way at this very moment."

Her remark encountered heavy silence.

Standing taller and straightening her shoulders, she said, "I am Princess Kaleela, daughter of King Kahled, High Knight of the Reclamation War, Royal Sovereign of the Kingdom of Blackburn; and of Princess Kaleel, Lady of the Forest, late passed and of your wooded lands. I demand you release us."

The apparent elven leader shot his gaze back to the elf from Dwyer's Pub, who said something under his breath that Dimitar didn't catch, even if he could understand the language. The leader approached Kaleela, his expression maddeningly unreadable once more.

"Then you are far from your home... Princess," he said with a touch of derision. He managed the common tongue with ease, the words smoothed by his elven accent. His eyes flicked up and down Dimitar and Olaf, the line of his mouth tightening. "One might wonder why someone of your nobility is traveling this far north with these *hal'rinn*."

"What did ya call us?" Olaf said, and Dimitar prayed he wouldn't start a brawl they couldn't finish, well outnumbered and at the wrong end of too many arrowheads.

"Baseborn," Kaleela answered, lowering her voice.

Dimitar clenched his jaw as red crept up his neck. "We're guardsmen protecting—"

"If you are guardsmen, then where are you taking your princess? Surely not into the Sun'Din, or we would've received prior word from High Knight Kahled."

Dimitar stared at the elf, searching for some excuse. The truth would entangle them further, and they had to be on their way. Nothing reasonable enough came to mind to explain why two men traveling under Blackburn's banner—packed away in his saddlebag—would journey unheralded this close to the Sun'Din with the princess of their kingdom.

"Ah, perhaps I know." The elf's eyes hardened upon the group. "Some of our people spotted you in Leighton last night. You not only held counsel with the Master of the Arts, but also gained much interest from foul, dark creatures. Perhaps the guardsmen of the Green Lands now seek to hide within our borders and are using their princess to gain access."

"Ya callin' me a coward?" Olaf said, heat rising, at the same time Dimitar said, "You can't be serious if you think—"

"They travel with me, that's all you need to know," Kaleela said, trying to regain the conversation.

"I'm afraid that's not enough." Swift and efficient, he stepped forward and grabbed her arm. Dimitar checked himself from interceding, fists clenched, as two fighters tightened the draw on their bows with an ominous creak. Helpless again, just like back in the alley. *But these arrows aren't false-tipped.*

Kaleela briefly struggled against the elf's hold, but in moments he bound her wrists before her. Dimitar didn't even hear the elves approach next to him.

He was grabbed from behind by rough hands, and in moments restrained in the same manner as Kaleela, as was Olaf. Elves gathered their horses and supplies, efficient and without care to Kaleela's growing distress.

"I *am* Princess of Blackburn and daughter of—"

"Enough. Whether you are who you claim is yet to be seen. Until then, we'll have silence from all of you." Reaching into his pack, he pulled out three lengths of hand-spun cloth.

Dimitar bit down on the cloth, powerless as all three were gagged. One of the elves picked up his sword, the point pushing against his back. The message was clear, and Dimitar marched toward the Sun'Din, not as a guest the way he'd often hoped, but as a prisoner.

20

KALEELA

The leaves' colors intensified the closer they approached. Something mystical extended from those limbs, the forest energy vibrating against Kaleela's skin. As they entered the Sun'Din, she walked through some unseen barrier. The power made the hair rise on her arms while at the same time, she exhaled as if she'd been holding her breath the entire time since leaving Blackburn. This unknown forest drew her in, intimately familiar.

The trails laid out before her, some wide enough to walk side by side, others so narrow they could only pass in single file by a sudden drop-off along the forest floor. At one point, elves walked along hidden pathways on the slope to her left. Their clothing and silent passage made it impossible to watch them for long before they blended into their surroundings. Kaleela managed to catch sight of their packed quivers and cocked crossbows: guards.

The brightening sunlight slanted through overhead, playing across the trees like fine-grained, liquid gold. A stream made its presence known nearby, skipping over rocks and roots. Occasional bird songs graced the branches above, and overall, peace surrounded them like a soothing blanket. The elves led them through the woods, walking with an unconscious grace that carried them with naught a sound, while Dimitar and Olaf cracked upon every twig or leaf underfoot.

The trees themselves stood taller and wider than anything Kaleela imagined. Summer sun filtered through the branches to the ground in patches, yet the canopy-shaded air was pleasantly cool. With each inhale arose scents of pine, balsam, cedar, and the mixed spiciness of new growth and ancient wood. Tree bark thrummed with unseen energy, encased in warm red and brown tones. Several hollow trunks split open at the ground, providing ideal shelter for travelers seeking refuge from a storm or for the night. If she wasn't marched at sword point, gagged and bound, Kaleela would've lost herself in the Sun'Din Forest's beauty.

After walking and weaving along countless trails, they were abruptly pulled to a halt. Dimitar and Olaf collided and threatened to drive one another to the ground. An elf snickered but lent a steadying hand. Dimitar shook off his help as he stood tall, and Kaleela sent a sympathetic look his way.

Low tree branches pulled aside, and two elves approached, followed by a handful of guardsmen—and guardswomen, who piqued Kaleela's interest. Throughout the Green Lands, women weren't often found in combat positions, although that was changing, led by her father and Conrad's efforts after the Reclamation War. *Father and Conrad learned the strength of women and wanted that for their kingdoms.* Kaleela stood out, in part due to her skill with bow and blade, but always attributed that to being raised and protected by two High Knight warriors.

This leading pair of elves, however, didn't seem to need protection from anyone. The first elf's features were quiet and fair, his long blonde hair braided back on the sides. Pale hazel eyes held both power and kindness. He carried himself in the manner of a poet or perhaps an assassin. The second elf followed at his side and in exact contrast, standing taller and with wider shoulders. Scars riddled his exposed, cool-brown forearms. Gold flecks highlighted his dark eyes, and his midnight-black hair was pulled up halfway in a topknot, the color unusual among the elven people known for their fair hair.

Like the elves before him, he took in the prisoners with an unreadable expression and absolute, steel authority.

"What do we have here?" His voice sounded gruff and harsh, as if from some terrible strain on his throat or perhaps an old injury.

Strolling over, he inspected the somber prisoners. Kaleela had the distinct impression that he promptly dismissed Dimitar and Olaf as unworthy of consideration. The elf's subtle expression changed once he turned to her.

"Gar'Ret, *hew thea*," he called over his shoulder to the fairer elf engaged in quiet elvish conversation with the troop leader.

Kaleela and Dimitar exchanged a quick glance at the mention of Gar'Ret's name. Despite ignoring Kahled's command to seek out this elf in the first place, they ended up doing as he wished. The fair elf approached, and as he turned to Kaleela, his eyes grew wide in shock, and he staggered back a few steps.

"*So'Gud roth!* Kaleel... but how?"

"Not Kaleel," the dark-haired elf said, slight rebuke in his voice; due to Gar'Ret's emotion or the switch to common tongue, Kaleela wasn't sure. "Look again. This is her daughter. Remarkable resemblance, is it not?"

A moment passed as the disbelief left Gar'Ret's face. Thinly veiled emotions flitted behind his eyes as he regained composure.

"Of course, Bela'Ruhn." Gar'Ret bowed to her in deep reverence. He pulled a knife from his belt and walked to her side, never taking his eyes off her face. "Forgive these guardsmen, my—Princess Kaleela. They're only performing their duties."

With a deft flick of his wrist, the cloth gagging Kaleela fell to the forest floor, then the ropes around her wrists.

"I've long hoped to welcome you back to your home, although not in this manner," Gar'Ret continued. "As of late, we've increased our protection around the perimeter. Rumors of vagrant Corruptors have become more frequent." He glanced at the troop leader. "My understanding is that these rumors hold more truth than the lands wish to face. You were in the attacked city last night, is it true?"

Although Kaleela had never known her mother, she kept one cherished portrait in her suite. Gar'Ret mirrored her mother's features and retained the same air of dignity. Kaleela didn't know who Gar'Ret was but had no doubt he shared a blood tie. For the first time in her life, she felt close to her mother, even if she did not yet understand why.

Gar'Ret read her hesitation and took her aside from the others, walking along a path opening before them. Kaleela glanced back to make sure Olaf and Dimitar were still in sight; Dimitar dipped his head her way, reassuring.

"I blame you not, fair elf. The world has grown dark, and these are times when sanctuary becomes priority." She avoided his question, falling on her learned courtesies to help ease the feelings within her.

On one hand, she remained guarded to protect her mission. On the other hand, the Sun'Din Forest filled her with such comfort and safety that Kaleela fought the impulse to loosen her tongue to this familiar stranger.

Kaleela tried once more to mute the forest's power over her, even as part of her wanted to fall into its energies and never resurface. Gar'Ret afforded her an indulgent smile, as if he saw right through her formality.

"You coming to these lands today isn't just a coincidence, I think," Gar'Ret said with ease. "You're long overdue here, among our people. Tell me why you've come to the forest's entrance. I promise you I'll help in whatever way I can."

The sincerity in his voice won Kaleela over as the trees sang out around her, paths open and inviting, calling her deeper into the forest. Calling her home. "I'm on a journey of the utmost importance. I implore you, let us go."

"My Lady Kaleela, you'd be best served by speaking with the king and queen first." Gar'Ret's expression was kind, almost affectionate, as if to soften his refusal. "They'll insist on seeing you, now that you're upon our lands."

"But we weren't trespassing! I wouldn't have come here unbidden if not for..." She trailed off, her words coming out all wrong in her haste to convince Gar'Ret. She blushed, then tried again. "Please, *please*, you must take my word. This journey cannot be delayed a moment more."

Bela'Ruhn stepped up, blocking the path. The pause gave enough time for the rest of the group to amble over, a few yards behind the small conference. Kaleela met Dimitar's eyes as they exchanged a silent understanding, both struggling to find a way to be released from the elves' hold.

Catching her gaze, Bela'Ruhn inclined his head ever so slightly toward Dimitar and Olaf, mild disdain twisting his expression before turning to Kaleela. "Yes, Princess. What's this so-called journey you're on?"

Kaleela turned to him, not unmindful of his disapproval. His rigidity stirred a memory from childhood, back in Blackburn Castle. Despite welcoming countless dignitaries across the Green Lands, her father never entertained visitors from the elven lands. She'd only met a fellow elf once, when this tall, dark-haired warrior visited him and summoned her to greetings. Bela'Ruhn did not have a smile for her and spoke to her father brusquely in the elven language, all the while scrutinizing her. Kaleela recalled the pain that had crossed her father's face as he listened. Bela'Ruhn did not return after that one visit.

As much as she hated to admit it, Bela'Ruhn intimidated her now as he had then, raising the unwelcome sensation of feeling like a child.

"My travels are my own concern," she answered, slipping into a dispassionate state. Unlike the helpful Lachans, these elves had accosted and taken them prisoner, and now interrogated her. She wasn't ready to be forthcoming.

"Is it true, what Cana'th tells me—you've fled a Corrupted attack?"

Kaleela's gaze slipped to the ground, but she kept her silence. What could she say without contradicting Cana'th, the elf at Dwyer's, or giving away their plans to rescue Kahled? Her silence, however, was enough for Bela'Ruhn.

"It would be my pleasure, Princess Kaleela, to escort you before the king and queen." He smirked, without humor in his eyes, and reached to take her arm. "This way, if you would follow—"

"No, no, I can't." She took a step back toward Gar'Ret. "With respect, I mean no intrusion upon your lands. Please forgive any misunderstanding we may have caused. I am... grateful for your offer to visit the king and queen, but I must decline. Perhaps upon another trip we could arrange a meeting; I'm sure my father would be pleased."

"Aye, there is a misunderstanding." Bela'Ruhn's voice scratched over the words, cool and unyielding, still without any great emotion. Here was a man completely in control and devoted to his duty. "It wasn't a request; you *are* coming with us."

Dropping any remaining courtesies, Kaleela turned her back on Bela'Ruhn to face Gar'Ret. If anyone would listen to her now, it was he; hadn't Kahled told her to trust him to begin with? With no choice left, she spoke the truth.

"I have a message for you, Gar'Ret, and you alone." She struggled to keep the desperation out of her voice. Speaking to Bela'Ruhn over her shoulder, she added, "It's not for you and your guards."

Bela'Ruhn curled his lip in response. "*Hal'ide daram, sith mehr haste thea.*"

Dimitar glanced at Olaf who shrugged, both unfamiliar with the elven language.

Kaleela whirled around and stood tall as if waiting to strike, head held high. She seethed with anger; it showed on her face, and she didn't care. *A half-witted human child, am I?*

Taking a step toward Bela'Ruhn she struck out, not with her fists but with her words. *"Mil'ish darath unde nyer anter wo'nath!"*

Gar'Ret's eyebrows shot up, and the other elves murmured among themselves. She dared to call the general ignorant, and judging the faces of the elves around her, the retort was deserved for his demeaning and patronizing remark.

Bela'Ruhn flickered an eyelid, trying to hide his acknowledgement of the mistake he'd made in assuming Kaleela didn't know their language.

"Your words have been noted," he said coldly, "and won't be forgotten." Now the one to turn his back on her, he added, "But it doesn't change our protocol. Guards, take her to the castle."

21

KALEELA

The elves continued their quick march, some melting off into the trees along the way to return to their guard posts. No city or signs of a kingdom were anywhere in sight. If not for the beauty of her surroundings, Kaleela would've lost heart long ago.

Her pulse quickened when Gar'Ret joined her side. She grew eager to learn more about the one elf she might find as her ally. Her father's words were not far from her thoughts or hopes: *Search out Gar'Ret in the Sun'Din Forest. He will know what to do.*

Equaling her stride, Gar'Ret addressed her in the common tongue. "You're truly a likeness of your mother, Kaleela."

"So I've been told. My father reminds me all the time just by the way he looks at me," she said. The same sadness haunting her father's gaze now shadowed Gar'Ret's hazel eyes when he spoke of her mother. Kaleela hesitated, unsure how to phrase her next question. "Gar'Ret... what relation do you have to her?"

He glanced askance at her with mild surprise. "Do you not know? Did your father not tell you of your lineage?"

Kaleela inwardly cursed herself for making her father seem at fault. "He found it too painful. My mother was his true love, and to speak of her recalls the heartache of her loss. He wouldn't impart such grief onto me."

"I do know of this love they shared." A small smile touched his features. "I carry her memory. Yet he hasn't mentioned my name to you, is all. What do you know of your mother's family?"

"My mother, Kaleel, was the princess," Kaleela said, hesitant to reveal her basic understanding of her roots. "Father met her here when he trained as a High Knight. He said her beauty was incomparable, and the moment she first smiled at him, she commanded his heart. The strength of their love was rare, more so because he's human and she, an elf. They wed and lived here, in the forest..."

Kaleela stopped, a sudden bitterness clenching at her throat. *Until she died in birth with me.* She pressed on. "Father named me after her, 'little Kaleel.' I'd have you tell me your relation to her, if it pleases you."

Gar'Ret stopped to turn and face her. "Prince to these lands they call me, and uncle to you. I'm your mother's brother."

Kaleela's heart leapt, but she made certain to contain her outward joy, holding back a gasp. It wouldn't serve her well among the elves to show her excitement like a child; such was a human reaction.

"Would you tell me about my mother sometime?" Her sudden eagerness almost overwhelmed her. She understood her father's directive now. Gar'Ret was her uncle; she had a family. The happiness dancing in Gar'Ret's eyes heartened her.

"Aye, that I could."

For the first time since leaving Blackburn, Kaleela felt safe and more so, connected to her mother. The pair resumed walking, and Bela'Ruhn yelled out a series of orders to his guards.

Kaleela lowered her voice to Gar'Ret. "Who's this Bela'Ruhn?"

"He's the king's *gar'guerr*—general—of the elven forces and commander of the elite guard. He's a rough one at that, but General Bela'Ruhn always does what he feels is right to protect the kingdom and royal family." He paused before adding, "He trained your father, you know."

To this, Kaleela raised her eyebrows, but deferred her next question when Bela'Ruhn called out to Gar'Ret, who excused himself from her side.

They began a heated argument, their flowing language sharpened in tone. Kaleela overheard bits of their conversation and understood enough: they debated what to do with Dimitar and Olaf. The two men might be part of Kaleela's company but were still humans, rarely invited into the elven lands and then only with express permission and reason. Kaleela lost track of their words as the trees ahead of their party separated.

120

They reached the city of Quinthal, the heart of the elven kingdom.

Almost as old as the dawn of the ethereal creations, the forest itself bent and bowed around the wondrous city. Each dwelling consisted of tree limbs woven in intricate fashion to form walls and roofs. Delicate knotwork was carved into the bark with unmatched craftsmanship.

The elves lived at ease, secure in the knowledge that no one could ever find their city without an elven guide. Women walked down the streets, some carrying wide baskets at their hips from the markets, with flowing hair and graceful movements. Only the eldest male elves sported beards, markers of their age. Children ran about, laughing as they chased one another among their elders or played some sort of game using small pebbles and a goblet. Many of the elves napped in hammocks. Street musicians played string or woodwind instruments. Others gathered to admire a new baby swaddled in a mother's arms and bestow a blessing.

As the group walked along the city street path, elves stopped to watch. More than one face reflected surprise and wonderment at the humans' presence, while others appeared unfriendly and challenging. Nonetheless, the entire city held a serenity that Kaleela had never before experienced.

Spiral wooden poles stood to either side of the castle base, displaying Quinthal's green and purple flags bearing a sun-framed tree crest. A long series of steps led to the main entrance of the fortress. The top boughs of nearby trees curved over the castle spires, creating a breathtaking arch and also a shield against outside view. Entwined branches revealed carved patterns of elven protection. Kaleela took it all in, wide-eyed and with an inherent connection almost visceral in its depth within her body. *My mother lived here.*

As Bela'Ruhn brought the group toward the base, a small lad ran to the general with a quick message. Bela'Ruhn answered and turned to a guardswoman who stayed by his side the entire march. She wore a sword strapped to her back and a second blade resting at the hip, instead of crossed in the back like the general's. The woman listened at attention to Bela'Ruhn, and at one point tilted her head to scan over Kaleela and the men. When the general finished, she gave a curt nod, and Bela'Ruhn turned to the group.

He spoke to Gar'Ret in elvish once more before facing Kaleela, adding in the common tongue, "I must see to more important matters now."

With the briefest bow, he turned on his heel and strode off down the main road, a handful of guardsmen leaving with him.

Gar'Ret shot a look at the general's retreating form, then addressed Dimitar and Olaf for the first time. "Welcome, humans, to the mighty city of Quinthal. You should feel honored. Since the High Knight training, no man has set eyes upon its glory. Time will tell if you're worthy of this distinction."

Olaf looked suitably impressed, but Kaleela could tell Dimitar's reaction was hampered by the bindings constricting him.

"I'll take your leave and arrange a meeting with my parents."

"Thank you." Kaleela placed her hand against her heart and bowed.

Gar'Ret returned the gesture before starting up the steps. Kaleela stepped toward Dimitar and Olaf, but the guardswoman Bela'Ruhn had spoken to blocked her path.

"Princess Kaleela. My name is Rialyn, Captain of the guards, at your service," she stated, straightforward and with a small bow. "You're to come with me."

"For what purpose, may I ask?" Kaleela tried not to sound alarmed.

"Guests such as yourself are offered time to refresh from your journey before meeting with the king and queen. I'll escort you to the bathhouse where you may bathe and change into more suitable clothing."

Kaleela nodded, finding this custom rather thoughtful. Suddenly mindful of the soot across her face and torn jerkin from last night's attack, she gestured at Dimitar and Olaf. "What of my companions?"

"I'll see to it they receive refreshment," Rialyn said after a moment's hesitation. She spoke with the other guards, and they led the troop in opposite directions.

Dimitar struggled, pushing against the guards. "Hey, you're not separating us. I stay with her."

One of the guards drew his sword, holding it before Dimitar's chest. Olaf elbowed Dimitar, and he stood down, even as his eyes flashed toward her.

Kaleela entered the bathing hut with Rialyn and a handful of ladies-in-waiting close behind. With quiet words, the ladies offered her a sponge bath, working with gentle, efficient hands to clean her arms, torso, and face. A deep green elven gown replaced her tattered riding shirt, the fabric long and airy, accenting her figure. The ladies in waiting brushed her hair into soft waves, hanging down the length of her back and plaited with smaller braids. The soaps and oils rejuvenated her skin's glow, and her dignified air returned.

She re-emerged a short time later and found Dimitar and Olaf waiting between armed guards. Their bonds had been removed, and they shared a water skin. Olaf saved the last few drops to drip over his sweaty face, shaking his head back.

He grinned as Kaleela approached and gave Dimitar a nudge. "Close yer mouth, lad."

Kaleela smiled back, Dimitar's attention flattering her like tiny bubbles tickling her sides, but then grew serious, eyeing the unsheathed swords of the guards leading the men. The courtesies extended to her were not given to Dimitar and Olaf. What would happen to them here?

She posed the question to Rialyn. "*Sera'th minast mil amae?*"

The conversation bounced between Kaleela and the guardswoman, Dimitar and Olaf unable to understand the elvish. Kaleela spoke in a quiet, respectful tone yet couldn't sway Rialyn. The warrior elf shook her head, her honeyed, short hair curved to her chin and tucked behind one ear, and her eyes not unlike Bela'Ruhn's, cool and unyielding. There was no apology to Rialyn's words, only orders. Kaleela turned away, tight-lipped, to face the men.

"We must wait a few minutes to see the king and queen. The whole council is assembling." She hesitated, not knowing quite how to say what needed to be said. "Dimitar, Olaf... when we go inside the castle you must be re-bound."

"What? Kaleela, that's outrageous!" Dimitar started forward but stopped when Rialyn's hand stole to the hilt over her shoulder with alarming speed. Settling back, he said, "What do they think we're going to do?"

"'Tis a common fact elves are distrustful of humans."

"We're men from King Kahled's court. They trained him, and he trained us. How does it make sense to treat us this way?" Olaf stared down the guards in challenge.

Kaleela tried to pacify them. "Please, both of you... if it was my choice, we wouldn't be here in the first place. But since we are, we must obey their rules." She lowered her voice. "Besides, the sooner in, the sooner out, so we can be on our way."

"If anyone was askin' 'cept you, Princess..." Olaf grumbled as he held his reluctant hands out.

She rewarded him with a thankful smile. Dimitar did likewise as the guards approached them with fresh ropes and constrained their hands before them once more.

"*Eir'guerr* Rialyn," hailed a voice above them.

Kaleela craned her neck to find the origin. An elf stood at the top of the castle stairs, serving both as messenger to the city and watch guard. Kaleela caught the rest of his message and translated for the men as Rialyn led the group up the multitude of steps.

"The king and queen will see us now."

My grandparents.

22

DIMITAR

T ell me you couldn't see the trails either," Dimitar said to Olaf as they began the slow ascent of the castle steps.

"Ach, no more than what's between me and yer pretty face," Olaf said, winded already.

"Thank the gods, so it wasn't just me."

Dimitar was relieved to be out of the forest, which loomed around him, thick and cloying. He made out the packed dirt and occasional stone step, marking a well-used route, but couldn't see past the elf walking in front. Undergrowth hid where the path ought to lead, revealing the way only as they approached. He couldn't understand how the elves kept on the trails, including Kaleela who had no apparent disorientation during the walk.

There's more elven blood in her than she's let on.

She ascended the stairs before him after affording him an encouraging smile. Sunlight shone against her golden hair, the small tips of her ears peeking out from the tiny braids done around her face. Some semblance of peace, at last, blossomed on her features. Her beauty intoxicated him, strengthened him to give his all in the name of her safety and joy.

Dimitar took in additional views of the elven kingdom. The streets appeared oddly arranged to him, as if a pattern should exist but couldn't quite be seen. The houses extended in concentric semi-circles, wrapping ever closer as they approached the heart of the city: the castle. The pattern conjured an ancient magic, similar to the forest itself, one that traced Dimitar's skin like a whisper of cool breeze on a summer night.

As they climbed, Dimitar tried to contain his labored breath, the day warm and the steps numerous. In fairness, it didn't help that they couldn't use their hands to wipe their brows or keep themselves steady. He discreetly tried once again to work a hand free from the bindings, hoping the thin layer of sweat on his wrists offered some advantage. As before, the knots didn't budge.

Entering the main hall, Dimitar caught his breath. The hall was colossal, tree trunks blending into the wall and stretching high enough to touch the treetops themselves. Dimitar couldn't remember spotting such a high ceiling anywhere outside, which he figured must be a trick of the eye. *And a mighty one at that.*

Colored glass filled the many spaces in between the branches, enveloping the room with a majestic dance of colors, not unlike Blackburn's throne room. *So this is what inspired Kahled.* On the walls hung several tapestries woven with such intricacy that Dimitar first took them for paintings. The floor itself displayed a mosaic of small stone pieces, again forming subtle patterns and symbols.

A guard grabbed the huge knocker in the middle of a massive mahogany door at the end of the hall and let it drop with a resounding crack. The thick doors didn't grind as Dimitar expected, but instead opened as if floating on air. If the main hall captured Dimitar's breath, the throne room made him almost stop altogether in his tracks. Olaf muttered his own amazement as Rialyn led their group toward the back of the chamber, guards spreading out around them.

Tall, thick trunks stretched floor to ceiling around the outer rim of the room, purple and green banners fluttering from higher reaches by an unknown breeze. Paintings of past elven legends filled the gaps between the pillars, their frames as large as doorways. They glowed with richness from the sunlight filtering through the numerous windows. Against the back wall, a large dais supported a pair of carved thrones. A dozen smaller chairs formed a crescent moon next to them.

The eyes of every elf in this half-circle focused on Dimitar and Olaf, the outsiders. Rialyn stopped next to the last chair on the right where Bela'Ruhn sat, his swords unstrapped from his back and leaning against his leg. He acknowledged her with a nod but kept his intense gaze on the two men. Gar'Ret sat to the nearest left of the thrones; he smiled at the group. The only two who ignored the humans in their presence were the king and queen.

An'Nadal and Elayis had eyes for Kaleela alone, their daughter's daughter.

As with heralding other kingdoms on behalf of King Kahled, Dimitar remembered his court etiquette, taking a knee and bowing his head to the elven king and queen. Olaf followed suit, but Kaleela walked forward a few steps and bowed gracefully in the elven manner. She placed her hand across her heart, gathering the folds of her long gown with the other, and curtsied.

To this, the king and queen nodded their approval.

"Rise, child of our most beloved daughter, Princess Kaleel, and of High Knight Kahled." King An'Nadal's voice resonated through the wood of the hall, rounding out the rich sound. A thin beard marked his elder age. A crown of gleaming interwoven metals sat upon his ash brown hair, but his regal manner was most apparent in the way he conveyed himself. "Long have you been kept from your birth home, Lady Kaleela. At last, you're welcome in Quinthal."

"And rise, men of Blackburn." Elayis smiled behind pale-green eyes and faded golden hair framing an exquisite face. "You, too, are welcome in our city."

Dimitar's keen awareness of his bound wrists tempered Elayis's words. Her resemblance to Kaleela caught Dimitar off guard, and he once again marveled at her elven nature, having always thought of Kaleela as more human. *That's unfair to half her bloodline.* He sent silent encouragement her way as she stood before her grandparents for the first time.

An'Nadal and Elayis both regarded Kaleela with serenity, their smiles patiently expectant of her reply.

"Your Majesties, I thank you for the hospitality you've shown me and my guardsmen." Kaleela swept her gaze over the two men.

Dimitar frowned and glanced at his bound wrists.

"I should hardly think being marched into our kingdom at blade point qualifies as hospitality, my child." Sternness touched Elayis's words as she scrutinized Bela'Ruhn, who clenched his jaw in reply.

"Your guards did what was necessary," Kaleela replied with gracious courtesy, earning Captain Rialyn's quick nod of approval. "There are Corruptors in our lands."

Although a few of the elves sitting beside An'Nadal and Elayis murmured, the statement did not have the impact Dimitar expected.

"We've heard of their return and of your struggle with them last night." An'Nadal softened his next words. "We also received word of High Knight Conrad's fall. I'm sorry, child."

Kaleela closed her eyes for the briefest of moments. Dimitar ached for her and the sorrow she carried; she still reeled from Conrad's loss.

"Thank you, Your Majesty. He was like a father to me, and I honored his memory with a tree blessing." She left off the words with a gentle clearing of her throat. "But I'm not here because of King Conrad. I bear ill news of my true father."

This time, her words elicited quite a stir from the council. Even Bela'Ruhn sat straighter in his chair. An'Nadal quieted them with a raise of his hand and made a small motion for Kaleela to continue.

"The Corrupted captured my father when he ventured to investigate King Conrad's death, and are holding him prisoner in the mountains to the east."

An'Nadal glanced at Elayis, and for a fleeting moment, alarm flashed across his eyes. Council members turned to each other with rising whispers.

"Corruptors do not hold onto prisoners. He's fallen by now," Bela'Ruhn said.

"He has not," Kaleela replied, the general's words unsettling in their possibility. "Many of our knights were slain both during and after the attack. But not my father; they're keeping him alive."

"If his life wasn't taken by the Corrupted, then it was by his own hand." Bela'Ruhn spoke with finality, elaborating after horror crossed the faces of Kaleela and the men. "High Knight Kahled knows what will happen to any soldier who falls under Corruptor control, and would prefer death to the alternative."

"Out o' all the High Knights, I can't imagine King Kahled surrenderin' so easily." Olaf's words carried across the throne room chamber, tight with pride and defensiveness.

Bela'Ruhn's eyes darkened as he leaned forward in his chair, resting a hand upon the armrest. "Had you not been suckling on your mother's breast the last time the Corrupted attacked these lands, you might have an inkling of what they're capable of. Still, I would've expected your king's drillmasters to school you in these matters."

He paused as if daring him to argue further, although Kaleela raised a hand to silence whatever retort Olaf would bring.

"Perhaps it's time to consider the Corrupted are working on a greater plan," An'Nadal said, sparking new murmurs among the councilors.

"This explains much of the news we've received of late"—Bela'Ruhn trained his attention back on the three—"but doesn't answer why you're here."

"My father thinks I'm safer here and will find sound advice as to his rescue," Kaleela said with an even tone. "He also didn't realize this surety wouldn't extend to my guardsmen, else I would've come alone."

Bela'Ruhn sneered but didn't rise to the bait.

Risky; don't worry yourself for us. But the fact that she stood up for them shot a new sensation across Dimitar's chest, surprising and heartwarming. He held his head higher.

"Right of him to send you for help." Elayis's tone caressed as smooth and pleasurable as velvet. "Kahled remains bonded to our people, and his call for aid won't go unanswered."

This roused the council, conversations rising. Not all councilors seemed pleased by Elayis's words. One councilman in particular gestured adamantly to the elf next to him. As his amber eyes scanned over him and Olaf, the bright loathing shook Dimitar. He'd never seen the likes of it before.

Elayis's words brought Dimitar's thoughts into startling clarity. The all-too-recent memory of Corruptor claws striking at Kaleela's back and dark ebon's flame burning against the night sky pushed patience out of his mind. The elven kingdom was not where they desperately needed to be right now.

"With respect, we didn't come to your borders to ask for help," Dimitar said, ruddy heat coloring his cheeks. "That is to say, Your Majesties, in truth we didn't mean to come here at all."

"Then why *are* you here?" An'Nadal asked, his tone sharpening.

"As you were told by your people in Leighton last night, we came under attack by a dragon with Corruptors. The route to an escape led us to your borders. If your guards hadn't detained us, we'd be traveling a different path right now."

Elayis's eyes narrowed. "A path that would take you where?"

Dimitar didn't answer, tight-lipped.

Instead, Bela'Ruhn replied with a gritty laugh. "You mean to tell us that you two sapling guards were attempting to rescue a High Knight from a Corruptor lair?" Bela'Ruhn's voice lit with amusement, but the mirth didn't reach his eyes.

Dimitar looked at Olaf, startled, and found a similar reaction on his friend's face. Their brief exchange did not go unnoticed by the elven general's trained eye.

"And you just happened to end up on our borders?" Bela'Ruhn said as he leaned back in his chair, contemptuous.

"That wasn't our intent—" Dimitar started, his tolerance thinning.

"And yet, here you are anyway," Bela'Ruhn quipped. "I say the attack made you realize you aren't in drill this time."

Several councilors murmured among themselves.

"If I may remind you, General," Dimitar said, pride and more than a touch of temper fraying his diplomacy, "we're guards of King Kahled's court. We've been trained, and better than most."

"Of that, I've no doubt." Bela'Ruhn tipped his head, looking down at him. "But Corruptors fight back, unlike the straw dummies you've encountered until now. Or did your drillmasters leave out that lesson as well?"

The blood rushed to Dimitar's face. "Do you mean to blame—" he began, losing his composure, but was smoothly interrupted once more.

"I don't blame you for running to our help, no." The smile persisted on Bela'Run's lips, but any humor left his voice.

This is bull's shit. Dimitar held up his bound hands. "This is what you call 'help'? Cut these bindings, and I'll show you what I think of your elven help."

The smile melted from Bela'Ruhn's face, and a few council members grew agitated in their seats, unleashing what sounded like elvish curses.

Olaf stepped next to Dimitar, automatically protective, but two guardsmen pushed him back, and they began to scuffle. Several guards drew swords with a shout, leveling the blades at the large man. They surrounded him, and a guard held not one but two blade tips against Olaf's chest. Olaf halted in place, even if his eyes said otherwise.

A swipe of metal damn near cut his skin, and the ropes binding Dimitar's wrists came free. A guardsman faced him with a sword drawn in one hand; he held another sword extended toward Dimitar, hilt first. He sputtered in elven, but Dimitar didn't need to understand the language to catch the gist of these words. Speaking warrior to warrior, the elf expressed a sentiment Dimitar would've shared if anyone ever confronted Kahled in his presence: 'If you challenge my general, you must get through me first.'

A cacophony filled the throne room all at once. Rialyn shouted an order, and a guard pulled Kaleela aside, causing her to let out a small gasp. Councilors drowned out one another with their displeasure, not all aimed at him but rather among themselves. Bela'Ruhn remained seated, watching the events unfold, but Gar'Ret made his way down toward the group.

Damn it. We don't have time for this.

The elven guard gestured with his sword, growling another stream of elvish. Dimitar held up his hands; he wasn't going to fight. Although his words came out as a challenge, he hadn't meant anything past venting his frustration. He searched his mind to come up with some way to salvage his honor and recall his challenge at the same time.

The elven guard threw the offered sword at Dimitar's feet, the metal pommel clanging on the floor. Dimitar raised his hands higher and took a step back as the guardsman leveled his own blade in a threatening stance. Both Bela'Ruhn and Elayis considered his position, although neither did anything to stop the guard advancing upon him.

The guard let out a sudden cry as his sword flew out of his grip. He watched as it tumbled through the air, clutching his hand against his chest. The sword clattered to the ground followed by another, smaller metallic ringing. A short throwing knife bounced hilt to blade a few times before lying still.

As one, the hall fell silent as all eyes took in the foreign knife, then searched for the source.

Not surprisingly, Bela'Ruhn had already risen to his feet to face the spotted threat. Drawing a sword from the scabbard beside his chair, he pointed the tip at a window on the far side of the throne room. "*Hew rhea!*"

Several guards drew bows so fast, Dimitar couldn't even follow the movement. Following Bela'Ruhn's line of sight, a hooded figure crouched in one of the windows midway up the wall, blending too well among the afternoon shadows. Ral held a dagger poised between the fingers of his left hand.

"No! Don't shoot!" Kaleela cried out as Bela'Ruhn opened his mouth for the order.

He paused but didn't tell the archers to lower their bows.

Kaleela frantically wrestled out of the guardsman's grip and spun to face the king and queen. "This man is with us, Your Majesties."

"Impossible," Bela'Ruhn said, his sword still raised. When it dropped, the arrows around the room would let loose.

"He's the messenger who delivered my father's words"—Kaleela's voice wavered as she pleaded with Bela'Ruhn—"and my guide on this journey. *I need him.*"

"Impossible," Bela'Ruhn said again, brow creasing further. "No one can find their way into this city, unattended and unwelcome. No one."

With slow, emphasized caution, Ral tucked the dagger into his belt and signed a short response. Olaf began to translate, but Gar'Ret cut him off, apparently versed in the silent language.

"You couldn't follow us," Gar'Ret said from where he stood in the middle of the room. His voice was thick with confusion. "The trees won't reveal their path to anyone without royal blessing. And you would've been spotted... you would've been heard."

Ral shrugged and swung himself over the window's ledge. In three consecutive drops to various handholds, Ral lowered himself to the floor. A creak of bows chorused as the archers followed him.

'Perhaps the forest felt generous.'

"Do not mock this sacred ground," An'Nadal said in stern rebuke, and Ral answered with an apologetic bow. An'Nadal then motioned for the archers to lower their arrows. "Allow this man to approach."

A moment's pause, then Bela'Ruhn issued the command. "Lower your weapons." As he sheathed his sword with an angry thrust, he addressed Ral. "And don't think because your throw landed hilt first, you haven't committed a grave act in this room."

Dimitar considered this. Could Bela'Ruhn track the thief's intent, and in such a chaotic room? There was no way Bela'Ruhn could spot the attack before anyone else and judge the throw as purposefully non-lethal. Dimitar knew of the unsurpassed warrior skills Bela'Ruhn and his elite fighters held in legend, but he'd always thought the stories just that—legend. He now reconsidered.

A second thought then entered his mind: did Ral intend to startle the guard, or was it luck? To throw with aim and accuracy from such an angle and distance wasn't possible. Was it?

Around the room, the creak of bowstrings sounded as the guards released their tension, and blades slid into scabbards. Dimitar bent to pick up the guard's sword and return it as a peace offering, but the elf put his foot on the blade, glaring. Dimitar released his grip and turned away, heading toward Olaf and ignoring the guard's heated stare on his back.

Ral walked up to the group and gave a small wave, which only Olaf returned. The council members filled the room with debate in their flowing language. Gar'Ret returned to his seat, glancing over his shoulder at the group with suspicion clouding his once-warm eyes.

None of this is going how I wanted it to.

"Enough!" Elayis's words resonated throughout the room.

All conversation halted.

"You've brought us much to consider today," she said to the group. "I don't know how this messenger came into our city unbidden, nor do I appreciate your guardsman's open challenge of our offer to assist in rescuing his king."

"Your Majesty—" Kaleela stopped as Elayis spoke over her.

"But that's not to say we don't understand your position. We shall consult our councilors on this matter. You'll be summoned when we come to an agreement." She turned to Rialyn. "Lead them to comfortable chambers, and make sure they're seen to. Despite their actions, they're still welcome within these walls."

To this, she looked pointedly at each man in turn.

"As you wish." Rialyn came to a stand once more and walked toward the main doors. "If you please," she said as she passed the group, and indicated with her hand it was time to leave the elven throne room of legend.

23

KALEELA

The elven city's harmony soothed Kaleela, who sat in a large bay window seat overlooking the treescape, lost in wonder. The sense of belonging near overwhelmed her but for the peace that wrapped around her, a long-sought embrace. *These are my mother's people, her streets, her castle. What if this had been my home, too?* She let herself sink into her thoughts, taking everything in, calming in spite of their confinement within the fine suite.

Dimitar paced the waiting room, his footsteps switching from loud clops to softened thuds as he crossed from vibrant wood to the lush tapestry rug in the middle of the floor. He tried to settle in one of the plush chairs as Olaf did but popped back up a minute later, back to pacing.

His presence, too, served as a comfort to her. Not once did he make her feel irresponsible or her task a burden. She shifted her gaze to him, considering. Dedication could manifest as obligation, but that wasn't the case with Dimitar. No, his drive stemmed from genuine concern. This was a man who wore his heart on his sleeve; deception wasn't in his nature. *He's someone who'll protect me no matter the cost.*

Ral stood in one corner next to a bookshelf, idly flipping through the volumes. *Oh, I wonder if he likes to read as much as I do?* The smaller man had been stripped of his knife belts before leaving the throne room, Rialyn pulling blade after blade from within the cloak folds. She didn't, however, draw back Ral's hood, and Kaleela's esteem for the captain rose at this sign of respect.

"Do you see any good titles?" she asked, curious.

The hood tilted her way, Ral's face shadowed, as always. A calmness manifested from the cloaked man, peaceful in a way not unlike the elven forest itself.

He set a book back in place, then signed, 'I can't read elvish.'

"Well, you're teaching me your silent language. What if I taught you elvish?" She grinned at the humble bow he gave her. *A charmer!*

Footsteps sounded outside moments later. Kaleela slid from the window seat and joined the men at the front of the room. A guard opened the suite door, sword drawn and resting on a shoulder.

He beckoned them with an elvish word and small wave. Dimitar reached the door first, but the guard's sword lowered and blocked him. He pointed over Dimitar's shoulder and spoke in elvish.

Kaleela cleared the confusion. "He wants Ral to go first, so he can keep him in sight. I'm sorry, Ral."

Without any apparent sign of frustration or insult, Ral stepped ahead as if leading the group in honor. The guard directed them into the main hall, his sword never leaving his shoulder, but even more imposing because of his implied confidence with the blade. Her father's words echoed in her mind: *never assume a relaxed air means your opponent's unready to strike.*

Councilors regarded them with open stares, most in neutrality but some bridging on hostility as they sat with arms crossed. Kaleela could only guess what they'd discussed, but their decision appeared far from unanimous. Before the semi-circle of council chairs, a new elf stood off to the side. His silver-blonde hair contrasted with a thick green mantle, leather straps crossing his chest. Around his waist hung a wide rope belt with four distinct, intricate symbols woven into the braids.

Oh my gods. He's a mage.

The woven runes reflected the disciplines of magic he studied, but Kaleela had never heard of a magic-user mastering all four elements: air, water, land, and fire. This mage's power was unmatched, unless Kaleela misheard the stories of their trade. Her gaze pulled away from the mage as the doors slid closed, and An'Nadal stood from his throne to address her.

"It has long been custom for elves to let other races manage their own affairs," An'Nadal said, with several councilors nodding in agreement. "However, we'll do so only if you're capable of saving

Kahled without the need of our intervention. Princess Kaleela, will you attest to the skills and strengths of your companions?"

A fair question. She studied the councilors in hopes of finding what answer they expected from her. Their stolid faces revealed nothing.

"Yes, Your Majesty. They've been trained by my father's best knights," Kaleela said after a moment's hesitation. No; she needed to show more confidence. She raised her voice, as firm as if she sat upon the throne instead of standing before it. "They're brave and true to their blades."

"I don't doubt their physical strength. What I'm asking is, do you trust your father's life in their hands?"

Kaleela weighed his question in her mind. *Did* she trust this small group with her father's life? Turning, she looked over her companions.

Olaf scanned the room before meeting her gaze. He gave a slight nod, and in that small gesture offered both calculation and agreement, having judged what he found in the councilors' faces and now ready to support whatever she said next. As he proved time and time again, the strength in his massive arms paled in comparison to the force of his heart.

Ral stood to the side, arms tucked into his cloak folds. He'd saved her from the Corruptor's cold hands outside of Dwyer's, and the goblin's brutal intent. The cloaked man's presence brought a sense of security, and for reasons she couldn't quite explain, she trusted him implicitly.

And then Dimitar. There was no force in this world that would stand between him and Kahled. *Or me.* He waited with his arms crossed, his expression serious beneath dark locks escaping from his hair pulled halfway back, handsome at every angle. He retained a determination that reminded her of Conrad. Although a short time had passed since they left Blackburn's comforts, she'd grown close to him; not just from his unfailing protection, but also the way he reached out and listened to her. Where once she resented his assignment to her, she now wanted him beside her. *I can be myself fully around him.* The thought brought a smile to her face and warmth low in her belly.

They'd come this far and risked their lives before goblins, Corruptors, and a dragon. And not one of them said a single word about turning around. They pressed forward, together, for her. For Kahled.

Still smiling, she turned to the king, conviction ringing in her words. "They will save my father."

An'Nadal returned her smile and beckoned to the mage. "Mage Willem, please approach."

With a rustle from his mantle, the mage came before the king and queen with a low bow. His movements were elegant and subtle, capturing the mastery of his art.

"We'll not leave Kahled, a High Knight and beloved of my daughter, alone to a Corruptor feast," Elayis said. "This mage will accompany you in your pursuit to save him."

A clamor of low murmurs spread among the councilors, some whispering words of dissent. Elayis turned in her throne and addressed them. "We've made our decision, and you will heed our word."

The whispers stopped immediately.

"I thank you for your kindness and generosity." Kaleela bowed low, keeping a level expression as annoyance rose within her. Was this someone else to watch over her? "But I don't think we need this mage."

"We don't send Mage Willem with you on a whim," An'Nadal said. "He's skilled in the arts of defense and healing. He could prove vital to your rescue. Have you considered that your father may be injured when you arrive? What would you do then?"

Kaleela acknowledged her grandfather's words. She didn't want to be responsible for another person on this mission, but his points were sound.

"I see your point, Your Majesty. Thank you for your thoughtfulness." Bowing again, she backed away from the throne. She met Dimitar's questioning look as he stepped beside her.

"Do we really need a healer with us?" Dimitar asked in a low voice. "Olaf and I know quite a bit—"

"It's Mage Willem, if you care to remember it. I've earned my title." Willem's tone conveyed a stinging mix of boredom and reprimand, as if speaking to children.

The group turned to find the mage joined them. His arrogance created an aura rich with intimidation and confidence.

Olaf addressed him first, grabbing Willem's hand and pumping it a few times. "Well, Mage Willem, it's awfully nice to have—"

"Save your words." He pulled his hand from Olaf's. "King An'Nadal gave me an order, and that's why I must travel with you. If our formalities are over, I'll begin my preparations for departure."

With this, he swept out of the room, leaving Olaf with his mouth open and hand still hanging in mid-air.

"Warm fella', ain't he?" Olaf wiped his trousers as if he'd touched something offensive.

"He'll show his worth when the time comes," Kaleela reassured them. *He's here to help us, not get in my way. Gods, please let that be true.* She turned to Rialyn as she approached. "We should all get ready. Please return their weapons and armor."

"I'll also send servants to attend to your arrangements for provisions."

Kaleela gave thanks as Rialyn set out to her duties, and the troop started toward the main doors.

"Princess, a moment." Gar'Ret descended from his throne to her. "May Kaleel's spirit help guide you to your father. Good luck to you and your company, *mil'ine*. We would have you return as soon as possible."

He held out his arms, tentative but inviting. Betraying the calm façade she'd worked so hard to maintain all day, Kaleela met her uncle's hug in a rush, grabbing on to him. A part of her heart had mended the moment she discovered Gar'Ret was her uncle, a hole she knew existed but never with the painful clarity that became apparent when she stepped into the Sun'Din. Parting after a long moment, he backed away with a small smile as he regarded Kaleela once more. With Gar'Ret's familial greeting—*my niece*—and encouragement, Kaleela hurried off to her duties, torn between her new family left behind and her father waiting ahead.

24

KALEELA

Activity around Quinthal Castle increased as word spread of a mission underway to rescue Kahled. Servants hurried with smooth proficiency throughout the grounds, fetching supplies and exchanging messages. Cana'th, the elf from Dwyer's, aided Dimitar and Olaf by interpreting their requests for food and basic supplies. Ral waited off to the side, ostensibly to avoid drawing any more attention to himself on top of his throne room entrance. Willem was nowhere to be seen, and Kaleela assumed he tended to his own business.

She changed into new leather armor and bundled up several packets of food and water flasks a servant put together. She recalled Dimitar's earlier lessons back in Blackburn's stables, and this time worked efficiently, eager to be off. Part of her wished to stay, to learn more of her heritage and find answers to questions formed since childhood. Stronger still was her desire to find her father and growing uneasiness over wasted time. She went about her tasks, setting herself to leave within the hour. Her intentions halted when Captain Rialyn approached.

"Queen Elayis wishes a word with you. Come with me."

Trying to shake any preconceived notions about what the queen wanted with her, Kaleela followed behind Rialyn, contemplating the captain's back. One blade slung over her left shoulder, and a second rested on her right hip. Her cool, straightforward manner was not so different from Bela'Ruhn's. Kaleela's stomach sank every time the general looked her way, but with the captain, her curiosity surfaced. Rialyn's angular elven features were pleasing, beige like the under-bark of a birch tree, although her demeanor and self-assured way she carried herself caught Kaleela's attention. The captain expected her orders obeyed as readily as Bela'Ruhn's.

As if sensing Kaleela's gaze, Rialyn half-turned toward her without breaking stride. She tucked a loose strand of honeyed hair behind one pointed ear. "May I speak honestly with you, Princess?"

Kaleela murmured assent as she hurried a few steps to match Rialyn's stride.

"You're so similar to our sovereigns' daughter and yet nothing like they expected," Rialyn mused aloud. "There's much you shall learn here."

"What do you mean? Have I caused some offense?"

A corner of Rialyn's mouth tugged upwards. "No, at least not to the royal family. Your presence is long overdue, and it'll do the family well to spend time with you. But tell me—do you know who Bela'Ruhn is?"

"Gar'Ret tells me he's General of your army."

"Aye, that much is true. T'would seem you don't know his reputation, though. He's not one to accept, ah, how shall I say... *dispute* from those under his command." Humor touched Rialyn's gaze.

Kaleela stiffened. "I'm not his to command."

"Perhaps not, but you're under his protection and will be forevermore. Our first duty is to serve the royal family, whom you've joined with at last." Rialyn now contemplated her with an open stare, and Kaleela wasn't quite sure how the wheel of scrutiny had turned around on her. "Yet I don't think any prior knowledge of General Bela'Ruhn would've stilled your tongue. Much like the queen that way."

With that statement, Rialyn pushed open a door and gestured. "She awaits you here."

Kaleela exited the castle walls into a blooming garden. Flowers of every color grew tall and plentiful, perfuming the air with sweetness. In the center of the garden rose a granite fountain. Water glistened in a steady cascade, casting small crystal drops in the afternoon sunlight. A low stone bench encircled the fountain, carved with flowing knot work curved like the tree root twisting its way around the base. Queen Elayis sat upon the bench, her long pale gown forming a small pool on the ground.

Finding her courage, Kaleela walked to her and curtsied. "You sent for me, Your Majesty?"

The queen regarded her with intensity before motioning her closer. "Come, my child, sit next to me." While Rialyn assumed Kaleela preferred the common tongue, Elayis spoke in her native language.

"I'm honored you'd meet with me, and lay myself upon your good graces." Kaleela answered in kind, her own voice sounding foreign as the elven words flowed from her tongue with practiced lilt. The words carried respect, but once again Kaleela fell back upon learned courtesies out of nervousness.

She wanted to ask about her mother instead.

She wanted to lean her head onto the elder woman's shoulder, accept a mothering embrace, and be reassured she'd see her father alive. As with Gar'Ret, the sparks of common blood passed between her and Elayis as they regarded one another, yet these words would not come. Her grandmother was still a stranger.

In a soft voice, Elayis said, "I despised you."

Kaleela's breath caught in her throat, as startled and wounded as if the queen had slapped her.

"When I learned my daughter had been taken from me, I cursed you, for your birth brought her death. What's more, you aren't even full with our blood. You're half-human..."

So, it was true: they did blame her for her mother's death, echoing the self-accusations Kaleela harbored all her life. Elayis's words spoken aloud now, left Kaleela defenseless. Heat and dismay suffocated her, and she swallowed with effort, a thousand apologies stuck upon her insides, pricking like thorns.

Elayis gazed afar as if conjuring old memories, unaware of her words' effect. She touched a lock of wavy, silken hair that lay on Kaleela's shoulder, but Kaleela jerked away, unable to look at the queen any longer. She stood abruptly, backing away a few paces.

"I'm... I'm sorry my presence causes you such distress." Kaleela's throat clenched with the effort of choking back her disappointment and guilt. "Please excuse me, and forgive me."

"*Garin'ah.*" Elayis's tone was calm and smooth.

Kaleela stopped in her tracks, the elvish name washing over her as easily as the fountain's waters. *Granddaughter.*

Elayis came to stand before her, just short of her height. She might as well have stood as tall as Conrad himself, given the same effect on Kaleela, who held her ground but whose eyes stung from holding back tears.

"My child, my granddaughter, you must understand this." Elayis's gaze held steady, and Kaleela was shocked to realize the queen pleaded with her. "As soon as you were taken from us, another piece of me was lost. I've been so wrong. And when you stood in our hall for the first time today, I so vividly saw my Kaleel in you. Granted, you share a great deal of her beauty. But beyond that, you carry her virtues of intelligence, strength, and passion. You keep your mother's spirit in you. I didn't realize how much I missed you until we met."

The hurt of Elayis's earlier words receded, replaced with dawning hope. Kaleela couldn't keep a tremble from her voice. "All I've ever wanted was to learn who my mother was."

"And we want to know you." Elayis grasped Kaleela's arms in an embrace, the elder and younger generation sealing a long-absent bond. "And now, too soon, you're leaving. You must bring back Kahled, and I know you can. He's a good man, blessed with the greatest gift in this world: you."

"Aye, I can't delay any longer. But... I want to come back. I've spent my whole life wondering about you—my mother's family. My family."

"I know, sweet girl. May the gods protect you and your companions. Come home to us. We've waited so long for you." Elayis stroked her face and kissed her cheek in goodbye.

Rialyn waited for Kaleela at the arched doorway, unfazed as Kaleela pressed her palms against wet eyes.

"Please take me to my friends," Kaleela said. "It's time to leave."

She walked deep in her thoughts, no longer interested in her guardswoman or surroundings. Before long, they reached the front entrance. Rialyn pointed to the bottom of the stairs where Olaf and Dimitar readied their horses, Dimitar laughing at something Olaf said. Ral sat astride his horse, stretching around to feed it a carrot. Willem also waited on the main road, separated from the others by a good distance. The warmth of pride touched Kaleela as she looked over her companions.

This is going to work.

Rialyn tapped her arm, holding out a bow. "This is for you on the remainder of your journey. The weapon is mine, but I hear it's of better use in your hands."

Kaleela accepted the bow, marveling at its craftsmanship. Customary knot work threaded the pale yew wood, etched in shallow marks so as not to compromise the wood's strength and filled with rose copper filament. The leather hand wrap felt worn and indented from Rialyn's grip, but the string was freshly attached. Kaleela tested the draw stroke, bringing her arm up and noting the power behind the pull. Her own bow, lost on the back of the horse in Leighton, couldn't have a better replacement.

"Here." Rialyn handed over a bundle of cedar arrows. "Why don't you try it?"

Sticking two fingers between her lips, Rialyn whistled short and loud, drawing the attention of the escorts waiting below. She shouted a brief command in elven, and a guard stepped forward, raising his shield to cover his torso. The men waited next to him, their attention turned to the top of the stairs where she and Rialyn stood.

"I'm not going to aim at him." Kaleela shook her head. "I don't want to risk his safety. I'm sure this is a fine weapon, and thank you for its use."

Rialyn appraised Kaleela with a sideways glance. "If your skill with a bow is what I'm told, there shouldn't be concern for his safety."

Although Rialyn's tone came off cool and neutral, the challenge in her eyes said otherwise. Kaleela bristled and replied by wetting her thumb and choosing an arrow, notching it onto the string. In almost the same movement, she drew back, aimed, and released. The arrow sailed through the air with surprising speed, driving home into the center of the guard's shield.

"Hey, hey! Why ya tryin' to pick us off?" Olaf hollered, throwing up his hands as the guard next to him lowered his shield, working the arrow back and forth to pry it loose.

Kaleela flexed the bow string once more, appreciating its quality. The captain smiled at her with genuine approval, and Kaleela smiled back.

"Thank you," Kaleela said. "I'm fortunate you'd lend me your bow."

"Until we meet again. May the Corrupted who cross your path discover just how unfortunate they are at the receiving end."

Elven guards escorted the company through the Sun'Din, stopping within sight of the northeastern forest edge. The group needed two travel days to reach the Great Basin and then three days traveling southeast before coming to the base of the eastern mountains. They were about to embark on the more treacherous half of their journey.

With a final murmured goodbye, Kaleela urged her horse forward. Crossing the boundary from the Sun'Din Forest into the Green Lands, intangible energies stretched against her as if to hold her back in, soft like a spider web's sticky threads. The next moment, the connection ended; the strand snapped. She kept her eyes on the road ahead where her greatest success, or unthinkable failure, awaited.

25

KAHLED

Kahled awoke in his cell. A moment of disorientation washed over him. Propped along the back wall, his body ached. His neck cramped with knots from hanging against his chest for so long. A few small trickles ran between his shoulder blades, and he swiped at the irritation with a clumsy hand. His fingers dragged across thickened stickiness, and instant pain flashed over his back. Kahled had no recollection how he returned to his cell, but the stinging gouges across his upper back made the case that Corruptors carried him. They knew no delicacy with their claws.

Resting his head in his hands, he relived the last few minutes in the perversion of a throne room. How could he miss the obvious? Somehow, he'd known all along but didn't want to believe the truth. It was too unthinkable.

Stretching his neck with a groan, Kahled hoped Kaleela had delivered his message to the elves. He knew instinctively he wouldn't live much longer. A point would come when he'd choose between death and submitting to the Overlord's will, and gods willing, he'd have the strength to choose death.

Kahled closed his eyes and sought to regain his composure. He breathed in and out, methodically and with intention, trying to ignore the developing rattle in his lungs. The hum of thoughts slowed with each intake and left his mind with each exhale.

The clatter of bowls dropped in his cell brought him out of his meditation. Kahled eyed the water with suspicion, but the Overlord wouldn't try the same trick again. The water was far from fresh but wasn't poisoned with the Corrupted seed. Still, as the liquid sluiced down his throat, the innate urge to spit it out made him choke, so vivid was the all-too recent memory of the Corrupted violation.

He took the bowls with him to the back of the cell, alarmed at how weary he became just crossing to the other side. Taking another small sip, it occurred to him that Conrad likely shared the same cell when he was held by the Corrupted. Did Conrad fare better during his time in the caverns, his fortitude always edging out Kahled's?

Tears welled in his eyes at the thought of his dearest friend, and a wave of guilt bit into his stomach. Kahled always showed greater intuition than Conrad, yet he didn't consider the Overlord until too late. If he'd seen the truth earlier, Conrad would still be alive. Together, they could've defeated this evil. Apart, the odds became much narrower.

"Damn it!" Kahled's voice echoed in his cell. He lay on the stone floor, exhaustion and despair running over his body. The solitude imposed by the Overlord took its toll, breaking down his strength, his will, his hope, until the fractured shards scattered on the ground beneath him. For the first time, Kahled didn't know if he wanted the elves discovering him in this wretched state.

As the weight of desolation shut his eyes, a naked truth came to him: the Overlord wanted him demoralized. Along with discovering his true identity in the crude throne room, Kahled now recalled the history of the man's manipulation. Nothing was done without some wicked purpose. His very mention of Conrad's name acted as a spike of hopelessness driven into Kahled's heart. Kahled was letting the Overlord's words destroy his will.

I'll be damned if I allow him to control me.

Forcing his eyes open, he used the remaining strength in his arms to push into a sitting position. With a shaking hand, he pulled the water bowl to his lap, along with the piece of bread. He needed the sustenance and would be damned if the elves discovered him lying down dying when they came to rescue him. He wouldn't disgrace Conrad's memory and their achievements as High Knights.

He wouldn't dishonor their relationship.

Kahled sent his mind outside the cell to distract himself from the reality confining him. Images flooded his thoughts, all battling for his full attention. He let them fight it out, knowing somewhere in his heart a memory would surface that could help him find the strength to outlast this ordeal.

A singular recollection took precedence. Kahled began to turn it away, not wanting to touch old grief on top of the new. But he'd taken no time to grieve for Conrad, and here in their shared prison, his will alone could no longer hold back the sorrow.

The memory returned.

As sister cities newly ruled by fellow High Knights, Blackburn and Stormgard relied on one another. Conrad had arrived at Blackburn Castle that day, having left from a previous visit only three weeks prior. Always the center of a crowd's attention, he was a charismatic and natural leader, lighting up any room. Conrad took to establishing his reputation and rule at Stormgard, the city having mourned their fallen king, then welcomed him to the throne with delight and reverence. His frequent trips were practical and strengthening as the Green Lands rebuilt after the war.

Kahled spent most of his time pacing the halls of his new home, carrying his tiny child, wishing Blackburn Castle would swallow them up.

Kaleel, his soulmate, his greatest love, was dead. The Reclamation War flashbacks hit him every night. He was thrust in charge of an entire kingdom. And his baby, achingly beautiful and innocent, looked at him with her mother's eyes.

If Conrad's visits became more frequent, Kahled hadn't noticed at the time.

It took both his and Conrad's efforts to settle the baby that night. Kahled refused to let any staff take up Kaleela's care, and kept her bassinet in a room connected to his master suite. Kahled held her, spinning tales of a brave girl saving helpless animals. Conrad rocked her, crooning song after song, not in the boisterous way he did at his many parties, but low and soothing. That night she cried the moment she was placed on the plush bedding, time and time again, and Kahled wouldn't leave her to sob. He couldn't bear the sound of her distress.

Kahled rested on the edge of his bed, already undressed to his underclothes, when Conrad came in, arms empty.

"Success?" he asked, and Conrad nodded with an exasperated grin.

"I sang 'The Mage Warriors' Stand' three times." Conrad placed his hands on his lower back and stretched. Instead of heading out to his suite, he took a seat next to Kahled and scrubbed a hand through his dark, cropped hair.

"Aye, that's a whole ballad. She'll sleep til dawn now. What's that, in an hour or two?"

Conrad chuckled, then turned serious. His gaze traveled over Kahled's face. "You look ready to collapse."

Kahled didn't reply at first, staring at some distant point. "I won't fall asleep right away."

"You haven't been sleeping well." It wasn't a question. *How did he know?* "Kahled... tell me what's going on. Let me help you."

Kahled looked down, unable to express the weight of everything upon him. He didn't want to burden his friend, nor give voice to the whirling torments that ravaged him day and night.

"I know you." Conrad placed his hand over Kahled's. "You can keep your thoughts if you wish, but I can still read you. It doesn't have to be this way. This pain you hold, it doesn't have to define you anymore."

Kahled looked at him then, the stormy gray of his eyes meeting Conrad's. "I don't know how else to be," he said, his voice cracking. "I've been given everything, yet I have nothing."

"That's not true. Think of your girl. Kaleel gave her life for her. Do not waste this gift."

Kahled's heart wrenched just to hear her name, his eyes brimming. Conrad had been there in the Sun'Din, to await Kaleel's labor and celebrate the birth of their child. Kahled recalled with a raw twist in his chest how he'd been first to hold their baby, overcome with joy and oblivious to the midwives' increasingly frantic ministrations on his wife. He rushed from the room to tell Conrad, shouting the news. Conrad embraced him, weeping in his ear, and Kahled laughed aloud, thinking his friend rejoiced. He no longer remembered who told him Kaleel died; only collapsing to the cold floor as his whole world ended. Conrad held him then, forced him to rise as the baby cried anew in the next room over, pressed against her mother's lifeless body.

Gods, he'd give anything for someone to take this pain away. The hurt washed over him in waves, electrifying his skin, suffocating his breath.

Conrad looked at Kahled, taking in the measure of his suffering, and his next words were very soft. "You also have me."

Kahled's expression shifted ever so slightly as Conrad's words took effect. There, at last, cutting through his endless grief and rising from a place within, flickered a spark of comfort. Conrad held his gaze steady and leaned in, closing the short distance.

"Let me help you," he repeated in a whisper, and then their lips met, soft and safe. Conrad cupped Kahled's neck as their kiss deepened, unexpected and new. A slow, heated tenderness followed like sweet air to a drowning man.

The next morning, Conrad, half-awake, elbowed Kahled out of bed when the baby began to stir and fuss in the next room over.

Conrad kept his word and visited Blackburn at regular intervals, advising and supporting Kahled's new rule and parenthood. Conrad seemed to sense when Kahled needed their intimacy, and at those times took to his bed. In time, joy entered their shared space as the kingdoms flourished and their girl grew into a young woman. Conrad had extended every part of himself to raise Kahled above his grief.

Kahled clenched his jaw now in the little stone cell. This is when his enemy could break him, but only if he allowed. He was underfed, exhausted, and despairing, yet there was still fight in the last of the High Knights.

Kahled looped some chain around his hands, closing the links into a fist. The next Corruptor that got too close to him would find out just how much.

He would rise again.

26

DIMITAR

The following morning began in brisk air. The company's breath formed small clouds around the fire where they took breakfast, warming themselves against the chill. The plate of dried fruits, boiled egg, and slice of cooked ham proved both filling and tasty, and Dimitar soon shook off the remnants of his sleepiness.

Ral tended the horses and gestured as Kaleela shifted some items in her saddlebag. She paused to hold the worn leather book and traced a finger along the etched cover.

"What about the book?" She watched Ral's hand motions, then repeated his question to make sure she had it right.

"I always carry it on my travels." Kaleela flipped through the pages. "The stories connect me with my parents—my fathers, that is. The Mage Warriors always followed a cause, someone or something that bound them to their purpose. They shared a special connection to their chosen person and would do anything for them. I thought the Mage Warrior tales would lend me some strength. I know—it probably sounds foolish."

She blushed, but Ral just nodded as she tucked the collection of tales into her bag, then turned his attention to the remaining horses. Dimitar tracked their conversation with a distrustful eye before finishing his meal.

The day's travel passed without event, and Dimitar allowed himself to hope the rest of the journey would follow in the same way; that is, until the group settled down for dinner.

"Who gave you that?" Willem snapped, gaze rising from Ral's hands to his hooded face. The mage had said very little to anyone in the group since yesterday's departure from the Sun'Din, and all attention turned to him.

Ral paused mid-lift of the cheese slice to his mouth, freshly cut from a block and balanced on a small throwing knife. A wine carafe, as yet unopened, stood on the ground where Ral sat cross-legged. The cheese's rich fragrance wafted into Dimitar's nostrils, and he involuntarily inhaled, tasting the pungent, expensive aroma on the back of his tongue.

Ral looked at Willem and lifted one shoulder before bringing the cheese to the shadows of his hood; the small knife then lowered, empty. Dimitar's mouth watered.

"Is something the matter?" Kaleela asked, unpacking some of the food in her own knapsack.

"That cheese and wine is from the royal kitchen's *private stock*." Willem's voice dropped several degrees in temperature. "'Tis not the sustenance our servants would pack for him."

Kaleela turned to Ral, anxiety lighting her eyes. Ral sliced off another piece of cheese, savoring the bite before setting his knife aside to sign.

'That's why I didn't wait for them to give it to me.'

Olaf barked a laugh before catching Willem's hostile stare.

"You stole them?" Dimitar said. "For the love of the gods. I can't believe this."

"Oh, Ral." Kaleela sighed. She turned to Willem, faltering under his darkening gaze. "I'm sorry, I... Ral, give the remainder back at once."

"Naw, he really can't." Olaf's eyes danced with humor. "It'll spoil 'fore we reach the Sun'Din on our way back."

Kaleela looked crestfallen as Willem's offense grew, and Dimitar muttered a curse under his breath.

He's nothing but a gods damn thief. We'd do best to remember that's all he is.

Olaf patted Kaleela's hand. "Hand over the wine, boy-o," he said to Ral, gesturing at the unopened bottle. "That much will keep in the mage's bag."

"And give him the chance to rifle through my possessions in order to retrieve it later? I think not." Willem turned to present his back to

Ral, settling into his affronted meal in stony silence. As such, he didn't notice when Olaf helped Ral finish the cheese and wine.

As they traveled throughout the next day, the terrain became more difficult to cross, reducing their pace at times. Instead of the more frequented paths across the central Green Lands, these northern fields were less worn with travel. Clear skies opened up to the full strength of the summer sun, hot and without a breeze. Under the blazing sun and repetitive landscape, slowed by a length of loose rocks underfoot, silence grew among the group.

Dimitar considered the elven mage's back, the way he rode without any apparent concern toward those in his company. Willem had journeyed in silence over the past few days, keeping a distance between himself in the lead and the others. Willem spared the group little attention since their meeting in Quinthal's throne room, much less since Ral's blatant thievery. *Arrogance, confidence, or disdain, I wonder. Maybe all three.*

Olaf squirmed in his saddle, and Dimitar shot him a knowing look. A day's travel in relative silence was enough for the big man. His friend had just about reached the breaking point, and Dimitar inwardly groaned.

"So, Willem," Olaf said, as if on cue. Ral motioned to Olaf the title reminder of Mage, which Olaf dismissed with a hand wave. "What kind o' magic can ya control?"

At the front of the pack, Willem didn't bother to turn before answering, and Dimitar strained to hear him. "I can call all four elements into my power."

Olaf pulled out a small sack from the side of his saddlebag and popped a few shelled chestnuts into his mouth, considering this. "Does this mean ya can conjure me some shade from this cursed sun?" He chucked to himself.

"No, I will not," Willem said, clearly pained at engaging in any conversation with the large man.

"But ya didn't say ya couldn't." Olaf tossed another roasted nut into the air and caught it in his mouth. "So, what else can ya do, then? What about turnin' stone into gold pieces? Oh! How 'bout casting a spell so that m'beer is always full, like right up to the top, no matter how big a gulp I—"

Willem spat something in elvish that sounded like a curse. "Really, human, is that the length and scope of your imagination when it comes to power bestowed by the gods themselves? How fortunate to be you."

Kaleela looked over, jumping in before Olaf retorted. "King An'Nadal told me you have valuable healing skills."

Willem's frosty tone warmed toward Kaleela but still dripped with haughtiness. "I can attack any foe, offer protection from bodily harm, and heal physical wounds."

"We got a man in the sellers' district back home who can palm fire," Olaf said. "*Very* popular with the ladies come wintertime."

"Humans cannot obtain any serious magic skills. You need two of your lifetimes of dedicated study to even consider entering the Dark Woods. These street performers are never serious about the craft."

"The Mage Warriors were all human, though," Kaleela said.

"That much is true. Their abilities were a gift and a blessing."

"Is there a limit?" Dimitar asked, curiosity getting the better of him. Willem shot him a sour look. "I mean, is there a limit to the amount of magic you can do?"

"No." Willem hesitated. "Not unless you expend all your magic, all at once. But that type of spell isn't performed; it takes all." He lifted his chin at Olaf. "It's difficult for humans to comprehend, when they're so occupied by trivial matters."

With that, Willem gave his reins a flick, urging the pack to pick up their pace and ending further conversation.

Olaf sat back in his saddle, his horse slowing to a stop as he frowned at the mage's rigid posture. He hefted the satchel in his hand, and a slow grin crept across his face. "How 'bout a demonstration," he muttered.

"Keep up," Dimitar said as he passed by, shooting an exasperated grin at his friend.

Bringing his horse back up to join the others, Olaf reached across to nudge Dimitar atop his horse, motioning to the mage's back. Dimitar shrugged him off, too tired and hot to care about the mischief in Olaf's gesture.

Olaf eyed the rigid mage thoughtfully before pitching a small chestnut at him. The first one fell short and landed on the horse's rump, sending a shiver up the animal's flank as it swished its tail. The second one landed on Willem's shoulder and bounced off.

"Knock it off, idiot." Dimitar swiped a bead of sweat off his temple.

The mage didn't flinch, riding along at a steady pace. At this lack of acknowledgement, Olaf screwed up his face in a scowl and tossed another small nut at Willem, this time off his arm. One after another nicked Willem, who continued to ignore their assault.

"Olaf, would you grow up? Seriously." Normally his friend's willing accomplice, Dimitar's interest drooped, lackluster under the heat of the day.

Olaf debated a moment, popped one last savory nut into his mouth, and shrugged. He then lobbed the rest of the handful at the mage's back.

Without turning around, Willem raised one hand, short waves of energy—*magic*—burning off his fingertips like heat off a slate roof on a scorching hot day. The chestnuts stopped in mid-flight, mere inches from his back. Dimitar didn't dare blink as Olaf gaped at the hovering objects, both astonished. With a twitch of his fingers and a brief murmur under his breath, the nuts shot backward at twice the force, pelting Olaf in the chest, head, and arms.

Olaf bellowed in surprise, cursing, and Dimitar laughed aloud. With a half-glance back at the two men, Willem flashed a small, triumphant smile. Olaf sulked a while afterwards and kept a wary eye on the mage, picking chestnut pieces off his chest and lap.

Upon nightfall, they stopped to rest for the day, all groaning as they dismounted their horses, who were just as grateful to be free of their riders and saddles. Despite the heat of the day, nights brought cooler temperatures. The group circled their bedrolls around a campfire, smoke and the occasional pop of a spark drifting up toward the stars. The sun rose before Dimitar even remembered closing his eyes, his body complaining from the previous day's travel.

Midday, they arrived at the Great Basin, approaching the edge on foot. Ever since they were children, Dimitar and Olaf heard stories about the ethereal power growing within the Great Basin. Centuries ago, the Basin was a land of extreme beauty, with pure spring waters flowing from within to meet the start of the Tempest River. The surrounding lands curved into a bowl shape, lined at the rim with tall, ancient trees and coated with a multitude of wildflowers, overrun with nature's glory. Before the Age of Blood sent the elves into their bordered forest, they used the Basin for ceremonies, coronations, and festivities.

All races ventured to look upon the Great Basin's glory and revel in its tranquility. Unaffected by the seasons, the Basin bloomed in full color throughout each year.

Once the Corrupted touched the land, however, their malevolent purpose tainted the soil, and the Great Basin decayed. Dimitar knew it now held little of its former grandeur but was unprepared for this desolation. The decomposed soil and stale air reeked of rot. Instead of flowing, crisp waters, stagnant pools of muck congealed upon the ground. Empty branches twisted from the trees, and no birds or wildlife remained. In the distance, hidden between tangled weeds and spiked vines, sat a singular white flower. It stretched to the sky, attempting in vain for salvation, the sight more discouraging than reassuring.

"This land was once more dazzling than the dwarven treasures of lore." Willem surveyed the Basin, pacing among the outer trees. "And in one lifetime, the Corrupted turned this perfection into an atrocity."

The others exchanged worried glances.

"Something isn't right here," he said. "We're a quarter century past the Reclamation. So little time, yet enough that these lands should be healing."

Kaleela touched one of the trees, tentative as if not wanting to cause further damage. Ral squatted in the dirt and held out his hands like sensing an unseen force. He then stood and motioned. For the first time since the confrontation over dinner, Willem acknowledged Ral.

"Aye, the land is held back," Willem agreed. "Poison still taints the ethereal forces' essence here. How could we not know about this?"

Dimitar took one more look at the distant flower before heading back to the horses.

A fair distance away, the troop found a sparse grouping of trees that provided some shade and put the Basin out of sight. The company ate a midday meal, silent, each lost in their own thoughts.

The Great Basin's rotting left a profound effect on Dimitar. It symbolized more than the evil of the Corrupted and much more than the simple deterioration of beauty. Not for the first time since Dimitar left Blackburn, he faced the power of the shadow forces ahead. The image of that one, struggling flower reminded him of Kahled trapped in the heart of the Eastern Mountains.

The late-summer sun's rays continued their sweltering assault, a nuisance as Dimitar gathered up their belongings once more. He wiped sweat off his brow as he worked, filling a satchel. Standing, he rolled his shoulders and looked around. Olaf hadn't yet returned from refilling their water flasks in a nearby brook. In the horses' direction, he picked up Kaleela and Willem in a heated discussion.

"I know I put it in this saddlebag. I wouldn't forget such a detail," Kaleela said, distressed.

"It's not here now, my lady. Perhaps it fell from the bag as you traveled. 'Twas a small thing; many other books are for your choosing back at the castle library."

"'Tis a gift from my fathers. I wouldn't lose it so carelessly, and nothing could replace it." Kaleela searched her saddlebag with increasing urgency, emptying its contents onto the ground.

All at once, Dimitar knew what they spoke of and where it was. In his mind's eye, he envisioned Ral taking the Mage Warrior book as he fed the horses that morning. He recalled his conversation with Kaleela in Blackburn's courtyard, of the stories shared between her, Kahled, and Conrad about the great Mage Warrior Ruarc. The words and memories in that volume were priceless to her.

Storming into the clearing with fury in his eyes, he grabbed Ral from behind. Twisting away, Ral backed off from Dimitar, his hands raised.

"Why did you take it, thief?"

Ral turned his palms to the sky, indicating he had no idea what Dimitar referred to.

You know damn well what you did. He swiped at Ral again, who dodged away.

"What's going on here?" Kaleela said, hurrying over to where the two men stood opposite each other, and Ral turned toward her.

Dimitar took advantage of the distraction and swung his fist. His intensity caught Ral off guard, but he managed to duck. Feigning the next punch, Dimitar brought his shoulder into Ral's stomach, tossing the smaller man against a large boulder. Ral thudded against the rock, falling to his knees. His cloak tangled between his legs as he tried to stand.

Drawing his sword, Dimitar kept Ral kneeling with the point of the blade leveled at his chest, both of them panting. "Do you have the book?"

Ral paused, as if contemplating that any answer he gave would incite further violence from Dimitar. His shoulders sagged, and he nodded. Reaching into a fold of his cloak, he removed the book, its worn leather cover etched with the likeness of a warrior from old ages. Mindful of Dimitar's blade still trained on him, Ral eased back onto his feet and handed over the book to Kaleela with an apologetic gesture. She took it from him, cradling it to her chest.

"I don't understand," she said to Ral, who held his empty hands up to his shoulders as Dimitar's blade tip remained on his chest. "Why would you take this from me? Why this, and leave my purse of coins untouched?"

Dimitar startled at this, glancing over in disbelief as she spoke. That the thief took a book—written in elvish, no less, and therefore meaningless to him—and left valuable coins made no sense whatsoever.

'I didn't intend to keep it,' Ral signed.

"You're full of bull's shit," Dimitar said before Ral could continue. He couldn't identify the strange conflict whenever Ral turned a hooded, unseen face toward him. The sensation of butterflies tickled in his stomach, as if his life's greatest desire manifested right before him, yet he couldn't quite see it. Dimitar didn't understand it, nor Ral's theft of the book or excuse, fueling his anger toward the thief. He dropped the point of his sword and stepped forward, lashing out with a backhanded slap.

"Dimitar, don't!" Kaleela shouted.

With a grunt, Ral caught himself with his hands upon a boulder to keep from falling to the ground. Expecting a flash of satisfaction from putting the thief in his place, instead Dimitar's stomach dropped like a weighted brick. He'd made a terrible mistake. The look on Kaleela's face said everything. Her face blurred into his mother's, a mirrored expression from when his father raised hands against them.

Don't act like him. You promised to never *turn out like him.* Angry at both himself and at the secretive man, Dimitar grabbed the back of Ral's cloak to jerk him up once more, unsure what he intended to do next.

The strength of Dimitar's pull snapped the material back. Ral's hood fell.

157

Kaleela gasped, covering her mouth with both hands. Swift as a river's current, Dimitar's anger drained from him. *Who did this to you?*

As he met Ral's eyes for the first time, the same resonance passed between them, this time without the uneasiness that always crept up on him. How could he bother with anger when all he felt was pity? Dimitar's sword dangled from his fingertips, the tip resting on the ground.

From a distance but drawing closer, Olaf and Willem approached. "Whaddaya mean, he's fightin'?"

Willem murmured a reply as the two men joined the rest. Olaf strode up, heavy water bags slung over his broad shoulders, and took in the scene, following Kaleela's stricken gaze.

Ral leaned against the large rock, his cloak the only indication this was the same man. Across the side of Ral's face cut a series of deep gouges, starting under his chin. What remained of the front of his neck held a slash of grisly scars, traveling to his right temple. Jagged scar work branded his warm-olive forehead in the shape of a pair of foreign letters. Early gray strands streaked through Ral's choppy, black hair. His dark brown eyes filled with resignation.

Finally seeing Ral's face only raised more questions. *How is this man still alive?*

Ral pushed himself up the boulder, coming to a stand. Dimitar bowed his head and sheathed his blade as he took a step back, emotions warring inside him.

"I'm sorry." Hollow sentiment, but no further words could capture his sudden shame.

Kaleela approached Ral, compassion in her touch as she clasped his hands in hers. "How did this happen?"

Ral gave a squeeze before releasing his hands from hers and, although they trembled slightly, began to motion.

27

RAL

For centuries, the town of Flamberg benefited from living in the shadows of the Eastern Mountains. The spring run-offs provided a limitless supply of clean, crisp water for both drinking and the irrigation of crops otherwise unable to root in such rugged terrain. Bountiful groupings of mountain berries traversed the lower plateaus, which turned into fresh pies, fruit preserves, and refined wine when fermented. The mountains tempered the valley in the winter months, shielding the town from the worst of the gales.

The Eastern Mountains were kind to Flamberg, which is why the townsfolk had no way to anticipate the enslavement that erased them from history on a midsummer morning.

Ral and his parents lived in the highest house outside of town, the hillside acreage abutting the mountain rock face. His father's stables grew in renown over the years, kingdoms far and wide sending their wildest horses to his hands. It wasn't just the horses returned saddled that created his reputation, but that they were controlled with their nobility unbroken. None knew exactly what Bertald did in the stables, and most considered his work unrivaled.

On the day of Flamberg's destruction, Ral woke from a deep sleep to a none too gentle shake and the rooster hollering in the fresh sunshine.

"Awake, my son."

Even when he'd been a baby, Ral was a deep sleeper, and nine years later he still needed a nudge out of bed each morning.

"Today is a special day," Bertald said a little louder, again prodding Ral. The words sank through the edge of sleep faster than the jostling, and Ral cracked open his eyes.

"Whyisitspeshal," Ral yawned.

"Today you'll join me in the stables."

It took a second for the meaning to find traction in Ral's head, and Bertald laughed out loud when he bolted up, bright-eyed.

"You mean it?" Ral asked, his voice pleading and sweet with youth.

"Yes, I mean it. I was your age when my father taught me, and you're twice as bright as I ever was." Bertald chuckled again as Ral hopped out of bed, throwing his clothes on. "But first..."

Ral's face fell, his joy fleeting at the catch, and he whined. "Awwww, Da—"

"But first," his father insisted, "go to town, and pick up my order of horseshoes. They should be ready, and there's a new mare you'll be able to shoe by the end of the day."

Ral didn't overlook the fact that Da said *he* would shoe the mare, and his excitement returned. "Can I go now?"

Bertald nodded, and Ral sprinted down the stairs, stopped by his mother who insisted he have breakfast. He grabbed a chunk of sharp cheddar off the table, cramming it into his mouth as he shoved on his boots and ran out the front door. His feet beat a pattern against the well-known paths from his homestead to the village center, where the townsfolk set up their tents and wagons for the day.

Ral paced inside Herond's blacksmith shop. He couldn't wait to get back to the stables with his da. But Herond was taking his time just to tease him.

"I know I put yer da's order 'round here some'mere," Herond said in his toothless mumble. The horseshoe bag sat in the far corner of the shop, but Ral knew better than to hurry one of the most respected elders in town. Herond saw it as his civic duty to teach the young'uns a bit of patience.

"Just let me know when you find it." Ral slipped out the front door to get a breath of fresh air. The smithy was stifling from the forge's great fire, and Ral hoped that if Herond thought he was no longer annoying him, he'd stop playing his games. By now the market flowed in full swing, tradesmen and farmers setting up their booths.

From atop a hill just outside of town came a sudden, foreign sound: the thrum of stretched rope coupled with a creak of strained wood. Shielding his eyes against the sun, Ral searched for what created such an unnatural noise. Impossibly, several boulders wandered around the hillside next to a wooden machine still rocking from some kind of effort.

Those aren't boulders, they're monsters! On the heels of this realization, Ral dropped his hand, the sunlight blocked out by a sizable rock mass arcing straight toward him.

"Here's yer da's order, young master Ral." Herond's words cut off in a cacophony of splintering wood and an explosive whoosh of flame. Where the smithy stood moments before, a stone block sent a wave of dirt, wood, and embers into the air.

Ral stood transfixed as Herond opened his mouth with a choking sound. A piece of wood protruded from his chest, blood pouring in rivulets from the corners of his mouth. Nothing could be done as Herond met Ral's gaze before the old man's eyes fell sightless, and the shop burned in earnest.

All at once, the world came back to Ral in a rush, along with horrified screams in the marketplace. His feet moved well before he knew where he was going; it didn't take long to get to the familiar path. Ral ran at breakneck speed as inhuman growls and terrified cries swelled behind him.

As he approached the last street before the pathway to his house, an immense goblin stepped in his way. Ral slid to his knees instinctively, the creature swiping air as he slipped between its legs. The second goblin didn't miss. Ral pounded his fists as hard as he could against the goblin's arms, like trying to stop the wind with an outstretched hand. Only one vulnerability presented itself as he was lifted into the air. His little fist struck the middle of the enormous creature's eye.

As the goblin cupped its eye with a snarl, Ral dropped to the ground and twisted his ankle. The pain swept through his leg, and his limping wasn't fast enough.

"*Asdrov krug zhoval!*" The goblin tongue grated against his ears, but Ral understood the meaning: he was going nowhere.

Frustrated tears sprung to his eyes as all the fight he mustered was useless. Flung over the goblin's shoulder, he watched through tear-filled eyes as they herded the rest of the town. Those foolish enough to resist were either taught submission or beaten to death. Most of the townsfolk were chained together in a long line, shackles hanging heavy on their necks. The goblins gathered the people of Flamberg like cattle toward the Eastern Mountains.

Ral scanned the lines ahead, hoping against hope someone could help him. One line comprised the older folk in town, many his parents' age. His line consisted of children and those on the brink of adulthood. At his age, Ral didn't understand the purpose of separating the two groups, but a nearby voice yanked his attention.

"Momma?" he called in a hoarse voice, his eyes searching. There, twenty yards to his right, stood his parents. Da slumped in his chains, his face a dull gray and his arm twisted at a severe and unnatural angle. Momma shuffled behind him, her hand resting on his father's back in a simple, loving gesture.

"Momma!" Ral yelled as loud as he could. He feared his voice wouldn't reach over the clamor, but she looked up. Their eyes locked, and a sob exploded from her body. Bertald saw him, and a smile crossed his lips, replaced with a torturous grimace almost as quickly. Ral understood their grief right away. They were happy he was alive but anguished over what they would all now face.

"We'll come for you, son." Ral read the words on his da's lips more than he heard them.

A goblin stepped up and slapped his mother for slowing the line, her head jerking back with the force and a spray of blood into the air. Ral twisted as hard as he could to get free from the goblin holding him in place, achieving little beyond annoying the beast. The lines diverged, his parents disappearing from view, and the sobs wracking his body tore him apart.

As they entered the mountains, their first stop was a large chamber of jagged hewn rock. A fire pit roared in the center, small, steel pokers buried deep in the embers. The sickly smell of burnt flesh filled the air enough to cause most of the prisoners to retch whatever remained in their stomachs. One by one, forced to kneel beside the fire, they received a brand on their foreheads, the metal splitting the skin and burning all the way to the bone. Ral, like many others, passed out from the searing pain the second the brand touched his skin.

When he woke, he was chained alongside children his own age next to an enormous wall of sheer rock face. Next to his feet lay a crude pick.

No one questioned what they were to do, and few bothered to consider alternatives.

Ral thought about ways to free himself. After all, they used a tool that severed metal, given enough time. But the patrols came too often, and the sound and sparks of metal hitting metal were too noticeable when compared to the steady *tink* of the picks hitting rock. Those who tried were punished, often killed outright. Death served as a constant companion inside the Eastern Mountains.

The brandings to mark the humans as property of that particular goblin tribe took the lives of several prisoners around Ral, their wounds festering. They spent their last few hours of life in an infected, feverish nightmare. Ral often wished his fate would join theirs, but one thought alone sustained his will to exist: Da's last words. Ral had to believe his da would find him and take him away from his bleeding hands, torn muscles, and horrific nightmares.

Ral didn't remember the time that followed—how much, he couldn't guess—although neither could he forget. Days had no meaning without sunlight to juxtapose the endless darkness. He only knew the long, tedious work of setting pick to stone, broken by a pause to drink stale water and eat hard bread. At times, the goblins tossed their prisoners meat from a source Ral avoided thinking on. The possibilities of its origin were too terrifying to consider, especially as more and more people collapsed. Whether from exhaustion or giving up the will to live, the people of Flamberg died off at an alarming rate.

When enough time passed that Ral's hands callused over to resemble an elder farmer's, his pick shattered against a hard bit of ore. A goblin beat him senseless for the waste of the tool, but a small shard lay on the ground after Ral was given a new one. The thin metal piece wasn't much of anything but had a peculiar shape in the middle—almost a bend. Without thinking, Ral pocketed the shard and continued with his work.

When the next break came, he took out the shard and considered it. Not quite sure what he hoped to achieve, Ral slipped the shard into the shackle on his ankle, twisting and probing with shaky fingers. Just as he was about to give up and recognize his folly, the metal gave with a small click. Scared he'd be discovered, Ral closed the shackle and pocketed the shard. A fire lit in his heart, long since extinguished: hope.

He worked with the shard every chance he got, his skills improving to the point where one or two twists would release the catch. Even then, it took him many more days before he mustered the courage to unlock both his right and left shackles to stand unfettered. Ral took his first unsteady steps around the long tunnels, no more than a few strides away from his place on the wall.

The time between freeing himself and roaming the tunnels in secrecy might have been unbearably long to anyone outside the mountains, but his acts of stealth came with a terrible risk. Goblins' vision penetrated the darkness, and the tunnels gave few places to hide. Ral discovered every niche in his immediate area and expanded his walks. If he searched long enough, he'd find his parents. He had to believe they were still alive.

Ral couldn't guess at the time he spent exploring the tunnels. He found no trace of his parents or anyone else in the other line from Flamberg, only countless other folk from different villages. Some glanced at him with curiosity, but most ignored his passage as they mindlessly dug the stone.

The painful truth of his parents' deaths could no longer be denied. If Ral kept the false hope of finding them, he, too, would lose his life in the tunnels. With the last sliver of his childhood cut from his heart, he made plans to escape.

Every day around the same time, several goblins headed down a certain path where Ral caught the whiff of fresh air coming into the tunnels. After years of breathing the mountain's fumes, the outside air was hard to miss. Ral had never followed them before because of the risk, and he didn't want to be caught before he found his parents. Now, he had nothing to lose.

He picked his lock and waited as two goblins headed side by side toward the pathway. Ral hid in a concealed niche and counted to twenty before following. Several times he curled himself into a recess to avoid detection as goblins lumbered up and down the hall. He glimpsed a dim light in the distance, not from a torch: the way out.

With agonizing patience, he made progress, and the illumination defined a doorway. Even at this distance, his eyes burned from the natural light, a pain he gratefully accepted. The last few hundred yards were the hardest of all, both due to goblin activity and Ral's anxious anticipation to be free.

When at last he stepped outside onto a sheer mountain path, wind whipped through his threadbare clothing and almost made him stumble off the cliffside. Ral had forgotten the crispness of autumn. A bitter chill stole his breath, working into his lungs with icy tendrils and shaking loose the years of inhaled dust. Coughs wracked his body and made him fall to his knees, even as his eyes searched the sky in a blissful reverie.

Try as he could to stifle the noise, his coughing didn't go unnoticed. One of the two goblins starting down the path turned back. Ral knelt without strength on the ground, gasping for air. His body left the ground as he was lifted, and he knew death would follow. Somehow, he didn't care. He'd tasted fresh air again and had nothing else to live for.

"You can no show others way out," the goblin grumbled in broken common tongue, holding Ral aloft with one fist clenching his tattered shirt, pulling back its other arm.

Through the haze of his overloaded senses, Ral instinctively reacted as best he could, twisting and bracing. He still took the brunt of the hit, claws dragging across his face and neck. He thought he cried out in pain, but perhaps it was the wind shrieking along the ridge. The goblin dropped Ral to the ground and kicked him over the side with a pinwheeling of arms. The first rock plateau stunned him so completely, he tumbled like a rag doll down the rest of the cliff.

Ral landed at the bottom in an explosive burst of pain. His face and neck burned like a stoked furnace, and he couldn't tell which bones weren't broken. Looking over, he followed his path down the mountainside, a trail of blood sprayed at various points. Warm stickiness spreading across his chest suggested some blood remained in him, leaving in a hot rush.

A hawk—*No, it's too big for a hawk*—circled lower in the sky, probably waiting for its meal to finish up dying.

Gods, let me go, let me go to join my parents. He prayed as the world swirled sickeningly before his gaze. With all the energy he could summon, he turned his gaze to the pale sky one last time. Instead, his view was blocked by the largest person he'd ever seen, looming over him. As the giant reached down, Ral fell unconscious.

After untold time in dark unawareness, Ral awoke to find himself in a bed, a large quilt pulled up to his chin and a down-filled pillow under his head. Soft candlelight flickered on a table, illuminating a one-room cabin. The wind moaned low outside the cabin walls, promising a night of dropping temperatures. His disorientation was complete, and in a frenzy, he tried to throw off the covers and come to a stand. A sharp pain ripped through his body as Ral twisted about, collapsing against the pillow with harsh panting.

"You're still healing," a deep voice said across the room.

'Where am I?' Ral tried asking, but nothing came forth. He couldn't move his jaw at all, such was the pain. When even his whimper remained silent, caught in his throat, Ral panicked once more.

"You won't speak again," the person said, coming into the light. "The goblin saw to that."

To call this person immense was like calling a mountain a bump in the road. They matched the height of goblins, with cool, dark skin polished like a river stone. Their features held a mix of masculine and feminine angles, radiating a deep power that surpassed their physical size. Hair as pitch black as a new-moon sky was skillfully box braided and laced with gold clips. A loose, beige linen shirt layered under a long vest, tucked into brown pants: simple clothing for an extraordinary being.

"In fact," they continued, their voice a distant rumble of thunder, "you're very lucky to be alive. Even my talents wouldn't have saved you if Sevak found you a quarter hour later in her search for an evening meal."

In response, a sharp, brief cry came from the far corner. A hawk-like bird sat on a high perch, preening its jet-black feathers.

Images, terrors, and bewilderment flooded Ral's mind, and he tried again to speak. Nothing issued forth. Frustrated tears leapt from his eyes. He had no means to release his thoughts or his pain.

"You need rest."

Sleep came over him in a relentless wave, his body betraying him as he collapsed upon the pillow once more.

There's power in this voice. His last thought echoed in his mind as he drifted off.

He roused sometime later; as in the misery of the Eastern Mountains, hours or days might have passed, Ral couldn't tell. The waxing moon set to rising on the other side of the window pane and a roaring fire illuminated the small cabin. He was alone. A large cauldron sat in the hearth, liquid bubbling and giving off a delicious aroma. His stomach growled as he eased back the blankets.

This time he came to his feet with more care. Even then, pain shot across his back. With a will born from the enslavement of his childhood, Ral forced himself to walk. Drops of sweat beaded on his brow, and a wave of nausea swept over him, but he managed to shuffle over to the table in the middle of the room. He sat down hard and laid his head against the cracked wood, trying to not pass out from exertion.

"Well done," a deep voice said. Ral raised his head wearily, yet with a spark of curiosity. The person wasn't there moments before; how had they entered the room unseen? For the first time, Ral noticed the person's compelling eyes, one green, the other blue.

"I never introduced myself," they said in a manner unconcerned about the etiquette blunder. "My name is Karn. Someday, I will teach you to tell me yours."

Ral accepted this dully, too exhausted to care anymore. Karn crossed to the fireplace, giving the stew a steady stir. When it came time to eat, Karn spoon-fed Ral, who had no strength left from the effort of crossing the room.

The next few months proved almost as hard as the years prior for Ral, although much more satisfying. Karn pushed him each day to rediscover the atrophied muscles in his broken body, now crossed into awkward adolescence, starting with walks in the countryside that grew into runs along a twisting riverbank. Karn taught Ral about the lands: what plants were edible, which could heal, and those that could kill. Depending on the lesson, Karn's eyes would shift colors, as if a different person led the conversation.

Over and over again, Ral opened his mouth to ask a question, and each time surprised himself anew at the forced silence. As innately as Karn understood Ral, even anticipated his questions, on occasion Ral could only grab Karn's elbow and shake it.

When the time was right, Karn looked down at Ral's latest attempt to get their attention. "We have to work on your communication."

Karn taught him a system of language using his hands. Re-learning every word frustrated Ral at first, but Karn was a patient teacher. Once he mastered the basic letters and phrases, gesturing more complex thoughts wasn't as difficult. Over time, Ral forgot the sound of his own voice, another piece of himself lost forever within the Eastern Mountains.

One day, Karn came back from their regular outing to find Ral attempting to give himself a haircut with a pair of shears. His black hair stuck out in short pieces, chopped away from his face. Ral quit running his hand through his shortened hair when he caught sight of Karn, who carried a bundle of red cloth tied with several lengths of twine under their arm.

"This is for you."

The bundle unfolded into a deep-red robe of extreme quality, the fabric smoother than anything Ral had felt before, with a sturdiness that guaranteed many ages of use. Leather straps crisscrossed over the shoulders and around the waist, tightening the fabric to his form and providing a place to latch on a pouch or a blade or several. Sewn to the inside tucked leather pockets, and a fitted hood slung down the back. Ral fingered the hood before touching the scarred strips that riddled his face and the concave spot on his throat.

With a resentful flush, he understood why Karn had brought him a robe with a hood. 'Why do I need to hide my face from others?'

Karn answered by speaking aloud while also signing his words. "Let's just say I know what it's like to stand out in a crowd. You'll thank me for the ability to hide someday."

Ral explored further and further from Karn's house, his sense of purpose growing beyond the walls now that he was an older teen. On one such day, he happened upon a worn road. Curiosity got the better of him, and he followed the path. As the sun reached noon's apex, he came upon a village where wonderment stole over him, drawn to the main gate.

"Har there, boy!" Ral turned to the gateman, who winced and curled his lip. "What 'n dark blazes happened to you?"

He motioned him forward to keep the line moving as much as to wave Ral out of sight.

Ral pulled up his hood, wandering and trying to remember what life among people was like. A few townsfolk looked him over, and some peered into the cloak's hood, but none shared the guardsman's reaction. His cloak acted as more than a simple bundle of cloth. Able to observe more freely now, Ral scanned the market. The booths and storefronts weren't all that different from Flamberg's markets, at least, what he remembered of them.

Anger built in his stomach, growing into a powerful rage. Storming through the crowd, Ral searched out the nearest guard post with one driving thought: the goblins must be held accountable for the atrocities they committed on his people—and his parents' death.

Several guardsmen sat at a long wooden table playing some game with flagons and cards. Ral grabbed the closest one's arm and signed. Years of pent-up frustration made his hands a blur as anger fueled his silent words.

"Whoa there." The guard looked at Ral in confusion. He peered into the cloak's hood, met only with shadows and the glimmer of eyes. "What's gotten into ya?"

'Damn it,' he gestured, signing faster, 'listen to me!'

"I dunno what yer aimin' at, but I'm not understandin'." The guard clasped Ral's hands, trying to soothe the furious motioning.

Ral pushed the guard's hands away and signed again, this time slower.

"What's with the hands?" one of the guards asked.

The third guard shrugged and took a swig of his ale. "Enough, boy. If ya got something important to tell us, then do it. Otherwise, leave us be."

The guard shook his head and turned back to the others and their game. Ral grabbed the guard's arm in a final desperate act, but the guard mistook the action as aggression. He shoved Ral's chest, sending him tumbling backward. Ral pushed himself up once more and, facing the guards square on, lowered his hood to get his point across.

"What the hells! Gods of mercy." The guard's face was a mask of shock. Several other people in the market looked over at the guard's outcry, and Ral became the center of attention. No one moved to help him, yet every villager eyed him with fear, revulsion, or both. Tears sprang from his eyes, and he turned to run.

"Stop, lad! What did this to ya?" the guard called, but his words fell on deaf ears.

Ral tore out of town as fast as his legs carried him and didn't stop until he couldn't catch his breath, a stitch worked deep into his side. Collapsing against a tree, he sobbed with silent grief. Years of hidden pain and torture came back, ripped from him and wracking his body. He sank to the ground and buried his face in his arms.

The cry of Karn's bird sounded a short distance ahead. Karn pushed through a row of trees a minute later and came to stand before him. Ral teetered to his feet before collapsing into their arms, and Karn helped him the rest of the way with a steadying arm. Back in the cabin with Ral bundled in a thick blanket, Karn asked him what had happened. He told them everything.

"I'm sorry I never mentioned how few would understand your signing," Karn said after Ral finished. "'Tis a special language, one humans don't usually take the time to learn. That doesn't mean there are none you can speak with. Just a few. They're the ones who matter."

That night, Ral spent hours in front of the hearth until the flame became a glowing ember, thinking about the day but mostly remembering his past. He came to a decision in the early morning hours.

'I'm going to find the ones who matter. I need to figure out my way in this world.'

Karn considered Ral before coming to a stand. Together they went around the cabin and assembled a few weeks' worth of supplies. At the door, Ral hefted the pack and turned to Karn.

"You'll learn in time why I found you and why saving you was my fate, just as moving on today is yours. If there's need in the days or years to come"—Karn tapped the side of Ral's head with one finger—"center your thoughts on me. I'll find you. We're connected now."

Karn turned back to his cottage without another word, and Ral set off.

The first town Ral approached netted similar results to the one he'd fled from. No one understood his gestures, and many assumed he'd gotten a horse kick to the head. The few times he lowered his hood drew winces and shrieks, so the thought of using that for sympathy passed.

When town after town ended the same, Ral started to lose heart. More importantly, his supplies ran out. He tried taking small jobs in stables in exchange for a room and meal, but none would hire a man who hid in the shadows of a magicked cloak, and he refused to become a mockery by lowering his hood.

Outside one stable sat an apple crate for the horses. The owner taunted his simple gestures asking for food, so Ral felt justified and hungry enough to sneak back and grab several. Taking food became a regular practice, and before long he escalated to small coin purses from nobles who walked the streets. The stealth skills he'd learned in the goblin mines translated well to city streets.

Ral couldn't know that although he escaped the guards' notice, others had been watching him for some time. So, he was surprised when he awoke one day not at his own bidding but by a blade pressed against his throat.

"Think it through," the man said with a dangerously casual air, before Ral could jerk away.

His skin was a polished brown, his features sharp, and his attire meticulous. A spark in his eyes tied to either inquisitiveness or bloodlust. Ral hoped for the former. The man pulled back Ral's hood, and Ral cringed, waiting for the intake of breath or exclamation that always followed. Instead, the man flipped the hood up and removed the blade from his neck.

"If you're a thief against the Guild, then I'm a knight," he muttered to himself, offering a hand.

Ral pulled himself to a stand, further perplexed but not without noting the first act of sympathy he could remember since his days with Karn.

"Do you know whose territory you've been encroaching on?"

Ral shook his head.

"You're on Guild lands. Not a Guild member, not yours for thieving." When Ral remained silent, the man pinched the bridge of his nose. "What's your name?"

Ral pointed to his throat and shrugged.

"Mute then." Against all hope or expectation, he gestured, 'Do you sign?'

28

DIMITAR

Duncan brought me into the Thieves' Guild. I had a place to belong. Took me under his wing, taught me some skills.'

"Ya mean like pickpocketing?" Olaf asked.

Ral tipped his head, then looked between Dimitar and Kaleela, guilt resurfacing on his features. 'It's easy for me to take without asking. A bad habit. The Mage Warrior book seems important to you, and I was curious. Turns out, Karn never taught me any elvish, but the pictures were interesting. I never intended to keep it.'

And like that, Dimitar believed him. The clarity with which he now viewed Ral was like a summer's river, crystal clear down to each pebble at the bottom of the waters. All his suspicion, all his doubt washed away, exposing his inability to see past his prejudice. *And that's for me to own.*

Ral started to sign something else, paused, and let his hands fall to his sides. Nothing else needed to be said.

Kaleela stood and without hesitation wrapped her arms around Ral, resting her head on the side of his arm as she held him. The weight of his story lay heavy upon them all, binding. Ral patted her outstretched arm across his chest. He then turned to face her and tilted up her chin with a gentle finger.

'No more tears,' he signed, brushing her cheek. He replaced the hood of his cloak, shadows once more obscuring his scarred face.

Dimitar inhaled, releasing his breath slowly and with it, the distrust and judgment he'd held toward Ral. He'd justified his uneasiness by blaming Ral as a common criminal and nothing more.

He met Ral's hooded gaze and looked at him anew. Dimitar still felt something, indefinable yet present between them, but the pull was no longer shrouded in resentment. He stepped forward and turned over his sword, pushing the tip into the ground, and knelt beside the blade.

"When we left Blackburn, I judged you as nothing more than a thief," he said. "Yet, you could've told us, 'Bad luck,' and moved on when we found the bridges down. You could've left us to die in the goblin attack or facing the Corrupted in Leighton. And you didn't have to stand with us in Quinthal's throne room. You've shown yourself to me many times over, and still, I couldn't look beyond your way of life." Dimitar paused before adding, "I've been taught better and ask your forgiveness."

Ral gestured for Dimitar to stand. 'I grant it to you and ask for your forgiveness in return.'

"Why would you ask that of me?"

Ral reached into the folds of his cloak and held out a stone wrapped in thin cloth. Dimitar glanced at his own whetstone. His head whipped up, and the astonishment on his face was enough to set off Olaf into a storm of laughter. An edge shaped his friend's laugh, releasing some of the shared grief from Ral's tale, and after that came pure delight.

Olaf leaned over and thumped Ral on the back. "Oh, aye, yer fittin' right in with the rest o' us. For fuck's sake, of all the cheek..."

"I s'pose you were going to 'return' this, like the book?" Dimitar feigned offense, this time without the flash of anger usually stirring within his chest.

Ral snickered within the hood. 'No.' He shrugged with a nonchalant air, sending Olaf howling once more.

"It's time we ride," Willem said, heading over to the horses.

Kaleela shared a parting look with Ral, clutching the book to her chest.

Dimitar stepped up to her. "Kaleela, I'm sorry for what I did. It was wrong of me, and... I'm not like that. I'll do better."

Kaleela held his gaze, her face sweet and forgiving. "You're driven to fight; I see that in you. But it's not fighting so much as protecting. You apologized to the one who needed it."

"I need you to hear it too. That's not who I am."

She searched his face, then a slow smile tilted her lips. "I hear you. And I see your truth."

Her words unwound something in his chest, and for a second, he couldn't respond, a lump in his throat. *I'll do my best for her, always.* He followed her to their horses, helping her astride and lingering until she took up the reins, situating herself. The rest followed their lead and rode as if to chase down the day's lengthening shadows.

Large, menacing clouds gathered as they set out the next day. Dimitar was both relieved to be out of the blazing sun and worried bad weather could slow their progress. Luck favored the group, and the rain held until mid-afternoon when the skies opened with a fury, lashing at the ground with pelting rain. When lightning flashed and the horses balked, they sought shelter under a large rock outcropping.

The group took advantage of the break. Olaf spread his bedroll, soon in a doze. Ral curled into a hollow in the stone wall, tucking himself in as he drew his hood far over his face. But Kaleela paced under the rock ceiling, pushing aside wet strands of hair and glancing at the darkened, waterlogged sky.

"I promise to wake you as soon as we can travel again," Dimitar said. "You need your strength, Kaleela. Take this time to rest."

He laid out a blanket for her and she curled up on top, knees pulled to her stomach and a loosely clenched hand tucked under her cheek. Her earlier words came back to him. *I see your truth.*

Dimitar tried to unwind against the stone wall, perhaps take a quick nap like the others, but his eyelids wouldn't stay closed. His gaze returned to Kaleela and his thoughts to Blackburn's royal stable when they crouched over ill-packed riding supplies. Then, too, she'd been little at peace, her mind no doubt running at high speed since news of Conrad's death. Dimitar wished he could bring back the joy and happiness that lit her face before he delivered Conrad's message to the kingdom and grief to her.

I'll see that you have it again.

Kaleela stirred, murmuring in her sleep before falling quiet once more. A blush tinted her cheeks and lips as she napped, her breath coming in regular flow. Her leather armor shaped against her body, and Dimitar's gaze traced the curve of her side, dipping down to her waist and back up at her hip. He imagined how her body would feel if he nestled his hand there, soft and pliable to his touch. The touch expanded in his mind to his entire body pressed against hers, cocooning behind her, hugging her warmth and softness to him. In spite of the rain's coolness, the small shelter shot up in temperature.

Sighing, Dimitar sought distraction from his wandering fantasies. He moved over to the outcropping's edge, rain pouring in sheets. Willem kept watch a few yards out, an invisible shield over his head blocking the rain as he gazed at something in the distance. Dimitar squinted through the downpour.

A forest this far north? He pictured a map in his head; did they still travel along the outskirts of the great Sun'Din Forest as it curved over the Basin? All at once, the answer came to him: not straight north of the Basin, but north and east.

Willem stared into the Dark Woods.

The people of the Green Lands knew well of the Dark Woods, the peril and mystery of its forbidden trees. After the Age of Blood, the foul creatures and beasts ravaging the lands had been confined within the Dark Woods's borders. The taint of the shadow forces now permeated the Woods, woven on the wind and in the pores of those who ventured too close. Even passing by the edge, darkness seeped into a traveler's unconscious; uneasiness at best or worse, indefinable, sweaty nightmares long after their journey ended. Parents throughout both the northern and southern lands scolded their children into behaving upon threat of some darkling from the Dark Woods, come to snatch the disobedient.

Willem fixed his gaze upon the forested border, and Dimitar took in his intensity. Other than the deranged or the damned, only magic-users entered the Dark Woods willingly. Those who survived the shadowy depths earned the title of Mage. Still, the Woods claimed lives each year as magic-users ventured in, thinking they'd outlast the trials within, never to return. Those who did survive were forbidden to speak, or perhaps were incapable of speaking, about their experience among the damned trees.

Dimitar pulled out of his thoughts as the rain started to let up. Willem turned to the outcropping and acknowledged him with a nod as he headed back to gather his pack. The thought struck Dimitar that a mage was not unlike a knight. They both trained and survived countless challenges to bear the title.

No, not the title. For the honor.

175

The troop roused, saddling their horses and starting a gallop to the east. The rain turned fields muddy and slippery, but the horses didn't let conditions slow them, as if they knew the journey's end approached.

Over the next four days, the terrain changed. The troop entered the Barren Lands, a region aptly named for its striking lack of life. Strewn across the ground lay patches of gravelly sand and misshapen, parched trees, stark in contrast to the lush Green Lands. The Barren Lands sat too far from the Tempest River to receive its nurture and too close to the Dark Woods to avoid any lingering taint upon the land. The rocky terrain increased, treacherous to travel at high speeds, and progress slowed.

The Eastern Mountains rose before them, tangible its nearness. The mountain rock was black as coal, crags reaching to the sky like sharp, jagged teeth. The irregular terrain became impassable for the horses, and Ral pulled the group to a stop.

'The path to the mountain opening is right up this bend. The horses have to stay here. They make too much noise, and we'll lose whatever surprise we have going for us.'

Leading their steeds to a patch of dry grass under a leafless tree, they took water flasks from the saddlebags to bring with them. With a low murmur, Willem carved symbols with his hands in the air around the horses, which shimmered as if surrounded by a heat wave.

"That ensures they won't run from us," Willem said. "'Twas a constraint spell. They won't move far from here until I release them."

Dimitar expected Deepshade to appear different or have an altered look in his eyes, but he seemed unchanged. If not for the brief bending in the air, he wouldn't believe anything affected the horses.

Gale-force winds and harsh weather over centuries had beat down the broad pathway. Puffs of dust rose with each step, the rock searing and dry. Dimitar tied back his hair and sipped water from his flask before resting a hand on the pommel of his sword. He couldn't shake the feeling something was wrong. They'd traveled for too long in supposed Corruptor territory yet without a trace of the vile creatures. His hand gripped the hilt tighter, instincts ablaze.

On a boulder up ahead, a black bird screeched as it took flight, and the entire troop jumped.

I'm not the only one nervous. Dimitar let his blade slide back into its scabbard.

Ral paused to allow them all to settle their nerves, then started up the pathway. At the boulder where the bird had flown off, an echoing hiss greeted them.

Without further warning, Corruptors tore around the bend. Blacker than pitch and startlingly agile on all fours, they scurried with bloodlust-driven speed. Teeth dripped with saliva, and protruding spikes across their backs glinted in the fading sun. Olaf swore in surprise as he pulled Lucky from its holder, and Dimitar drew his sword from his sheath with a directed shout.

"Watch out, Kaleela!"

Pulling knives from his belt, Ral killed the front two Corruptors with quick throws, black blood arcing to the sky with the impact. Another Corruptor barked a wordless command to the others, and two more broke off to surround Ral. With oily slickness, they circled him and closed the distance enough that Ral spun his knives into a defensive hold. One reared back and hissed as it raised its hands. With a sickening crack, its claws extended further out from its fingertips.

Dimitar recalled with cold clarity the length and depth of the scratches across the High Knight armor in Blackburn. He and Olaf raised their weapons together, stepping back in defense as the remaining five loped toward them, claws rending rock shards. Olaf swung his axe in an arc that would have decapitated the Corruptor in front, but it ducked under the strike as it slithered around the men. Dimitar and Olaf spun in place, caught off guard by the Corruptors ignoring them.

The Corruptors headed straight for Kaleela.

She notched an arrow on her bowstring, chose her target, and released. The lead Corruptor fell with an arrow buried to the feathers in its neck. Kaleela pulled another arrow and released in the same breath. The next Corruptor fell, dead before it hit the ground. The three remaining grew too close, and she back-pedaled as they leapt at her. The air around her shifted and curved, and the Corruptors slammed back as if running into a stone wall. Off to the side, Willem wove his fingers and mouthed a protective invocation. Kaleela took that moment to pull a short blade from her boot.

Dimitar and Olaf caught up with the Corruptors, attacking them from the rear. The creatures' aggression overwhelmed Dimitar, not knowing where the next attack would fall. His training proved true as he blocked each blow aside, but he couldn't find a hole in their flurry of attacks to counter as they forced him back a step. Dimitar's muscles fatigued as he tried to second-guess the next strike. He then remembered something Kahled once told him during an impromptu lesson.

Dimitar and the other new guardsmen had spent the morning practicing the art of defense when Kahled stopped by the training grounds. He decided to fill their noontime break with a story, no better tale to Dimitar's ears than the Reclamation War with its hours, days, and weeks of non-stop fighting. Dimitar couldn't understand how a fight lasted so long when his own arms grew tired after a few minutes.

"A knight's sword doesn't weigh in his hands," Kahled had said. "It's an extension of his arm, and you must always remind yourself of that. The trick is to convince your enemies that they have no power over you. By reacting to their attacks with the slightest blocks, they begin to believe nothing they do will get through. They'll misspend their strength in frustration and needless strikes. Then you attack."

Dimitar waited for the Corruptor's next attack. This time, instead of a grand sweeping parry, he stepped to one side and flicked his wrist, knocking the Corruptor's claws to the side. Dimitar's switch in defensive style puzzled the Corruptor as it splayed its claws in a counter-attack. Again, Dimitar blocked its strike with ease. The Corruptor followed with an endless string of attacks, none thrown with any semblance of aim or consideration. Dimitar dodged to the side without even needing his blade's protection. Kahled's words proved true, and the Corruptor stepped back in obvious frustration, bearing a defensive stance. When Dimitar swung his blade, the Corruptor didn't react in time as Dimitar dipped low and sliced its middle.

Turning to help the others, he instead found Corruptor bodies at their feet. One burned and smoked, the oily stench nauseating, courtesy of a magicked fire attack from Willem. Olaf regarded Dimitar, then nodded with a grin of pride. Ral rejoined them, his dagger still dripping with Corruptor blood. Kaleela inspected the corpses strewn on the ground. She nudged a worn rope coil with the toe of her boot, clutched in the claw of the Corruptor closest to her.

"They were here for me," she said.

Something skittered on a boulder next to them. A Corruptor jumped off the top of the rock and loped away up the path. Dimitar started after, but Ral stopped him with an outstretched hand.

'Where there's one of them, there's sure to be more.'

29

DIMITAR

Dimitar's sword hung with a different weight in his hand, heavier than usual, almost awkward. He'd trained for years but never imagined he'd fight and kill the Corrupted. One hundred High Knights challenged their presence in the Reclamation War, and all but three died for their efforts. Yet here he was, still training to be a common knight, and he'd lived through the fight.

How is it fair that so many died, yet I survived? No matter. We have to get him out. Hang in there, sire.

Ral guided them up the rugged pathway shrouded in the dying light of dusk, halting the group from time to time to listen for Corruptor patrols. With each passing step, he grew more and more tentative. The Corruptor that ran off would've made it to the lair by now, and the group should encounter some kind of resistance. But the early night stayed silent, and the path remained clear.

Dimitar couldn't spot any sign of threat ahead in the path, yet tension knotted his stomach. He closed his eyes and strained his ears as taught.

Something was coming.

Ral spun toward the group. He pulled a dagger from his belt and signaled to the others to spread out. Willem swept his arms in summoning. Fire after fire sprung from the ground and surrounding boulders, forming a controlled ring of light to illuminate a large area around the group. Dimitar's breath came tight, his sword gripped with both hands, sensing the incoming attack with every fiber of his being.

The first Corruptor launched into the center of their circle without warning. It crouched low, growling and gnashing its teeth, its oily skin reflecting the firelight as if engulfed in flames. Solid-black ink eyes boiled and churned in their sockets. Sharp, deadly horns protruded across its body and limbs. When it spoke, its voice hissed like hot metal plunged into a forge's water barrel.

"Kaaa-leeee-laaaa." It directed its lidless eyes at the princess and licked its lips with a long, black tongue. "Give girl. Rest live."

The troop froze, bewildered at its proposition. Although the Corruptor's words didn't give a reason, it confirmed they were indeed searching for Kaleela. They didn't care about those with her, which explained why the Corruptors ignored Olaf and Dimitar during the earlier attack.

"Give girl!" the Corruptor screeched, high and shrill. It didn't seem possible, but its hide turned a deeper shade of black.

Kaleela raised her bow. "I'm not to be given."

Before the Corruptor could move, it fell with an arrow in the center of its chest, shrieking as it hit the ground. The cry was answered with another, and then a multitude of unhinged screams up the path. Kaleela pulled back a new arrow, patiently waiting for a target.

From the darkness surrounding the ring of fire sprang an onslaught of Corruptors, their claws cracking as they shot out from their knuckles. A mass of writhing blackness encircled the small group. The Corruptors advanced in concert, separating the group from each other, and Dimitar swore as Kaleela was forced to back up out of his reach.

Much as before, Kaleela was split from all except Willem. She let loose her notched arrow, nailing a Corruptor. With amazing speed, she pulled two arrows from her quiver. Drawing them both back, she released, burying the shafts into the hides of two more. She strung another arrow but hesitated at the Corruptors' change in behavior.

The Corruptors advanced toward her, hissing and growling in checked hatred. Kaleela retreated in kind, yet they didn't instigate any attack. Several burst into flames, unable to escape Willem's targeted attacks, but the others paid no mind as they crept with determined focus on their prey. Not until the net surrounded her from behind did their intention become clear. The net engulfed her, tightening, clawed hands pinning her striking arms. The Corruptors threw her to the ground, Rialyn's bow skittering aside.

No, no, no. Dimitar swung his sword with mad fury, desperate to reach her, but Corruptors now surrounded him and Olaf.

As Kaleela fought and kicked the webbed netting, undulating light surrounded her. A Corruptor flew backwards into a large rock with a sickening crack while the others hissed, trying to find the source of magic. A blast of protective light surrounded Kaleela again, tossing another aside.

Buy me some time, Mage, I'm coming.

"Dim, get m'back," Olaf growled, and Dimitar squared up behind him, encircled by Corruptors. "Time to dance."

Years of sparring together lent fluidity and precision to their tandem movements. Yet for every Corruptor that fell beneath their blades, another took its place. This was the Corrupted way of fighting Dimitar had learned about in training. The creatures weren't skilled fighters, yet their sheer numbers could overpower the opposition. Dimitar couldn't imagine fighting an entire Corrupted army, losing ground as he was.

Ral whirled by him in a flash of cloth and blades. He took out a number of the creatures with his knives but soon ran out. Resorting to his long dagger, he pushed back the Corruptors with quick thrusts and a whirlwind of spinning cloak. With graceful agility, he bent over his victims and regained his throwing knives while still keeping his guard with the dagger. As more Corruptors joined the attack against him, they backed him into a corner between two large rocks. Ral turned away from them, running toward the boulders. They gave chase only to watch as he jumped, landing high on the stone's face. Pushing off from the rock, Ral twisted in the air, launching knife after knife into the Corruptors' upturned faces as he spun over them. Landing in a roll, he came up and sliced through the next Corruptor's throat.

A Corruptor broke off, slipping into the shadows toward the mage who cast his spells from atop a boulder. Still, Dimitar couldn't reach them, the damn creatures hissing and swiping at him with deadly intent.

Despite recalling Kahled's advice, Dimitar's arms grew tired pushing back the almost endless number of Corruptors. His hands became slick with blood, theirs and his. Razor sharp claws tore his bracers and cloth beneath, and Dimitar resorted to a defensive stance. Olaf continued to win with brute strength, cleaving Corruptor head and limb clean from their bodies. But as with Dimitar, a new Corruptor replaced each one he felled.

Just when they were outnumbered, Ral attacked the Corruptors from behind. Now faced with a battle on both sides, the Corruptors started to make mistakes. Dimitar and Olaf found holes in the creatures' defense, gaining ground to maneuver. A number of them found their feet suddenly encased in magicked stone, unable to move when Dimitar's sword sliced the air. What had seemed an infinite number of Corruptors became a small mass of dead bodies.

"Ral, to me," Dimitar said when the two men carved out enough space to rejoin. Kaleela's small cry of despair across the clearing banished any weariness from his limbs. Ral took a knife in each hand as he joined Dimitar. "They're trying to take her!"

Olaf turned to follow but paused. "Go," he shouted to the men and headed off toward Willem, tracking something with his gaze. "Somethin' ain't right up there."

Olaf circled behind the large boulders, and Dimitar lost sight of him. Moments later came the sharp crack of metal on stone, but Dimitar couldn't stop, the remaining Corruptors dragging Kaleela toward the mountain. Ral ducked in low, coming up with his knife on the first Corruptor, slicing it from belly to throat. Dimitar brought his blade across the face of the next and stabbed another. In little time, he and Ral killed the final Corruptors surrounding Kaleela.

Cutting the net around her, Ral pulled Kaleela to a stand, her gasps loud in the now quiet night air as she clung to his arms, finding her footing once more. Ral stepped away to survey the area, making sure no more Corruptors remained to fall upon them. Dimitar planted his sword into the ground and embraced Kaleela, noticing her shaky legs. She drew a sharp intake of breath as Dimitar supported her, wincing in pain. Dimitar frowned as he assessed her bloodied and bruised wrists from the Corruptor claws that pinned her.

"Did they hurt you?" he asked.

Kaleela shook her head as Dimitar looked her over, evaluating the extent of her injuries. His fingers grazed the tears in her leather jerkin, acute reminders of the attack. Coldness stole over him once more.

"Let me check." With care, he traced each ragged opening with his fingertips. When he was satisfied her skin was unscathed, he turned to her, cupping her hands more gently. Kaleela returned his gaze with a new strength behind her eyes. Her trembling lessened, and she squeezed his hands, interlacing their fingers. Dimitar smiled at her, reassuring. *We're okay, everything's going to be—*

"Dimitar! Come quick!" Willem's voice didn't carry its normal authority. Across the clearing, he knelt before Olaf's unmoving form, blood pooling beneath them.

"Oh gods... What... Is he...?" Dimitar couldn't bring himself to say it as he ran to them and dropped to his knees, heart pounding in cold fear.

Willem lifted Olaf's left arm, severed just above his wrist. He now ignored Dimitar, whispering the healing spell as he pushed with his palm toward the bloodied stump to stanch the flow, a few inches of space wavering between the two. Olaf moaned and stirred, and Willem touched the large man's forehead, then chest, all the while in low incantation. Olaf fell into a deeper unconsciousness, as was Willem's intention based on his next ministration. A short, controlled burst of white-hot flame shot between Willem's outstretched palm and the stump of Olaf's arm, cauterizing the wound with a sickening smell that made Dimitar want to vomit. He swallowed the lump in his throat, determined to be strong for his friend.

"He's out of danger now," Willem said, trying to soothe the wild look in Dimitar's eyes. He wrapped Olaf's arm in a cloth stitched with potent runes, engulfed in gleaming light streaming from his fingertips as the healing incantation came to an end. "He saved my life, and I likely saved his in return."

Olaf lay unmoving with sweat beaded at his temples.

"What the hells happened?" Dimitar's emotions whirled, panic wrapped in pure relief that his friend was alive.

"I didn't see the creature behind me. I turned, too late." Willem described the events in a cool and neutral manner, as if discussing the weather and not near death. "Olaf saw what I did not and stepped between us. He didn't hesitate. He blocked the attack intended for me with his arm and cleaved the Corruptor mid-leap, cutting straight through to the boulder."

He gestured behind him; Olaf's axe lay on the ground next to a dead Corruptor, half the blade broken off from its impact on the rock.

The bandage around his friend's mid-forearm mesmerized Dimitar, thriving with living energy from the spell and ending in a stump. Kaleela knelt beside them, and without thinking Dimitar laid his head on her shoulder. His thoughts were too many, his emotions all over the place. She placed her palm against the side of his face, and he took a shaky breath.

"I'm so sorry," she said, quiet and sad. "I didn't want this to happen."

Dimitar pressed her hand with his, sighing into the touch and its comfort before turning to face her. "None of this is your fault."

Her gaze swept downward.

"Look at me." He cupped her face. "This doesn't change anything." And he meant it.

Willem turned to the troop's wounds. Corruptor claws had marked each of them, and blood dripped from Dimitar's arm. Willem efficiently bandaged cuts that would need stitching; now, haste was necessary. Ral rummaged among the Corruptors' bodies to collect his knives and Kaleela's bow and arrows.

"You can ease your minds." Willem noted Dimitar's impatience and Kaleela's worry as she touched Olaf's brow. "I put an enchantment on him so he may rest. A few minutes will act like hours to him and his body. There's been enough time for recuperation, if you wish for me to wake him."

"Do it," Dimitar said.

Willem passed his hands over Olaf's forehead once more with soft-spoken words in the ancient tongue.

Olaf groaned and opened his unfocused eyes. "Is she safe?"

Kaleela laid her hand against his chest, smiling for his sake as her eyes brimmed over.

"Aye, you big oaf," Dimitar said between gasps that were half-sobs. "You've been hurt. You're okay, but it's real bad. Your arm..."

Dimitar glanced down as he said this. Olaf regarded his wounded limb, turning it back and forth a few times.

"I s'pose I have you to thank," he said to Willem, who simply held his gaze.

Olaf closed his eyes and with effort, pushed himself up to lean against the rock. He struggled to pull himself to a stand without the use of his left hand. Dimitar moved to help, but Olaf shook him off. His second attempt was steadier, and he achieved his footing. Olaf hefted what remained of Lucky, swinging the axe side to side. With half of its double-blade remaining, the weapon now weighed for a one-handed attack.

"Gods and forces of good, I thank ya for leavin' me with m'favorite half." Olaf clutched the axe to his chest.

"You need to go back to the elves. Dimitar can go with you," Kaleela said. Dimitar shot her a look of refusal, but she pressed on. "Gar'Ret will help you."

"I'm not goin' back to any elves. I'm stayin' right here. Do ya think a little scratch would stop me?"

"Listen. You listen to me," Dimitar said, heat rising in his voice. "You need to go back. You can't—"

"No, *you* listen. I'm not goin' and that's final," Olaf yelled.

Willem cut between them, raising both hands. "I shouldn't have to remind you about the urgency of our situation. 'Tis dangerous to remain here any longer. Other Corruptors will wonder what happened with their planned attack. We must move."

Willem turned away from the group and extinguished the fires one by one. Dimitar and Olaf locked stares for a moment before Olaf started up the pathway. He stumbled a few steps but regained sure-footedness after a couple of strides. Ral and Kaleela followed; Dimitar shook his head in defeat and joined them. Willem put out the last fire, and the cool, dark night descended once more.

30

KAHLED

Jolted out of a doze—the closest he'd come to sleeping in the past several days—Kahled was surrounded by Corruptor guards. Hissing, they dragged him to his feet and out of his cell, back toward the abhorred throne room.

Surely to my death this time.

His feet slipped, pulling him to the ground, and on reflex he reached out to catch himself. His hand landed between two thorny protrusions on the Corruptor next to him. Kahled recoiled at the inky sliminess crawling under his flesh. Revolted, he cursed his frailty and willed himself to stand without aid the rest of the way.

Corruptors pushed him to the far side of the chamber and chained his wrists to the stone wall. The chains hung long enough for Kahled to either stand or sit, but he couldn't step more than two paces away. Struggling to free himself was useless, so he tried to save his strength both physically and mentally.

Kahled crouched against the wall. A few minutes alone was enough to find his composure. He surveyed the hellish pit, Corruptors scrabbling by in the hallways, but none entered the throne room.

A deep unease settled in him. He was a patient man but wondered when help or death would arrive. It seemed an eternity ago he'd sent the thief to Blackburn—almost too long. He questioned, not for the first time, whether his instincts were wrong about the cloaked man. Facing the Corrupted on the battlefield answered all his training; but here in their underground lair, his body and spirit in their claws, forced Kahled to examine the possibility of defeat.

He twisted in his chains with fury and despair. Slumping to his knees once more, Kahled buried his head in his hands and brought up the one image to calm all restlessness.

He thought of his Kaleel.

31

KALEELA

Kaleela clutched her bow as the company drew ever closer to the mountainside entrance. A few hundred yards away now, she found little comfort so close to their goal. Instead, deep dread filled her. They'd been overtaken so easily in the last attack. Her small troop might have won, but she couldn't shake the sensation of the binding net and Corruptors grabbing hold of her. If not for Willem's quick healing magic, Olaf's severed limb would've meant the loss of his life. Her hand kept opening and clenching around Rialyn's bow as she thought about the possibility of failure and her father falling victim to the Corrupted, like Conrad.

Kaleela sensed being watched, and turned. Although he attempted to smile, Dimitar's jaw locked in grim resolve. Something about the certainty in his eyes, however, made Kaleela relax her grip.

When they were close enough to the mountain face that the path ended, Ral huddled the company together. Willem created a small light before Ral, so his hands could be seen in the darkness, pale blue flames giving off minimal luminescence. After a moment's hesitation, Ral lowered his cloak hood, meeting each of their eyes.

'The entrance is up ahead. This place is Corrupted territory now, but goblins created their passageways. I recognize their handiwork.' His face scrunched, a mixture of disgust and torment. 'When goblins begin tunneling, they create two side-by-side tunnels, one for hauling stone out and another to return the empty carts.'

He pointed to the others as he continued, his mutilated face casting unnatural shadows from the magic flame. 'Take the long, curved hallway on the right; it leads to an intersection. Turn right again, and Kahled is in the third cell if he remains where I last saw him. However, a problem lies with the Corrupted. Before, this place crawled with them, and now we're expected.' Ral turned to Dimitar. 'I'll go in first... alone. I'll lead them off down the other tunnel. That should give you enough time.'

"What?" Dimitar said. "We can't let you go in alone. It's too dangerous."

The side of Ral's mouth quirked. 'They cannot kill what they cannot catch.'

"At least take one of us with you."

Ral didn't answer at first, then pointed to Willem. 'Your fires. We can trap them within the tunnel.'

Willem nodded once in agreement.

'Once you hear the Corruptors' alarms, open your eyes and ears to judge when you should follow us in. Don't be too hasty. And remember: tunnel on the right, then first right, then the third door. Don't try to find Willem or me. We must not forget our goal.'

A long silence followed as each member of the group considered Ral's plan. Kaleela saw no sign of hesitation in his face. Somehow his loyalty hurt her, because now she knew what the mountains had already cost him.

"Ral, you don't have to do this," she said. "You don't have to go back in there."

Ral placed a hand over his heart, then extended it toward her. 'I'm here to see this through.'

He looked over the group before raising his hood, stealth once again. He gestured 'good luck' and led them a small distance to the mountainside.

The jagged, menacing rock face seemed uncut at first. Ral cocked his head as he studied the surface, then led them a short distance to a gap between two outcroppings. A widened hole sucked in the darkness around them, and the tunnels Ral described opened in front of them. He turned, bowed, and disappeared into the shadows.

"May your elven ancestry prove true, Princess," Willem said. To Olaf and Dimitar, he added, "And may you fight with the honor and courage of your king."

He picked up an arm's length branch. Setting the tip on fire with a touch of his fingers, he handed it to Dimitar and vanished into the mountainside after Ral.

32

RAL

Within the mountain, Ral relied on his instinct to make out the dips and turns along the tunnel, torchlight sparse along the crude walls.

'Wait here,' he signed.

'We must stay together,' Willem signed back.

'I think I hear them ahead. Wait at the midpoint of the tunnel. I'll drive them to you.'

Willem gave a quick nod, and Ral entered the gloom, feeling his way along the hall. His breath came steadily in and out, an unconscious gesture to ease the stifling confinement of the goblin tunnels and memories brewing just below the surface. In his mind, echoes ricocheted: the ping of pickaxes against the rough-hewn rock and dying gasps from people starved not only of food, but sky and fresh air. With his next inhale came the noxious smell of festering wounds and sour tang of sweat that never totally dried. Ral spiraled inwards as he slumped against the tunnel wall.

They need me.

The singular thought came unbidden to his mind but brought him the weight of clarity and purpose, much like the night he'd strayed from his path because he spotted an encampment of knights. Duncan would've called him a fool for taking on such a risky mark, but a strong impulse to approach them compelled him all the same. That same force drove him to rescue the man they called king when he should've escaped into the night. And now, it compelled him to protect those who would call him guide.

Who might call me friend.

He didn't know where this loyalty stemmed from, but it was unbreakable. A bond so deep, it felt natural. Like the beat of his heart or the intake of breath into his lungs, he didn't have to think about the obligation toward this group. It was simply the path before him.

He shoved off from the wall, pushing away the crushing claustrophobia like a shield deflecting a sword. Ral pulled out one of his daggers and gripped it as he continued. The halls stayed too quiet, the scratch of claws on rock silenced. Without so much as a whisper, he made it to the intersection. Warning lit in his gut.

I shouldn't have made it this far. He turned to his left, the dull glow from a distant torch providing the barest light. Searching the path as far as his eyes could see, he perceived nothing but dark stone. Where were the cursed creatures?

A scrape from above drew his gaze up. Coating the tunnel ceiling, Corruptors clung to the rock in a weaving mass, needled teeth bared as they closed on him. Startled, Ral threw his dagger as hard as he could, impaling the Corruptor above him. He dropped into a backward roll as they fell one by one from the ceiling, unleashing sibilant cries. Dashing to his feet, Ral sprinted down the hall, his heart pounding.

The Corrupted moved like oil on the path outside, but they weren't in their natural terrain. Here, they thrived inside the mountain tunnels. The Corruptors ran on all fours across the ground, walls, and ceiling, long claws fastening themselves deep into the rock. They hissed and screeched with each pass of their spiny legs, a crashing wave of pure wrath. What little light made its way into the mountainside reflected in their greasy hides.

Ral led them, his cloak billowing as he ran. A small prick of light flared down the hall, growing in size and intensity, as Willem called the fire element. His fingers glowed with the power of the building spell: a beacon.

The shimmer of Willem's motioning hands illuminated the hall, catching the attention of the encroaching Corruptors. The foremost barked an earsplitting shriek, its speed doubling. It overtook Ral with a loping pounce. Ral rolled with the creature before coming to a stand and continuing his run, barely breaking stride. The Corruptor lay on the tunnel floor with a knife handle protruding from its gaping mouth.

The reddish light surrounding Willem's hands grew in intensity and Ral gestured with an outstretched arm. 'Release the spell.'

Willem, hands poised, needed a final word to let loose the torrent of elemental flames building in his hands. He hesitated, waiting for Ral to cross the threshold.

Two more Corruptors launched themselves from the ceiling onto Ral, taking him to a knee. One landed on Ral's upturned knives, but the other gained his back. The crack of its claws extended, followed by swift pain as it sliced across his side. Red cloth flew back in tatters as he threw himself sideways, knocking the Corruptor loose against the tunnel wall. Even that brief motion gave the remaining Corrupted enough time to reach him at last. Ral slammed a dagger over his shoulder into the Corruptor on his back, threw another into a Corruptor coming at him from the front, and gained only enough time to turn to Willem.

'Release the spell.'

Dismay etched Willem's face as unspoken understanding passed between them. Ral stood too far away to be safe from the spell.

Blood dripped off Ral's hands as he signed again, not all of it the black blood of the Corrupted. *'Release the spell!'*

Flames shot forth, encasing the hall with a blazing river of fire. Heat washed over Ral along with the shrieks of the Corrupted as they dropped, encapsulated in flame, unable to stop in time before running into the fire wall. Ral twisted, knives in hand, as Corruptor after Corruptor fell upon him, bringing him to the ground.

33

THE OVERLORD

The Overlord sat at a low table, studying a map spread over the stone surface. He waited for the princess to arrive, watching in his mind as Kahled's daughter continued along the path and entered the lair. He held the eerie connection with the Corrupted, allowing them to share a collective albeit crude consciousness. The Overlord smirked as he sensed his minions closing in on the cloaked one, but his attention shifted as the next guest arrived.

The Goblin Master was large, even by goblin standards. His tusks had long since broken off near the base, their torn and jagged edges protruding upwards. The youngest Goblin Master in centuries, his skin still held a deep, mottled shade of green. What he lacked in experience, he more than made up with brute strength and cunning. He was a strong leader, and the Overlord knew better than to underestimate him.

The Goblin Master sat unceremoniously, without a word to the Overlord, and scanned over the map detailing cities across the Green Lands. Dispersed red and black circles indicated who would own particular areas after the goblins and Corrupted conquered them. One place was not yet circled: the city of Tildare.

Situated in the southern region of the Green Lands, Tildare lay deep in the future territory claimed by the goblins. The Overlord wasn't willing to give it up, however, and refused to negotiate. The Goblin Master viewed Corrupted ownership of Tildare as an intrusion on his land and treated the Overlord's demand as a sign of invasion. With full battle preparations days from completion, one of them would have to sacrifice their claim on the city.

"For too long you've been forced to live within the mountains," the Overlord said. "You may take ownership of the southern lands we conquer. I care not for the slaves you need to do your work, and now you'll have plenty." He pointed to Tildare. "Except this one. This city is mine."

"I not likes this." The Goblin Master slammed his fist down, the common language broken and harsh. Small figurines representing Corrupted and goblin armies scattered as they jumped from the table onto the floor, bouncing off the stone.

"It doesn't matter whether you like it or not." The Overlord leaned back in his chair, unbothered. His Corruptor guards slithered across the floor, picking up the small models and placing them back on the map. "This is how it will be."

The Goblin Master turned a deeper shade of green as fury tightened the muscles in his massive arms. Already enormous, he stood to full height in his anger, dwarfing the seated Overlord. Froth dripped off his jagged tusks, landing in slow splatters upon the map.

Narrowing his eyes to slits, he growled again, emphasizing each word. "I not likes this."

The Overlord stood from his chair. His fist struck with such speed and force that the Goblin Master hit the wall behind him before he could blink. Shaking off the blow, he came to a stand with a murderous growl. As he reached for the knotted club at his side, Corruptors descended out of the shadows. They thronged around him in a hissing, churning blackness, claws dangerously extended.

A Corruptor slipped forward, ignoring the cornered goblin. Growling, it delivered a short message. The Overlord turned to the messenger and answered low in response.

Everything's in position. Oh, High Knight, I'm glad you were difficult. The breaking of you will be my first victory.

"We're done here," he said to the Goblin Master. He walked over to the table, eyeing the map once more before raising his gaze, pointed and lethal. "I trust the matter of Tildare is settled?"

The Goblin Master snarled at the writhing Corrupted. Baring his teeth, he nodded.

"Excellent." With a flick of his clawed finger, the Overlord scratched a circle around Tildare. "Then I suggest you begin with the preparations."

He turned on his heel dismissively and followed the Corruptor messenger out the door.

34

KALEELA

Mercy of the gods, please let us find his cell. Kaleela peered into the tunnel with the magicked torch light that burned hotly yet didn't so much as blacken the branch.

They waited for any sign of Ral, Willem, or the Corrupted. A sharp screech pierced the night air and echoed its way down the long corridor. Olaf grabbed his axe as Dimitar leaned into the entrance, head cocked. Kaleela made out the tapping of the Corruptors' claws in the side tunnel. As louder shrieks bounced along the walls, Kaleela reeled back, her heart pounding. The air grew thick and foul.

Dimitar turned to her, fear and determination brightening his eyes. "Let's go!"

The torchlight wasn't enough to illuminate the path that breathed obscurity as they traveled deeper into the mountain. Her instinct screamed at something amiss, that they should've run into Corruptors by now. But this close to her goal, Kaleela ignored her gut and concentrated on their task. She had to trust that Ral and Willem succeeded in distracting the Corruptor patrols. She had to focus, or her father would die here.

The end of the tunnel came quicker than Kaleela expected. Turning right, she slowed her pace to feel along the warm, damp stone. Her fears grew; had they passed the doors somehow, or did Ral misremember the directions? Just as she was about to go back, her searching hand touched the first door. If not for the metal bars, she couldn't discern the door apart from the wall, the wood long since petrified. A few strides later and she found the second door. Her heart pounded in her chest as she reached the third.

As her hands fell upon the scarred wood, something felt wrong, an instinct that smothered all hope. Peeking in, the cell's blackness sat like a buried coffin. She called through the bars in a hushed voice. "Father? Are you there?"

Kaleela jumped when Olaf rested his hand on her shoulder, guiding her back. Grabbing onto the door handle, he pulled with all his might as if to rip the door off its hinges. Instead, he stumbled backwards, hitting the opposite wall with a thump. The door wasn't locked.

Dimitar rushed into the cell, planting the torch in a crack in the wall. Kaleela fell in after him, calling for her father.

Empty.

The two stood dumbfounded, unable—or unwilling—to comprehend what Kahled's absence implied. Kaleela choked back a sudden cry. Along the wall hung broken shackles and a streak of blood that formed a puddle on the ground, blackened by the torch light, signifying the unbearable.

"No...." she said in a small voice, any and all strength sucked from her body.

Behind them, Olaf growled a warning.

"Stay your hand." Willem appeared, gasping for breath. "I trapped the Corruptor guards in the tunnel. It should give us enough time to escape."

"Where's Ral?" Dimitar asked. "Willem—what happened to Ral?"

Empty. Empty... Gone.

Willem lowered his head, an unaccustomed timbre to his voice. "He didn't survive. There were too many, and they caught him; he fought, but it wasn't enough. In his last act, he made me seal the tunnel with flame, so we could continue."

Kaleela's throat clenched, wanting to scream in frustration and sob in despair. The grief she'd coped with and shielded away over the past weeks came back to her a hundredfold. She couldn't breathe, not without agony coursing through her chest.

"Where's Kahled? We must go." Willem peered into the cell.

"This must be the wrong cell." Dimitar's words rose into an uncertain question. "Or did they move him?"

"He's gone." Kaleela's gaze couldn't leave the blood stain. "I lost him. My fathers, they're both gone from me!"

Her cracked words slipped into a wail. Strength drained from her entire body, doubling over as she clutched her middle. Sobs wrenched from her chest, her eyes flooding with tears. Dimitar lifted her to him, and she broke against him then, weeping as she clung to him.

"This cannot all be for nothing," Dimitar said, hopelessness hitching his voice.

"It's a trap." True horror seeped into Willem's words. "They knew we were coming all along."

Chittering Corruptors turned the corner at the intersection, becoming louder as they approached. Willem raised his hands; he didn't get out a word of the spell before they slammed into him, knocking him to the ground.

The Corruptors surrounded them, forcing their surrender.

Their mission had failed.

35

DIMITAR

Dimitar's leaden steps dragged against the ground as Corruptors drove them deeper into the mountain. The image of the empty cell pierced his mind. He failed Kahled on every level. Never had he felt so defeated. Never had he felt so alone.

Even with the creatures prodding and snarling at them, the troop remained unresponsive. Failure extinguished any struggle within them, and the ropes binding their wrists were almost unnecessary.

Firelight flooded over the group as they rounded the last corner, entering the Overlord's throne room. Dimitar lifted his arms to shield his eyes from the sudden brightness, blinking a few times. He took in the fire rivulets creeping along the walls and lingered on the throne before coming to the far corner of the chamber. There, a huddled form leaned against the wall. Three silver, embroidered rings intertwined on the back of the man's tattered tunic, the glorious emblem of Blackburn. Dimitar's heart skipped a beat, hoping one of Blackburn's knights had survived.

There's something familiar about that man's posture. Dimitar's thoughts were sluggish, slow to form around the obvious. *Something about the way he—*

Dimitar stopped in his tracks and exhaled the name. "Kahled."

Grabbing Kaleela by the arm, he spun her to face the corner. Kaleela's head rose as if waking from a trance. Her eyes settled on the thin, drawn man in the corner as he turned. Only then did Dimitar's statement find her ears.

"*Father!*" she screamed, her voice echoing off the walls.

Kahled's mouth dropped open at the sight of his daughter and closed again in a smile. Tears fell from his eyes as he sank to his knees. "My Kaleela," he rasped.

Kaleela burst into furious action. Swinging her fists low and driving them up, she caught the Corruptor next to her off guard, knocking it to the ground. Breaking into a run, she sprinted toward her father. Dimitar sprung clear of his guard seconds later. His long strides pulled him even with her as they rushed across the vast room.

Corruptors started after them but slammed backwards off an invisible wall. Willem mouthed an incantation, twisting his hands within his bindings, fingers beginning to glow. The Corruptors tried to stand, only to get thrown to the side as Willem chanted and gestured with his bound hands, churning the air to bend to his power.

Olaf used Willem's diversion to search out the Corruptor carrying their weapons. Barreling toward it, he grabbed Lucky's handle and kicked the Corruptor to the floor. Their weapons scattered across the stone ground. Olaf raised his axe, but the Corruptor jumped on his back before he could strike. Spinning, he tried to fling it off, but another one joined the first, claws sinking into the meat of his back. It took a third one to knock Lucky from his hand, and not until the fourth Corruptor latched onto his wounded arm was Olaf forced to the ground with a gritted cry of pain.

A Corruptor shot out and wrapped around Dimitar's legs; he buckled and fell hard onto the floor. His bound arms dug into the weight of his body, knocking the wind from him. Another jumped onto his waist, grabbing a claw full of hair and yanking his head back. From the corner of his eye, Dimitar glimpsed more Corruptors crawling through a second entrance into the hall.

Kaleela paid no heed to the Corruptors scrabbling through the door as she ran to where her father knelt just beyond the second entrance. Dimitar watched, helpless, as a hulking figure rose in the final doorway, and a wordless cry of refusal escaped him. There was no way he could reach her in time, even if he could break free.

She skidded to a halt, sliding to the floor in a backpedal.

The Overlord appeared in the entranceway as if emerging from the stone mountain itself. Tall and intimidating, he strode with purposeful movements, the strength of his body in stark contrast to Kahled's weakened state. He wore a battle helmet adorned with metal spikes in similar fashion to the horned protrusions upon his body and the Corruptors' hides. Although the helm partially obscured his face, his eyes and their coldness pierced the room.

His gaze swept over the unchecked prisoners, and he raised his arms high and unleashed a monstrous roar filled with command. An impossible number of Corruptors flooded out, slinking between his legs and over his shoulders as they ran into the room.

Kaleela tried getting to her feet but was engulfed by them, her shriek piercing into Dimitar as sharp as any blade. He twisted beneath the Corruptors' claws, fighting to get to her even as the grip tightened in his hair, pulling against his scalp with eye-watering pain. Willem began his magic anew with steady precision, throwing Corruptors away from Kaleela and himself as the creatures attempted to bring him to the ground.

"Go for the hands, you fools!" the Overlord shouted.

Willem had no choice but to cease his incantation and cup his hands together, lest the Corruptors rip his fingers off. Their fight was over.

With Willem's protective shields disabled, the Corruptors dragged the rest of the group to the far wall and attached them with long ropes to hooks protruding from the rock. The rope circled their wrist bindings, leashing them to the wall. With Willem, they tied extra bindings around his hands, immobilizing them.

The Overlord sauntered over to Kahled, the fires casting a long shadow over the kneeling knight. Kahled tore his gaze from Kaleela to meet the Overlord's stare, tight-lipped.

"I grow tired of your resistance, High Knight," the Overlord said. "I'm going to ask you again, and I warn you, answer with care: Will you join me?"

"No, sire!" Dimitar struggled against the restraints.

The Overlord held up his hand. A Corruptor standing next to Dimitar backhanded him, the sound echoing in the hall. A trickle of blood dripped from his mouth, and he spat upon the ground.

Without turning to face the prisoners, the Overlord said, "Next time, they won't strike with their claws in." Raising his voice, he directed his full attention to Kahled. "Give me your answer!"

"My answer is the same as before and will forever be," Kahled said through clenched teeth.

The Overlord turned to the bound group on display, ignoring Kahled for the moment as if expecting this reply. Unhurried as he approached, he cupped his hands behind him, the back of one hand tapping against the other. Stopping at the end of the row of prisoners, he took in Willem first, tipping his head in question. "Of all your kind, they send you to accompany these saplings?"

Willem's gaze held steady and unblinking, and he said nothing. His fingers flexed, but the bonds were too secure, leaving him without the maneuverability to cast and guide his magic.

The Overlord turned away dismissively. "They sent the wrong elf to challenge me, perhaps because your death will be meaningless, *Elea Magai*."

The Overlord didn't see Willem's forehead crease upon hearing his title in elvish. His attention now found Olaf and Dimitar. In the same fashion as with Willem, he judged the two young men. What the Overlord assessed made him snicker.

"Kahled," the Overlord drawled, his voice low and menacing, "the kingdom sent *guardsmen* to your rescue? I'm once again disappointed in your judgment. Perhaps you're not worth my time after all."

Dimitar stared down the red-tinged eyes behind the helm with growing hatred. He quickly understood his purpose as bait for his king.

"You've murdered the rest of my men. If you think to win my allegiance bringing harm upon these two, then you've underestimated my resolve!" Kahled's last words ended in a ringing shout, full of power and command.

Dimitar's pride in his king dampened with bitter realization at the sick truth: Blackburn's knights were indeed dead, each and every one of the men Dimitar trained under and respected. Reason stood that he and Olaf would join them in death sooner than not. He twisted against his bonds.

A sadistic grin spread over the Overlord's features. "Perhaps you make a point. I have little use for them. But my army, there's a different story. They're always eager to feed upon flesh. Shall I hold a banquet in my hall?" The Overlord nudged a toe toward Olaf. "This fat one would make a feast."

Olaf bared his teeth in response even as the leather bindings cut into his wound, bringing fresh blood through the wrappings. Dimitar's stomach clenched; he caught the fear that stole into Olaf's eyes.

With a chuckle, the Overlord began to step past him. "Now, what have we—"

"Stop," Dimitar said before the Overlord looked upon Kaleela, tied beside him. He kept talking, wanting to keep her out of the Overlord's path. "Your words are easy to come by behind your cowardice. Make your threats and promises, but do it without the Corrupted to help you. You know that you'd be beaten if we weren't bound."

"Oh?" The Overlord's brow arched in amusement mixed with growing anger. "Prove it."

With lightning speed, the Overlord drew his sword and thrust through Dimitar's bonds. Dimitar untangled his hands from the severed ropes as Olaf renewed his struggle. He locked eyes with Kaleela, her tear-stained face filled with distress, and his chest tightened.

"I can't protect you here anymore," he said, his voice ragged with determination, "but I will always fight for you. *Always.*"

The Overlord strode between them, facing Dimitar. "I am no coward, boy. Your ignorance is pathetic, but I'll grant you one boon." He tossed his blade to the ground at Dimitar's feet. "Pick it up and face me."

"Dimitar, no," Kahled ordered. "Stand down now."

Dimitar hesitated, then broke his king's command and took the weapon, circling away to draw the Overlord's attention further off Kaleela. *Over here. Look at me, asshole.*

The blade quivered in his hand, and the Overlord matched his steps, arms wide with palms upwards as if in a bow, mocking him. Dimitar narrowed his stance, trying to keep himself as guarded as possible. He knew better than to assume he had the upper hand because he was armed and the Overlord wasn't. Risking a quick look, Dimitar judged how fast he could cover the distance and free Olaf or Willem.

"*Tsk,*" the Overlord chastised, "this fight is between us, just as you wished, boy."

With a snap of his fingers, Corruptor guards swarmed Kaleela, Olaf, and Willem, baring their claws and placing razor edges against their throats or above their hearts.

"You'll find my guards much faster than you." Placing his hands behind his back once more, the Overlord fully faced Dimitar. "You wanted to play the hero. Now's your chance."

"No, Dimitar!" Kahled yelled again.

His warning was futile as the Overlord charged Dimitar, who matched the aggression with equal force. Dimitar brought his sword in a tight overhead strike aimed at his shoulder. His swing fell short as the Overlord twisted at the hip and met the blade's arc with his fist, punching the flat of the blade out of harm's way. He then threw his other fist squarely against Dimitar's chest.

Pain exploded through Dimitar's entire upper body as he flew backward, landing on his back in a skid. His vision swam as an eruption of heat spread throughout his chest. His breath rattled into his lungs, but the tightness in his chest increased. Dimitar had tussled in his share of fistfights over the years, but this was different, the power behind the blow unnatural.

A hand grabbed his shoulder and hauled him to his feet.

"Here," the Overlord said with cold indifference, offering his sword once more. "You dropped this."

Dimitar grabbed the hilt and ignored the pain stitching its way down his side as he circled the Overlord. Using one of the skills he'd recently mastered in training, Dimitar reversed the direction of his circling and took a step closer. In doing so, he now stood within striking distance even if he didn't appear to move forward.

Dimitar thrust out, hoping to catch the Overlord unawares by the reach of his strike. As Dimitar anticipated, he twisted at the hip again. Spinning to the opposite side, Dimitar brought the sword in low, aiming at the Overlord's middle. This move had great success in training and worked against several Corrupted on the mountainside.

The Overlord stepped toward Dimitar and caught his sword hand mid-strike, the fingers tightening over Dimitar's fist in a vise-like grip, knuckles popping from the pressure.

Oh shit.

Dimitar's head snapped to the side as the Overlord threw his other spiked elbow in a tight strike. A gush of blood arced into the air from the cut across his forehead. The Overlord wrenched Dimitar's sword hand around, pain exploding up Dimitar's arm, driving him to his knees. In one swift move, the Overlord kicked Dimitar's side, sending him sprawling once more like a rag doll.

Laughter filled the throne room, evil and merciless, as the Overlord came to stand over him. Rolling onto his side, Dimitar clutched his ribs—*broken?*—with a grimace. Blood pooled from the cut on his head, which he had trouble lifting. Tears squeezed out as pain wracked his body with each breath. As if from afar, Kahled shouted, but Dimitar couldn't make out the words in the fog of his mind. He could only hold on to his best friend's voice, piercing into him with urgency and anguish.

"Stay down, lad," Olaf begged in a hoarse voice. "For the love o' the gods, end this! Stay down, and give me a chance at him."

Stay down. The words repeated in the hazy cloud of his mind, and he clenched the dirt beneath his fist. *Stay down.*

The Overlord laughed again, clearly pleased at the beaten body, signaling victory.

The laughter stopped as Dimitar flexed his palm against the ground and pushed up with the last of his strength.

From his hands and knees, Dimitar grasped the pommel of the Overlord's sword. His body pulsed in agony, not one place untouched from the fire of throbbing pain. It hurt to lift his head to face the Overlord, which he did as he came to a slow stand. Dimitar brought the sword around, tip dragging on the ground from his weakness and resolution.

A lifetime of hatred burned behind the helm, and the Overlord pulled back a fist leveled at Dimitar's head. Dimitar swayed on his feet; even if not knocked over, he'd surely collapse, yet he fought with all his will to never bow down to a tyrant.

"Please," came a heartbroken cry across the room. "Please, stop this! Leave him... You've won, can't you just leave him?"

The Overlord lowered his fist and turned to the source.

Kaleela pleaded through brimming eyes. "*Please.* You've won."

The Overlord turned to Kaleela at last, sick pleasure lighting his eyes, and waved a hand in unspoken command. A Corruptor slipped forth to yank Dimitar back to the wall, who stumbled, left with no physical strength left to resist. The Overlord's sword clattered to the ground from Dimitar's numb fingers. Corruptors rebounded his wrists and hoisted him once more to the hook where he hung without strength, clinging to consciousness and unable to respond as both Olaf and Kaleela called his name.

The Overlord turned toward his throne after pausing to grab and sheath his blade. As he walked, he spoke with a lighter tone as if unmindful of—or energized by—the brutal beating that had just occurred.

"I don't think much of her traveling companions," the Overlord said, sneering at the bound men and lingering with sadistic pleasure over Dimitar's beaten form. "But he lasted longer than your knights."

Before Kahled could react to this biting insult, he continued.

"How amusing... After all my efforts to search out your daughter, she comes to me in the end. Perhaps you should follow her lead, Kahled." The Overlord's smile was cruel. "And such a lovely young woman. Truly her mother's image."

He drew out the last few words as he leered at Kaleela. Her head snapped up in response, and she peered into the dark helmet.

"It's too bad, really." He reached his throne but didn't sit upon it. Instead, he turned to face Kahled, whose face betrayed sudden, awful comprehension. "I didn't want things to come to this. All you needed to do was join me, Kahled. One word would've been enough. Now, I'm afraid it's too late."

Snapping his fingers, he ordered, "Bring the girl here."

36

KAHLED

Kahled shot to his feet, fighting against the chains holding him to the wall. "Don't you touch her," he growled, blood running down his hands as the cuffs cut his wrists. The Overlord's laughter echoed throughout the chamber.

Two Corruptors removed Kaleela's rope from the hook, snarling as if they'd just as soon rip her limbs off. Force proved unnecessary; Kaleela held her head with set determination as she walked toward the Overlord. She kept her gaze fierce and pinned on a point against the far wall.

When she was within distance, a Corruptor handed the rope leash to the Overlord. He tilted his head to capture her gaze, but she shifted her eyes to another point, cold and defiant. Kahled ached with pride as he watched his daughter.

The Overlord gave a quick tug on the rope, jerking her forward a few steps. Her eyes darkened in humiliation as he continued to reel her toward him, but still she refused to acknowledge him. Her attempts at evading his piercing stare faltered as the Overlord leaned closer.

"Just like your father," he said, glancing at Kahled, who closed his eyes in despair.

Kaleela recoiled, and the Overlord lifted her chin, forcing her to meet his gaze. "You have the fight of your father in you, young lady. I admire that. It reminds me of another man who died right where you're standing. A brave man, to be sure, but not terribly bright. I believe you knew him. He resisted me for hours, even after the torture. I just had to break him, and he'd be mine. 'Tis a pity..."

Pausing, the Overlord stood behind Kaleela and cupped her face in his hand, directing his next words to Kahled. "Conrad went through a lot of pain before I killed him. I doubt she'll last half as long."

Kahled stood taut, filled with furious anger, blood dripping down his wrists with the strain. "Let her go," he said through clenched teeth, "or you'll regret it."

The Overlord snickered in response. "Oh, I doubt it, good Knight. I'm not the one in shackles." He leaned in close to Kaleela and spoke to her even as his gaze burned at Kahled. "It shouldn't surprise you that Conrad begged me to let you live in peace before I sliced his throat. But I do have a secret for you. I made sure to tell him my plans for you, sweetling. He died knowing he couldn't protect you; that he could do nothing to save you. I've never seen such a face of misery in my life."

He glanced at her and wiped away a tear that slipped down her cheek with a dark, clawed finger.

"Leave her alone! This is between you and me," Kahled cried hoarsely. Never had such hate entered his heart before this moment, watching his daughter intimidated and threatened for his sake.

The Overlord spared him another cruel smile, then threw Kaleela to the ground. She collapsed on all fours, landing hard on her knees and bound hands. The Overlord placed a foot on the other end of the rope, pinning her there.

"This is your final chance, High Knight. Join me, or your daughter dies here, where your beloved Conrad died. Your choice."

Kahled stopped struggling and stared in fury at the Overlord. Demanding he choose his code or his life was dishonorable enough. Now, the Overlord forced him to choose between his one remaining love in life or all he stood for as a knight and as a man. Looking into Kaleela's eyes, Kahled no longer saw just his daughter. He glimpsed Kaleel in her, and pain wrenched his heart.

"Do not try my patience!" The Overlord drew his sword from its scabbard. He raised the blade as Kaleela struggled in vain. When the sword reached shoulder level, he added, "Don't erase Kaleel completely from existence."

Kahled flinched, blood rushing from his face. The Overlord's words struck him deep within, voicing his innermost thoughts. Every emotion, every image, every smile he'd shared with Kaleel came rushing back. Dizziness overwhelmed him as he sagged against the wall. Conrad joined the flash of memories, his great smile and hand in friendship held out for support. Kahled tried to grab hold of his friend's strength but couldn't reach. No matter how he extended himself, his loves couldn't help him now.

The Overlord's sword paused at the peak of its arc. In a voice resembling those of his minions, his command echoed across the cavern in an ear-piercing shriek. "Choose now!"

Kahled raised his head and straightened his shoulders. Kaleela would die if he chose honor, and her life was worth everything to him, even at the cost of his own damnation.

Forgive me.

Kahled leveled his stare at the Overlord. "I surrender to you."

The Overlord leered within his helm. Lowering the blade, he beckoned to the nearby Corruptors, sharing an unspoken command. Two Corruptors flanked Kahled, grabbing the chains holding his arms and yanking them back. Kahled cried out as he was immobilized. A third Corruptor crept toward him, carrying a crude goblet. No guise of fresh water cloaked the tainted liquid this time; black oiliness swirled as if with a life of its own.

"Thirsty again, Kahled?" the Overlord asked, mocking and eager. "Time for a drink. Let us toast."

One of the Corruptors wrenched Kahled's head back, forcing his mouth open. Kahled involuntarily struggled, despite his resignation. He knew all too well what would happen next. He remembered every minute of it in the cell, gods help him. When the Corruptor raised the goblet at last, Kahled braced himself for the transformation that would take him completely this time.

As the Corruptor extended the foul cup, it stopped with a low hiss. At the same time, the Overlord bent backwards, howling in pain, and spun toward the far wall with a snarl. A large, smoldering wound burned in the Overlord's lower back. He cried out as another burst of flame slammed into his shoulder, spinning him further around.

Willem's incantation came on whispered breath yet losing none of its potency. The mage had managed to burn his bindings free, but at a terrible price. Without the guidance of his hands, the fire spell ran unrefined, burning his flesh as well as the rope that fell away. His fingertips turned a charred red, flesh bubbling with bright blisters. The pain must have been unbearable, but Willem's face twisted into a mask

211

of pure concentration as he chanted under his breath, stepping forward with more fire attacks shooting at the Overlord and the surrounding creatures. The Corruptors holding Kahled took off across the room and rushed to attack.

Kahled locked eyes with his daughter, breathless on the floor at the Overlord's feet. His back faced her, legs crossed from spinning to face the attack and his weight partially removed from the rope. With a cry of refusal, she sprung off the floor, driving her shoulders into the back of his knees and coming to a stand. The Overlord's legs buckled as he fell, but not before a fireball hit him in the face. The spiked helm turned molten, steel dripping in rivulets into the Overlord's upturned face. The Overlord screamed in agony, his body flailing. His movements diminished until, with a final twitch, he lay still and smoldering.

With a burst of desperate energy, Kaleela ran to Kahled. She fell into his fettered embrace, tears streaming from both their eyes.

"What are you doing here, my darling girl?" Pushing her back, he undid the ropes around her wrists. Kahled fought hard not to tremble as he cupped her face. "You could've been killed."

"I didn't trust anyone else, Father. Couldn't wait, not after Conrad."

Kahled held her to his chest, shielding her, overwhelmed by the need to protect her from the surrounding chaos.

As Corruptors closed in, Willem freed the two men with quick utterances and a pointed gesture with his other hand, the ropes binding their hands and wrists unraveling. Dimitar staggered over to Willem, yanking the rest of the charred ropes off. The mage started a new chant and focused his gestures toward Dimitar, detailing symbols in the air. *A numbing conjuration; his pain will be dulled.* Within seconds Dimitar stood straighter and firmer. He placed his hand on Willem's shoulder in a quick gesture of thanks.

Dimitar ducked under a Corruptor's strike and ran to where his weapon had fallen to the floor. Sliding along the stone to reach his sword, he grabbed the hilt and swung it in one fluid movement, decapitating the nearest Corruptor. Dimitar worked to clear a path for Olaf to get to his axe, which had skittered across the floor in the earlier struggle, but the Corrupted were too numerous. Wavering light engulfed him, throwing the Corruptors back. Willem continued the protective spell, albeit with lines of pain now etched into his face with each gesture. Yet he gave Dimitar all the advantage he needed, and Corruptor after Corruptor fell by his blade.

"Let's get you out of here." Kahled let go of Kaleela and came to a stand. As much as he wanted to rip out of them, the metal bracers cut into his broken skin, and he bit back a groan.

"Olaf!" she cried out. Kaleela pulled at the chains attached to the stone wall and called his name again.

"Willem, get me to her!" Olaf shouted in return. When the air around him bent, he thundered forward, knocking over the Corrupted in front of him. Without breaking his stride, he picked up Lucky as he passed by.

"Olaf, please help me!" Kaleela gasped when he got close enough. "I cannot break these chains."

Olaf pulled her aside and hefted his axe high over his head. With a loud grunt, he threw his weight behind the fall of the blow, bending one of the links in half. The next blow snapped it in two.

Stepping back, he bowed. "A pleasure havin' ya back, Yer Majesty."

Kahled placed his hand on the back of Olaf's head but slumped to one knee in exhaustion. Olaf sheathed Lucky, then hoisted him up, looping his arm around Kahled's waist. Kahled looked at him gratefully and gave a nod. His will would not fail him now.

The Corruptors became confused without their leader's guidance and scattered. With Olaf leading the way, the three ran to the far entrance where Dimitar and Willem cut through Corruptors.

A groan cut from behind them. The Overlord pulled himself onto his hands and knees, struggling to stand.

Kahled spun to the others. "We must go! Now!"

A few Corruptors blocked the path that led to the exiting hallway, the group's last chance at escape. Willem mouthed the commands upon whispered breath and carved out a spell with his charred hands, a mix of sweat and tears running down his cheeks. Torch flame leapt from the nearest wall as Willem directed the elements, rushing across air turned wind, and cast aside the remaining Corruptors guarding the exit. Dimitar seized the opportunity and led the group into the hallway.

"Mage, wait," Kahled said, turning back. "He won't let us go so easily. Block him."

Willem stood at the entrance next to Kahled and started a new, lower chant. The Overlord rose to his feet and caught himself against the side of his throne as he tripped, damaged muscles and nerves re-knitting together. He picked off pieces of molten steel attached to his face, still raw but with restorative power underway. With increasingly stronger steps, he made his way to the entrance.

Just as he drew within a couple strides, a large, translucent wall of wavering light filled the hallway entrance. The Overlord reached the doorway and pounded the hardened air, but it held strong. He tore off his ruined helm, at last revealing his face, the broad, angular planes accentuated by the inky veins of the Corruptor seed. Kahled met his eyes one last time, then ran down the tunnel.

The Overlord's howl echoed behind them. "A war is coming for you...!"

37

KAHLED

The sun rose over the mountains behind the group, shedding blessed light on the trail as they hurried along its winding path, chilly morning mists separating with their passing. Although no sign of the Corrupted followed them out of the mountainside, the troop's weapons remained brandished, ready for any indication of a pursuit. Kahled's eyes widened as they passed the Corruptor bodies among the boulders. *So many carcasses.*

Reaching the trail's end, they collapsed against the larger rocks lining the pathway, exhausted. Willem was the first to remember their horses, nearby and under his spell. A unified sigh of relief exhaled from the company as he went to retrieve them.

As the adrenaline wore off, Kahled surveyed the group. *Gods, what they all endured for me.* Olaf gritted his teeth, his left arm bleeding through the wrappings. Dimitar held his sword steady but clutched at his side, blood matting his hair from the gash on his forehead. Kaleela remained the most unscathed—the Corrupted had seen to that. However, Kahled knew his daughter's face well enough; she struggled to remain composed.

"Sire, we can—" Dimitar began, but Kahled shushed him.

Dimitar spun into a defensive stance, raising his sword with shaking arms.

Several boulders of different sizes lay behind them, nothing more. The dawn's light brought a softness to the dry landscape, at odds with the dangerous area promising more violence. Dimitar glanced back at Kahled, his unspoken question hanging silent between them.

Kahled closed his eyes and extended his hearing. "Something's here, about fifty paces ahead."

A small scrape of rocks tumbled near a boulder off to the left. Everyone jumped and turned to face the Corrupted onslaught... but none appeared. Kahled stepped forward, struggling with his weakened body.

"Show yourselves!" he shouted, at the end of his patience.

Moments later, more rocks fell across the path in a trickle.

"So'gud roth! Ath slinth ar'anistal," swore a familiar, gravelly voice, and Bela'Ruhn appeared between two boulders followed by a troop of armed elite warriors. He stumbled over the loose gravel, causing another small trail of rocks to tumble along the ground, and let out another vibrant curse.

Dimitar and Olaf lowered their weapons and stared at Bela'Ruhn in shock as he regarded them with equal wonder.

"It's been a long time, General Bela'Ruhn. I wish we met under better circumstances." Kahled extended his arm.

Bela'Ruhn sheathed his sword and grasped Kahled's forearm in a firm grip. *"Nath eirah tas.* We were sent to rescue you, High Knight." He added without intonation, "It appears we weren't needed." Facing Kaleela, he bowed his head. "It seems I underestimated you, Your Highness."

Before she could respond, Willem turned onto the path, the horses in tow. He stopped in his tracks when he saw Bela'Ruhn.

"General, did the king doubt my ability to carry out this mission with success... or was that your own thought?" Willem asked, irritation in his voice.

"Kahled's one of mine," Bela'Ruhn answered with a rasp. "And the Royal Majesties wanted assurance the princess would return."

Willem retorted in elvish, and their conversation continued with growing heat.

For the love of the gods, elven pride is going to get us all killed.

Kahled stepped between them, holding out his shackled hands. "Now isn't the time to argue over competency. The ground upon which we stand is far from safe."

Although Kahled stood with all the dignity of a High Knight, his utter fatigue could no longer be hidden. He wavered on shaky legs.

Willem gingerly handed the horses' reins to the group. One of the elven guardsmen attended to him at once, bringing out a salve from a pouch. Cupping his hands—flesh mangled and nerves tortured—Willem called over one of the elite warriors and spoke with her in low, hushed tones. Doubt crossed the elf's face, but she, in turn, conferred with Bela'Ruhn, who shot Willem another pointed look before granting his permission. Two of the elite squadron members slipped aside and headed up the mountainside path.

Turning to Kahled, Bela'Ruhn said, "I have a warhorse to carry us both back to Quinthal." He lifted his voice to the group. "We ride out."

With a grunt, Kahled pulled himself onto the horse, accompanied soon after by Bela'Ruhn. The others followed suit, turning away from the mountains.

As they rode, the last of the strength left Kahled's body. He slumped against the horse's neck and would've fallen off if not for Bela'Ruhn's steadying hand. With the rhythm of the horse's hooves hitting the ground and fresh air filling his lungs, Kahled slept.

PART THREE

38

DIMITAR

The journey back to the Sun'Din Forest passed without event but was arduous nonetheless. The pain in Dimitar's ribs grew with each day, Willem's numbing spell giving way to the constant fall of Deepshade's hooves. They took little time to sleep and gather nourishment from satchels of rations the elves brought, before General Bela'Ruhn bid them to continue. The general's grueling pace shaved off two days from the time it had taken them to reach the mountainside. In doing so, the group had little time to converse. Perhaps no one was ready to speak of what they'd endured.

The air thrummed with energy as the troop made their way to Quinthal. Scouts sent word ahead that Bela'Ruhn returned with Kahled, and the streets lined in anticipation. The people remained respectfully silent as the party made its way to the city's center, coming to a halt at the castle base. When Kahled lowered himself off the horse, the crowd roared to life until one continuous cheer lifted the sky. Kahled smiled in return, but Dimitar saw him hide his shaking hand against the horse's side. Dimitar, along with the rest of the group, dismounted and stood before the clamoring crowd.

The elves quieted with the low peal from a large horn. Turning to face the entrance, each elf bowed in deep reverence, hand or fist upon their hearts. Dimitar did the same, glad to stretch his saddle-weary back. The castle doors opened wide, and Queen Elayis and King An'Nadal appeared in the doorway, both garbed in fine robes, crowns shining in the sunlight. They walked forward hand in hand and descended the stairs. Gar'Ret emerged next, his hair hanging free past his shoulders, and followed his parents. When he reached the bottom, he walked over to where Kaleela bowed, sharing a smile as he offered his hand, raising her to stand with the royal family.

Elayis and An'Nadal stopped before Kahled. Murmurs threaded through the crowd as Elayis embraced the High Knight. An'Nadal placed his hand on Kahled's back as the great man's chest heaved. Although most mistook his tears for happiness at being freed from the Corrupted clutches, the truth dawned on Dimitar: Kahled grieved for Kaleel. This marked the first time since her death that he returned to Quinthal and faced the king and queen.

Kaleela started forward to offer her support but was stayed by Gar'Ret's hand.

Bending close, he said, "He's asking to be forgiven. Her death still weighs heavy on his soul. Leave them in a moment of peace."

Truth be told, Dimitar had never figured out why Kahled held such limited contact with the nation that bestowed upon him the High Knight rank and all the glory that followed. Watching his king now, he began to understand.

The three remained in that embrace for some time before Elayis broke away and spoke in soft tones to Kahled, clasping his arms. Dimitar strained to hear what she said, only catching bits and pieces of elven words. Elayis hugged Kahled again, then turned to face the crowd, welcoming them with open arms. Gar'Ret translated her elven words for Dimitar and Olaf.

"This morn marks a day that will not be forgotten," she said. "A day when elf saved man in an effort not given grudgingly, but out of genuine fellowship. Our top general led this band of troops and guards. His commitment to his duties, and to the life of another, shall be praised."

All eyes turned to Bela'Ruhn, who raised both hands to quiet the crowd's applause. "This honor does not belong to me." He gave a hard look at Kaleela, Dimitar, Olaf, and Willem as the crowd murmured. "I served to lead this company back to our lands; nothing more. Princess Kaleela, Mage Willem, and these men deserve the honor of High Knight Kahled's liberation."

At this, the crowd ignited once more. Dimitar grinned as confidence flamed. For the first time, victory overcame his weariness. *This must be what it felt like for the High Knights, coming home heroes.*

Gar'Ret faced Kaleela and brought her into a strong embrace. "You've honored your mother." He then turned to the men and bowed. "I welcome you again to Quinthal, guardsmen. You've proven your worth, and the trees shall ever guide you here."

An unseen force washed over Dimitar upon Gar'Ret's pronouncement, as if a breeze not so much rifled by him but through him. His senses sharpened reflexively, the entire forest opening to him. The pathways were well-delineated, and the patterns made sense. No longer did an unyielding woodland wall surround him; instead, the royal proclamation altered the Sun'Din's relationship to him. Dimitar intuitively knew he could now navigate the elven lands without constraint.

The street-side celebration would have continued if Kahled's weariness didn't get the better of him. Even the kingdom's admiration could no longer forestall the group's exhaustion. Elayis instructed her servants to lead him and Kaleela to the royal suites within the castle. Kahled couldn't manage the stairs in his weakened state, and two guards assisted him. Kaleela followed, encircled by her grandparents and uncle, but turned to look back at Dimitar. He caught her gaze and tipped a wave. He longed to follow, but this moment wasn't for him. She needed her family, both immediate and extended. *Gods willing, my time will come.*

Moments later, Bela'Ruhn spoke with Rialyn, and she brought the men to their large, shared suite. The soft, down-filled beds were nearly irresistible, even more so the water steaming in porcelain tubs in the corner. Olaf sucked in his breath at each inch of hot water as he lowered himself, submerging with a long groan. Dimitar eased into his own tub, the water darkening with dirt, soot, and blood, lacerations screaming even as the dull throbbing in his shoulder and ribs receded.

Servants drained the dirty water while adding back fresh, and dipped cloth in clean water pails, washing his limbs. Dimitar thought to protest, having never experienced the luxury of being bathed, but the thought left his mind as soon as gentle, deft hands massaged and cleaned his body. He closed his eyes and sank back into the water, drifting.

An hour later, part of which was spent working a short blade against the stubble built on his jaw, healers entered the quarters and began their ministrations. Salves were worked anew into his muscles and his cuts deep cleaned and bandaged, stirring up fresh pain. He gritted his teeth as they wrapped sturdy cloth around his middle, securing cracked ribs. Although his sword arm throbbed, the healers confirmed it hadn't fully dislocated and no lasting damage would come.

Olaf remained worse for wear from the amputation, unable to keep from shouting out when the healers unwrapped the original bindings around the cauterized stump, freshly oozing.

"Drink this blend," one of the healers offered. "It will dull your pain so we can treat your arm."

"Ya don't have to ask me twice," Olaf panted, tossing back the tangy brew in one gulp.

Only then could he tolerate the cleaning, treating, and re-wrapping of his forearm. After the healers left, Olaf sobbed with great, heaving breaths, staring at his bandaged arm. His tears weren't from physical discomfort, but instead a deep, heartrending ache, a cry that Dimitar hadn't heard since they were kids. Dimitar sat in silence, arm tight around him, as Olaf wept against his shoulder. Eventually, Olaf pushed away to crawl into his own bed and a deep sleep.

Dimitar lay down with a careful stretch, the brown, supple underclothes silky soft, soothed by a strange combination of a gentle breeze from the window and deep aches. Sleep should've come the second his head hit the pillow, but his mind wouldn't stop racing. The healers offered a sleeping tea he declined; perhaps he should've taken it.

His thoughts circled back to Ral. Somehow, Dimitar couldn't find any overwhelming grief associated with his death, as if his heart wanted to convince him Ral still lived. Scrubbing at his closed eyes with the back of his hand, Dimitar scowled, unable to understand how he still sensed that intangible connection with Ral, telling himself to face death's finality.

Frustrated, he gingerly turned over onto his side as his thoughts turned to Kaleela. She'd been with him since Kahled first assigned Dimitar as her guardian. Something more now stemmed from his desire to protect her. As a young boy, he'd catch sight of the fair-haired girl nestled between towering guards marching along the streets. He never dared approach, but something about the little princess gave her a twinge of loneliness that made him want to cup her hand in his.

Dimitar grinned to himself. His boyhood dream had come true, but his smile faded as a new wish surfaced. Like the first, this desire was unspoken, yet growing with every new sun that touched the horizon. They were no longer children, and Dimitar wanted to give more than his friendship.

Kaleela's face lingered in his mind, her green eyes sparkling with far greater brilliance than any hue in Quinthal. Lulled by Olaf's regular, deep breathing, Dimitar drifted off to a dreamless sleep.

39

KAHLED

Kahled took his time venturing through the forest, at once longing for and dreading his destination. A full meal and several healer treatments had rejuvenated him enough to make this walk, although he feigned sleep to slip away from the castle. He needed to do this alone. Twenty-five years had passed since he buried his wife, yet his steps didn't falter, the path a fundamental memory. The clearing came to Kahled faster than he was prepared, but any remaining trepidation disappeared as he stepped into the spacious grove.

Peace filled him as he walked among the pale bark of the *colah'sol* trees. The glow of their leaves sparkled with the lives they memorialized, and Kahled swore the wind carried laughter as it danced through the grove. Searching among the trees, his breath caught as his gaze landed on one in particular. Not yet as large as those around it, the tree illuminated a radiant energy, far outshining any other. Kahled remembered when he last stood before Kaleel's memory tree, freshly blessed, as if it were yesterday.

He stopped an arm's length from the tree, bathing in the emotions that washed over him. Dropping to his knees, he rested his forehead on the tree trunk and lovingly caressed the smooth bark. Tears welled in his eyes as his breath grew ragged.

"Oh, Kaleel..." he managed before grief overtook his ability to speak.

After a time, Kahled sat back on his heels and wiped his cheeks dry with an absent-minded swipe.

"I don't know where to begin," he said in a broken voice, trying in vain to sum up decades of yearning. He fingered the bandages around his wrists as his thoughts found a home, and with a smile he began. "She looks just like you, Kaleel..."

Kahled spoke to the tree, his words coming easier as time drew on. His laughter rang through the trees as they listened to tales of Kaleela's youth; branches creaked as he relived the Reclamation War's dark days; the wind whispered comfort as he spoke of Conrad's lifelong friendship and death.

When he finished, a radiant green leaf drifted from Kaleel's tree and landed on the back of Kahled's hand. He spun the leaf a few times, marveling at its simple beauty. With a sigh, he tucked it into a pocket and once more placed his palm against the trunk. "Thank you, my love."

A twig snapped, drawing his attention away from the memorial tree. Bela'Ruhn stood at the grove's edge, having intentionally made his presence known. Kahled's question was cut off before he even opened his mouth.

"I only just arrived. Whatever you shared, I didn't overhear."

Bela'Ruhn stepped into the clearing and offered Kahled his hand. He accepted the help and pulled himself to a stand. Bela'Ruhn clapped him on the shoulder before regarding the tree.

"One reason we choose this type of tree as the heart keepers is their remarkable hardiness." He looked up at the long trunk. "They withstand the weather like no other, not even wilting in winter's long freeze. Some trees have never lost a leaf, such is their resilience."

At this, Bela'Ruhn looked pointedly at Kahled.

"Just arrived, did you?" Kahled asked, bemused.

Bela'Ruhn tipped his head and grew serious. "Your captivity took more from you than just your strength."

Kahled started to respond, but Bela'Ruhn silenced him with another look. Kahled took a few moments to think on his words and gave a shuddering sigh. "You're right, *Gar'guerr*. My heart isn't in my blade. I've suffered much, and I fear we face more ahead than we're ready for."

If Dimitar and Olaf could witness the look in Kahled's eyes at this moment, they'd see him turn to Bela'Ruhn the same way Blackburn's knights looked to him for guidance.

Bela'Ruhn regarded Kahled. "Then we must remind you of your honor. Before sunrise, meet me in the training quarters. I trust you still remember where they are?"

"Of course, *Gar'guerr*." Kahled brought his fist to his chest.

"I give you tonight to remember your losses. Tomorrow you'll learn to use them for your gain."

With that, Bela'Ruhn put his hand to his chest in salute and marched from the grove. Kahled waited for him to leave before turning to Kaleel's tree marker. Bela'Ruhn spoke the truth: his strength would rebuild not on the pain of his sorrow, but on the love of those surrounding him.

40

DIMITAR

The next few days brought blessed rest, safe within the Sun'Din Forest. Healers visited Dimitar and Olaf's suite at regular times, checking their injuries and supplying fresh wrappings. Servants brought simple, nourishing meals to them, and Dimitar was grateful. He napped, more than he thought possible, and at night took a sleeping tea to send himself into dreamless slumber. Even with that much respite, his body responded with stiffness and fatigue.

Healers had entered the room an hour ago to check on Olaf's arm, escorting him out for further therapies. Dimitar now sat in the early evening light, alone with his thoughts.

He cradled his head in his hands. The hours spent inside the Corrupted cavern had felt like days at the time, yet now blurred together too fast to recall in detail. Emotions waged battle within him, a mix of relief at Kahled's freedom toppled with grief over the loss of a friend taken too soon. At times, involuntary body shudders would bend him in half, especially when he recalled Kaleela on the ground, the threatening blade above her. He felt years older in the time of a fortnight.

A small knock cut Dimitar's thoughts short. Padding over and opening the door, he recognized Kaleela's lithe frame silhouetted by a torch in the hallway. Whatever concerns had been troubling him moments before slipped from his mind as he beckoned her in. Her skin glowed in the candlelight, and an airy gown, silver like moonlight upon a pond, draped off her bare shoulders.

"Kaleela," Dimitar said, and then she hugged him, tight and grounded, sending his senses reeling. His arms encircled her, and Kaleela dipped her head upon his shoulder, melting against him with a slow, soft exhale. Dimitar soared at her body's warmth coupled with the fresh smell of her hair cascading down her back. *Right here. Right here with her in my arms is where I could stay forever.* She nestled against him longer than he expected, yet never long enough, before drawing back—but only enough so that she could look at him. Their bodies still touched, heated and centered around an unspoken gravitation.

"I never had a chance back there to tell you this," she said in a quiet voice, "but thank you."

He raised an eyebrow then winced, touching the bruised cut along his forehead. "For what?"

"For everything," she answered with a little smile. "For convincing me to wait when I only had impulsive thoughts of revenge. I'd be among the bodies of our knights right now, if not for that wisdom."

Dimitar lifted her hand, pressing her palm against his heartbeat.

She stayed in his arms as she continued. "Thank you for defending us not just with your sword, but with your heart. And most of all, thank you for saving my father."

"I fight for Kahled because he's the closest thing to a father I've known." A tide of safety swept past Dimitar's vulnerable thoughts, and he spoke the full truth. "I went to save him, not for duty or honor, but because he means more to me than I can possibly say. And I stood by your side because you..."

Dimitar stopped, searching her face, struck as always by her beauty. He wanted to voice what had built in his heart since long before they faced each other upon the archery range in Blackburn. He held her hand in his own, tracing each finger as he gathered his courage, searching for the right words. Patiently expectant, Kaleela watched his movements before catching his eyes, a smile growing upon her face.

As he opened his mouth, floorboards creaked, followed by a not-so-delicate cough. Olaf leaned on the doorframe.

"Olaf!" Kaleela threw herself into his outstretched arms, almost knocking him back.

"That's m'girl!" Olaf said, lifting her one-armed as if she weighed nothing.

Kaleela squealed as he spun her around, setting her down with a gentleness that belied his size. He placed a lavish kiss upon the back of her hand, then made his way to the cushioned chair next to the fireplace and flopped down. His tiredness, too, was still evident. With a head tilt, Olaf's gaze fell upon Dimitar and appraised him. To the unspoken question, Dimitar gave a brief nod—*I'm better now*—and Olaf winked, turning his attention to Kaleela.

"How does your arm feel?" she asked.

Olaf smiled and flexed his right arm. "It's a wee bit sore from all the axe-swingin'. I'm thinkin' those Corruptors are worse for wear though."

Kaleela smiled back and gave him a look. "I'm being serious, Olaf. How does your *other* arm feel?"

"It's okay, Princess," Olaf replied, faltering. "I mean, I can't believe I lost m'lefty. Bastards. Willem—'scuse me, *Mage* Willem—said it's a couple more sessions with him 'fore he'll call me healed. Couple too many, if ya ask me," he added with exaggerated annoyance, drawing a giggle from Kaleela. Looking over at Dimitar, he said, "Besides, now it'll make our sparrin' more even."

Dimitar scoffed. "You'll have a new excuse for why I whoop your arse, you mean?"

"Them's fightin' words, lad. Ya find yerself lucky I got this beauty of a lady 'twixt you and me, renderin' me helpless with her charms."

"Impotent?" Dimitar asked with mock concern, only for Olaf to lunge out of his chair at him.

Kaleela put out her arms, laughing as they both made a show to come up short. "Behave, you two! Father asked me to bring both of you back to his suite. He wishes to hear our tale."

Dimitar had delivered many messages over the years, but this was the first time he was among the key roles. *It's my story to share this time.* He considered his sword belt and decided to leave it. They were safe here. Dimitar and Olaf followed Kaleela through several passageways, servants bowing in deference as she passed.

Coming to a halt before a large oak door, Kaleela turned toward them, a crease upon her brow. "He's much improved, but the mountains have taken their price."

Olaf and Dimitar both nodded their thanks for the warning as Kaleela knocked. A bustle and low voices issued from inside the room, and one rose louder than the others.

"Come in," Kahled said.

Dimitar held the door open for Kaleela, bracing himself. After Kaleela's words, he expected the worst. Instead, Kahled sat on a chair similar to the one in his room, if not more ornate, with several elven healers tending to him. Kahled appeared noticeably thinner, especially around the face, but bore a healthy flush. Dimitar and Olaf both saluted and dropped to one knee as Kaleela moved to stand at her father's side, resting a hand upon his shoulder.

"There's no need for that," Kahled said to the men, patting Kaleela's hand with affection. "We're all equals here. Besides, I would hear your story, and I'm afraid it'll lose some of the dramatics coming from the floor."

As healers collected various potions and balms, departing with respectful bows, Dimitar pulled up a chair and went over the first days in Blackburn after Kahled departed. When the story introduced Ral and his willingness to guide them, the air in the room grew somber.

"I've noticed his absence and can only assume the worst," Kahled said. No one answered him. "I've jumped ahead in the tale, t'would seem. Please continue."

Kahled listened in respectful silence, but as the story unfolded, he once again interrupted. "You went to Leighton to meet with *whom*?"

Dimitar sat back in his chair, confused by Kahled's disbelief at what he thought was a clear statement. "We went to meet Karn," he repeated. "Why do you ask?"

"No reason, other than... Well, it's just... No one speaks with Master Karn," Kahled said, perplexed. "If not for you telling me this, I wouldn't believe it."

Dimitar described the dragon's ebon fire, his voice heavy with remembrance. Kahled didn't press him, the king's eyes darkening with new understanding at the lengths to which the Overlord had gone to attempt to kidnap his daughter.

Kaleela then took over, detailing their inevitable encounter with the elves and meeting her family for the first time. She spoke with halting words of the Corruptors' attempts to take her and the fight in which Olaf lost his hand. When she got to Kahled's cell, the strength in her voice wavered and her bottom lip trembled.

"I thought you were dead," she managed, her breath hitching. "And I couldn't bear it, not after Conrad was taken from me."

Kahled opened his arms, murmuring calming words as she composed herself.

"I know the rest." He leaned back with a sigh. "You've made our kingdom proud, but you must hear what I've learned during my imprisonment. I'm afraid the real fighting has just begun."

41

KAHLED

K ahled summoned a servant to build a small fire in the fireplace
to rid the room of its nighttime chill and chase the remaining
shadows from the corners.

"The council that called me to attend was nothing more than a
trap," Kahled said, several logs now snapping against flame. "The
Corrupted attacked my company, numerous beyond reckoning. Our
knights fought well but couldn't match their numbers. By the time I
realized they came for me and I put my sword aside, more than half our
force was dead. The knights spared at first were brought to the caverns
and murdered, one by one. I heard each and every one of their deaths."

Dimitar and Olaf hung their heads, and Kaleela murmured a brief
prayer. The volume of their deaths was too much to comprehend.

"At first, I believed it was a matter of time before my turn arrived,"
Kahled said. "However, the longer I lived, the more it became apparent
I was kept alive for a purpose. I wish I knew then what I know now. I
could've avoided much death. They were good men."

Kahled's words trailed off, his thoughts falling into memory. He
tried to picture Blackburn's training grounds with half the knighthood
absent, and failed. The pit of his stomach turned with grief and anger
at the needless loss of life.

"Who did this?" Kaleela asked, her eyes blazing.

"That thing you faced in the Corrupted lair is behind all of this,"
Kahled said, heat creeping into his voice. "I sent Ral away with the
message for you to deliver to the elves because I wanted you safe,
darling girl. And I thought with their backing, I could stand against

the Overlord. I needed to confront him, but as his prisoner, I wasn't on equal ground. I didn't know who ruled over the Corrupted, but I suspected his identity. And I was correct."

Kahled looked at each of them in turn. "The Overlord is High Knight Rippold, First Knight of Tildare."

Shocked silence met his words, as if the room froze.

"That kind of betrayal, not just to the knighthood but to... well, everyone." Dimitar's face twisted in repulsion.

"High Knight Rippold?" Kaleela repeated, recognition dawning. "But how? And for the love of the gods, why?"

"Likely the same reason he held you down with a sword at your neck." Kahled looked over at Dimitar. "Or offered you a blade when he held none. For sheer dominance."

"I could tell something was familiar about him," Kaleela mused. She sat straighter in her chair. "I remember this man. I met him once, didn't I, Father?"

"Aye, a long time ago and much against the wishes of both Conrad and me. Even in High Knight training we didn't trust him. He was skilled in combat, make no mistake about that, but not like us." Kahled grasped for the right word. "He was... vicious, almost feral. He gave no regard to his opponent, striving instead to inflict physical and mental damage. It wasn't enough for Rippold to knock his opponent to the ground; he'd stand over them for humiliation's sake. At times, Bela'Ruhn commanded him to take his blade off a beaten knight's throat, else he would've held it there until the man begged."

"What was he like in the war?" Olaf asked. "'Cause I'm still not understandin' how he turned his back on the High Knights' honor."

"Rippold killed more Corruptors than most of us combined. He *reveled* in the slaughter. The elves weren't as impressed with his ferocity, concerned about what he'd do with complete autonomy. They specifically withheld a kingship. General Bela'Ruhn thought Rippold should continue to report to a higher authority."

"But to fall from High Knight to the lord of the enemies he killed..." Dimitar said, thinking out loud.

"Rippold is obsessed with gaining power and prestige. Before the Reclamation, when we trained to become High Knights, your mother"—here Kahled nodded to Kaleela—"ignored his advances. That she showed very little interest enraged him; he felt entitled to her attention. When she and I fell in love, it antagonized him further. Her decision ultimately united Conrad and me, but it struck Rippold to lose, in his eyes, what was meant for him."

"She would never," Kaleela said, indignant.

Kahled hummed in assent. Kaleel had in fact taken Rippold's measure before any of them. "Rippold was furious at being denied kingship. We anticipated a backlash but didn't see nor hear from him for many years, and I thought he'd come to accept his position. I was proven terribly wrong one afternoon. Rippold arrived at Blackburn Castle unannounced. Conrad was visiting at the time, no coincidence, I'm sure. Conrad wanted me to refuse his presence, but I couldn't dismiss a fellow High Knight. Rippold insisted on holding a private meeting between the three of us. He revealed a plan to overthrow Algernon, the king of Tildare at the time, and asked for our assistance. Said we owed it to him as comrades to instate him in the kingdom's highest position."

"Did ya kick the bastard out on his arse?" Olaf asked.

Kahled's smile flickered to life. "I'm afraid it wasn't that dramatic. We both demanded he give up such notions, and he stormed out. I worked on getting messages to King Algernon and to Quinthal, but within the week, Rippold disappeared. That's when I sent Dimitar to collect tidings for the first time."

The room fell quiet as the group mulled over the tale. Kahled rose from his seat; a deep fatigue crept up on him. "Enough for one night. I admit, I need more rest. Bela'Ruhn thinks waiting for sunrise is a waste of good training time, and the night's getting on."

"Training?" Kaleela asked, surprised. "But you're still under the healers' care!"

"They can heal my body, but not what matters most to me right now." Trying to assure her growing look of concern, he said, "I know my limits."

Kaleela bit her lip and murmured, "Does Bela'Ruhn know your limits or care to respect them?"

"For now, I'll let the healers' elixirs do their purpose. I'll see you on the morrow."

The group rose to leave, bidding him goodnight. Kahled placed a small kiss on Kaleela's head before making his way over to his bed. The door closed, and he ran a hand down his face, weight settling upon his shoulders.

42

KALEELA

K aleela beckoned them down the hall. Olaf offered her his arm and she accepted, again amused at the size of his hand dwarfing her own.

"Ach... a High Knight," he said. "I didn't think they could, well, *do* that kind of thing. Traitor."

"He practiced with them," Kaleela said, thoughtful. She, too, had difficulty expressing her profound disappointment. "He knew Father and Conrad, trained in their brotherhood, and to do this to them..."

Kaleela delved into the memory, stopping at an open balcony at the end of the hallway. The night air was calm, starlight dancing between the tree branches far above. She inhaled deep in her chest, the light scent of wood and balsam fir both sweet and comforting.

"The day Rippold stopped to conference with Father and Conrad, I came upon them by accident; we weren't expecting to receive anyone in chambers that day. He stood as tall as Conrad, and even then, I recognized the lack of the deference he should've shown my fathers, given their kingships."

Kaleela paused against the railing as she looked to the treetops. Dimitar stood beside her, and she leaned against him, grateful for his closeness.

"Rippold took notice of me and came over. He smiled, but it just looked like a strained mouthful of teeth, more like a sneer. He stopped in front of me and stood too close." She held her palm up, illustrating the invasion of her personal space. "I remember Conrad's hand slid to his sword hilt; I caught it just out of the corner of my eye. At the time,

I didn't understand why he'd do that, only, it made me uneasy. I'd just come of age, you see."

The memory's discomfort returned. She wrapped her arms around herself in an unconscious gesture. "He looked me up and down in a way that wasn't proper and said I looked just like my mother, the same way he did in the mountains. That's when Father spoke his name, sharp enough that he turned back to them. He went off with Father and Conrad, and I never saw him again."

Dimitar pushed off from the railing and paced, his face darkening. Kaleela watched him struggle; something deeper cut at him.

"I'm sorry you ever faced him, both then and now," he said, his voice tight. He clenched and unclenched a fist, turning away.

Olaf stepped up to him with a knowing look. "Ya good, lad?"

Dimitar shoved a hand through his hair. "I looked up to the High Knights. My mother told me so many tales of how they're the best among us. Better than my father, and how a man should be."

Kaleela wondered at this, but Dimitar only said, "You know what I'm talking about, Olaf."

"Aye," Olaf said, unusually solemn. "I guess even High Knight trainin' can't erase a man's true nature."

"It's not right. A man should protect the people around him. What Rippold did to you, Kaleela, is no better than what my father did. And where were the other knights to stop him? Men like Rippold, unless someone stands against them, they'll push and push until something breaks."

Dimitar broke off as his voice wavered, pacing again as if to escape his past. Olaf cut in and wrapped his arms over Dimitar's shoulders, leaning down to rest his forehead on his. Grounding. Calming.

"There's nothin' you could've done, little pup," Olaf said, repeating the words under his breath. Dimitar held onto Olaf's forearms, eyes clenched shut as he took a shaky breath followed by a deliberate, slow exhale.

Kaleela let them have a moment, unspoken questions caught in her throat and compassion coursing through her. *What—or who—broke this little boy? How can I tell him that he's one of the bravest men I know?*

Both men accompanied her to her suite in silence, then bid her goodnight. Olaf bowed with a flourish, but Dimitar lingered a moment longer. She met the troubled, fair blue of his eyes as he bowed to her, drawing out the motion as if reluctant to take his leave. Without thought, she reached for him, yearning with an ache in her chest that took her by surprise. He clasped her hand and brought it to his lips, a mark of need and longing.

Inside her room, she held her hand against her chest, his kiss a brand upon her skin.

43

DIMITAR

That night, Dimitar dreamt of the singular moment when Kaleela fell into his arms, and the feel of her, the smell of her, completed him. In his dream, the moment didn't end there. It continued as naturally as if they had coupled countless times already. Gone were their shared fears over what harms would come, anxiety over Kahled's fate, and despair from failure. In its place hummed safety, a balance in the world made all the more true as Dimitar drew her further into willing embrace. Her body responded beneath his caress, and he lowered upon her with a need almost wild but for the tenderness that took over. Dimitar awoke at some point, lightly sheened in sweat and with a new ache issuing forth from his body.

Morning arrived with golden light slanting through the window coverings and a fresh, dew-tinged breeze curling over his face. Birds chirped wild songs in the surrounding trees as Dimitar pulled the blankets aside. Yawning, he appraised the room in daylight, eyeing the intricate knot weavings upon the door and ceiling. Airy and spacious, ancient tree trunks melded into walls and ceilings with sturdiness more akin to stone than bark. A few embroidered tapestries adorned the walls, wafting as the breeze coasted through the room, carrying a sweetness he tasted on the back of his tongue.

Servants had retrieved their saddle belongings the night before, and both Dimitar and Olaf adorned themselves in their guardsmen's tunics, freshly cleaned and mended. Dimitar's pride in his city rose as he slipped the sturdy cloth over his shoulders, noting the three entwined, silver circles marked upon the deep-blue material. The familiar uniform brought him a measure of comfort as well. A knock happened upon their door as Dimitar finished lacing his boots, and a messenger entered.

"Coffee," Olaf croaked, eyes still blurry and his brown hair tousled in every direction.

The servant nodded rather graciously at this before inviting the two men to breakfast with the king and queen. As they readied themselves and exited the room, Dimitar licked his fingers and mimed smoothing down the back of his hair to Olaf, who did so but managed to send his hair spiking in new directions. Dimitar shook his head, smiling. Some things never changed.

Guardsmen stood at the entrance to the main banquet hall and opened the doors for them. Olaf released a low whistle, and Dimitar marveled at the room's sheer extravagance. Large tree trunks lined the walls, covered in airy drapes of colorful silk entwined with gold and silver threads. The table in the center of the room stretched an impressive length but without a seam along its polished surface. Not until the rich aromas of warm bread loaves with apple butter, honeyed meats, and ripe fruits reached him did Dimitar realize he was famished.

"Please have a seat, good men of Blackburn." Elayis smiled, indicating two chairs just beside Gar'Ret. Dimitar and Olaf shared a quick glance, both recognizing the honor of sitting so close to royalty. They touched their chests in unison and bowed before walking the length of the table to the chairs pulled out by servants.

As always, Dimitar was drawn to his purpose: Kaleela. In conversation with Gar'Ret, she sat next to her father, radiant and tranquil. The sight warmed him even as all eyes turned toward him and Olaf, and they made their way into the room.

An'Nadal and Elayis, their serenity permeating the room, graced the head of the expansive table. Kahled, having received leave from Bela'Ruhn's training for the meal, wore signs of working hard to deserve the break. Gar'Ret sat across from him, as did Bela'Ruhn and Rialyn. Several other elves occupied the table, and Dimitar recognized most as council members from the throne room.

"Are you well this morning, Your Majesty? Your Highness?" Dimitar addressed Kahled and Kaleela formally, heartening as she broke into a brilliant smile and nodded her assent.

"Well enough, with thanks to my *gar'guerr* for making it so," Kahled replied, earning a noncommittal grunt from Bela'Ruhn.

Dimitar and Olaf thanked the elven king and queen for their accommodations and healer treatments, and the royals in turn inquired about the men's health and comfort. Olaf heaped a pile of food onto his plate, unmindful of the side-glances he earned at his impressive portion size. Dimitar took a bite of the warm apple pastry, the fresh fruit a song of sweet cinnamon in his mouth. He settled into the conversation at hand, much more at ease this morning compared to his prior visit which, he recalled with clarity, had ended in a diplomatic meltdown.

An'Nadal clinked a spoon on the side of his jeweled goblet. "For the bravery of these humans and the return of one of our own, we shall hold a feast tonight."

A ripple of excitement coursed down the table. An'Nadal then addressed the men. "We welcome you again to our city, guardsmen. I invite you to explore our kingdom and the way of life among our people. Captain Rialyn will accompany you for interpretation."

This time, Dimitar didn't find himself questioning whether the elite warrior hung at their side for guidance or guarding. He accepted the terms as good will and bowed his head in appreciation. While servants cleared the table of dishes, An'Nadal bid everyone a fair morning, and he and Elayis left the room, bringing Kahled and Kaleela with them. Dimitar's spirit fell, as he hoped to spend more time with Kaleela, but said his goodbyes to the royal family and headed out with Olaf and Rialyn.

He stepped into the morning sunlight, the breeze carrying a lightness that infused his body, pulling the cares off his shoulders. The freshness invigorated him, allowing him to take in the famous elven nation with new eyes and curiosity. Rialyn pointed out various homes, storefronts, drinking gardens, and meditation groves. A buzz carried across the streets in anticipation of the feast that evening, and a fine aroma of baked goods filled the air as preparations began. Several elves bowed in greeting to the men as they passed, catching Dimitar and Olaf off guard the first few times.

Yet, Dimitar wasn't immune to the less-than-friendly stares he received from others. He knew better than to ask Rialyn about this affront; as sure as some humans questioned an elf within the Green

Lands, some elves felt likewise about his and Olaf's presence in their city.

When they passed a play area, several children surrounded the two men, their bravery spurred on by their numbers. Small in stature and each breathtakingly beautiful, the young children begged for a story of their daring rescue.

"So there we were, fightin' the ruttin' arseholes with our bare hands," Olaf said, before adding, "if ya pardon m' language," behind his hand to Rialyn as she translated his words too late, her shift in expression a sure giveaway.

The children shrieked and giggled in unison, eyes wide as he continued. Dimitar had seen Olaf intoxicate children with his tales before, and was comforted to know the art of storytelling extended beyond races.

Rialyn led the men onward, calling out a sharp greeting in elvish as they neared the next building. With tall windows thrown wide and billows of smoke issuing from the chimney, there was no mistake what lay within. Dimitar and Olaf eagerly approached as a voice—a woman's voice, Dimitar noted with interest—returned the greeting. They ducked out of the sunshine and into firelight. As his eyes adjusted, Dimitar took in the forge at the center of the back wall and a large, floor-standing vise not too far from it. Along the walls hung iron tools: hammers, tongs, punches, and clamps.

The blacksmith's hammer fell in constant, swift strokes upon the anvil, each strike tossing a small shower of sparks into the air. The smith's long, leather gloves protected her from hand to elbow, but pocks crossed her muscled, umber upper arms from decades of errant particles. A top knot pulled her caramel-brown hair out of the way, and her middle-aged face hardened with concentration and effort, but didn't appear unkind. The blacksmith set the hammer aside and studied the blade's length. With a grim nod, she turned and put the blade in the fire, then gestured for the men to come over as Rialyn propped herself against the wall, crossing her arms.

"Sera'Lan." The elf stripped off one of her gloves and extended her hand. Dimitar clasped her hand, impressed as always at the near-painful strength of a smith's grip.

"Dimitar and—"

"Olaf." Sera'Lan cut him short as she gripped hands with the big man. "I heard your names around."

The elvish accent ran thick in her voice, her broken common challenging to understand. "Not hard to figure out you are *hal'ade* everyone is talking about."

"I hope with favor," Dimitar replied, half-joking.

"Depends on who's speaking." Sera'Lan chuckled, turning away to stoke the fire. Dimitar shared an apprehensive look with Olaf but put on a smile as Sera'Lan lifted the blade, its length glowing with radiant-white heat. "Look at this *belan* and tell me what you see."

Dimitar examined the blade for any distinction as it dulled to a screaming red. Wider than most—a broadsword in the making—it appeared as any other blade fresh from a fire. The small edges became clearer as the metal cooled. *Not just edges, but letters.*

"Runes," Olaf said, as if reading his mind.

"With each layer of iron I fold into *belan*, I strike *el'van* runes. Some for strength of bearer and others for strength of *belan*." Sera'Lan returned the blade to the kiln, hefting the bellows before turning to the men. "I am working on twelfth fold of iron."

"This must've taken you months to forge." Dimitar's eyes widened with admiration.

Sera'Lan laughed, a deep, rolling wave of delight. "The runes take months to strike, years to set before magic works into steel."

"You've been workin' on this one piece for years?" Olaf asked, incredulous.

"I make many *belans*, many orders for the kingdom," Sera'Lan replied. "When I have some time, I do this one. Off and on... two hundred fifty years."

Dimitar's jaw dropped. Centuries dedicated to the craftsmanship of a single weapon from a single hand. Elves lived a hundred years for each human decade, and Dimitar couldn't quite wrap his mind around the scale of time involved in a singular project like this.

"Who is it for?" he asked, unable to keep the wonder from his voice.

"Ah, now there is a story. You want I tell?" Sera'Lan glanced at Rialyn, who gave an almost imperceptible nod. Something unsaid hinted in that gesture, but Dimitar turned his attention back to Sera'Lan. "Take a seat and let me finish next striking. Then you will hear tale."

Sera'Lan took the blade from the flames and struck the iron, now turning to rippled steel as she completed this fold. Dimitar and Olaf sat at the table in the corner of the forge, watching the elf with new respect. A few more spark showers lit the air, and Sera'Lan regarded the blade before setting it aside on the anvil to cool. She dipped the tongs in a water barrel, the hiss of stream a tremendous burst, and laid them next to the blade. She then removed her long gloves and thick apron, setting them on a workbench beside the anvil.

"*Gar'guerr* Bela'Ruhn once had a student like no other. An *el'van* large of size and power," Sera'Lan said, sitting across from the men. She reached over Dimitar's shoulder and grabbed a waterskin, taking a big gulp. "He learned with speed and even quicker made perfect. Bela'Ruhn had an *eir'guerr*"—Sera'Lan took another drink from the skin, face scrunched as she searched for the common word—"a second leader?"

"A captain," Dimitar supplied. "Like Rialyn?"

Sera'Lan gestured at her. "Aye, that is the word. This *el'van guerr* is very strong, full of skill and power. Never anyone see a *guerr*—a warrior, aye?—like him before. Bela'Ruhn very proud. He comes to me one day with order for special *belan*. Tells me he wants runes in each fold. Does not care how long it takes me. Does not care how much it costs him. I make his other *belans*, so he trusts me. That all he tells me, but I know: this *belan* is for the *eir'guerr*. Too heavy for anyone else."

Dimitar considered this last statement. Sera'Lan claimed the sword was too heavy, yet moments ago had lifted the blade in its raw steel form like it weighed nothing. Dimitar had learned long ago there were two types of people you never challenged to a contest of strength: woodcutters and blacksmiths.

"So. I start *belan* and Bela'Ruhn's *eir'guerr* continues training. He becomes quicker, stronger. Bela'Ruhn plan to make *eir'guerr* into a *gar'guerr* after him, a great honor. But first he must prove himself. *Gar'guerr* Bela'Ruhn tells him to watch outside Sun'Din with guards. Watch from the trees for enemies. *Eir'guerr* not happy with order. Not good enough for him. But he goes to make the general happy.

"While out there, he sees small group of *hal'ide*. Some humans. They come running from something, other *hal'rinn*."

Dimitar and Olaf exchanged a glance at this, and Olaf mouthed what they both were thinking: mercenaries.

"They ask *eir'guerr* if they can hide in trees, in Sun'Din. If *el'van* can help. *Eir'guerr* refuses. *Hal'ide* beg him, but that bad choice. *Eir'guerr* already insulted with guard duty. To then bring them into our great forest? No.

"He decides to help but not like *hal'ide* ask. He helps them with his *belan*. At first *hal'ide* fight back but are no match for *eir'guerr*. He kills them, and not just the men. Some guards come to tell Bela'Ruhn. He goes to stop his *eir'guerr*."

Sera'Lan took another sip from the skin before hanging it back on the wall. Dimitar wasn't sure what to make of the blacksmith's story. He knew the age-old contempt elves had over humans, but an outright slaughter? His stomach twisted to think upon it.

"Bela'Ruhn is outraged at *eir'guerr* and demands his *belan*. *Eir'guerr* is in *anist'histar*—in blood rage, aye? He turns on the general. He catches himself, his *belan* in front of Bela'Ruhn's face." Sera'Lan held her thumb and forefinger apart to show how close the sword came to Bela'Ruhn.

Olaf whistled, which made Sera'Lan smile.

"What did General Bela'Ruhn do to the *eir'guerr*?" Dimitar asked, the elvish word awkward on his tongue.

"Ultimate punishment. He cut *eir'guerr* ears and sent him from Sun'Din. He no longer *el'van*. He now diminished to *hal'ide*."

"Your ultimate punishment is to make an elf look like a human?" Dimitar frowned, incredulous and insulted at the same time.

Sera'Lan had the self-awareness to look chagrined. "'Tis a custom from ancient times."

"Then why are ya still makin' the sword for him?" Olaf asked.

"Not for *eir'guerr* anymore. For Bela'Ruhn now. He wants *belan* so he remembers not to trust so easily. To remember his shame."

More questions came to mind, but Dimitar caught Rialyn's expression by the doorway, one that indicated she wouldn't permit much more of this tragedy to unfold. Perhaps she regretted allowing Sera'Lan to tell them in the first place.

Dimitar dared another question. "What was the *eir'guerr's* name?"

"Vin'Saar," Sera'Lan said, a small shiver visibly running down her back.

Dimitar narrowed his eyes. "He wasn't just cruel to the humans, was he?"

Before Sera'Lan answered, a voice hailed across the street, calling for Rialyn. She stepped out to receive the messenger, and Dimitar and Olaf followed as Sera'Lan returned to her work. They thanked Sera'Lan for allowing them to watch her craftsmanship of the blade, then pushed back the heavy leather door covering, stepping into the waning light.

As Rialyn spoke in rapid elvish with the messenger, Dimitar looked around the streets and inhaled the fresh air, catching a familiar smell for an instant. The fragrance's identity lay on the tip of his tongue, yet he couldn't place it.

"So, lad," Olaf said, interrupting Dimitar's thoughts as they waited for Rialyn to finish speaking with the messenger, "are ya gonna stand around thinkin' of her all day?"

"What?"

"That smile ya gave just now. I know that look. Yer fallin' for her." Olaf's smile brimmed with wicked teasing.

"What are you talking about?" For a second, Dimitar thought Olaf paired him with Rialyn. But before Olaf answered, Dimitar remembered what the scent reminded him of. How could he forget? Last night, when Kaleela hugged him, her hair carried the freshest, most intoxicating scent. The air in the Sun'Din, perfumed with hundreds of different flowers and trees, only hinted at the refreshing and wondrous essence Dimitar caught in Kaleela's embrace. The whiff nonetheless contented him enough for Olaf to notice.

"I'm not falling for her," he mumbled, kicking a stone with the toe of his boot.

Olaf responded with a roar of laughter and threw his arm around Dimitar's shoulders, eschewing any and all subtlety.

"Don't think I haven't noticed, lad. Who'd a' thought you'd set yer heart on a princess, though. She's a mighty fine woman." Olaf glanced down at Dimitar, growing serious. "And yer a mighty fine man, deservin' of such a beauty as her."

A small, self-conscious smile brimmed on Dimitar's lips. His mind's eye recalled the fire in Kaleela's eyes, as much when she didn't get her way as when she sighted an arrow. Her faith in his strength was like a calling that compelled him to answer. And most of all, her smile upon him, compassionate and enchanting, ignited his heart.

I can't deny it.

Ducking closer to Dimitar's ear, Olaf lowered his voice. "And if ya ask me, which ya didn't, I think she might like ya too."

Dimitar pulled back in surprise. The big man held up his hand.

"You'll need to trust me on this one, Dim. I've had my share of looks o' love from women, and she's full of 'em your way."

A thousand questions ran through Dimitar's mind at the same time, and they came out in a stammer of "whens" and "whats." Olaf laughed and gave Dimitar a shove, sending him stumbling a few steps.

"The sun's sinkin'. Quit yappin' and pick up yer feet," he said with a grin. "In an hour or so, you'll see for yerself."

"Guardsmen." Rialyn's sharp tone drew both men's attention. Dimitar knew a voice of command when he heard it, and tried to push Olaf's words out of his mind as the elite warrior hurried over to them. "We must return to the castle now."

"For the feast tonight?" Olaf asked, but Rialyn shook her head.

"Not yet." She turned and set a quick pace down the pathway. The two men hurried to catch up with her. "I will take you to him first. He's back."

44

KALEELA

Inside the castle, Kaleela stood beside King An'Nadal and Queen Elayis as they introduced her to the court. Along with her father and the royal family, she mingled with the councilors and esteemed elven families throughout the Sun'Din Forest. Elves filled both the outside courtyards as well as the main banquet area, their curiosity piqued by her, sole grandchild of the king and queen. Silk banners hung upon the walls softened the rooms, and a harper plucked a mellow song. Kaleela relaxed yet caught herself searching out her father across the room, reassuring herself he was there; he was safe.

A light touch upon her arm drew her attention.

"I'd like you to meet someone," Gar'Ret offered, leading her to a quieter spot.

Kaleela glanced back at her father once more, but forced herself to shake off the habit and focus on a woman of striking beauty who gazed out an open window. She turned as they approached, her hair a rich chestnut brown, rare and prized among the fairer elves. Her sun-kissed golden features were smooth and flawless, with a kindness glowing about her eyes as she reached for Gar'Ret.

"I present my lady and wife, Aurie." Gar'Ret weaved an arm around the woman's full-figured waist.

"My honor to meet you, my lady." Kaleela curtsied yet held back her surprise, thrilled to learn of her new relative. *I didn't even know I had an uncle, for that matter.*

"Welcome, *mil'calah*," Aurie replied with unexpected warmth and familiarity as she placed her hand against her chest to mirror the elvish endearment: *my heart.* "We're honored to have Kaleel's child among us at last. You look so much like your mother; 'tis something you know well enough by now, aye?"

Kaleela smiled and nodded, enjoying Aurie's gentle friendliness. "You knew my mother, then?"

"Kaleel was as dear to me as a sister of my own blood. I cherish the memories of my time with her. Oh, it fills my heart, you standing here today!"

Although old enough to be Kaleela's own mother, Aurie's true age hid behind youthful features and a childlike enjoyment with those around her. Time had yet to weigh upon her the way it did Kahled in his late-middle-age years. Elven centuries passed like human decades, and Gar'Ret and Aurie looked like peers, not Kaleela's elders.

Her open kindness drew Kaleela in, but her next words stole her breath away. "I still have some things that belonged to your mother. Would you like to see them?"

"Aye." Kaleela's heart thumped in her chest. "Very much so."

Aurie slid out of Gar'Ret's embrace after a quick kiss and wove her arm around Kaleela's waist, yet another unexpected gesture of familiarity. Slipping out of the main hall, the two women traversed the castle hallways before entering Aurie and Gar'Ret's suite.

Kaleela paused inside the entrance, taking in the expansive chambers. Like her suite, the large rooms contained several pieces of ornate wood furniture. An encircling balcony terrace peeked beyond gossamer drapes toward the back of the room. Yet unlike her own visitor's suite, this one evoked a personal intimacy, evidenced by paintings of Gar'Ret and Aurie hung upon a wall, a line of bookshelves holding favorite volumes, and various knickknacks displayed on shelves. This space held its own welcoming feeling of home.

Aurie knelt beside a cedar chest on the far side of the main room. The thick wood and black iron hinges looked heavy, but she raised the top without effort. She sifted through the items, lifting one out. "Here, my little dearest. 'Tis a portrait of your mother and Gar'Ret when they were children, not yet of age."

Kaleela cupped the small watercolor in the palm of her hand. The miniature painting was exquisite, completed by a careful hand at such a small scale without losing any of the color and vibrancy in the two solemn, pale-haired children looking back.

"These are letters your father wrote, when they were courting." Aurie handed over a bundle of thick parchment, tied with a black satin ribbon.

Kaleela recognized her father's handwriting right away, the elongated letters slanted and steady.

"I considered sending these to Kahled when I found them, some time after your mother passed," Aurie continued, shifting her long, dark hair over one shoulder. "I wasn't sure he'd find comfort in them, though. So, I waited and am glad I did; now you can keep them. Don't be shy to look upon them, as these words sealed your father's love in Kaleel's heart. Your mother would want you to understand how much they loved one another."

A lump formed in the back of Kaleela's throat. These items were priceless to her: a glimpse of her mother as a child, a peek into her parents' newfound love. Already Kaleela's connection to her mother strengthened its fragile ties. The feelings warmed her and stoked a fierce ache at the same time.

Aurie talked on, not unmindful of the tears brimming in Kaleela's eyes. She caressed Kaleela's arm, a loving gesture, as she spoke. "I have a few of her clothes, saved in my boudoir. They're all yours now. And your mother's wedding dress! The queen brought in a dozen hands to complete the embroidery alone, with thread spun from the richest of the Valpurga gold mines. She and Kahled together, well, 'tis no wonder they made such a beautiful young woman as yourself. Oh, she loved you so much, Kaleela, as she carried you in her body."

Kaleela's voice lowered, thick with emotion. "Thank you for your words and all these memories. I can't tell you what it means to me."

"I know." Aurie drew her into a hug.

Kaleela clung to her, the lushness of Aurie's round body a primal embrace. Aurie rocked her in a slight motion, soothing and lovely. Kaleela's head rested against her chest, and her ear cupped the steady rhythm of Aurie's heart. Had the beat of Kaleel's heart thrummed against Aurie's when they hugged as sisters-met decades ago? Was this the echo of her mother's heart, a memory from the womb, her first and only connection to her?

Is this what it's like to be mothered?

Aurie tilted her head at a knock at the door.

"*Sul'ren,*" she said, loud enough to be heard across the expansive suite.

A guard entered the room and bowed. "Sorry to interrupt," he said in broken common, "but Princess is to come with me."

"For what purpose?" Aurie replied, coming to a stand.

"Not you, my lady. Her."

"Is my father all right?" Kaleela blurted out, instantly ashamed of the foolishness from her hasty reaction, color flushing her cheeks.

Aurie gave her a reassuring smile.

"I am asked to bring you to your companion. He is injured but returned."

Kaleela's thoughts tumbled anew—had Dimitar and Olaf fallen into trouble in the city?

"Go, *mil'calah.* I'll have your mother's things brought to your room."

She returned Aurie's sweet smile and followed the guard out, the lightness of her step growing heavier as the guard's message settled past the warmth of Aurie's embrace.

"What happened? Which man returned?" Kaleela asked in elvish as they crossed a long corridor.

The guard didn't break his stride, answering her over his shoulder instead. "The cloaked one."

Kaleela stopped in her tracks, which earned her an exasperated glance.

"Come, my lady." He continued in elvish since she understood the words well enough. "His room is just ahead."

Kaleela hurried her steps to catch up, sure she didn't misunderstand and yet not daring to hope. They headed down a short flight of stairs and came to a door graced with carved runes. Herbs and an underlying smell of soaps permeated the air, the scents growing in strength as the guard opened the door for her.

Two familiar faces turned as she entered, Dimitar's smile lighting his eyes, albeit strained. Olaf also broke into an anxious grin before moving to the side, revealing a low bed. Several elven healers circled the battered man on the bed, deftly avoiding the multitude of bandages soiled anew with fresh blood. A mage murmured an incantation with focused intent, his gaze never leaving the body. Willem stood at the foot of the bed, directing the healers in a low tone, layers of bandages still swaddling his hands.

Ral's eyes flitted beneath his lids, and a fevered sweat dampened his brow. Sheets covered his waist for modesty's sake; he'd been stripped of his cloak, tunic, and leathers. Long-faded scars suffered at the hands of goblin slavers lined his exposed skin. Combined with the bloodied bandages, injuries riddled him from head to toe.

"Ral," Kaleela cried as she stepped forward.

In unison, the healers chastised her with stern looks and warning shushes for breaking the silence, and Dimitar raised a finger to his lips. She reached out to take Ral's hand, to touch him and his warmth to prove he was alive, but a healer intervened, holding up her hands to block the interruption. Dimitar elbowed Olaf in the side and pointed at the door, nodding at Kaleela to head back into the hall. She looked at Ral one more time, unresponsive upon the bed and surrounded by busy, silent healers. Her heart went out to him.

He looks so damaged. Gods, what this poor man has endured.

When the door closed, Dimitar turned to Kaleela and pulled her into a tight embrace. "He's alive."

"How is this possible? When did he return, and how?" She let Dimitar's words push out her pain for Ral, instead focusing on his recovery, holding on to life.

"As we left the Eastern Mountains, Willem requested a few of Bela'Ruhn's elite guards to check if Ral survived."

"Why would he do such a thing when there was"—she paused, guilt seeping in—"no hope?"

"Somethin' about how he sensed Ral still livin'," Olaf said, clearly at odds with the explanation Willem had left them. "His life energy could still be read or somethin' like that. Unnatural what these mages pick up on, I say."

"Well, it turns out he was right, thank the gods," Dimitar said. "They found Ral dragging himself through a tunnel toward the entrance. Barely alive, but breathing for all that. The guards rode as fast as they could but had to stop often to nurse the wounds. They arrived a few hours ago."

"And the healers have been on him without stop." With a grimace, Olaf added, "At first they were afraid Ral was tainted."

"Tainted?"

"Aye, with Corruptor essence. It's not a pretty sight from what I hear, Princess. Somethin' like that, it turns a man, fouls him. There ain't turning back once it's been forced on ya and takes hold, either."

"But that wasn't the case," Dimitar jumped in, catching Kaleela's horrified look. "Ral's cut up bad, real bad. He's lost a lot of blood, has burns on his body, and is feverish, so they haven't ruled out infection yet. The healers are working their craft on him, you can trust that."

"Willem says he needs undisturbed sleep for hope of recovery, and they're workin' a magic to keep him slumberin' for now."

"You should've seen what they did to Olaf when he came bursting in with a roar," Dimitar said as Olaf shrugged, not looking very apologetic.

Kaleela absorbed their words, the message almost too much to comprehend for all the "whys" and "hows." She turned to Dimitar and searched his face. "Will he be all right?"

Dimitar's grin faded. "Willem says Ral must be gifted by the gods to still be breathing. His injuries are..." He trailed off, searching for the right words.

"Extensive," Olaf finished.

"But the healers are making progress. They said because his body hasn't given in yet, there's a good chance they'll heal him in time. They just don't know how much time he needs."

Kaleela looked back at the door, tempted to peek in again.

As if reading her mind, Dimitar said, "There's nothing we can do except leave the healers to their trade. I already asked, and they just told me to be quiet. We need to have faith in them and Willem—and in Ral. He's still fighting, by the gods."

"I'll thank Willem later at the feast," Kaleela said, cupping her hands to her chest. "If not for him, Ral would've crawled out of those tunnels only to die on the threshold."

"Speaking of the feast," came a soft voice down the hall. Aurie approached with a sympathetic smile for Kaleela. "I'll escort you to chambers for preparation. Our servants await you."

A guardswoman alongside her gestured at Dimitar and Olaf, indicating they were to follow her, and the group parted ways once more as the red-orange hues of sunset struck across the sky, not dissimilar to the color of Ral's now tattered cloak.

45

DIMITAR

"They couldn't even match m'eyes," Olaf grumbled.

An enormous, gilt mirror leaned against the wall in their room, brought to them along with their custom attire and silver bowls of water, soap, and grooming blades to freshen themselves up. The men's Blackburn tunics were set aside for the night as they prepared for the elven celebration, donning their new finery. Tailors had sewn a rich, embroidered summer dress coat, pants, and linen undershirt in forest green for Olaf. His sleeve ended just below his amputation in a neat tuck, yet looked no less grand.

Dimitar finished wrapping a wide satin belt several times around his middle and knotted it. Vines in dark thread weaved a pattern across his dress coat, the color of a deep lake. His hair just kissed the top of his shoulders, except for a lock that insisted on sweeping his forehead, still bruised and scarred from the Overlord encounter.

"Well, they got the sparkle in mine just fine." Dimitar said with a smirk. "I guess they didn't have shitty brown in their shop." Standing next to Olaf, their reflection in the mirror, Dimitar gave his most charming smile. "See?"

They admired their appearance together. Caught between the past and present, memories of their childhood orphan history together shimmered beneath the rugged, handsome looks of manhood as Dimitar met Olaf's gaze in the reflection. The moment ended when his words sunk in, and Olaf took a backward swipe with his elbow, which Dimitar ducked.

IN THE NAME OF HONOR

"Like hells you say," Olaf muttered, adjusting his robing in the mirror. "Yer lucky it's tight around m'arms."

A knock stopped Dimitar's retort, but he still laughed out loud as he headed over to open the door.

"Good evening."

"Sire." Dimitar was taken aback to find Kahled, and bowed, as did Olaf. He'd assumed a guard had come to summon them as usual. Kahled still looked tired, as if he carried some burden upon his frame. Dimitar's gaze was met steadily enough beneath the thin crown of gold-carved vines. "How do you fare, my lord?"

"I arrived here as an old, brittle man from my imprisonment. My recuperation came in the form of training with General Bela'Ruhn. 'Tis a bitter, if necessary, medicine to take."

Dimitar and Olaf chuckled in sympathy.

"Shall we, then?"

The men followed Kahled out of the room where Rialyn waited off to the side, attending to him. She nodded at the men in a gesture that reminded Dimitar of Bela'Ruhn's stiff formality. She'd changed out of the elite guard uniform and into evening wear, but not a gown. Instead, she donned a tight, sleeveless leather vest topping even tighter leather pants, with arm bracers to match. The darkened leather was simple and protective, supple enough to bend around muscled curves. Her double swords bowed against her body, hanging on her back and hip, a natural complement to her form. Rialyn presented as a constant warrior, just like Bela'Ruhn.

Olaf moved to grandly offer Rialyn his arm in accompaniment. She raised an eyebrow as if to say, "You must be joking," and fell in step next to Kahled without a single word.

"Well, that just might be a first," Dimitar murmured in commiseration to Olaf, who looked like he would nurse the rejection all night. They both turned their attention to Kahled as he addressed them.

"We're headed to dine with the royal family and those who mark tonight as a celebration," he said, coaching them on the expected etiquette. "Many toasts will be offered, but few words. The elves don't need to recite the great deeds you've performed. The proof is in the result, as we stand here before them. They'll salute you, and you shall return the gesture; to do otherwise risks insult."

Kahled paused, and Dimitar noted with some alarm that the king needed to catch his breath.

The mountains took their toll.

Kahled gathered himself and lifted his arm out to Rialyn. She slipped her arm through his, and they continued on once more. Behind them, Olaf gesticulated in silent disbelief, mouthing wounded pride, but Dimitar shushed him. He couldn't tell if Kahled meant to cover his weariness with the gesture or worse, needed to lean upon a sturdy figure.

But Kahled's voice remained steady. "Best remember to salute each toast to you, else you'll find yourselves on the wrong side of Bela'Ruhn's favor. Then again, I don't believe I've ever seen a right side to the general's favor."

The men laughed aloud, and Dimitar could've sworn Rialyn shared a surreptitious wink with Kahled as he patted her hand.

She led them out a castle side door and along pathways lined with luminaries, the glow matching evening's last light as the first stars peeked through the treetops. The night entered on a breeze, sweet and refreshing against the tinge of bonfire smoke it carried. A short set of stone steps led them to a large clearing, lined with chairs and tables on one side and musicians assembled in another corner. Lanterns hung from tree boughs, lighting the area with soft, golden hues. One raised table served as the head of the clearing with reserved seats for the royal family, council, and honored guests.

Rialyn led the men there, and Dimitar appreciated that she respectfully seated Kahled before taking her own chair. No sooner did they sit than servants set out food platters and filled their cups with wine. Dimitar didn't recognize half the fare offered but helped himself anyway. Mouthwatering aromas rolled off fresh herbs and sauces that Dimitar swore he could taste by smell alone.

"Where's the meat?" Olaf whispered.

None of the usual venison or bird that graced Blackburn's plates was present. Instead, the meal consisted of vegetables, sauces, breads, cheeses, fruits, and sweets. Yet after the first bite, Dimitar didn't think another moment on what might've been missing. The food's freshness was unparalleled, the flavors expertly matched, and the wine cool and honeyed.

The music timbre changed, and a murmur passed through the guests. Looking up from his meal, Dimitar wiped his mouth with the cloth napkin before laying it aside, already forgotten.

Bela'Ruhn stepped into the courtyard with a practiced survey of the area. He marked where Dimitar and Olaf sat—the human outsiders—but the general was the least of Dimitar's focus. The royal family entered next, with Kaleela between Gar'Ret and a chestnut-haired woman, arms entwined and heads tilted in conversation. Behind them followed King An'Nadal and Queen Elayis, also arm in arm.

Dimitar's gaze fixed on Kaleela alone as he rose to stand along with those in the courtyard. The music and chatter of the party faded as all his senses focused on her.

Gone was her leather armor and the riding wear he'd grown accustomed to. Instead, bare arms peeked from gossamer sleeves. The long gown formed around her waist before flaring out, ombre blue like the evening sky's first darkening. An untold number of tiny jewels threaded up the gown and sparkled in the candlelight. A large gemstone came to rest above the swell of her breasts, revealed by the cut of the bodice. Several small braids and flowers were plaited throughout her hair, loose and curled. A thin, intricate headpiece of silver and gold marked her as elven royalty.

Kaleela met Dimitar's gaze evenly as she approached the main table, and a rosy pink tinged her cheeks as he continued to stare while she took her seat. Not until a rough tug pulled on his arm did he break his gaze. Olaf motioned in between forkfuls for him to sit. He was the only one left standing, earning some curious looks from those around him. Blushing, he dropped into his seat, grateful as Olaf passed him a goblet, taking a gulp.

"Lad," Olaf said with exaggerated patience. "Did ya not hear a thing King Kahled told us? Yer manners appall me, they really do."

Olaf lifted his goblet higher and saluted an elf across the clearing who'd raised his glass in toast to them. Dimitar did the same, earning a nod from the elf, before taking a more measured sip as Kaleela settled between Kahled and the woman.

The elf king and queen remained in the middle of the courtyard until all were seated; meals and conversations came to a stop. An'Nadal and Elayis turned as one to face their guests, and all around the gathering, goblets raised in utmost respect. A musician struck a long, low note on a pipe, joined in by a string, a drumbeat, and then a woman's clear voice. With a hint of a smile on her aged features, Elayis stepped into An'Nadal's arms, their formal dance marking the start of the celebration.

Intricate steps unfolded, and they quickened the pace as if to defy their elder age. An'Nadal and Elayis fixated on one another, a private connection for all to witness. The effect drew Dimitar deeper into their dance. The song called to him in a language he didn't know, the melody haunting but for the lift in his spirits as the woman's voice soared. The elf king and queen shared their intensity with one another, yet the emotion behind their dance was for the listeners to interpret themselves.

The complex dance came to its inevitable end, with An'Nadal and Elayis stepping ever closer and slower to one another, spinning together at last as one before coming to a stop, their mutual respect tangible. Strong applause followed as they took their seats at the table, and An'Nadal motioned for his guests to continue with the feast.

Eating and conversation began once more as the musicians struck a new tune, notes lifting high into the air, seeking the next dancers. The elves in the courtyard came alive along with the new song, partners exchanging hands in a circular dance similar to those across the Green Lands.

"I think I'll try m'hand at this one," Olaf announced, downing his goblet after saluting a pair of elves across the clearing.

With a whoop as the music picked up tempo, he dropped into the dance and swept up an elven woman, twirling her among the others. Dimitar grinned into his cup but held back from joining his friend. Scanning the crowd, he spotted Kaleela among the dancers, joyful in the arms of a young nobleman and then alongside the next elf as they switched around the dance floor.

Dimitar yearned to receive that smile, to bring her the unbridled happiness she deserved after their trials in the Eastern Mountains. He struggled with jealousy that settled in his gut, telling himself he was unreasonable and out of line even as instincts demanded he sweep her into his arms.

Damn these feelings, heavy in his chest and jangling his nerves so that his thoughts muddied, worrying about everything and nothing all at once. He pushed back his chair, seeking distraction. A few tables down, Kahled settled back in his chair, arms crossed over his chest. Despite the revelries playing out, his forehead furrowed and his jaw locked in a tight grimace. He raised his glass in toast to those around him, but Dimitar could tell his mind wasn't upon the act.

Crossing the distance between them, Dimitar took the empty seat next to Kahled. He raised his glass to his king, and only then did Kahled draw back to the present. A moment's pause, and Kahled clinked his goblet against Dimitar's in a decidedly human gesture before taking a drink.

"My lord, if I may ask, what bothers you?"

Instead of answering, Kahled gazed across the courtyard at his daughter with fatherly pride. "I've always known Kaleela as my child, yet now more than ever, she seems so much more like her mother's daughter. If I could keep her carefree and without sorrow, I would. Tomorrow can wait."

Seeing the concern settle upon Dimitar's face, Kahled exhaled with a huff. "For now, the elves have proclaimed a night of merrymaking in our honor. Such a thing hasn't happened since the High Knight celebratory feast. 'Tis an honor indeed for us mere humans," he said dryly, and Dimitar chuckled. "Though a shame Ral couldn't be here."

"He deserves the praise as much as any of us, if not more. I hear he's responding well to the elven healers. They say his fever broke."

"This is good news. We'll need him again before long." Kahled became distracted in thought once more. Dimitar grew solemn at these words, but Kahled cut any questions off. "Tonight is cause for celebration. Do not spare your time on a tired old man."

"But sir—"

"Save your words, Dimitar," Kahled said with a wave of his hand and an uplift in tone. "Go; be merry. I order it."

Dimitar hesitated, then nodded, and Kahled clapped him on the back. No sooner did he leave than Bela'Ruhn approached and took the seat next to Kahled, striking up conversation in low tones. Dimitar sighed, torn between the shadow over Kahled and the laughter of those in celebration.

The musicians paused in their set and Olaf strolled over, somewhat out of breath.

"Olaf, you've outdone yourself this time." Dimitar perched on the edge of the table and offered a fresh wine glass to his friend. "Did you manage to dance with absolutely all of the available ladies?"

Olaf wiped his forehead, kicked back his drink like his life depended on it, then turned to Dimitar with a delighted grin.

"Absolutely," he answered, and Dimitar laughed. "The ladies, the bachelors, even our beauty of a princess."

Dimitar raised an eyebrow, then Olaf's eyes widened. He dropped a heavy hand on Dimitar's shoulder. "No, lad, I take it back. There's still one who owes me a dance."

"Oh?" Dimitar followed Olaf's line of sight. "Oh, no. You aren't serious. Tell me you're not serious. I wouldn't joke with that one if I were you."

"Jokin'? Who said anythin' about jokin'?" Olaf said a bit too loudly as he drank again.

Dimitar shook his head at his impossible friend. Glancing over at the tall warrior, Dimitar couldn't picture Rialyn being asked to dance by any man.

"Why don't you take a pass this time." Dimitar knew full well Olaf had no intention of listening to him.

Olaf opened his mouth to retort, but the words sat unused in his mouth. He gaped at the elite warrior as she headed out to the middle of the dance floor, the musicians beginning anew. Her partner met her there, gazes fixed on one another as lovers reunited, and the two women intertwined arms. Swaying to the slow song, Rialyn brushed the woman's long hair off her neck, planting a kiss on the swell of her throat. The elven woman smiled fondly at Rialyn as she rested her hands low and familiar upon the warrior's hips.

"Well. All right then." Olaf ran a hand through his untamed hair and exhaled from deep within his chest.

As one, Dimitar and Olaf tossed back their drinks. Rialyn and her partner swayed against one another with casual familiarity, their hands caressing one another, intimate and joyful. Olaf sunk into a seat at the table, settling in.

"I'm afraid this just isn't your night, my friend."

"Ach no, lad, I'm good." Olaf popped a morsel in his mouth and raised his goblet to salute his friend. "As long as I have yer pretty eyes on me, it'll be m'best night ever. Eh? Lad?"

Olaf's goblet was left hanging in empty air. Like the Tempest River ever drawn to the waters of Lake Lachlann, Dimitar's attention wandered to Kaleela once more. She danced and laughed with those around her, her happiness warmer than the hundreds of lanterns lighting the courtyard.

Olaf gained his attention with a poke in his side. "Dim, that's the biggest look of longin' I've ever seen. Don't tell me ya haven't danced with her yet."

Dimitar started to give an innocent response, then shrugged his shoulders in defeat. He couldn't deny it any longer.

As if reading his very thoughts, Olaf added, "Ya can't keep hidin' it, m'boy."

"Best night ever," Dimitar echoed as he pushed himself off the table edge and entered the dance, making his way to Kaleela through curious stares, some friendly, some impassive. With deliberate intent, he crossed the clearing to where Kaleela stepped in gentle rhythm alongside Gar'Ret. She paused when she caught sight of Dimitar, eyes bright with some emotion he couldn't yet place. Her unreadable composure, so much like that of the elves around her, threw him off guard, at a loss for words as Gar'Ret turned expectantly to him.

"You've honored me with this dance, *mil'ine*," Gar'Ret said to Kaleela after a moment's pause; more like a lifetime to Dimitar. "I must now ask the same honor from my own lady wife."

With that, Gar'Ret graciously stepped away from the pair, leaving Dimitar and Kaleela to face one another. Surrounded by dancers yet alone at last, Kaleela met his gaze with a smile lighting the corners of her eyes. Dimitar stepped forward and extended his arm to her, and she blushed under the weight of his gaze.

"Kaleela, you look more beautiful than anyone I've ever seen." Even as he spoke the words, they didn't do her justice. "Please honor me with this dance."

She placed her hand atop his arm, stepping beside him in rhythm with the thrum of the music. She cast a glance at him from under long lashes. "Would it surprise you to know I've waited all evening for you?"

Her question landed like a jolt, and for the first time, Dimitar dared to hope her affection matched his. "Yes," he answered truthfully.

"'Tis no matter." Kaleela stepped closer to him, her words soft and vulnerable. "I know you'll always come for me."

And with that, Dimitar's hope sprung into elated realization that her feelings grew alongside his own.

He swung her to his other side, in tandem with the other dancers, eyes locked with hers. His hands never left her waist, and a thrill raced through his core. The music's pace rose, dancers whirling, yet Dimitar slowed his step, drawing closer to her. The maelstrom of dancers faded, caught in the eye of a storm electrified by his desire.

Kaleela responded by circling her own arms around him, resting her cheek on his shoulder. Dimitar bowed his head, inhaling the rich fragrance of her hair that had eluded him all day. His heart soared from the scent he'd come to yearn for, coupled with her body pressed against his.

With a light touch, Dimitar tipped Kaleela's chin up. He traced the curve of her jaw to the tip of her ears, her beauty irresistible. Kaleela's lips parted just so, and her fingertips brushed aside the lock of hair on his forehead. Dimitar started to lower his lips to hers, the air between them alive with energy. As he cupped his hand behind her head to draw her to him, the song ended and a swell of applause rose from the crowd.

Startled by the sudden rush of noise, Kaleela drew back before their lips met. Dimitar looked around as if coming out of a fog, and half-heartedly clapped for the musicians even as he silently cursed their timing. Another spirited tune burst forth, and the elves danced anew with boundless energy. Dimitar turned back to Kaleela, but their moment was broken. Instead, they exchanged a knowing look and joined the dance once more, breaking away to switch partners as custom in most of the elven dances. They never strayed far from one another, always finding a means to rejoin. Although they twirled and laughed as before, something deepened in their relationship.

Olaf's right. She has my whole heart. And I'll protect hers, always.

Late into the night, Dimitar took his leave from her, Kahled, and the elven royal family. He yearned to tell her his feelings for her, to touch her again and recapture that one sweet moment, denied. Instead, he led a stumbling Olaf to their room. The large man swayed as he tossed an arm around Dimitar's shoulder, attempting to sing an elven tune while recreating the words with some of the more vulgar lyrics Dimitar had heard in a while. Olaf fell into slumber the second his head hit the pillow, leaving Dimitar in blessed silence.

And in that silence, as Dimitar drifted off to sleep, he replayed his dance with Kaleela in his mind, intensifying his greatest desire, and felt complete.

46

Olaf

Olaf opened his eyes when the mid-morning sun peeked its way past the curtain's edge. The world took a few moments to catch up with his head as he rolled over on his side, the effects of last night's wine no longer his friend. With a groan, he scrubbed his face with his good hand. When the lights stopped flashing behind his eyelids, he scanned the room. Dimitar's bed was empty, the sheets made. Spotting a large water pitcher on an end table, Olaf pulled himself to a shaky stand.

The door flew open.

"Good morning, king of the cups," Dimitar said, way too loud for Olaf's taste.

"Ach, what's so good 'bout it?" Olaf staggered toward the pitcher.

"Just because one of us drank too much last night, doesn't mean he has to ruin everyone's mood," Dimitar joked as he plopped himself into a chair.

Olaf turned to respond in an uncharitable way—*I'm gonna ruin yer ever-lovin' life if you don't shut the fu*—but the words stopped on his lips. A beaming smile lit Dimitar's face ear to ear, the likes of which Olaf had never seen before on his friend. Olaf searched his clouded mind for anything about the previous night's festivities. His frown eased, and despite his aching head, a grin deepened upon his face as he remembered Dimitar and Kaleela in each other's arms.

"Ah, lad. She's got yer heart, she has."

"When we were dancing, it just felt so... so right." Dimitar's smile widened, boyish and exuberant.

Olaf raised the glass of water. "May yer days be long together and yer nights even longer."

Dimitar laughed, but Olaf was just warming up.

"May the gods bless ya with many years of baby-makin'. May ya sheathe yer sword and plow yer fields every day of ya wakin' life. And in the long nights together—"

A knock at the door interrupted Olaf. They shared a wide-eyed look.

"Do you think it's her?"

"Aye, if she's as happy 'bout last night as you. Sit over there. I'll answer it." Olaf waited until Dimitar sat in a chair and smoothed out his shirt before opening the door. His breath left in a rush; an elven guard stood in the doorway. Olaf gestured for the guard to enter as he downed his glass of water and turned to refill it.

"I am sent to retrieve you." The elf remained in the entrance and pointed at Olaf.

Leaning close to Dimitar, Olaf murmured, "Did I do anythin' last night I should know about?" In a louder voice, he replied, "Where ya takin' me?"

"King An'Nadal and High Knight Kahled sent for you."

Olaf reached for the water pitcher. "Okay. If ya give me a few minutes—"

"No. You must follow now," the elf said, the order rife with irritation.

"What *did* I do last night?" He scrubbed a hand down his face.

Dimitar shrugged, and Olaf threw on some clothes. Dimitar helped him with the fastenings, and Olaf was struck anew at his missing hand, an ache in his chest as much as his phantom limb. Dimitar stood to follow as he headed out, but the guard held up a palm.

"My command is only for this one."

Olaf shared a concerned look with Dimitar, then pasted a smile to cover his uneasiness. "You sit here and wait for the little lady to come 'round. I'll be back soon."

Olaf racked his mind for any recollection of last night. Had he asked Rialyn to dance after all? Perhaps he inserted himself between her and her partner, and caused some offense. Olaf rubbed his forehead. *Ach. Pretty sure I dreamed that part.*

Dimitar scowled at being left behind as the guard led Olaf out of the room. Olaf lost track of how many turns they made through the castle hallways. He had a vague idea they were heading toward the heart of the castle, which made him more nervous. His stomach rolled treacherously.

The guard came to a halt before a large, wooden entrance with simple carvings. Ushered inside, Olaf sobered right up.

King Kahled and General Bela'Ruhn sat on either side of King An'Nadal in the castle's war room. A handful of councilors flanked the three on both sides, including Captain Rialyn. They surrounded a large, circular table covered with a map of Mirodaigne. Dispersed across the Green Lands were figurines, with a heavy concentration of red pawns in the east.

Conversation halted as Olaf joined the room, attendees turning to see who entered. Without so much as a greeting, the discourse continued as if he wasn't there. Only Kahled recognized his presence, motioning Olaf to sit in the chair next to him.

Olaf took all this in before piecing together that Kahled and Bela'Ruhn were in a heated discussion.

"We cannot allow them to advance further west, General." Kahled's tone wearied as if trying to get this point across for some time. "These people suffer enormous loss. It's my duty—our duty—to come to their aid."

"We must approach this with greater judgment." Bela'Ruhn sounded just as tired of proving his point. "There are casualties with waiting, but—"

"But nothing!" Kahled shouted. "These are human lives you're talking about."

Olaf had never seen his king lose his temper before. *Shit all, this is serious.*

Kahled took a deep breath. "You cannot use them as a means to slow the enemy, so you can take your time with preparations."

"I realize that, High Knight," Bela'Ruhn shot back. Raising his voice over the murmuring councilors, he added, "You know better than this. Or have you forgotten your training?"

Kahled sat back in his chair as if slapped. "Of course not, *Gar'guerr.*"

"Fight with your mind first, then your blade, and lastly with your heart. I trained you better than this."

Olaf recognized the elven phrase as one of the High Knight commandments. Kahled had impressed this wisdom on Blackburn's knights and those in training.

Kahled shifted in his seat, considering the general's words but clearly opposed to Bela'Ruhn's suggestion.

"If we rush to their aid, we'll meet this horde weary, unprepared, and on their terms," Bela'Ruhn continued, like a teacher to his student. "We must think beyond the lives at stake."

Kahled shook his head to refuse, but then An-Nadal raised his hand. "Enough. I will hear from our newest member."

Everyone turned in their chairs to face Olaf, looking expectantly at him.

"I'm not sure..." Olaf croaked. He couldn't have been caught more off guard than if Bela'Ruhn sprouted a second head. Clearing his throat, he tried again. "I don't know what we're talkin' about here."

A few elven councilors sighed in frustration, but An'Nadal quieted them with a stern glance. Kahled turned to Olaf as he brought him up to speed.

"We received messengers from Stormgard and Blackburn last night in the midst of our celebration. You may recall my original order to send my daughter to Gar'Ret's care here in the Sun'Din, and that every indication of her destination was given to both Blackburn's and Stormgard's councils?"

Olaf swallowed heavily as Kahled continued.

"When the eastern cities were attacked, their first thought was to send word to Kaleela here, thank the gods. The scouts deployed since our return earlier this week also arrived back to confirm."

Olaf braced himself. "Attacked, sire?"

"The Corrupted invaded the Green Lands. Harlow in the northeast and Cyril, Arista, and Paxton in the mid-east are overrun. Some survivors escaped to get the word out. Arrowsfall Queendom is putting up a good fight, but the rest are fighting a losing battle."

"The messengers brought strange tidings, as well," Rialyn added. "Goblins fight alongside the Corrupted down south. Our enemies took our strategy to heart and united their strength."

"But not united in their efforts." Kahled swept his hand at the red dots on the map. "Like before, the Corrupted attacks are unfocused... too widespread."

269

"Don't goblins attack weak points first to spread fear before movin' onto larger targets?" Olaf said, gaining a few approving nods around the table.

"Usually, aye," Kahled said. "But these cities aren't weak points. There's no clear advantage gained from these attacks."

"At least, none we've identified yet," Rialyn said.

Another elf followed Rialyn's point, but Olaf tuned them out as he concentrated on the map. Something about the figurine placement tugged at his memory, yet the more he focused on the pull, the more it slipped away. It had to do with something Rialyn said.

There's a pattern here we're not seein'. Somethin' gained by attackin' these cities first.

Olaf came back to attention when the table grew silent again, looking at him. "Sorry, what's the question? I was lost in m'thoughts."

"Don't be dense," came the snide remark from an elf toward the end of the table.

The elf's derisive tone and very words rang through Olaf's head, stirring a critical memory. Only then did Olaf remember when he first heard these exact words, straight from Karn's mouth at Dwyer's Pub, and the connection clicked. *Karn was right all along.*

"I know what they're plannin'," he said, interrupting Kahled who'd begun to retort in his defense.

"Please, enlighten us." King An'Nadal rested his chin on steepled fingers.

Olaf took a few more moments to put everything together in his head before speaking. "When we met with Karn—"

"You met with *Master Karn*?" Bela'Ruhn interrupted in disbelief.

"Well, more like they met with us, but aye. One o' the things they said was the Corrupted had a weapon this time that they didn't in the Reclamation. Somethin' that would make the difference this time 'round."

"What is this weapon?" one of the councilors asked.

"Karn never did get a chance to tell us on account of the dragon breakin' loose all kinds o' fury. I spent days tryin' to figure out what they were referrin' to. Thought about all the great blades in our lands or yours, or even somethin' the dwarven clans down south might have. But now, I don't think they're talkin' about an actual weapon."

Olaf turned to address Bela'Ruhn. "Rialyn said the Corrupted are takin' strategies to heart, and I think yer more right than ya know. Why did we win the Reclamation?"

"Superior strength," Bela'Ruhn said matter-of-factly.

"But why was it superior?" Olaf prodded.

"Because we combined our forces," Kahled said next to him, the High Knight's mind following his line of thought.

"Exactly," Olaf continued, gaining momentum. "But why would the Corrupted now decide this was a good idea? And why would goblins, known for not gettin' along with anyone, not even themselves, join with the Corrupted?"

"Because someone gave them the idea," Rialyn replied.

"Rippold." Kahled spat the name in disgust, and the war councilors struck up conversation anew.

Bela'Ruhn's steely gaze didn't waver.

"That's the weapon they have, General," finished Olaf. "It's Rippold. He's providin' them all with guidance. These aren't random or weak cities they're hittin'. Look again."

They all stood to study the map. Olaf had the elven grand general, a High Knight, the elven king, and the Sun'Din councilors captivated. *Gods, thank ya for the sobriety right now.*

"They're splitting us up," Kahled said. Olaf turned red as his king looked up from the map at him with a proud smile.

"*So'gud roth*, he's using our own tactics against us," Bela'Ruhn spat out.

"Rippold combined the Corrupted and goblin armies and placed them between major human cities," Olaf said. "There's no way the Northern and Southern Lands in the east can get to each other now, not cleanly."

"And if the elves attack from this side of the Tempest," Kahled said, "the enemy could pull together and form a unified front."

"With no reinforcements coming from the east," Rialyn said.

"That's right, 'cause the goblins took out the Arlan Bridge down south," Olaf said.

Silence fell across the room, everyone taking in the layers of strategy at play.

"I'm guessin' you were arguin' about meeting 'em head on here?" Olaf pointed to a narrow pass in the path of the northern threat.

Kahled nodded.

"I'm thinkin' that's what Rippold wants us to do. It's a trap."

"All the more reason to wait before advancing," Bela'Ruhn said.

Olaf's stomach clenched, not from the ill effects of last night's drinking but a new realization. *Oh shit.*

"Ya can't wait," he said, eyes intent on the map.

Bela'Ruhn gave a withering glance and began to reiterate some of the points he'd sparred over with Kahled.

Olaf cut him off, ignoring the warning that flashed in the general's eyes. "Ya can't wait, 'cause Rippold isn't just aimin' for our cities. He's aimin' for yer lands. He's coming *here.*"

"It matters not," a councilor said. "Despite what you think about that thief following our guardsmen into the city, no one enters these woods without permission. The forest won't allow them."

An'Nadal passed a hand over his eyes, and the gesture alone drew up any further comments as the room quieted, waiting for his pronouncement. "Rare are the outsiders who are granted royal permission to walk unhindered within the Sun'Din. General, tell us the worthy who received this honor."

Bela'Ruhn straightened and recited, "All who are of elven blood are born with this inherited right. In history and legend, the Mage Warriors served as peacekeepers and champions to all, including the elven nation, and thus were granted free access. There is the Master of the Arts, known as Karn, whose present form does not preclude them from their birthright. The High Knights of the Reclamation War were honored with the rights of passage."

Bela'Ruhn hesitated, and Kahled ever so subtly cleared his throat.

"And a few select others have been granted freedom within the forest," Bela'Ruhn finished, casting a sour eye toward Olaf.

The enormity of what Gar'Ret conferred to him and Dimitar on the steps of Quinthal's castle sunk in. The Sun'Din Forest's enchantment blocked and turned out anyone not elven or bestowed access. This explained why the Sun'Din's paths were unnavigable to him and Dimitar when they first stepped foot in the forest, but then appeared clear as day after Gar'Ret's pronouncement that the two men were now welcome visitors.

An'Nadal nodded in satisfaction. "We bestowed upon the High Knights freedom across our lands. And now a High Knight leads this combined army. We cannot delay action and risk the Corrupted army being escorted into the Sun'Din. They will march upon this city once they cross the threshold."

Olaf bowed his head as An'Nadal reached the same conclusion as he. Rippold had full rights to the Sun'Din lands, with Corrupted and goblin armies at his command. Nothing stopped him from penetrating the forest wall and heading straight for Quinthal.

"Then what do you suggest we do?" Bela'Ruhn asked.

In the momentary silence that followed, Olaf raised his head and glanced around the table. He caught himself from gulping; Bela'Ruhn addressed him. Sitting back in his chair, Olaf looked to the ceiling and gathered his thoughts, wishing his head wouldn't pound so hard.

This is gonna be a long day.

47

THE OVERLORD

"P l... pl... please," the man pleaded, his nose shattered and tears streaming down his face in a mix of pain and fear.

"Please what?" Rippold leaned closer as the man scuttled backward, collapsing upon a broken arm.

"My wife and ch... children—" His words cut off with a rattling cough.

Rippold grabbed the man behind the neck and pulled him close, death's embrace. "I won't kill them," he said into the farmer's ear, pulling apart just enough to see some semblance of peace pass over the man's face. Rippold then plunged his sword through the man's stomach. "My minions, on the other hand, will enjoy feasting on their flesh."

He watched with uninhibited pleasure as the man's eyes grew wide in disbelief, then hopeless despair. Bored already, he ripped his sword free, the man's raw gasping subsiding into silence and drowned out by the screams piercing the air.

Rippold inhaled deeply, the afternoon breeze carrying the scent of blood across town. While he reveled in the destruction, slaughtering small villages like cattle failed to satiate his bloodlust. He needed the challenge of clashing arms, the satisfaction of conquering those who believed they held power to match his own. The elven response couldn't be far off, if he knew Kahled and his godsforsaken honor.

Let them come.

Sitting on a corner of the town's stage, once used for auctions and traveling players and now coated with swatches of blood, he studied his wet sword. An elegant weapon, the blade's smooth, polished metal cut razor-sharp. Printed upon the pommel was a shield surrounding a full-leaved tree: the High Knight insignia.

Rippold had trained harder than any other High Knight and met every test General Bela'Ruhn served him. Yet Conrad, not he, was praised above the other knights for his skill and strength. And Kahled, not he, won the heart of Kaleel, the most beautiful woman he'd ever dreamed to lay eyes upon. Out of one hundred men, only three remained to uphold the High Knighthood, yet Conrad and Kahled received so much more: kingships, respect, and favor among the elves.

Rippold had endured enough of his subservient position.

Locking his jaw, Rippold dragged the sword edge along the thick of his palm, wincing. Black blood welled along the cut before congealing around the wound. As always, he marveled as the blood reversed its flow, and his skin came back together. A few minutes later, not even a scar remained. Even the Corrupted hadn't anticipated this benefit when they came to him with their proposition years before.

Kahled and Conrad had rejected his plan to take Tildare's throne, and he couldn't pull off the insurrection without their help. Even now, Rippold recalled how they stood united before him, denouncing his actions as one.

"You sonofabitch," Conrad cursed him, shouting in his anger. "You swore an oath to serve as First Knight and now you think you can take the place of the king?"

"You're dishonorable," was all Kahled said in that quiet, arrogant way of his.

Any comradeship Rippold held among their brotherhood was cast out that day.

Rippold arrived back at Tildare in a cold fury. His frustration overwhelmed him, spurring his anger. He considered hunting down a serving maid, but didn't want to deal with the weeping. Pacing the castle corridors, early winter's wind moaning outside, Rippold seethed at the hopelessness and unfairness of his position. He wanted more. He deserved more.

Emboldened, Rippold walked up to the king's throne and sat upon the dark velvet cushion, surveying the empty room. A window clattered open, cold wind chilling him to the bone. His instinct, honed under the elite elven training, brought all his senses to attention.

With a guttural snarl, a Corruptor launched itself through the opening, coming to rest on the wall of the chamber's far side. Rippold was already on his feet, sword drawn. Nothing prepared him for what the Corruptor rattled off in ragged common. It promised Rippold endless power, the strength of twenty men, and the chance for revenge. Its sibilant voice wove images of an army at Rippold's control and countless thrones across the land under his rule.

Rippold listened, yet the hatred toward the Corrupted that coursed in his veins on the battlefield still pulsed. War memories raged in his mind, which ended with images of Kahled and Conrad ensconced on their thrones. Gritting his teeth at the unfairness, Rippold reconsidered the Corruptor's proposal as he pictured himself larger and stronger, driving his sword into the hearts of the other two High Knights.

"Grant me this strength," Rippold declared upon the throne, verbally signing the pact that would transform him forever, "and I will rule all."

The Corruptor hissed and unfurled, thrusting its clawed hands into its own chest. When its hand reemerged, covered in a dripping, writhing mass of blackness, it proceeded to throw the substance in Rippold's face.

He screamed in terror as the black liquid burrowed into his skin and down his throat, its chill spreading through his entire body. His fists gripped the side of the throne, body contorted in painful spasms as the change began. Horns and spikes burst from his skin as his joints popped out of socket to readjust to his growing form. Just before the pain consumed him, the agony stopped.

Rippold held his breath, bracing for more pain, but his arms and legs thrummed with newfound strength. The last of his humanity departed in his exhale. The High Knight was now the Overlord.

Storming across the room, Rippold reached to rip open the door, thoughts of Kahled and Conrad fresh on his mind. He was stopped mid-stride by the Corruptor, who hunched low, hissing. Rippold grabbed his head as a loud, screeching cacophony shattered his mind. Conrad and Kahled once again surfaced, but this time, countless Corruptors prowled about his mind, pushing forth images they wanted him to see. The collective consciousness presented him with an irresistible summons, and plans started to form.

Yes, death is too easy for them.

The images crystallized: instead of driving his sword through the High Knights, Rippold ordered them like dogs. Kahled and Conrad called him master as they ran to where he pointed, laying waste to everything and anything in their paths alongside the Corrupted. Kingdoms fell to him, people subjugated and pledging themselves to him as their new leader. Next to the enormity of Rippold's power across the entire Green Lands, Kahled and Conrad became insignificant, eclipsed by his rule.

Rippold left Tildare on that cold night, guided by the Corruptor into the deep recesses of the Eastern Mountains where an inner fortress awaited. All the Corrupted promised him came to pass over the next dozen years. They answered only to him, submitting to his tactical plans with bloodthirsty eagerness. His neighbors within the mountains, the goblins, were natural enemies to the rising Corrupted numbers yet not so stupid as to dismiss Rippold's offer of alliance, and his army doubled.

Still, there was more: the unnatural strength that belied his fifty-some years, the healing powers, and then the mythical dragons of yore who slumbered in the deepest caverns, awakened to do his bidding. The day drew near when he would unleash them upon Kahled's doomed armies.

With his forces gathering and preparing over the years, he turned toward the two disloyal brethren who owed him their service. Rippold tried his best to convert Conrad, fuming at Conrad's automatic and unyielding resistance. It didn't take any of his pleasure away when he shoved a long dagger through Conrad's neck. He stared into the great warrior's eyes as Conrad choked out the last of his life from his pierced throat. Rippold then turned his thoughts to Kahled, admitting that perhaps he'd been too hasty. No doubt Kahled would prove as resistant and need persuasion.

An unlikely ally presented to Rippold in the form of the elven messenger. *The exile.*

One of several elves cast out from the Sun'Din Forest for unspeakable acts, and who hated the idea of elite warriors training humans, the exile was more than willing to deliver the false message to Blackburn. Rippold didn't reveal his true identity to the elf at the time but hoped to do so someday, just before killing him for disrespecting the High Knighthood that had trained Rippold all those years ago.

The false message worked, and Kahled fell right into his hands. He'd been so close to dominating him. Rippold wasn't as angry about Kahled's escape as his own error that day in revealing his healing powers. The magic strikes had wrecked his body with a terrible, heated pain, which would've burned any other person's innards in a horrible death. Yet he had risen before them all as his body healed itself in mere minutes. Now his enemy knew this special advantage he held.

Rippold perched upon the bloodied town stage, and a sneer curled his lips into the briefest smile. "Let them know my powers. If I cannot be crowned, then I'll be feared. Let them revere my strength, for they cannot kill me, and now it is known."

Satisfied with the town's utter destruction, Rippold stood, eager to meet the last High Knight upon the battlefield.

He will taste my blade yet. He'll look into my eyes as he dies, and know that I am king.

48

DIMITAR

D imitar paced the room with deliberate steps, trying in vain to calm his nerves.

I should've received some tidings by now.

The sun traveled well along in the cloudy afternoon sky. A servant delivered simple fare during high noon, which Dimitar picked at. Voices from those around the castle grounds carried through the window, heightening his frustration at his own inactivity.

He couldn't stand to remain in the room any longer and headed out into the castle alone. Stretching his legs felt good, and Dimitar walked as if with purpose, although he had none. He received stares from the servants he passed along the way, but they returned his broken elvish greeting fair enough. Dimitar wandered until he came upon a familiar route, then quickened his pace. Taking the last short flight of stairs in two steps, he knocked with a light touch, opening the door unbidden.

The air remained tinged with the scent of herbs in the healers' room, but this time carried a freshness from the open window behind the bed. Ral reclined on pillows along the headboard, napping.

Dimitar studied the man's olive, golden-tanned face. His brow no longer creased in pain, although ever marred by the crude goblin brand. The mutilated flesh along his neck was disturbing to behold, but after a few moments, Dimitar saw past the scars and branding. Ral's choppy, chin length black hair had been washed and combed back. He had about a decade on Dimitar in age, handsome and in the prime of manhood.

Kaleela sat on a cushioned chair, leaning forward on the side of the bed, her head resting upon her arm. She clasped Ral's hand in hers. Her eyes were also closed in rest, and she stroked the back of his hand with her thumb as she sang a soft song on whispered breath. Dimitar's heart stirred at the unexpected sight of her.

Kaleela raised her head as Dimitar shut the door. She smiled, sleepy and content, and reached for him with her free hand. Dimitar captured her hand and raised it to his lips. For an instant in time, the three were connected. Although he couldn't say why, the moment felt profound.

Ral stirred, and Kaleela withdrew her hand from Dimitar as she sat up, leaning toward Ral and speaking his name gently. His eyes blinked open, coming to focus on him.

"Hello, my friend," Dimitar said, and Ral managed a weak grin.

Ral raised his hands, his movements slow yet understandable. He tapped his forehead, then gestured at Dimitar along with a *tsk* click of his tongue. Running his fingers along the rising scar near his scalp, still bruised and tender, Dimitar shrugged.

"'Tis nothing." Dimitar was touched and embarrassed that Ral's first thought was for his well-being when he'd endured far worse. He tried to ignore the scar work and branding upon Ral's face. He focused on his eyes instead, piercing despite the dark circles.

"Nothing compared to yours," he finished awkwardly, gesturing the length of Ral's bandaged form and not knowing where to begin naming the man's injuries.

"We had a chance to talk earlier," Kaleela offered, when the silence between the two men stretched. "I told Ral about Father's rescue and the man behind the Corrupted insurgence. Although he's more monster than man," she added on a bitter note.

"He shouldn't have said those things to you about King Conrad," Dimitar said, remembering the level of maliciousness in Rippold's words as he said whatever it took to shatter Kaleela and thus break Kahled.

Kaleela brushed off the concern, although her voice was small. "I know he wasn't telling the truth about Conrad. Yet, we'll never know either way."

Ral pushed himself into a better sitting position. Kaleela handed Ral a nearby cup of tea, infused with healing herbs judging from the tangy aroma.

"Ral," Dimitar said, his words slow with sudden, tremendous guilt, "we thought you were dead. Willem said as much and had we—had I— thought there was a chance to find you..."

Ral raised a hand as Dimitar trailed off. 'My good fortune that Willem had his doubts,' he signed, but Dimitar shook his head.

"I'm so sorry. We should've searched for you, and I don't know how to make that right. But... How, for the love of the gods? How did you escape?"

Ral set down the healing brew, flexing his fingers and looking away.

Dimitar's gut twisted. *Going back into the mountains even in memory is painful for him.*

'I carved a death for as many Corruptors as I could. Willem's spell cut me off from him but took out a number of the creatures as well. With those in the corridor, it became a fight of knives against claws.'

Ral's gaze became distant and his signing hesitant. 'I cut the breath out of every last one, but they got to me as well. I thought I might bleed out, there on the tunnel floor among the Corruptor bodies. Gods, the reek of them... I had to wait until the fire wall subsided before I could try to move, and by then it was damn near too late.'

Ral clenched his hands into fists, bringing them to rest against his forehead, eyes squeezed tight.

"It's all right," soothed Kaleela, her eyes mirroring his pain. "You don't have to say any more."

Ral looked at Dimitar and motioned once more. 'I refuse to die in that cursed, godsforsaken mountain. There's a different purpose at work for us.'

Dimitar sensed more Ral wasn't articulating, perhaps unable to describe, but wouldn't press him further. He didn't understand what Ral meant; yet somehow, he sensed it, deep in his body: a resonance.

"You've repaid any debt to our kingdom a hundredfold." Dimitar eyed the many bandages on the thinner man. "Your service is done, and not without a lifetime of thanks."

The corner of Ral's mouth tugged up. He took another drink before setting the cup on the side table. 'Did you kill the Overlord?'

Dimitar paused. "No."

'Then it isn't done.'

A knock at the door sounded, and Dimitar was relieved to see Olaf's large frame taking up most of the doorway as he followed Kahled into the room. Kaleela stood and embraced her father as Dimitar approached Olaf.

"Where have you been all day?" Dimitar asked mid-stride. Olaf opened his mouth, but he jumped in. "I mean, I figured you were in a special meeting. What did you talk about?" Again, he halted Olaf in his response. "I know it's about the Corrupted, so you don't—"

"Lad! Enough!" Olaf snapped, rubbing his temple. To Dimitar's disappointment, Olaf pushed past him, muttering the whole while about idiocy and poor upbringing. Swinging his good arm around Ral's shoulders, Olaf gave him an affectionate shake in greeting and declared the elves absolutely indecent to give Ral nothing but tea to drink when clearly, he needed a line of pints.

Ral patted Olaf on the back as if to reassure him that he'd survive in spite of this outrageous treatment. The room then fell silent as Ral and Kahled assessed one another.

Ral placed a hand on his chest, then extended it to the king. 'I owe you an apology for trying to steal from you.'

Kahled raised an eyebrow at this. "It's complicated, isn't it? On one hand, you brought my daughter to the very last place I ever wanted her to be. But on the other, if you hadn't, well... 'tis likely I wouldn't be standing here before you."

"It's like you were meant to find Kahled's tent," Dimitar said. *A greater purpose for us all started that night.*

Kahled rumbled his assent, then dipped his head at the thief. "My debt is to you, Ral. Perhaps I could repay you with a lifetime of King's Cheese once we return to Blackburn."

"King's Cheese?" Olaf repeated, glancing between the two.

Ral shrugged, but a blush swept over his face. 'Aye. It's what I was going for.'

Dimitar shoved a hand through his hair, then held his palms out face down, emphasizing his words by patting the air. "Wait, wait, wait. You're telling us you tried to steal *cheese*?"

"It is really good cheese," Kaleela offered with a blossoming smile. "Honestly, the best I've ever had, so smooth and buttery, with this addictive flavor. Eating just one piece is impossible."

Ral swept up her hand once more and brought it to his chest, bonding in mutual adoration. Olaf chimed in with his appreciation while Dimitar sputtered a response.

Kahled cleared his throat, and the room fell silent. "At any rate, I've come to summon you." His somber tone set aside any other questions from Dimitar. "That is, if you're well enough to walk."

Ral nodded, set aside the bed covers, and came to stand next to Kaleela, who took his arm with a worried eye. Stripped of his magicked cloak, leather gear, and layers of knives, Ral appeared frailish, faded linen clothing hanging loose on his thin frame. He bowed to the king, meeting Kahled's gaze with questioning eyes.

"What is it, Father?" Kaleela asked. She, too, didn't miss the change in Kahled's demeanor.

"Just come, my child," he said, weariness plain upon his face. "We're called to another meeting—all of us."

Walking the hallways together, Kahled shared the news from the war room, then Dimitar and Kaleela took turns asking questions.

"I don't have all the answers to this invasion." Kahled stopped at the throne room entrance. "But now we'll meet with the one who does."

As with Dimitar's previous audience in the great hall, An'Nadal and Elayis sat upon their thrones surrounded by councilors seated in a semi-circle to either side. Bela'Ruhn and Rialyn sat to Elayis's right this time, although Dimitar had a hard time seeing them, his view blocked by a massive figure.

Not until the group crossed the length of the throne room did Karn break from their conversation with the elves and turn to acknowledge them. Even then, they faced only one among them: Ral. Karn's unreadable, dark eyes assessed Ral's numerous bandages and tired posture. Ral hunched his shoulders and kept his head lowered; whether cradling his injuries or self-conscious with his face exposed, Dimitar wasn't sure.

Karn's gaze lingered on Ral as they addressed the rest of the group. "You've brought your father back, Princess. Now do you understand what's at stake?"

They gave a brief nod at Kahled's presence, perhaps Karn's attempt at respect to the High Knight.

"Aye, we understand, all too well," Kahled said. "The Corrupted amassed their numbers and declared war upon our lands, under the guidance of our own High Knight Rippold."

"Bah!" Olaf exclaimed as he spat upon the ground.

Elayis raised an elegant eyebrow at Olaf's outburst and stared pointedly at the stain upon the floor, then back at him.

"Oh... uh, sorry," he said, scrubbing with the toe of his boot as he turned bright red.

Karn ignored Olaf as they addressed the royal family and councilors. "Rippold is the tool, the weapon with which the Corrupted wish to strike their victory across these lands—all our lands," Karn emphasized. "The Corrupted themselves won't stop until another Age of Blood is upon us. They'll never stop. The shadow forces compel them evermore."

The councilors stirred and murmured among themselves, but silenced as An'Nadal spoke. "The Corrupted were first banished a lifetime ago."

"Several lifetimes," Karn corrected under their breath, although their voice, like themself, was far too large to be concealed.

An'Nadal continued, unfazed. "The Reclamation War saw the resurgent Corruptors exterminated upon every battlefield. Every last one was tracked down and fell to our blades, were they not?"

"I swear it." Bela'Ruhn touched his sword hilt in memory.

"Then how is it these creatures of shadow seek to spoil our lands yet again, and so soon after the Reclamation?" An'Nadal asked.

"The source," Karn said, and a chill ran up Dimitar's spine. Ral shivered beside him as well.

"The Storm of Banishment that ended the Age of Blood worked too well," Karn continued. "We slashed a closure into the void with such strength, such combined power, a new crack formed as a result. Every spell has a consequence, and the bigger the spell, the larger the reverberation. The wound healed at the cost of a scratch, since festering. This crack between our world and the shadow forces lies within the Eastern Mountains and remains their source for crossing into our world."

"And what of the dragon's return, Master Karn?" Willem asked, seated among the councilors. His hands remained bandaged, still healing from the self-inflicted burns. "The arrival of even one upon the lands is an ominous sign. No dragon has breathed our air since the Age of Blood."

"More than one legend from these dark times has returned. The Corrupted and now dragons—they're the spearhead of the shadow forces' minions. The source will birth creatures from the Dark Woods that will render our lands into their playroom."

Dimitar caught himself holding his breath as he envisioned all Karn described. The enormity of the situation hit him, and he spoke up.

"To defeat the Corrupted once and for all, we need to destroy their source, their point of entrance into our world," he said, earning a baleful eye from Karn.

"No; you need to figure out how to win this war against Rippold and his horde." Deliberately, Karn turned and faced Ral. "*We* need to destroy the source."

A heartbeat's pause, and Ral stepped forward in service to Karn even as their intentions sank into the others.

"No. No, you can't do this," Dimitar said, stunned that Karn thought to ask anything of Ral in his current condition.

Karn ignored him and instead lifted the flap of a large messenger bag slung over one shoulder. They rummaged inside, withdrawing a dark, folded cloth.

"Here." They tossed the cloak to Ral. "Try not to shred it this time."

Ral fingered the soft cloth and gave it a shake, unfolding the layers before fastening the new cloak around his shoulders. He pulled the hood over his head and in that instant, obscurity hid his face once more. The look was all too familiar to Dimitar, yet merely hid Ral's wounds.

"There's no way ya can ask him to help," Olaf said. "Look at him. Ya breathe on him too hard and he's fallin' over."

Ral gestured for Olaf to settle, but the large man was having none of it.

"Don't quiet me! Has everyone lost their damn minds? If ya need someone that badly, I'll go. What, ya think because I lost m'lefty that I can't fight anymore?"

"Ral is to accompany me," Karn said with finality. "We are to depart as soon as you ready us horses and supplies."

Olaf threw up his hand in disgust and argued anew with anyone who dared to meet his eye. Dimitar didn't know what Karn intended to do, other than it involved the most dangerous mission of all. The weight of uneasiness draped over his own shoulders. Selfishly, he wanted Ral to fight beside him in the war to come, should the man even recover his strength in time.

"Father, please, this is madness," Kaleela said.

Kahled shook his head. She turned to face the entire court, coming to stand next to Ral.

"Your Majesties... General... I beseech you to intervene. Without this man, my father would be lost to the mountainside, to the Corruptors and filth within there. Do not ask Ral to return when he has yet to heal. It isn't fair, and it isn't right."

"It's not for us to decide, my child," Elayis said in her gentle way.

Tears glimmered in Kaleela's eyes, wordlessly pleading for anyone to help. Sympathetic yet unmovable faces were her only reply.

"You ask too much, Master Karn," Dimitar said.

Karn turned to him with eyes that flashed a warning, shifting to hazel and dark brown.

Dimitar meant no disrespect, even as he held his ground. "Of all people, you know exactly what Ral's been through in those mountains. Now, for a second time, he almost lost his life within those walls, but this time he did so willingly, in the name of honor to our king."

Dimitar looked at Ral and no longer saw a mangled, hooded thief, but a hero and friend. "If you ask this of him, to enter the mountains a third time and in this state, you're asking to take his life."

"Humans!" Karn uttered in apparent disgust and exasperation. Their voice boomed throughout the spacious chambers, silencing those around them. Karn's ebony forehead deepened in a frown as they appraised Dimitar, Kaleela, and Olaf.

For one brief moment, Dimitar hoped his words had penetrated through to Karn and changed their mind.

"I'm not *asking*," they snapped.

In response, Kaleela clasped Ral's hand in hers in silent, stubborn protest. Her bottom lip quivered.

Karn sighed in vexation, then held out their hands in supplication as if willing them to understand. Again, their dichromatic eyes changed, now green and blue. Through the authority permeating their voice, Karn's next words just slightly softened. "I'm also not looking to take his life. I'm looking to save all our lives."

The room remained silent at this. Dimitar sensed that whatever Karn needed to do, they needed Ral. As if reading his thoughts, Ral stepped forward. All eyes were on him as he held Kaleela's hand and walked over to Dimitar. He placed a delicate kiss on the back of her hand, then unlaced his fingers and switched her hand into Dimitar's. Reflexively, Dimitar closed his hand around hers as she did the same. He met Ral's eyes from beneath the hood, the meaning clear: he was meant to stay with Kaleela.

Ral turned to Karn and signed a simple message. 'I'm ready when you are.'

He nodded once to Olaf, who looked wholly miserable, and then to Dimitar, who still held Kaleela's hand. 'I'll see you again, on the other side.'

49

DIMITAR

Blacksmiths arrived at sunrise with weapons and armor for the men. Dimitar was pleased to find Sera'Lan among them, and exchanged somber greetings as the elven smiths laid out their equipment on a table.

"These *el'van* armor, we made already and remake to fit you, aye?" Sera'Lan said.

Dimitar nodded, impressed at the armor's quality, its metal cool and heavy under his inquisitive fingertips.

The smiths had received the measurements taken by the tailors prior to the celebration feast. The refitted armor and chain mail coat Dimitar wore underneath formed around him like a glove. The chest plate glistened, made of strong dwarven steel and emblazoned with Quinthal's insignia in gold relief. Soft, supple leather straps pulled the cuirass and arm guards tight.

"This, though, I picked just for you." Sera'Lan passed Dimitar a blade.

He picked up the long sword as if touching a weapon for the first time. The blade's craftsmanship was flawless, metal polished and oiled to a high shine. Tight wrappings surrounded the grip, embedded with a thin silver thread. Quinthal's insignia stood out on the otherwise unblemished steel pommel. Dimitar slid the blade into its scabbard with a slight hiss.

"It's too good," he said, honestly overwhelmed. "The best blade I've ever held. Thank you."

Sera'Lan nodded in approval before turning at Olaf's exclamation.

"By the gods, lass, ya dressed her up for dancin', ya did!" He hefted Lucky in delight and twisted back and forth in his new armor.

Sera'Lan gave a puzzled smile, not understanding but accepting Olaf's appreciation nonetheless. "You... dance?... with this axe?"

"Oh aye, on the battlefield she's m'favorite partner."

This time Sera'Lan joined him in uproarious laughter.

The blacksmiths had been informed Olaf never wielded anything but his favorite axe. They'd melted and reformed the jagged, broken edge into a long, deadly butt point. To balance the weapon, they removed portions of the unbroken side, the bit shaved into razor sharpness. It now weighed at least half as much as before. Olaf chuckled in satisfaction as he set Lucky on the table, clasping Sera'Lan's forearm as she returned the gesture.

Dimitar half listened to Olaf and Sera'Lan talk, fixating on his reflection in the armor. No distortion of his mirrored image cast back despite the curve of the breastplate, yet he was estranged from the reflection. The darkness in his eyes, unfamiliar to him, evoked something deeply serious, almost eerie. The face he gazed upon was the same one he'd looked into for years with reverence and a touch of longing. His eyes had deepened into the unbounded storm of Kahled's.

"Lad? Are ya there?" Olaf clapped his hand on Dimitar's back.

Dimitar blinked, breaking the trance, and Olaf tipped his head toward the guard who summoned them at the door.

The men gathered their things, and a knot formed in Dimitar's stomach. He didn't even have the chance to see Kaleela before they left.

He ached for her.

50

KAHLED

The elves worked with efficient haste, readying weapons, armor, and supplies with set determination. General Bela'Ruhn gave the order to march out of Quinthal and head east once more. Elven messengers sent out after Kahled's initial return met the army on their way back to the forest, and all reports read as one: the Green Lands' outer cities were falling hard and fast as the Corrupted forces clawed over them, seeking ever westward. Kahled sent a messenger to Blackburn to report back on his kingdom's status, but the man hadn't returned. Dark thoughts hovered in his mind, troubled at his kingdom outnumbered and ill-prepared for the Corrupted horde bearing their way. He silently prayed to the gods.

Three days of hard march brought the army to the northern point in the lands where they expected to meet Rippold's forces. No sign of the enemy presented, yet Kahled was confident in Olaf's prediction that the two would meet here. The area sat in a direct line between the Sun'Din and the reports of Corrupted strikes across the lands, connecting the two sides in a straight path. The flat plain extended large enough to spread out the army and avoid the tight quarters the Corrupted preferred, and surrounding hillsides provided clear sighting for the archers.

As planned, the elven army split when they reached the plain. The larger of the forces held ground behind the swell of open hillside, while the elven elite broke off toward the rocky outcroppings on the far side, lush landscaping fast giving way to the first jagged signs of Eastern Mountains territory.

Gorge walls towered over the elite guard formation as Bela'Ruhn led them down the narrowing path. Their armor gleamed in the sun, gold and purple insignias emblazoned on shining chest plates as they entered the shadowed valley. Each elf bore a large, rectangular shield and the elite squadron's signature two swords, signaling Bela'Ruhn's best warriors. There was no mistaking this group of five hundred as anything but the very best the elves would throw at an enemy.

"Your man best be right about this," Bela'Ruhn muttered to Kahled, not for the first time since they left the Sun'Din. Risky and clever at the same time, Olaf's plan held the distinct possibility of failure.

Kahled glanced ahead to their destination. "He's never let me down."

Halfway along the length of the gorge, a rock outcropping formed a natural arch reaching over the entire width of the ravine. Bela'Ruhn and his troops could have chosen another passage to meet the Corrupted army head-on, but none got them there as quickly. From a tactical viewpoint, Smuggler's Pass was the best way to go. Once Olaf pointed this out, everyone at the war table agreed: the arch made an excellent point for an ambush.

And they were marching straight into it.

"Show yourself," Kahled said under his breath as he scanned the path.

Bela'Ruhn glanced at him, his eyes dark with a warning Kahled had seen before, a lifetime ago during High Knight training. *Control your emotions.* The unspoken command echoed in his mind.

Kahled took a steadying breath, then another, and stilled himself as he extended his hearing. He focused past the creaking armor and marching footsteps, listening for any Corruptors approaching up ahead. Collectively, the elite squad quieted at once, and the air imperceptibly shifted, a breeze whisking by Kahled's cheek as if to escape the imminent confrontation.

"They are coming." Bela'Ruhn's gaze searched the dark, shadowed pockets along the gorge walls, skimming the archway and darting back to the winding pathway.

The wind gave one last sigh, and on it carried a trace of sickening, rotted flesh.

The Corrupted weren't coming; they were already here.

All at once, Kahled realized the shadows upon the stone *were* the Corruptors. Packed together, their hides blending into the stone, hundreds perched high on the cliffs. With a piercing screech, the first Corruptor let go of the rock face and hurtled toward the elven troops. Hundreds more joined the first, and before the elite squadron looked to the blackened sky, the trap was sprung. Within seconds, the Corruptors would smother the elves from above, the elves' ground formation useless against an unprecedented assault from the sky.

Without further hesitation, the elite squadron executed their plan, bending at the knees and pulling their shields up. Taking one of their swords, they pushed the long blades through a small opening in the shields. The Corruptors, shrieking and hissing in triumph, now found themselves hurtling toward a lethal pincushion of elven blades.

The falling Corruptors tried to react in time, twisting in vain to evade the sword tips. The majority impaled themselves upon the blades, clunking against the metal with horrific thuds, death instantaneous. When the last of the Corruptors landed, the elves threw their shields aside and unsheathed their other blade, one in each hand. They quickly put to death the few Corruptors that survived the fall.

Bela'Ruhn surveyed his squadron. Not a single elite warrior suffered more than a scratch, whereas Corruptor bodies piled around them. Kahled recalled Olaf pounding on the table in front of him as the councilors tried to oppose the plan. *His mind is made for strategy, that one.*

"I'll be damned." Bela'Ruhn inclined his head at Kahled, an acknowledgement of the man Kahled trained.

With a sharp whistle and hand gesture, Bela'Ruhn issued his next order.

The elite squadron then did something they'd never done in its history: they turned on their heels and ran.

"Let's hope the rest of his plan works," Bela'Ruhn said as he followed his regiment.

Kahled fell into a jogging pace next to Bela'Ruhn, his attention on the next steps: rejoin the main elven army and begin strategic placement of the troops—elite warriors, foot soldiers, magic-users, and archers—to meet the incoming enemy. There, both Dimitar and Olaf remained to serve under his command, waiting for him with the secondary foot soldiers. Kahled's gut twisted as he searched the high points of the hillsides. The archers were still out of sight.

"I ask you for nothing but this one thing," Kahled had said to Bela'Ruhn within Quinthal's walls before their march. "Order Kaleela to stay in the Sun'Din Forest. Send her to the king and queen, and let them keep her safe until this destruction ends. The war front is no place for—"

"For a fighter?" Bela'Ruhn cut him off. "We have need of every warrior in this battle, else these shadow forces breach the Sun'Din borders. You know this is true, as well you know Kaleela is more than capable. Your emotions as her father cloud your judgment."

"Enough about human emotion!" Kahled shouted, stopping Bela'Ruhn who'd begun to turn away dismissively. "She's my daughter and only child; Kaleel's only child. She's not a soldier in my army. Look at reason, for the love of the gods. This is no place for her."

"Kahled, keep your sense," Bela'Ruhn said, his patience wearing thin. "I won't have her removed from this battle when her skills match some of my best archers. I'll hear no more of this overprotective sentiment."

The two men faced each other, eyes locked and heated. The sting of Bela'Ruhn's rebuke raked across his skin, as did Kaleela's own echoing, angry words when she'd refused his insistence that she remain behind at the castle.

"General... please," Kahled had beseeched, but the look in Bela'Ruhn's eyes crushed any hope of convincing the general his daughter should stay out of the war. Deep down, Kahled knew nothing except dungeon chains would keep her at the castle. Nonetheless, he hated the risk she faced—that they all faced.

A roar started at the front of the line. He and Bela'Ruhn turned as one to the troops in front of them. Incomprehensible shouting and jarring movement rippled back to where the two stood, searching for cause. Both men ran up the last swell of land to survey the disruption among the army.

Corruptors descended the southern hillside, pouring in vast numbers and launching themselves into the middle of the elven army. A mass of teeth and claws, the foul creatures thrust into the middle of the troops with frightening speed. Their numbers were staggering, multiplying beyond the soldiers and instilling an automatic sense of hopelessness. The Corrupted swarmed upon the ground, splitting through the troops, and Kahled's memories of the Reclamation War mirrored the scene before him. He steeled himself as Bela'Ruhn shouted a series of orders to the elite guard. The Corrupted outnumbered their army, but numbers didn't count for everything.

"Is Rippold so eager to face us?" Kahled turned to Bela'Ruhn, frowning. Back in Quinthal's war room, the councilors expected to meet the ambush and then travel further eastward before reaching the bulk of the Corrupted army. "What's the advantage striking here?"

"Rippold's pride is unchecked, as is his vengeance," Bela'Ruhn growled. "If he wants a war, by the gods he'll have one."

The elven army reacted as one, closing in on both sides to meet the Corrupted, the shine of their blades soon dulled with inky blood. Corruptors fell by the hundreds as archers joined the fight. Their arrows struck with great speed, sailing over the main army and landing a dark rain of death in the Corrupted forces. Kahled tore his gaze from the battle, searching once more among the line atop the ridge, but even his skilled sight couldn't find Kaleela among the formation.

Mages stood alongside the archers, casting spells of protection and defense on the front lines. From a distance, Kahled caught the subtle shift and bending of the air around those soldiers who would've otherwise been overtaken. Sharp claws scraped uselessly against the magical shields, Corruptors cut down by the blade. The crash and chaos of war grew deafening.

Bela'Ruhn barked another command to the elite warriors. Kahled repeated his words, the elvish language quick to return to his tongue, and troop leaders called the orders down the lines. The elite guardsmen charged forth to meet the enemy, and in minutes surrounded the bulk of the Corrupted army on two sides. Although smaller in size, the elite guard's skills were unmatched. Double blades became a whirl of death. It was impossible for the Corrupted army to last more than a few hours.

Something isn't right. Rippold knows far better than this.

Kahled unsheathed his blade but hesitated before joining the troops. Rippold's line of attack was utter foolishness. By charging into the middle of the army, the Corrupted were encircled. He glanced at Bela'Ruhn, a similar uncertainty in the general's eyes. Bela'Ruhn surveyed the soldiers' movements on the field, searching for the unknown threat. He, too, observed the senselessness of the Corrupted attack.

Kahled shook his head in frustration, cursing aloud. "I don't trust this attack, General."

And in that moment, with dawning dread, Kahled recognized Rippold's greater strategy. He knew Rippold's next move with utter certainty, as if some of the Corrupted taint still traveled in his blood and thus gave him a glimpse into the shared consciousness. He pivoted, half-hoping his intuition was wrong.

Behind the slain Corruptors in the gorge, moving with frightening speed, the Corrupted army in its entirety swarmed out of the mountain paths. They appeared as a stain coating the ground, noxious and polluted. The initial strike battling the elven army wasn't the entirety of Rippold's force, but approximately a third. The rest of the foul creatures charged the battle from behind.

At once cowardly yet tactical, the maneuver put the elves in a deadly predicament. The archers couldn't reach over the main elven army, the initial Corrupted army, and the fractured half of their army to hit the new Corrupted forces. Likewise, the magic-users stood too far from the surrounded soldiers to cast their protective shields. Both Corrupted and elven armies would now fight a two-front war, confusing and bloody.

In short, the Corrupted were about to find elven troops without archers or magic aid, their general on the wrong side of the fight, and their backs turned. Kahled shouted to the elite squadron, drawing their attention to the encroaching Corruptors, closing with unnatural speed. Bela'Ruhn cursed to the sky as the first alarm cries rose from the far side of the battle. He unsheathed his twin blades, brandishing them as he turned to face the hated enemy.

The massacre had begun.

51

DIMITAR

Dimitar and Olaf stood in line with their squadron, among thousands of soldiers in the army. The anticipation heightened to an unbearable impatience. No one shouldered the weight of time more than his friend. Dimitar glanced at Olaf, who shifted from foot to foot, scanning the hillside where the elite guard should reappear. If they didn't return in full, or at all—

Dimitar cut off his train of thought. He clenched and unclenched his sword pommel, a rhythm to the pulse of his anxiety.

The elite guard crested the upper ridge of the hillside, marching with the strength of victory in their movements. A welcoming cheer struck up among the main army as the entirety of the elite warriors breached the hilltop to rejoin the rest of the troops. Olaf whooped so loudly that Dimitar's ears rang, his relief palpable. Dimitar smiled as his friend punched him across the arm in exuberance.

"Do ya see that, lad? Look at 'em; they did it!"

Dimitar clapped him on the shoulder, but the swell of different cries swallowed his words of praise. He turned and in the blink of an eye, before the elation of victory settled, Dimitar's insides curdled. A black tide of Corruptors poured down the southern hillside and barreled upon the soldiers. His grip tightened on Olaf; the same fear mirrored on his friend's face.

"They're not supposed t'be here. This ain't a strikin' point for them." Olaf's fear shifted to anger, swift and terrible as he drew up his full height. "Those bastards. You bastards!" he shouted, raising his axe to the sky in defiance.

Corruptors cut their way through the army ranks, their numbers boggling to behold. Dimitar had thought he was prepared to fight them again. His armor and weaponry were of unparalleled quality. But here, staring down thousands of the creatures stole his breath and weakened his knees. They clawed closer and closer to where he and Olaf stood, weapons at the ready. The troop leaders shouted commands, but Dimitar couldn't follow the elven words.

"Where's Kahled?" Dimitar tore his gaze from the approaching horde to the other side of the field where the elite guard had almost finished joining the main army.

The troop leader yelled again, this time at Dimitar and Olaf as he moved down the line of soldiers, calling out directions.

"I don't understand," Dimitar said, but the leader stepped out of earshot. Without Kahled to navigate both languages, Dimitar and Olaf were cut off from all communication. The battle began, and suddenly Dimitar felt lost and alone, the same helplessness woven into him as an orphaned boy.

Olaf yanked him back to his senses, planting his axe and grabbing him in a rough hug. Like when they were children, Olaf put his forehead against Dimitar's, resting a free arm over his shoulders. Dimitar did the same, locking arms with Olaf.

"You and me, little pup," Olaf said with a fierce intensity. "Side by side, together."

"Together, my brother," Dimitar echoed, his strength surging to match Olaf's.

With a wordless growl, Olaf separated from Dimitar, hefting his one-handed axe and lifting the shield fitted to his amputated arm. Dimitar raised his sword, facing the incoming enemy as elvish words ran unchecked around him. The men might not understand the elven language but were trained, skilled, and prepared to fight.

As the swing of his sword descended but before it sliced a Corruptor's spiked hide, Dimitar thought of Kaleela up among the archers. He understood her desire to fight in this battle, and moreover, he trusted her competency. Every Corruptor became an entity that separated him from her. Dimitar focused on the foul creatures with a purpose. *I can't be with her again until the war is won.*

Dimitar's blade swept through the first Corruptor with vengeance. His world became hyperfocused on the swing of blades met by the swipe of dark claws. Somewhere in the recesses of his mind, he noted the urgent, wild hits against the first Corrupted wave as his heart pounded and his breath came in heaves. And then later—how much later, he didn't know—his actions became less frantic and more methodical. Dimitar paced himself against the unending flow of Corruptors. At all times, he was aware of Olaf's presence on his right, the two working in tandem as they struck down the Corruptors, over and over. Over and over.

The sun traveled across the sky, bearing witness to the hours of battle. Any initial fatigue wore off, replaced with a hardened certainty that any misstep, any flagging of his sword arm could end in a fatal error. A deeper weariness took hold of Dimitar's muscles, but a fresh wave of elven soldiers swarmed around him, Olaf, and the other fighters in their line. This allowed them time to step back and breathe. Many followed their instinct of checking themselves over for cuts, abrasions, or deeper wounds now allowed to protest fully.

Olaf leaned upon his axe pole, breathing hard from the day's exertion. Dimitar turned at a sharp rap on his shoulder.

One of the elven soldiers pointed to the back line. "Rest."

Grateful, the two men headed away from the fighting. For now.

Dimitar and Olaf took respite in organized, if irregular cycles alongside the other soldiers in their regiment. The battle's ebb and flow dictated the opportune time to step away from the front lines, switching places with those newly rested. The elves didn't need sleep as often or as long as the two men, and this battle continued day and night, the Corrupted needing no sleep at all. Dimitar and Olaf were spared fighting at night, their human sight no match for the elves' superior vision.

When night descended, the men made their way toward the back of their forces. Shielded by the hill slope, makeshift tents huddled together, sheltering the wounded. Small campfires heated gruel for sustenance and boiled water for the healers. Those needing rest curled up on the ground, sometimes with backs against one of the few, knotted trees in the area, other times close to the fires if the night carried a cold breeze.

On one such night, Dimitar sank next to a campfire, setting his blade aside with tired arms. Olaf did the same, too exhausted to groan aloud as he usually did. Warm bowls of food were handed to them, and the men ate in haste and without thought. After the flavorless yet hearty meal sank into his stomach, Dimitar studied Olaf. His friend looked him over with the same weary expression and cracked a smile, the gesture fleeting.

Olaf pointed at Dimitar's left shoulder. "That one nearly had ya."

A deep, ragged scratch raked down his armor. He couldn't remember when the blow happened, but Olaf was right. If he hadn't been wearing armor, he'd be dead.

"Same thing happened to me here." Olaf raised his arm.

Dimitar scooted around the fire to run his fingers along the dented metal. He traced the smaller, concentric dents around the edge. "Damn thing looks like it bit you."

"Bugger certainly tried, I can tell ya that. But it's nothin' compared to this."

He turned his back to Dimitar. A thin line ran the entire length of the cuirass, joined halfway down by two other lines. Dimitar pictured the clawed hand raking across the metal. This brought back a memory.

"Check this out." He shifted a layer of armor covering his hip, revealing the chainmail underneath. A fistful of rings twisted around each other, some near the point of snapping.

"What the hells did that?"

"One of the damn things got its mouth latched on before I chopped its head off." To Olaf's incredulous look, he added, "A couple elves kept turning the head in a circle until its jaw popped. You know, like trying to snap a green branch."

Olaf started to laugh—a deep sound rolling up his barrel chest.

"It's not funny," Dimitar said, offended. "It almost bit my leg off."

This made Olaf laugh harder. Soon both men hung onto each other's shoulders as unchecked laughter ran through them. The mirth left them gasping for air as they leaned back, sharing a drink from a water pouch.

"Damn, I needed that." Olaf wiped the tears off his cheeks, smeared with dirt. When he looked at Dimitar again, the smile left his face. He pointed at Dimitar's shoulder. "Ya need to be more careful, Dim. That's a killin' blow, and I need a few more of these laughs before the end."

A scream filled the camp, inhuman and terrifying.

Olaf and Dimitar grabbed their weapons and ran toward the source, too close. Another pained scream pierced the night as people shouted to each other in the healer's tent. In unison, Dimitar and Olaf threw open the front flap, weapons bared, only to stop dead in their tracks.

Willem crouched beside one of Bela'Ruhn's elite guards, chanting as he splayed his scarred hand wide over the elf's face. Four other elves each held one of the elf's limbs with all their strength and nearly failed to keep the guard on his back.

Black veins coursed in time with his heartbeat. His exposed skin undulated in waves, cracking open at the joints, small protrusions jutting out. The elite warrior's mouth stretched into a scream alternating between throat splitting and basso growling, the corners of his lips bleeding with the strain.

The soldier was infected with the Corrupted essence.

"Dear gods, look at his eyes," Olaf said, his axe still raised, frozen in horror.

The elf's eyes sank back into his head. A swirling mass of black churned in the sockets. They reminded Dimitar of boiling tar used to seal barrels. Small trickles of the inkiness dripped down the guard's cheeks and fell to the floor.

Willem intensified his chanting, but the warrior's cries became more inhuman. A commanding officer shouted across the tent to Willem, yet Dimitar understood the meaning. His heart sank.

Willem hesitated, then closed his hand and stopped chanting. With an involuntary cough, he fell to his knees, bent over and exhausted from his magic expenditure. The commander pushed his way forward and pulled a sword from his scabbard. As the elite guard started once more with a high-pitched scream, his skin corrupting into foulness, the commander decapitated him. The body jerked on the cot, then fell still, the other elves releasing their hold on his arms and legs.

Olaf walked over and offered his hand to Willem. The mage looked at the hand as if considering shaking it off, but instead took it and allowed Olaf to help him to his feet.

"I thought we got to him in time. I saw it happen. I was on the hillside a few yards away when the Corruptor threw its taint in his face." Willem looked at Dimitar, the mage's normal arrogance replaced with a shaken vulnerability. "His name is Ret'Kar. Rialyn's brother. One of their finest..."

Dimitar stepped forward and made a motion to ask for the commander's sword. The elf raised an eyebrow but did as requested. Dimitar placed the sword on Ret'Kar's chest, wrapping his two hands around the hilt. Whispered voices traveled around the tent as the gathered elves offered prayers. Behind him, Olaf's low voice murmured a supplication.

Dimitar remained silent, the words caught in his throat.

52

KALEELA

S traight through the eye," Rialyn announced with satisfaction, and Kaleela murmured her approval at the elite warrior's bullseye.

Kaleela drew her own arrow back and sighted, ignoring the steady heat in her aching arm. She released and watched her target fall before drawing another arrow from a seemingly endless supply. Corruptors clawed at the hillside, gnashing razor-sharp teeth below her in vain against an impenetrable air shield maintained by a group of magic-users. Kaleela had learned days ago to ignore the churning mass beneath her, focusing instead on her next target. Only the occasional hissed "Kaaa-leeee-laaaa" that issued forth gave her an involuntary chill.

Along the hill ridge bracing the sides of the battlefield, elven archers and magic-users worked their craft. Air shimmered from mages' hands as spells shot into the battlefield, encircling the elven forces with protective shields. Their spell casting lent a monotonous, low tone contrasted against the clashing and snarling among the fighters. The archers had released a deadly wall of arrows when the Corrupted first attacked, riddling them by the hundreds. But now, with the troops interspersed, a unified archer assault was impossible. The archers now shot at will.

At first, a detail of soldiers and mages had flanked Kaleela. She argued long and hard with her father to claim a position in this war, and the extra protection frustrated her.

"This is a waste of our resources," she said to the troop leader, who refused to budge, although his demeanor indicated he didn't disagree with her.

It was Rialyn who convinced the private security to disband. She described Kaleela's competency with the bow and arrow, referring to the time in the Sun'Din when Kaleela shot into the crowd, picking out the center of one guard's raised wooden shield. As the two argued, Kaleela grabbed a stash of arrows, planted them in her quiver, and fired. The troop leader turned just as Kaleela sent a single shot that pierced not only one, but a second Corruptor directly behind it.

"I'll serve as her personal guard," Rialyn said in dry amusement as the two Corruptors toppled over dead.

Kaleela ignored them, picking off troublesome Corruptors, more satisfying than any target practice. The troop leader had no further argument, reassigning the guards to larger ranks and giving Kaleela a place in line among the archers.

With her unfailing accuracy, threading the needle between countrymen and enemies time and time again to land fatal shots, Kaleela moved to the front of the archers' line. She and Rialyn now worked in tandem.

Rialyn took her eyes off the battle to assess Kaleela. "Do you need a break?"

"No," Kaleela lied, picking another arrow and notching it. She couldn't, wouldn't stop; not when this filth threatened her everything and everyone. "Where to?"

Rialyn pointed across the field to the tangled middle where Corruptors and elven fighters mixed in a chaotic, ugly mess. Kaleela's sharp eyes spotted the problem: three Corruptors lined up back-to-back, creating a swirling circle of deadly claws the surrounding fighters had yet to penetrate. Kaleela aimed high, unleashing the arrow with her breath less than a second behind Rialyn's shot. They shared the same grim expression as their joint arrows flew true. With two now taken out, the foot soldiers ended the third Corruptor seconds later.

Rialyn nodded once to Kaleela and scanned the field for their next target. A breeze rippled across the field, sweeping up to the ledge where the archers and mages aided the fighters below. The stench of death, and something darker and fouler, couldn't be ignored. The wind whipped loose strands of hair away from Kaleela's sun-kissed face, and her gaze remained steady as she surveyed the battleground.

She wasn't looking for a target.

Kaleela searched for her father, outfitted in the best elven armor and blended among her mother's people. A born leader and true fighter, he'd be issuing orders to elven warriors with centuries' more training, and they'd obey without question. She couldn't lose him now, not after everything.

She looked for her friend, Olaf. *You'd think I'd spot him in a heartbeat.* Why couldn't she find the extra-large man wielding an axe one-handed and likely bellowing at the top of his lungs?

And she thought of Dimitar with a longing in her heart. The troops blurred together, yet she'd know him anywhere. She sensed his absence all the time, separated after weeks together when she'd come to feel safe with him. Kaleela didn't need Dimitar to guard her, yet she sought him on a more profound level. She had to see him again, to recapture the way his smile touched the corners of his eyes, how a lock of midnight hair always spilled down, and the ease at which he carried himself, wearing his heart on his sleeve.

A shiver caressed her spine as Kaleela recalled their dance in the Sun'Din, curving her body against his as he guided her to the music. The strength in his arms punched a wave of desire low in her gut, and more than anything else, she wanted to return to his embrace. *Dimitar, where are you?*

She shivered again, this time uneasy as something darkened the sun, bathing her in shadow. Her heart raced even before the new threat arrived.

An unholy scream pierced the air as the shadow whooshed above her head.

Kaleela recognized that cry, and icy fear erased the warmth sheltered within her. She ducked as the dragon rushed overhead, wind from its great wings staggering her backwards. Its scream echoed another and then a third. Three dragons crested the hillside and, like a living nightmare, descended upon the battlefield.

Kaleela stood on shaky legs, taking in the great creatures in full daylight as they swirled above the fighters. The deepest black of night, the dragons' diamond-shaped scales seemed to absorb the light around them. White steam plumed from elongated snouts filled with piercing teeth the length of a forearm. Pointed heads lined with cruel spikes crowned long, flexible necks. Each guided their flight with a spiny tail tapered into a spiked tip and wings almost as wide as their bodies were long.

The same instinctual panic that had threatened to overwhelm her at Dwyer's Pub swept through her. Kaleela's memories of that night in the tavern and outside streets came flooding back, filling her with dread and hopelessness. She knew first-hand the destruction these creatures wrought. And she didn't know how to defeat them.

Working as if directed, the dragons swooped among the fighters, lashing out in deadly strength with both teeth and claws. Although some Corruptors were caught in their attacks, the dragons plummeted into the elves' forces, ripping into them. The dragons were too large and fast to catch at the end of a sword. Kaleela shot at the closest dragon in futility. The archers' arrows bounced off their scaly hides.

In a flash, Rialyn gripped her arm. "Wait here, and don't die," she ordered.

Rialyn took off running through the battalion of archers to the other side of the ridge where the mages continued to fight, shouting commands as she went. In less than thirty seconds, Kaleela's ears picked up a new vibration: a change in timbre from the mages as they cast a collective spell.

One of the dragons made its next dive toward the soldiers. Invisible to the naked eye save for a ripple in the air, a magic shield formed over the soldiers' heads by about ten feet. The first dragon crashed into the barrier and reverberated off with a howl. The other two dragons also came down hard, repelled by the shield. A cheer rose among the archers, who continued their strike at the dragons. Although few arrows penetrated, the dragons slowed under the assault, large wings swatting at the swarm as a horse shakes away cluster flies.

One dragon made a lazy circle over the field and headed toward the ridge. A lump rose in Kaleela's throat and, paralyzed, she couldn't cry out. She was powerless as the dragon took a slow inhale, recoiling its serpentine neck.

The ebon fire coated the first row of magic-users, and just as on the streets of Leighton, a moment's pause hung in the air before bodies erupted in flames. Those touched by the black flame collapsed in agony. Their screams and scrambling spread, formations and protocol forgotten. In a matter of seconds, the orderly and formal lines shattered, and the entire hillside of the elven army fell into complete disarray.

The enchanted air shield receded and broke down. Kaleela whipped her attention back to the dragon above the mages, now circling. They were open targets on the ridge line. The crowd jumbled against one another as the next spurt of fire hit, this time closer to the archers.

"Run!" came a shout from among the archers, someone who'd come to the same conclusion as her. Others took up the exclamation. "Run! Run!"

Kaleela was pushed aside as bodies rushed to escape the dragon's fire, its victims' terrible screams filling the air. The Corruptors' snarls grew louder as the shield keeping them from breaching the hillside began to fail. Kaleela spun in place, overwhelmed. Where could she run to? Where was safe?

"Ah, good, you're still here, Princess." Rialyn reappeared beside her.

Kaleela whirled around, astounded to reunite in such chaos. Rialyn seemed unfazed and determined. She raised her voice above the deafening hillside panic.

"Soldiers!" she roared in commanding elvish. "To my side!"

Archers and mages halted at the pure authority in her voice.

"We are elves, by the gods! We do not run from our enemies. Now turn and present!" She issued orders to the soldiers nearest her who repeated the commands down the broken lines. "Archers, concentrate on the soft skin at the joints in the wings and neck folds. Defensive mages, protect and block. Mages on the offense, to me."

Rialyn turned and charged straight at the hillside's edge. She sprinted as if ready to leap straight into the writhing mass of Corrupted so eager to ascend the ridge. Kaleela's heart leapt into her throat as Rialyn issued one parting command to the mages around her.

"Upward bound, Mages!"

Rialyn kicked off the edge of the hillside. Kaleela held her breath, expecting the elite warrior to fall headlong, but against all rational thought, Rialyn ascended into the sky. Her legs churned as if still gaining traction, propelling her up with speed and strength. New tones rose from the magic-users next to Kaleela as they commanded the air around Rialyn.

One of the dragons turned to fly by the hillside, intent on reaching the soldiers on the battlefield. As if in slow motion, Rialyn unsheathed the two swords. Her back arched mid-flight as she drew both blades into a striking pose.

The dragon recoiled its head and screamed in anger at its surprise attacker, too late. Rialyn landed on its upper neck and drove both blades into its flesh to the hilt. The dragon shrieked in mortal agony, twisting as it plummeted to the ground. Kaleela lost sight of Rialyn as the great beast fell.

The dragon hit the ground with a tremendous *whump*. The fear building since the dragons appeared began to dissipate. Before their very eyes, the dragons became mortal, no longer the stuff of legends but simply the enemy. Soldiers set at once to the dragon, whose movements slowed to a stop.

Kaleela searched in vain to see if Rialyn survived the fall, but the chaos from the surrounding troops and dust kicked into the air was too great. At that moment, she realized Rialyn hadn't issued her a final command. It dawned on her this might have been an intentional omission; Kaleela was free to make her next move.

Her people, her father, her friends were all down there, at the mercy of these dragons.

Dimitar's down there.

Only one choice presented itself.

Kaleela tracked one of the two remaining dragons, then took off running to the hillside. She called out to the mages while sending a prayer to the gods. The second her foot left the ground, a push from behind and below propelled her, as if she were somehow falling up instead of down. She recalled Rialyn's directives and notched an arrow, drawing and sighting aim as the unseen force launched her closer to the incoming dragon. Smoke stung her eyes as the dragon billowed forth its ebon fire onto the battlefield. Kaleela held her breath against the acrid smell and stifling fumes as the dragon pulled back its wings.

Her arrow landed true, lodging into the crease between the dragon's wing joint and its body. Kaleela had no choice but to drop her bow as she barreled toward the creature in mid-flight with seconds until impact. She hit the dragon's wounded side, grabbing at any hand or foothold.

She found none.

Kaleela slipped down its side, fingers swiping against smooth scales. She pulled out the long knife at her side and swung, hoping to impale the creature and save herself from a fatal fall. Her dagger hit the dragon's scales and nicked off with naught but a scratch. She tried another quick strike, but at that angle her blade again deflected. Kaleela had seconds to find purchase, and from a distance outside herself, uncontrollable terror and panic set in as her body fell through the air. With an outward dispassion that would impress any elf, Kaleela swung her blade as hard as she could.

Her knife pierced not the flesh of the dragon, but its wing.

With a steady ripping noise so tactile Kaleela felt as well as heard it, she caught herself in a slow descent along the dragon's left wing. Injured by her arrow, plus Kaleela's full body weight upon it, the wing became immobile. The dragon screeched, spiraling to the ground. Kaleela held on to the hilt with all her strength, bracing for impact as the ground came up to meet them. The dragon landed unevenly, toppling to one side, and at last, Kaleela was flung from its wing. The impact knocked her into blackness.

Into nothingness.

The first sense to return was sound: metal clashing, voices shouting, the screech of a dying dragon, and always the chittering of the Corrupted. Next came smells: noxious smoke from the dragons' breath, vile gore from Corruptor bodies, and the earthy scent of a hot, broken land. Blood.

Kaleela blinked with effort—*when did my eyelids get so heavy?*—as she regained her senses and sat up. The fight raged on around her. She gained her footing, unsteady but determined. She looked down at her empty, weaponless hands.

She looked up, and not quite fifty yards away, impossibly, stood Dimitar and Olaf.

53

RAL

At first, the journey across the southeast Green Lands seemed familiar. Ral and Karn retraced the steps Ral and the others had taken after escaping Leighton's dragon attack. Karn led them away from the great battle up north, crossing at first chance over the Hunter Bridge to head south along the east side of the river. Ral tolerated the constant, dull aches in his body as they rode.

Karn was an individual of few words; that hadn't changed in the years since Ral's broken childhood with them. When pressed on where they headed, Karn merely said, "South. An entrance lies at the base of the Eastern Mountains. There, we enter."

Ral couldn't bring himself to ask what would happen once they did.

The lush, forested hills evolved into the plains landscape of the southeast, the Eastern Mountains ever silhouetted in the distance. A tug stirred within him and old memories rose, feelings he hadn't remembered since childhood. He was coming home.

Urged by the long-forgotten memories, Ral sensed they traveled close to where he once lived. Karn didn't deviate from their determined course, pressing them ever faster toward this southern point. As they crossed the near-familiar countryside, a pang so acute struck him, almost a physical pain, such was his longing.

He stiffened; he had no village, no home to return to. Flamberg and his childhood were long ago lost to plunder and destruction. There would be no reminiscing of his earlier life.

At one point, Karn reined in and stopped, assessing the towns and villages laid out in a valley. Almost indiscernible to the naked eye, droves of people traveled away from their homes. Karn frowned.

"Something is moving these people." Karn spoke aloud while signing to Ral, just as they had done when Ral first learned to communicate with his hands.

They nodded toward the distance, and Ral followed their gaze. He just made out the groups of people headed west, away from the mountains. Now Ral furrowed his brow; this wasn't the expected number of tradesmen and travelers. He inclined his head at Karn for an explanation, but they urged their horses onward.

The answer arrived later the following day as more travelers passed along the well-worn paths. Some stumbled along, leaning on others' shoulders. Most bore makeshift bandages made from torn cloth. Beneath his hood, Ral caught a man's vacant stare, someone who'd seen atrocities so vile that a moment's pause to recollect would drive him to madness. All held this same hollow, distant look Ral knew too well.

'This is the work of goblins,' Ral signed, anger clutching at his mangled throat.

"Come," was Karn's quiet response, coaxing their horse onward. "We must make a quick detour."

Ral inwardly sighed. He knew better than to pepper the mage with his questions.

By nightfall, they drew up to the northern edge of the great Lake Lachlann. Through the darkness, Ral spotted various fire pits and torches lighting the expanse of land situated in the middle. They arrived at the safeguarded home of the Lachans.

"Secure the horses," Karn directed. No sooner did Ral finish knotting the steeds' reins to a nearby tree, than Karn faced the island and raised their hands. They dropped them to their side in one swift motion, a flash of light rolling forth on the wave of a deep vibration. The shockwave shot outward, reaching the other shore within seconds. The horses neighed and reared in protest as the magic reverberated over them.

Ral clenched his fists, magic pouring across his body, leaving his skin prickling with energy. As the air settled, an irresistible pull of his senses turned him toward Karn: a summons.

'Is this how you come calling?' he signed at Karn, who almost looked bemused as they fixed their stare out to the island.

Distant shouts echoed from the far shoreline, followed by a soft splash as a boat launched. The boat light grew closer, and hailing was unnecessary. The boat approached their shore with half a dozen Lachans aboard. Each held a spear at ready, sharpened metal tips glinting in the lantern light.

The vessel came to ground with a soft scuffing as the bottom raked the sandy shore, and the Lachans jumped out. Their skin held varying shades of sun-tanned richness, and they wore form-fitting, fish-scale leather. Keeping their spear points at firm attention on the two, they waited for the remaining figure to join them.

Ral recognized her from all the many weeks before.

Feorn stepped off the boat, her bare feet whisper-silent as she moved through the water and came to stand before him and Karn on shore. Her spear was the only one not pointed at them, but her grip no less firm. One of the Lachans brought the boat lantern closer. Candlelight illuminated her smooth, brown face, wary eyes searching for an explanation. After taking in Karn, she relaxed her grip and bowed. The other lake people followed suit in obeisance. Feorn planted the end of her spear into the sand and then did something that surprised Ral.

"Master Karn," she greeted them, stepping forward and opening her arms. She hugged the magic-user with real warmth, comical in height difference as Karn towered over her and...

Are they embarrassed? Is that a blush?

Karn stared forward with stoicism through the embrace and did not return the gesture, though neither did they withdraw. Feorn continued her pleased greetings, her voice clipping over in the Lachan's unique language. Ral didn't understand, and waited off to the side until Feorn turned to him.

"Ah, the goblin executioner returns." She raised her hand to him with a clack of strung river pebbles adorning her wrist. Ral met her outstretched hand with his, her palm smooth to the touch, slight webbing visible between each finger. "So, you were able to find each other. I hope this bodes well for your princess's journey."

"The journey has evolved into something greater," Karn said, "and I come with a task for you, Lady of the Waters."

Feorn paused to take this in, then gestured at the boat. "I will hear more of this tale. Come join us back—"

Karn cut her off in their usual blunt manner. "We cannot afford time for pleasantries. Goblins bear down upon these lands. They'll cross around your lake within the day, perhaps by daybreak."

The Lachans murmured at this, and Feorn's eyes grew thoughtful, thin membranes crossing from the side as her eyelids blinked. "Aye, we've received word from our scouts that goblins are on a hunt. I've gathered our people home on the island. We'll wait them out, as before. Thank you for bringing us this counsel, Master Karn."

"No, it's not a hunt." Karn's voice deepened with warning. "This isn't a mere goblin horde, but an army. They're compelled by a war extending all the way up north. One attacking both humans and elves. A war joined with the Corrupted."

True horror crossed Feorn's face as Karn's words settled. "How can this be?" she whispered, her voice rising as the implications sank in. "Why would they seek such utter destruction of life, land, and waters?"

Ral was pretty sure her next words were a curse in her own language.

She composed herself and gestured to the island. "We'll keep our people safe on our land and wait out this violence until they've spent themselves and return to their mountain caves."

"Your task is not to hide and wait. You must leave your waters and join the humans to fight the goblins."

Feorn tilted her head and spoke with a firm tone. "Master Karn, your will does not secure my people's safety. The goblins would never brave crossing the depths of Lake Lachlann to touch our home. We're safe here."

Karn shifted from one foot to the other, and Ral looked up, catching the expression of one all too used to delivering grievous news.

"Perhaps, for a while." They towered above the group, and their ebony skin seemed to bring strength to the darkness of night. "But not forever. The destruction wrought around you will soil these waters. Your resources here are finite. You'll be forced to leave the island, and will find naught but carnage upon these shores. Your ending will come in slow and painful strokes. But it will come."

"They'll leave us if they've taken whatever else they want. This is their way," Feorn said, and some of the lake men nodded in agreement.

Conversation rose among the group, the Lachans speaking among themselves with worry across their faces and in their gestures.

With a small sigh, Ral stepped forward and raised his hands for attention. The Lachans quieted and all eyes turned to him. Karn translated, their baritone voice resonating through the group.

'You must fight because they'll come for you next. I lived through the nightmare you now face. They're going to destroy your people—all people. And those they don't kill...'

He paused a beat, then lowered the cloak's hood to reveal his face. Mangled. Scarred. Haunted. A few of the lake men murmured. He signed once more, his hands cradling his plea.

'They'll come for your children.'

Feorn stared at him, wide-eyed. Anger settled around her, and she turned to one of the lake men and issued a sharp command in their language. The man handed his spear off and slipped into the lake waters, beginning the swim back to the island shores with steady strokes.

"You say we have until our sister rises at dawn?" she asked, her voice tight with emotion. Karn nodded once. "Then we have much to consider this night."

"You won't fight alone. The humans nearby face your foes. Join them, and work together."

Feorn hesitated, and Ral could tell she wished for any other way. The same longing had swept through him many times in his life. The lake water lapped at their feet, and in the distance a loon gave a solemn cry, the call echoing around them. Feorn looked at him then, and empathy softened her features.

She nodded in affirmation. "And you, Master Karn? Will you stay to remove this filth from our waters?"

"No." They gestured to Ral. "We're going into the mountains to stop the source of this damnation once and for all. And we must leave now."

54

KAHLED

Bela'Ruhn and Kahled watched in unison as the third dragon crashed, the impact vibrating through their boots. Four elven warriors clung to its neck as they scrambled for purchase. The dragon shook its head, but they managed to hold fast. Rearing on its hind legs, its chest expanded with a gulp of air like blacksmith bellows. The elves tried to cut off the shadowed flame, plunging their swords into its neck. The blades sank deep enough to be fatal, yet not in time to stop the dragon from jetting out its flames in a mortal cry.

Kahled hit the ground, knocking the wind out of himself. The wave of blackened heat missed Bela'Ruhn by a hair's width but struck his entire backing squad in full force. Some managed to get their tainted armor free, but most combusted in spouts of nightmarish gore. Kahled got to his feet, assessing the situation. Bela'Ruhn yelled orders to regather his troops, then stayed his next raspy command. The dragon's last fire had consumed too many. Their squadron was no more.

From past the dragon's body came the sounds of continuing battle, including elven squad leaders shouting orders. What could've been a glimpse at reconnecting with their forces became layers upon layers of Corruptors scuttling into the space that held their one chance at retreat. They encircled Bela'Ruhn, Kahled, and the remaining handful of elven warriors, their teeming mass holding back like a predator playing with its prey.

Sinking dread filled Kahled's gut. "Well, shit."

An elven soldier echoed Kahled's sentiment with a curse of his own. Kahled sensed Bela'Ruhn turning so they stood back-to-back.

314

"Do you recall my lesson on effort, High Knight?" Bela'Ruhn asked.

"Never give your all, or you'll have nothing left to give."

"Very good." In his next command, Bela'Ruhn spoke louder, so the other elves could hear. "Now is not the time to hold back. Give your all."

Armor creaked as they dropped as one into battle-ready stances. The Corrupted charged en masse toward the small group with a chilling hiss. Kahled and the elite squad stepped forward to meet their end with swords ready.

Bela'Ruhn reached the Corruptors first, swinging his two blades with a speed and fury Kahled had never imagined. The elven general spun, dropped to one knee, and stabbed behind him, skewering a Corruptor. Stepping forward into a low squat, he spun free, his swords a whirlwind of death, slicing the chests of four other Corruptors. Bela'Ruhn twirled his blades flush against his forearms and dashed forward, every pump of his arms cleaving Corruptors in a flourish of blood. Each strike severed limbs and split skulls, wild in force and precise in execution.

Kahled turned away from Bela'Ruhn's blade dance to face the Corruptors encroaching on him. The wisdom in Bela'Ruhn's words echoed through him as he split the first Corruptor in half with an overhead swing. Every blow needed to be lethal. An initial rush channeled his determination into every strike, the Corruptors scrambling in vain to twist out of the way. But his power diminished exponentially as Kahled realized the logic behind not fighting at full strength. His arms grew weary, and twice the swing of his sword carried him off balance, leaving him almost defenseless.

Like Kahled, the other elves showed signs of tiring, and Corruptors steadily pushed the small group closer together. Only Bela'Ruhn maintained full control. His strikes drove him into the air, crashing back down with blades whirling in both directions. Corruptors fell, clutching fatal wounds. His blades swung in a blur, terrifying and hypnotic to watch.

Without warning, the remaining Corrupted stopped pressing. Kahled tucked his sword and took three strides back, giving him just enough space to assess how they fared. The group took any opportunity to rest, panting as they evaluated the Corruptors' hesitation.

"What is this?" one of them asked, an edge of desperation in his voice.

"I don't know," Bela'Ruhn said, "and I don't trust it."

The creatures stood in a tight circle around them, neither advancing nor retreating. It wasn't like the Corrupted to change strategy on the fly.

That's when Kahled knew. "Rippold has taken control."

"What do you mean?" Bela'Ruhn asked over his shoulder.

"Rippold knows they have us, sir." Kahled considered his next words. "They haven't broken through, so they've asked for guidance. Rippold is with them now."

The other elves looked at him like he'd lost his damn mind, but Bela'Ruhn grunted in response. As if on cue, one Corruptor broke from the mass and laughed in a slurry of hisses and barks.

"Very clever," it rasped. The limited vocalizations came from the Corruptor's maw, not by its own volition. "High Knight, you will be next. General... now you die."

The Corruptor shook its head as if to clear its mind, and the creatures advanced once more. This time they approached with synchronous movements, raising their claws. An impenetrable wall of talons slithered forward. One of the elves eschewed caution and charged. Three Corruptors fell, but they adjusted and closed around the elf. A brief scream, and they lost another.

"Any ideas, sir?" When he received no response, Kahled glanced at the general.

Bela'Ruhn scanned over the Corruptors, searching for some way to charge through. Getting to the other side of the encroachment where reinforcements lay was their one remaining option. "There."

Kahled followed his gaze. If any doubt remained that Rippold controlled these Corrupted, it vanished as Kahled spotted the weakness.

Rippold always held his sword higher than most. Against unskilled combatants, he used this as a feint, so they'd either attack low to try and get under the blade or attack high to knock his blade out of the way. During the High Knight training, Bela'Ruhn had tried to rid him of this habit, but Rippold refused to lose the tactic. He liked the subterfuge, and it worked quite well against a single opponent.

One Corruptor held its elongated claws higher than the rest. Rippold controlled all of them through the hive mind, but focused on this one: the lynchpin of the group.

"You go high and I go low?" Kahled asked.

Bela'Ruhn grunted his approval.

Charging together, Bela'Ruhn swung with both blades at the Corruptor's face as Kahled slid to his armored knees and aimed at the Corruptor's midsection. The Corruptor locked in confusion, not knowing which attack to counter, and therefore didn't block either. It lost its head and bowels at the same time.

With the commanding Corruptor's death, Rippold's control over the entire group wavered long enough that they no longer stood as one. Bela'Ruhn and Kahled pushed through in a straight line, slashing and slicing with calculated swiftness. For a split second, the last row of the Corruptors lay within reach.

A Corruptor rushed toward Bela'Ruhn, its claws held higher than the rest. It lashed out a wide, lethal strike at his unprotected back. With his last surge of strength, Kahled leaped between them as Bela'Ruhn turned, too late. In the same motion, Kahled flipped his sword over his shoulder and across his back, blocking the Corruptor's attack. As he pivoted to face the creature, it flung its other arm in a second strike, and Kahled couldn't bring his sword round in time. The Corruptor's claws bit into a gap in his armor, and the fire of pain exploded across his left midsection.

Another clawed hand came down toward him. Kahled hunched over, without defense. Bela'Ruhn swatted it aside and grabbed Kahled's shoulder, heaving him forward. Kahled tumbled over onto his back and braced for a mass of deathly blackness to rip him apart.

He had nothing left to give.

Instead, he faced the blue summer sky. They'd made it through.

Bela'Ruhn eased Kahled to a stand and brought him further away from the reforming battle line as reinforcements swept past, letting the High Knight lean on his shoulder for support.

"We're even," Kahled gasped as he clutched his midsection, the seeping pain blurring his vision. He could've sworn Bela'Ruhn chuckled.

"Perhaps. For now, you need a healer. I will see you there."

Kahled didn't remember much of the next stretch of time as Bela'Ruhn guided him to the healers' tent. They entered the cool enclosure where Rialyn lay unconscious upon a cot. Bandages swathed her arm in a splint. Bela'Ruhn left his side to go to hers as healers took over, helping Kahled onto a bed. The healers treated the gash over his ribs, the laceration deep. They poured a cold, green liquid over the wound, and Kahled welcomed the numbing agent with gritted teeth as they administered stitches. One healer wound a long strip of cloth around his midsection several times before moving on to attend to others. Kahled's eyes involuntarily closed, drifting off to Bela'Ruhn's whispered prayers over Rialyn.

Kahled didn't know how long he slept, and woke to a commotion outside the tent entrance, voices rising with insistence. Bela'Ruhn no longer sat with him or Rialyn. The tent flap opened, and a healer approached Kahled, carrying a small piece of sealed parchment.

"This is for you. I turned the man away because you're in no condition for visitors, but he insisted I deliver this to you with haste."

Kahled eased himself into a sitting position, grimacing as his side pulsed in new pain. He took the parchment and blanched at the sigil on the wax: the High Knight crest. He cracked the wax and read the twisted scrawl inside.

"Get me a waking draught," he said to the healer, who scowled.

"I cannot allow—"

"Get me a waking draught," Kahled repeated, his tone leaving no room for argument.

The healer clenched his jaw and went to fetch the vial.

Kahled had plenty of opportunity to use the waking draught during the Reclamation. The concoction dulled pain and enlivened the body, giving a false sense of vitality. Yet the price to pay for using the draught was just as damaging as the potion was uplifting. He'd no longer feel the wound at his side, and experience energy to fight like nothing happened. He also knew his coming actions would turn his already grievous wound much worse.

With the message repeating in his head, he took the vial and drank it.

He had no other choice.

55

DIMITAR

Dimitar rushed across the field as fast as he could, Olaf at his heels. He found it impossible not to watch the dragons raining destruction around the battlefield and then fall from the sky. He spotted the lone figure caught on the one dragon's wing, braided blonde hair whipping on the wind, and he knew. He *knew* that person was Kaleela. And he watched them both plummet to the ground.

Dimitar and Olaf hacked at any Corruptors foolish enough to confront them along the way, the elven troops outnumbering the enemy in this area. Dimitar approached the dragon, now in its death throes, ducking under its flailing, barbed tail. Elven soldiers rushed to end the creature. The felled dragon shrieked in pain and stumbled a few yards, collapsing once more to the ground. Its movements grew heavy and slow, and Dimitar and Olaf circled the dying beast, looking for Kaleela.

Dimitar's eyes locked with hers the second he saw her. She took a few unsteady steps toward him, and then they were both running, rushing into each other's arms. Dimitar crushed Kaleela in his embrace, and she clung to him, a small sound escaping from her throat. He buried his face in her neck, his cheek against her skin. He couldn't get close enough to her. Even through layers of the archers' leather armor, she felt soft against him. She was alive.

Drawing back, Dimitar cupped her face in both hands, taking in all of her. Silently he sent his thanks to the gods. The sounds of war receded, along with the fear, exhaustion, terror, and grief that had served as insidious companions since he stepped onto the battlefield. His cares fell away, and nothing else mattered except holding her.

"Are you okay? By the gods. What you did to that dragon..." Dimitar trailed off as he looked for any sign of serious injury. He ran his hands up her arms and down her back, seeking out possible wounds.

Kaleela clasped her hands around his forearms, drawing him back in, neither willing to part. "Aye, I think I just hit my head." The beginning of a smile lit her features as she gazed at him.

"I know a head knockin' when I see one," Olaf said. He never took his eyes off the battlefield as he spoke, guarding them. "We need to get ya to the healers, Princess."

Dimitar placed his arm around her shoulders, guiding her toward the back lines and healing tents. Kaleela leaned on him as they weaved away from the fighting. She kept her footing, but Dimitar suddenly stopped in his tracks.

A man skirted the edge of the healing camp. Even though the man was armed with a sword, he ducked away from the combat, working his way toward a rock outcropping at the base of a large hillside. A cloth wrapped around his forehead and ears, perhaps for shade against the summer sun. He wore an acidic expression, cruel and pleased, as he glanced at the battlefield. Dimitar's heart pounded in warning as sudden dread washed over him.

"Lad?" Olaf followed Dimitar's fixed sight and caught the scout behind the fighters and healers moving around camp. "I've seen that man before." Olaf scowled deeper. "No, not seen... I've heard 'bout him."

The answer came to Olaf at the same moment Dimitar also recognized the messenger.

"By the gods, Olaf... it's him!" Dimitar said, already taking a few steps forward. His steps quickened as he tracked the man—*no, he's an elf, I see that now*—who slipped between two large boulders at the trailhead. "He's the one who gave me Conrad's message. The false message!"

"Dimitar!" Kaleela cried out, and the plea in her voice compelled him to stop.

He's going to do something that'll destroy us all. I owe it to everyone to stop him this time. Dimitar turned to her, near frantic in his urgency.

"That's the man who deceived me... all of us," he said in a rush. "I'm sure of it, upon my life."

"I'll take her to the healer's," Olaf said.

Kaleela's eyes flashed in anger as the impact of Dimitar's words settled upon her. This scout had a role in Conrad's murder, her father's imprisonment, and this entire war. "No. You're no longer the only protectors."

Dimitar wrapped his arms around her, once more drawing her close. "I won't leave your side again." He kissed her forehead before releasing her and facing the path.

"Then let's get 'im," Olaf growled, handing Kaleela a dagger from his side.

In unspoken agreement the men stepped forward, Kaleela following as they crept up the path. Two sets of footprints appeared in the dry dirt: one set leading down the path and the other back up. Following the tracks, Dimitar approached every turn with caution. He held his sword at the ready as they came to the top of the path. Before them lay a long straightaway, and the tracks blurred at the far end.

When they reached the other end, Dimitar tilted his head to listen ahead of them, a slight scuffle unmistakable between the looming boulders. Olaf hoisted his axe, and Kaleela peered out behind him. Dimitar held up his hand and lifted three fingers, counting down. When the last finger fell, he and Olaf stepped forward as one with a yell.

An unexpected sound cut through their cries: *thadunk*.

Dimitar spun on his heel just in time to catch Olaf, who pitched forward into him as he staggered, lurching aside.

"The hells?" Dimitar snapped, at the same time Olaf said, "Who pushed me—"

Both men looked back.

Kaleela faced them, an odd tilt flashing across her face. The dagger slipped from her hand. Her voice issued forth upon a whisper. "I saved you. You're both safe."

She attempted to smile, wavering on her feet. Olaf dropped his axe and barely caught her in time as she collapsed, limp in his arms.

In her back, next to her right shoulder blade, was embedded a long, dark arrow.

56

DIMITAR

Kaleela...

With heavy feet Dimitar rushed to Olaf, taking Kaleela in his arms. He cried out a senseless refusal as he dropped to his knees, cradling her and repeating her name. Her head rolled against his chest.

Too late, the trap was revealed. The noise ahead served only as a distraction from the actual attack behind them. At the far end of the rocky clearing stood the messenger, a discharged crossbow resting against his leg. Olaf bent to collect Lucky once more with a look of absolute, unchecked murder. The messenger met his eye, blanched, and ran out of sight behind the nearest cluster of boulders. Olaf started to chase him, but Dimitar called him back.

"Oh gods... Olaf, help me." Dimitar's voice filled with desperation.

Olaf crouched beside them and helped turn Kaleela, so they could view the scope of her injury. The arrow cut into her back, deeply embedded, and blood seeped through her tunic. Her eyes flew open, the sparkling green now cloudy with pain, and the true extent of her wound realized.

"Hurts... hurts too much," she gasped. Kaleela squeezed her eyes shut as she struggled for a deep breath. She gave a strangled cry as Dimitar shifted her in his arms, her body trembling from the shock and pain.

"Ah, Princess... no, not you... not for the likes o' me," Olaf said, his voice hitching.

The two men shared an anguished look, both refusing to speak the unbearable. Wordless understanding passed between them.

"Watch her, brother." With the greatest care, Dimitar placed her once more in Olaf's arms. Dimitar shuddered, trying to regain a sense of hope. She still had a chance. The healers' tents weren't far from the path entrance.

"Dimitar." Kaleela fought for breath, reaching for him.

He grabbed her hands and pressed them to his lips. "Live for me. I'm going to find help." Dimitar leaned close to her. "I love you. I've always loved you."

Kaleela tried to respond, but words choked in her throat from the effort of breathing. A tear slipped out the corner of her eye, tracing down her dirt-stained face. Dimitar squeezed her hands, but she no longer had the strength.

"Shhh, it's okay, it's okay," Dimitar said, his voice breaking. He kissed her fingers once more, and willed himself the courage to let go and stand.

Before he took a single step, he froze at the sound of dark laughter. He whirled around, uncontrolled rage in his eyes.

At the end of the clearing, the Overlord crouched on a low boulder. Rippold's knees were level with his shoulders, spikes jutting out from cracked skin and blending together into a lethal patch of thorns. The black, sleeveless gambeson appeared at odds with the armored elves on the battlefield, dotted with rivets and flaunting Rippold's confidence. Dark corruption edged his face, flat and planed out in broad strokes as if by a clumsy painter.

"I told the messenger to shoot the first person to cross this path," Rippold said. "Of course, I expected Kahled. But for his daughter to die in his place? Well, if that isn't a delight."

"I'm going to fucking kill you," Dimitar said, shaking with anger.

Rippold sneered. "Peculiar though, isn't it? Two women of the same name and same elven blood dying well before their human companions. I guess their race isn't all it boasts to be."

Dimitar's breath came in ragged gasps, but under his barely checked emotions he faced a far greater dilemma. Kaleela's strained breath made his own chest hurt; she didn't have much time. Dimitar was faster than Olaf, and had the better chance of reaching help. But he couldn't leave Olaf alone to fight Rippold, who'd surely attack once Dimitar left. Furthermore, if he went for help and Olaf fought Rippold, who would protect Kaleela?

The intensity grew tenfold as Rippold lowered himself from his perch. "A shame I wasn't there when Kaleel died. She insulted my pride and her own race when she chose Kahled. A mistake she paid dearly for."

Rippold looked at Kaleela, not in regret but with a smile. Dimitar's indecision was answered: he grabbed his sword off the ground.

As if Rippold understood Dimitar's intention, he curled his lip. "At least I have the satisfaction of removing Kaleel from history. Now her child—Kahled's daughter—will follow her in early death."

"Nooo!" Dimitar cried.

Any remaining hesitation disappeared in a cloud of unchecked anger. His face twisted into a mask of pure vengeance as he charged. Dimitar threw all his weight behind a high, double-handed blow. Rippold twisted at the waist to dodge the attack, Dimitar's sharp elven blade nicking the edge of the gambeson.

Rippold reached behind his back and pulled out his High Knight blade. His counter-attack came in a fast frenzy of low and mid strikes. Dimitar had no time to recall his lessons, and improvised his defense, escaping the first flurry unscathed. He launched his own offensive, swinging his sword in tight arcs, and his impassioned strikes met with Rippold's clanging defense. Dimitar continued his vicious attack, forcing Rippold to step back in what appeared to be a defensive maneuver. He fell for the trick as Rippold sidestepped one of the strikes, parrying it with a quick swipe.

Cursing himself, he spun his blade to block the next attack just in time. Aimed at his neck, it would've proven fatal. The blow was powerful enough to send Dimitar reeling. Staggering back to distance himself, he rolled his ankle on a stone. Pain rushed forth, quick and blinding as he fell to the ground, his sword slipping from his hand.

Rippold laughed, cruel and full of malice, as Dimitar crawled backwards on his hands and feet. Grabbing him by the chest plate, Rippold lifted him. He stared deep into Dimitar's eyes as he brought the sword up to his throat. Instead, Dimitar threw the dirt in his clenched fist into Rippold's face.

Dimitar broke free from the grip and reeled back from the cloud of dust and pebbles, landing on his bad ankle. Gritting his teeth, he limped over to where his sword had fallen. Luck stayed with him as Rippold worked to scrub his eyes free of the dirt.

Stepping forward, his ankle yelling in protest, Dimitar drove his sword through the Overlord's middle.

Rippold roared as he twisted his body, ripping Dimitar's sword from his hands. Blinded from the dirt, Rippold swung his sword in a wild sweep, and Dimitar stumbled out of the way.

Planting his sword tip in the ground, Rippold brought both hands to encircle the hilt of the embedded sword. He pulled Dimitar's blade from his abdomen in one vicious tug, an arc of black blood following the tip as he threw the sword wide. Rippold bent back and bellowed in pain, fists clenched as his skin resealed.

Dimitar charged, landing a punch to the wound. Rippold doubled over with a grunt, and Dimitar hit him in the face, then again and again.

The next time Dimitar swung, Rippold grabbed him by the fist and yanked him around with unnatural strength. With a pop, his left shoulder wrenched out of socket, and Dimitar cried out, the pain instantly crippling. Rippold seized Dimitar under the jaw, lifting until they locked gazes. With his other hand, he wrapped long, clawed fingers around his neck, squeezing.

"I'm going to make your death hurt," he growled.

Dimitar fought the Overlord's powerful grip in vain, unable to move his dislocated arm. As his air supply slowly cut off, Dimitar looked into the face of his death, calm and defiant, his vision spinning. Somewhere deep inside, he knew he bested the High Knight. His strike had been fatal, and only the Corrupted healing powers saved Rippold from death. The Overlord lived, but High Knight Rippold lost. And they both knew it.

57

THE OVERLORD

R ippold watched the life drain from the guard's face. Suddenly, his hands relaxed their grip, and the young man collapsed to the ground in an unconscious heap. There wasn't a spoken command to do so nor any physical harm done to him.

Rather, there was a presence.

Smiling, Rippold whirled on his heel, his arms and legs already forming the High Knight battle stance.

Kahled had arrived.

58

KAHLED

The great High Knight didn't share the glance. Instead, he knelt beside his unconscious daughter, his face pulled tight in anguish. Closing his eyes, Kahled took a steadying breath and placed his hand on Kaleela's head. The world grew wholly silent as he collected his pain. *Conrad, give her all your strength so I can see this done.* Coming to a stand, still looking at his girl, he unsheathed the sword at his hip.

Slow and deliberate, Kahled turned to face Rippold. When their eyes met, a battle greater than any rivalry with swords took place. Between them flew sparks of living, thriving emotion, electric and powerful. Fueled by both honor and love, Kahled lowered himself into his fighting pose.

The two High Knights mirrored each other as they circled, swords within striking distance. Both men bent at the knees just so, their chests turned at the precise angle to present very little of a target yet still allow great mobility in their attacks. The blades crossed their bodies an exact equidistant width away, placed for both defense and attack. This was the High Knight stance for one-on-one combat, a blend of elven and human forms of swordplay, and both men were masters.

"Exceptional likeness she has to her mother," Rippold said, breaking the silence. "Pity she caught the arrow intended for you. Thus continues the luck of the bloodline, I suppose."

Kahled checked himself, trying to keep his anger at bay. His sword dipped a fraction, his emotions reaching his hand well before his training. Rippold tried to incite him to make a mistake—and it almost worked.

Kahled waited for the right time to break the standoff as the circling continued. Too sudden of an attack signaled desperation, an anxiousness to have the fight over. Too much patience tensed his muscles beyond fight readiness. Between those two moments was the prime time to attack, which, of course, was the hardest of the three to discern.

"Tell me, High Knight," Rippold continued. "Does her blood run as thick as Kaleel's? Oh, I forgot. You abandoned her while she died, didn't you?" Lowering his voice a notch, he added, "Just like you are now."

With a streak of metal, Kahled's blade broke through the air, ending the standoff. Rippold stood equal to the challenge, his own sword catching Kahled's in a wide parry. Rippold's counter-attack came swift and exact, but not enough to find Kahled unprepared. With a sweeping parry of his own, he struck the blade wide of the mark. His rage still festering, Kahled launched a vicious series of blows, all aimed at his neck and chest. Rippold stepped back in defense with quick measured steps, and Kahled pressed the advantage in hopes of overpowering him. He realized too late that Rippold had fooled him into an overly aggressive attack.

Rippold ducked below his next thrust, leaving the entire lower half of Kahled's body exposed. Kahled sidestepped the blade, but couldn't stop Rippold's fist from landing solidly. Fresh pain overpowered the waking drought's numbing effects, and new blood seeped through his bandages.

Grimacing, Kahled stepped back beyond striking distance to collect himself. He'd protected his leatherwear with only a pauldron in his haste to leave the healer's tent, knowing he'd have to match Rippold's speed in a duel. Of course, Rippold knew where to strike; he'd gained that collective knowledge from the Corrupted on the battlefield earlier. Despite his familiarity with Rippold's tactics, Kahled had fallen victim to his taunts. The sharp ache at his side made sure it wouldn't happen again.

Like predators on the hunt, the two High Knights once more found their stances and circled one another. Rippold smirked as Kahled favored his left side, dark red blooming the leather. He'd drawn first blood against Kahled—something he couldn't do in hundreds of sparring sessions during their training.

Rippold reached out from time to time with his blade to bounce the tip against Kahled's sword, trying to provoke another fit of attacks. But Kahled calmed his emotions, his mind settling into his High Knight training.

Rippold stepped forward, his sword coming in low. In a flash of memory, Kahled remembered him taking the same move against hundreds of Corrupted during the Reclamation. If he backed away in defense, Rippold would bring his sword up with amazing speed and thrust out his hand, his long reach burying the blade deep into his opponent's chest.

Kahled stood his ground and brought his own sword low to block Rippold's blade. He took the advantage. Twirling, he brought his sword around in an arc, aiming at his neck. The blade didn't quite meet its target, instead slicing through the shoulder spikes. With a grunt of unexpected pain, Rippold stumbled backwards, three long, black spikes falling to the ground as he retreated.

Kahled didn't give Rippold time to collect himself, and charged. His first strike met with a loud clang, but his second, quicker attack landed square on Rippold's thigh, his blade burying itself halfway into the leg.

Neither warrior moved, both wide-eyed as, incredibly, Rippold's thigh knit together and healed itself with Kahled's blade still embedded.

Rippold acted first, slapping Kahled with the back of his fist and sending him sprawling. As Kahled tried to stop the world from spinning, Rippold closed his eyes to prepare for the sword's removal. Taking two sharp breaths, he grabbed the hilt and yanked with all his strength. The pain made him cough and collapse to one knee. Locking his jaw against the agony, he turned to find Kahled, just in time for Kahled's fist to crash into his face, sending him tumbling.

Kahled lifted his sword and took his position once again. Rippold faced away from him as he got to his feet. When he turned back around, Kahled's heart skipped a beat. Rippold's eyes roiled black with the Corrupted soulless gaze.

Neither knight moved as they stared each other down, their rage tangible in the space between them. Both men knew the next strike would be the last.

"You fight well, High Knight," Rippold said. "But not well enough. Now you'll learn why I should've worn Kaleel's honor, why I deserve kingship, why I alone was chosen to rule the Green Lands."

Rippold raised his sword to shoulder level, pointing at him. "You should've joined me. We would've been unstoppable. But I'm afraid you're too weak of will. For that, you must die."

He advanced on Kahled, who anticipated a rush, not this deliberate, calculated approach. Stepping back, Kahled worked to maintain the distance between them.

What's he trying to do? Kahled analyzed Rippold for any indication of his next move. His hand ached from clenching his sword handle, the intensity churning in the air. Relaxing his grip for less than a second, he made a terrible mistake.

Rippold waited for this exact moment. He stepped forward with unnatural speed and threw his entire weight behind a strike aimed at Kahled's sword just as he loosened his grip. The blade flew out of Kahled's hand, reverberations numbing his wrist. Rippold's next strike missed as Kahled ducked, and he kicked Kahled in the chest. He slammed backwards to the ground, his arm narrowly avoiding the severed spikes. Spinning his sword, Rippold brought the tip down and drove the blade through the armor gap in Kahled's left shoulder, into the ground.

High Knight Kahled, King of Blackburn, beloved of the elves, and perhaps the greatest fighter ever known to humankind since the fall of the Mage Warriors, was beaten.

He tried to mask the painful fire radiating from his shoulder and shooting up and down his entire body. He reached for the blade with his right hand, wanting to free the sword in his daze of pain, but his entire body felt pinned. The more he struggled, the more his vision turned to gray in an excruciating haze. Swallowing his pride, Kahled fell still on the ground. If he had any chance to win this fight, he had to think—and falling unconscious from pain would limit that.

Kahled slumped as if accepting his fate, and Rippold sneered. "I'm far from finished with you, High Knight. A lesson needs to be taught."

It's the suffering he wants, always has been.

Placing both of his clawed hands on the cross guard of his sword, Rippold leaned with all his weight and ever so slightly rotated the blade. Kahled grimaced in pain-racked suffering, tensing his entire body against the sharp agony, but still he refused to cry out.

Rippold knew just what to say, leering over him. "You never deserved her, Kahled. You fought her fate, as well as your own. Kaleel died for your grievances. And now your cursed daughter, this foolish boy, and all these elven saviors will die along with her. Their blood is on your hands. Their deaths are your fault. You should be glad I'm going to kill you."

Kahled closed his eyes, fighting back tears of pain and sudden, overwhelming reality. He tried to block out Rippold's words, but couldn't find a way to alleviate the gut-twisting guilt drilling through his mind.

He should've known marrying Kaleel was a mistake. Kaleela would've never been born, but at least she wouldn't be lying in a puddle of her own blood, her young life cut short with the crossbow bolt intended for him. Even Conrad's death weighed on his shoulders. If he joined Conrad when he ventured north to investigate the Corrupted rumors, perhaps he'd still be alive. And Dimitar, coming into knighthood with so much of his life to live, now discarded awkward and lifeless on his side, his arm at an unnatural angle. All his loved ones, dead or dying because of him.

What have I done?

'You've taught us to love,' a soft, pleasing voice said deep within Kahled's mind, one he hadn't heard in a long, long time. Just the sound of her soothing lilt made his heart cry out.

"Kaleel," Kahled said, a tear escaping down his face.

Rippold smirked, understanding that the pain he caused with his words far outweighed the agony of the sword buried in Kahled's shoulder. "That's right, Kahled. You killed her. By breaking the laws of nature, you've killed them all. And now you'll die alone. A failure. You're nothing."

His words were now lost on Kahled. Kaleel's voice flooded his veins with staggering warmth and strength. The pain in his shoulder all but disappeared in the glow, and the guilt twisting his gut unbound. He hadn't caused anyone's suffering.

'You taught us to love,' Kaleel said again as if to confirm his thoughts. Kahled couldn't tell whether she was real or a pain-induced hallucination, but for some reason, it mattered little. 'You gave us the one thing that defies death and binds us eternally. They need you. Please, my love. Now is not your time to join me. Be strong, and live!'

Kahled's face flushed with renewed energy.

Rippold pressed his weight on the sword. "Look at me."

He wants my despair. Kahled opened his eyes, but behind them pulsed an emotion far from hopelessness.

Kahled struck out with his right hand against the flat of the blade buried in his shoulder. Although the pain sent a wave of nausea coursing through his body, Kahled forced himself to turn as Rippold stumbled forward, the source of his balance disappearing from under his hands. As Kahled rolled, the sword pulled free just enough for him to grab one of the spikes on the ground. Clutching the thorn in his hand, he gathered every ounce of his strength into one, tremendous swing. The strike landed in the soft, meaty part of Rippold's neck under his chin as he reeled forward, driving the barb deep into his jaw.

Rippold staggered backwards. He grabbed at the spike embedded in his neck, the point puncturing the back of his throat. The claws on his fingers prevented a solid grasp of the smooth, thin base. His eyes grew wide as his healing powers re-formed skin over and around the thorn, trapping the spike in his throat. Choking in pain and surprise, Rippold twisted as his breath cut off, black blood frothing from his mouth.

Gritting his teeth, Kahled pulled the sword free from his shoulder and came to a shaky stand. He staggered over to Rippold, who'd fallen to his knees, hands raking at his neck.

In a pained yet steady voice, Kahled addressed the dying Overlord. "You're wrong, Rippold. I helped them all to live. And you never should've touched Conrad."

With a merciful thrust, Kahled drove the blade straight through Rippold's heart.

Leaning close as the last breath left Rippold's lips, Kahled spoke in his ear. "I'm only the cause of your death, you bastard."

The two High Knights shared one last look before Rippold fell to the ground, dead.

Kahled contemplated the body in deep silence. The fallen Knight's leathery skin transformed, the Corrupted seed inking from his pores, sucked into the dry ground. Kahled didn't feel any grief nor sign of regret—only a deep-seated justice.

He turned at the footsteps coming up the path as a handful of elven warriors joined the clearing. Three immediately dropped by Kaleela's side, and one approached him. The man spoke to him in elvish, and although Kahled understood the language, the words came at him as if from underwater. Instead, Kahled searched inside himself for the sweet voice that called to him and spoke the truth of their love. He wanted to hear her again. But already, the voice faded into memory.

One of the soldiers caught his attention, pulling him out of his musings. "High Knight. Your daughter, sir, she doesn't fare well."

Struck with more force than any blow Rippold delivered, reality slammed into him. He spun too fast, his shoulder sending a crippling pain through his body while his midsection screamed from torn stitches. His footing staggered, irregular as he came to her side.

"You two!" he yelled to the guards nearest the trail. "Go get help!"

The guards looked at Kaleela, then to one another. Their glance punched Kahled in the gut with what wasn't said aloud.

Kaleela was dying.

59

DIMITAR

D amn it, she isn't going to die! Go get help now!"
Dimitar's head lolled to one side, eyes shut and drifting in and out of consciousness. *Whose voice was that?* It sounded like Kahled's. *Did he see how I failed...?*

Somewhere in the recesses of his awareness, he felt hands on his body, turning him over, probing the muscles of his left arm. With one push, the bone buried back into the joint.

The pain awoke Dimitar with a cough of nausea, eyes flying open and a yell on his lips. The elf worked his fingers around the shoulder to ensure the arm went back in place. Dimitar sat up, groggy, his eyes still blurred with dark dreams of death. The elf removed a leaf from his healing pouch, crumbled it in his fingertips, and held it under Dimitar's nose.

The powerful herb had an immediate effect, and Dimitar rose to full consciousness. "Wha... what happened?"

In response, the elf pointed to where Rippold lay in a pool of oily, black blood. Dimitar's eyes grew wide, trying to remember. Bracing his weight on his arms to stand, Dimitar winced when they both throbbed in resistance. They served as a painful reminder of his failure to defeat the evil knight.

The elite guard wrapped his arm around Dimitar's middle and helped him to a stand. He waited for Dimitar to grow steady on his legs, still supporting his weight as they walked over to Kahled.

When they drew close enough, Dimitar stiffened. Kahled sat on the ground, cradling Kaleela in his arms, the crossbow bolt protruding from her back. In a rush of memory, Dimitar replayed Kaleela collapsing, the weight of her body against his as he took her from Olaf and sank to the ground, his name on her whispered breath. A pain more acute than any wound slammed into him.

"Come here, lad," Kahled said, his voice wavering. "There's someone who needs you."

Dimitar couldn't stop shaking as he sank down next to them. Kaleela's face had drained of color, strikingly pale, her lips parted. Her chest rose with her breathing, but the time between breaths grew longer—*too long*—with each rasp. A crimson pool wet the ground where she lay. The sight of her lifeblood was equal to a slap across Dimitar's face, wrenching the agony from within him.

"Oh, gods. Please don't leave us, Kaleela. Hold on." Dimitar grew desperate, mindless of Kahled whose eyes clenched shut as he held Kaleela close, mouthing a prayer. He wanted to touch her, but dared not disturb Kahled's embrace. He willed her eyes to open so he could see the fire and beauty that captured his heart. A terrible loneliness descended upon his chest. He leaned in close to her, begging the gods to send her his words, and cupped her limp hand.

"Don't leave me, Kaleela." His voice came as a half-whisper, half-plea, fighting to stay strong as if his strength would regain hers. "You don't know what you mean to me. I can't... not without you..."

Grief wrenched from Dimitar's throat from his need to tell her all his love, and never having the chance. He could no longer breathe around the pain in his chest. The clearing fell silent as if withdrawing from the drowning sorrow by two broken hearts.

All at once, a voice shattered the silence—a loud, booming voice.

"For gods' sake, man! Would ya hurry up!"

Dimitar raised his tear-stained face as his friend came charging over. He'd been so engulfed with grief that he forgot Olaf was supposed to be here, guarding Kaleela. *Where did you go?*

His answer came right behind Olaf, Willem's tell-tale green robe rustling as the tall elf rushed to them.

Willem sank to his knees next to Kahled. Reaching out a scarred, trembling hand, he tried to free Kaleela from his hold. Kahled met the elf's cool gaze with vehement resistance.

"I need the room," Willem said.

Still, Kahled refused to release his daughter. "She's... not... breathing." He choked the words out, unable to say more.

"Please, Kahled," Willem urged. "Let me save her."

Kahled's heated gaze met Willem's, then his face crumpled. With the utmost care, he laid Kaleela on her side. Dimitar linked arms with him, as much to help his king to his feet as to gather his own strength, and the two took a few steps back. Olaf circled around and joined them, grabbing Dimitar's hand in his.

"I wanted to carry her to the healers, but with the ruttin' arrow stickin' out her back and m'arm... If I'm too late..." Olaf's words became lost in a checked sob.

They shared a quick, emotional look before turning to Willem.

Stillness fell over the clearing as the mage closed his eyes, his breathing slow and regular. Willem held out his hands a span away from Kaleela's chest. He chanted, low and methodical, his voice somehow overlapping in whispers and different pitches, twisted by the magic's potency. The words were ancient and the spell, almost an impossibility.

Willem said the price was always too great.

The air around his hands flickered, white-blue magic weaving itself between his scarred fingers in intricate patterns and designs. As Willem's words built, so did the light's braiding until his hands glowed with solid, dazzling brilliance. The magic worked its way up Willem's arms, his shoulders encompassed with shimmering, pale blue. His face twisted with strain, eyes flickering under his lids, lips a blur as words flowed from his mouth in ever-increasing intensity. Sweat pooled on his brow and dripped down his face as the conjuration engulfed his chest and neck, his entire frame shining with magic.

Without warning, his body bolted upright as he screamed the last word of the spell in a mix of pain and elation. Dimitar started forward, but Kahled tightened his hold, entreating him to wait.

The light encompassing Willem whirled with energy as it circled and rolled around his body. The mage's arms unfurled to either side, palms facing the sky and fingers stretched as far as the hands allowed. Streaks of golden light intermixed with beams of crimson and emerald formed from the elements themselves, their radiance increasing to match the air magic. He forced a hand down to curl around the embedded arrow. In a final blast of sheer brilliance, the combined elements flooded into Kaleela's body.

The magic blanketed Kaleela and Willem together. Then the energies leapt from his body to hers, throwing Willem back several feet. Kaleela's entire body arched, illuminated and enfolded by the magic spell as it glimmered over her, sinking in. Another flash of light ripped through the clearing, and the three men shielded their eyes. With a final crack like a lightning strike, the light vanished, the clearing at once calm and silent.

Dimitar and Kahled stepped forward together, their gait anxious and reserved at the same time. Their need to know if Willem's spell had worked was beset by the knowledge that if the magic didn't cast perfectly...

Dimitar steeled himself as the thought raced through his mind. The setting sun cast a deepening shadow as he bent to Kaleela. Kahled stood next to him, fists clenched at his side. The sunset's golden glow caressed her features. Dimitar turned her over, searching her face. A flush tinged high on her cheeks, and her chest rose and fell in a normal rhythm. Relief coursed through him like a balm, and he pulled Kaleela into his arms. Silently, Dimitar made a promise to her then, to tell her all he'd been meaning to say.

Kahled sat beside him, resting his palm on the back of Kaleela's head. He murmured endearments as he stroked her hair. Guardsmen and guardswomen surrounded the princess, checking vitals and calling for a stretcher. Dimitar was pulled to his feet, drawn into Olaf's embrace.

"He saved her, lad." Leaning back from the hug, he bellowed to the sky, "By the gods, he saved her!"

A groan from a few yards away cut the moment short. Willem rolled over, utterly spent and half-conscious. His hand fell open, and an object clattered on the rock. Olaf hurried over and knelt next to the mage as more guards rushed to attend him. Picking up the object, he murmured in surprise.

Olaf stood and turned to the others, his hand extended. In his fist was the long, dark shaft of the crossbow bolt.

60

RAL

R al stood at the mountain entrance, taking in the path's unnatural darkness. He inhaled, trying to fill the sudden hollowness in his gut. The summer sun fell upon his back, but a coldness within him rose. Every villager's scream, every goblin's throaty growl, every poisonous screech from the Corrupted, all echoed through his mind. The mountain swallowed him up before he even set foot inside, and Ral wished he were anywhere but here, even as he understood this was the only place he could be.

Karn stood next to Ral, side by side. They secured their long black braids on top of their head, tucked and overlapped. They, too, appraised the gaping slit in the mountain face, scowling. The goblin entrance had been cleaved into the rock with imprecise strikes, sharp and jagged, by unskilled hands. A foulness in the air lingered about the entry.

Karn's bird screeched as if to embolden them onwards as it drifted in slow circles overhead. Karn cast a baleful eye up at Sevak, then addressed Ral. "The goblins all left the mountain to head to their southern war, but that doesn't mean danger isn't waiting."

Ral half-heartedly kicked at a small stone underfoot with his toe.

'Master Karn,' Ral signed, hesitating long enough for Karn to turn and face him. Ral struggled with what he wanted to say, but a weakness born of enduring fear and trauma stole his courage. At that moment, Ral once again became a damaged child: unsafe, alone, and with no control over the pain that would happen next.

'I don't want this,' he motioned at last, gesturing to the opening and all that waited within.

Karn looked down at him, studying his face within the cloak's shadowed hood, Ral's misery and shame on full display.

"Do you sense it?" Karn asked in response.

Ral shivered involuntarily. Something lay within the mountain, vile and festering, something that would make him beg for his years under the goblins' cruelty over the alternative. A pull of absolute evil radiated from the entrance, as if its defilement seeped into his very pores. Ral had faced his suffering within the mountains twice now: once when seeking out King Kahled upon capture and again attempting his rescue. Mere steps away from a third return into a living nightmare, this time was different. Death was the favored outcome, as worse things than dying lay within.

This time promised the worst of all. And he didn't want to do it.

Karn nodded, as if hearing all of Ral's thoughts. They then did something unexpected.

Karn took a knee, lowering themself, so they were below Ral's eye level. Just as when Ral was a child, Karn took one of his hands. The gesture was calming and serious, and Ral knew that what Karn said next would be nothing but the complete truth.

"If what I suspect is right, you're going to be tested," Karn said, bringing both hands up to sign as they spoke, green and blue eyes never breaking contact with the hooded man. "That isn't why I brought you here. I'll lead us to the source, but I need you to guide me. I cannot do this without you."

A lump formed in Ral's throat. He swallowed, not without some effort; he hadn't permitted himself tears for a very, very long time. Whatever... *thing*... awaited them inside the mountain charged his emotions. Something this evil, this strong, couldn't be allowed to claim the Green Lands, no matter what it cost him.

"This isn't the end," Karn added, coming to a stand and facing the entrance once more. "This is a beginning."

With that, Ral came into his resolve, and he raised his chin and squared his shoulders. 'I am at your service.'

Karn selected a fallen branch and lit the tip with the touch of a fingertip, handing it to Ral as they walked into the passageways. The Eastern Mountain's interior came rushing back to Ral in a blast of remembrance that couldn't be helped. Along with the memories came overwhelming grief for the wasted years during his youth, the hundreds of people who lost their lives digging the tunnels, and most of all, his parents who could never be replaced. The dark, swirling energies seemed to feed off his pain, and Ral tried to block them out. He focused on his task at hand, which Karn explained to him as they stepped inside.

Karn followed Ral, eyes closed in the deepest thought. Their hands rested on Ral's shoulders for guidance as the great magic-user searched out with their mind, their body now a shell of life. They could no longer speak, hear, or see; all senses turned inward, focused on the pull of the source. Squeezing Ral's right shoulder, they indicated they should head toward the right when a tunnel provided access. Ral turned there and continued to guide them, waiting for Karn's next signal.

He led Karn through countless passageways, lit by the magicked torch, his eyes seeing for both of them. He sensed the abyss deep in the mountainside as it pulsed with a lethal iciness. Karn's next directional squeeze was much tighter than the rest, as if Karn held onto Ral for strength. After another right, the air became frigid. The tunnels were dank and often muggy but never this cold. Warnings rang in Ral's head.

A thick layer of ice encroached upon the rock face. Stone cracked in places, the chill biting the slab asunder. Ral tugged his cloak tighter, cold snaking into his robes. His breath crystallized in the air as he turned left, entering a large cavern with several side tunnels connected to the chamber. Ral's footsteps came to an abrupt halt, his feet slipping on the slick surface. Karn came to their senses with a great inhale, opening their eyes, now brown and black.

They reached the source.

The rock face at the far side of the cavern split into an endless hole in the fabric of reality. The abyss stretched roughly the size of a horizontal doorway, filling Ral's entire field of vision the longer he gazed upon it. The deep blackness appeared inert at first glance, but as Ral's sharp eyes focused on the horrific vision, the surface boiled with activity, deep shadows folding over onto themselves. As Ral stared into the void, he inhaled sharply, eyes wide in revulsion.

In the waves of the agitated surface rose the cold, cruel face of a forming Corruptor. A twisted and tangled larva, its eyes bulged twice as large as they should be. The hatchling Corruptor pressed to the membranous surface of the hole, its hands stretching out and extending beyond the boundaries of the abyss.

Ral jumped as Karn rested their hand on his shoulder and pulled him back. Ral stepped away, eyes locked on the scene, his attention fixed on the slimy, dripping arm that ended with the wicked claws of a Corruptor.

Karn surveyed the void, ignoring the creatures and scanning the edges of the hole. Its fluidity lapped against the rock like waves on a shoreline. The hole grew larger and churned with ten times the power as before. Almost as if...

"Gods of mercy."

The source, the very portal to pure evil cast deep into the Eastern Mountains, knew Karn stood to destroy it.

The larva Corruptor finished with its metamorphosis, its pointed head starting to crown through the surface. Karn and Ral simultaneously took another step back. The hole's churning wasn't roiling waves. Thousands of Corruptor hatchlings waited for their birth.

Facing this enormity, Ral's emotions shifted. All his fear and reluctance transformed into an absolute refusal to allow this filth to enter the Green Lands and beyond. The urge to stop this leap of evil became a calling upon which he must act.

Ral crossed the distance to the source, a dagger seized in his fist. He raised his hand high and swung a vicious strike aimed at the crowning Corruptor's head. His hand came too close to the abysmal void, growing painfully cold as his knife shattered against the surface. A split second later, darkness leapt off the rock face, seeking human flesh to defile. Ral's reflexes proved quicker, but not by much. The small, dark mass fell to the floor with a plop, melting into the stone at Ral's feet. He leapt back and automatically drew two new blades, his breath in ragged bursts visible in the air.

Karn, in turn, took a step closer to the hole. Ready or not, it was time. With the first ancient word uttered, the spell poured from their mouth with its own will, pulling itself from the collective power within the tenfold magic-user. Karn gestured with both arms, commanding the elements to them, ice crystals forming on the waves of magic in the air.

The void grew even larger in response, larvae rushing to hatch. Hundreds of Corruptors pushed against the abyss film, their faces newly formed on their distorted skulls. The first hatchling now crawled out to mid-chest, its legs trying to kick itself free from the source's membrane as it let out an inhuman shriek.

As Ral stood with a dagger in each hand, he began to rock back and forth on his feet. A certain rhythm pulsed to the undulations of the source, as if breathing. With each bend of his knees, darkness and malevolence pulsated within that tear in reality. Worse still, he understood it on a visceral level. Not a temptation, but a primal acceptance of its existence.

Karn increased their chanting, and the words tangibly unwound in Ral's mind. Karn's words manifested the true opposite of the tear. Where the source drove an ancient fury, Karn's spell unleashed purity. Ral sensed the magic flowing in time with the waves of darkness from the abyss, as if somehow one and the same yet also diametrically opposed. The pull and ebb of the two forces tugged something deep in his core, stirring ancestral memories long forgotten, some inner lock now released.

Ral tried to pull himself out of the powerful tide overtaking his entire being, but couldn't extract himself. He wasn't afraid; somehow the power belonged to him, rather than something the incantation or void did to him. Yet neither was he prepared for what was happening. The more he fought the rising power within, the stronger it became. Involuntarily, he dropped both blades, arms and hands going rigid, splayed by his side. He threw his head back, hood falling to his shoulders, as ripples of energy coursed across his chest and down his limbs.

I have to stop the source.

The void contracted, fighting the spell. Magic swirled throughout the cavern as if whipped by an outside gale. For a terrible moment, lightning crashed inside the source, illuminating innumerable Corruptor bodies and other creatures too horrific to name in a field of endless depth.

Faced with this terrible destruction, Ral's mind turned to the grace within himself. He pictured Kaleela and her sweetness, the first to smile at him in her gentle way, her innate ability to care about him as a person and not just for his assistance. And Dimitar, the young man's quiet strength, his capacity to own his mistakes, his passion to defend all those he loved. Ral envisioned the two of them together, Kaleela in Dimitar's arms, and the vision pierced his heart like a song note. Olaf's roaring laughter... the blessed relief when King Kahled first signed with him... the soothing energies of the trees in the Sun'Din, an old familiar comfort...

I have to stop it for them.

With that last conscious thought, Ral surged with power from within, uncontrolled, lifting him so his toes left the ground. He stared down the void and screamed with the impossible sound of his own voice.

Karn's recitation rose to match the maelstrom, power and magic extending through his hands and off his body to pound the edge of the source, releasing its hold upon the world. He spoke the last word of the spell with a thunderclap.

The shrieking of a thousand damned souls filled the cavern with ear-splitting harshness. Undulating in ever-larger strokes around the edge, the void struggled to maintain its hold on the rock face. Corruptor larvae pushed against the barrier, but could no longer break through. The surface boiling grew violent, as if the entire source poised to explode outwards. But the void's last attempt at spreading its evil was for naught. The edge of the abyss pulled back toward the middle, collapsing in on itself.

The Corruptor pulling itself free saw the edges closing inwards and renewed its efforts. With a grunting hiss, it pulled itself out halfway but no further. Fear churned in its eyes, and the void closed around it, cutting it in half. The source closed with a hiss of steam, the rock face once more unmarred.

Ral's eyes glazed over, lost in both inner thought and knowledge from countless prior lives. Power swirled unchecked around him. Karn laid their palm on his forehead.

"Now is not the time. Sleep."

A brief flash of light, and Ral collapsed to the ground, unconscious.

61

DIMITAR

D imitar's arm, shoulder, and ankle all hurt like hell coming down the hillside, his throat bruised and so sore that it hurt to speak or swallow. The elven healers harnessed his dislocated shoulder and bandaged his ankle, then plied him with numbing creams, healing treatments, and sleep draughts. What Dimitar needed most was rest. The concoction hit strong enough that he fell into dreamless sleep for many hours, the silent darkness welcome. He moved through a cycle of deep sleep over the next two days, punctuated with brief waking for sustenance and more treatments.

This time when he awoke, refreshment coursed throughout his body, enough that the lingering dull aches were tolerable.

"Hey there, little pup," came a familiar voice by his side.

Olaf slouched over on a stool next to his cot, his arms resting atop the edge of the bed. As usual, his hair stood out in wild pieces, and he was clean-shaven, wearing light-brown linen clothing and fresh wrappings around his left forearm.

Dimitar smiled as he eased himself into a sitting position, scrubbing the last of the medicinal sleep from his eyes.

"The war is ending," Olaf said with a grin of his own.

Dimitar froze, a range of emotions crossing his face.

"The Corrupted filth have been scatterin' since High Knight Rippold fell," Olaf said, but Dimitar interrupted him.

"Don't call him that," Dimitar said tersely, his voice still raspy. "The High Knight title—Rippold doesn't deserve it."

"Aye," Olaf agreed, then continued. "I caught some reports comin' in from the field. The Corrupted lost their cohesion and drive, all at once. Our forces overtook them, and they've been on the run back to the Eastern Mountains since yesterday. 'Tisn't a battle anymore, 'tis a chase. General Bela'Ruhn is personally leadin' a squadron to hunt down every last one o' the bastards."

"Is King Kahled with him?"

"No, lad, he's here recuperating," Olaf said with a twinkle in his eye, "along with someone else."

"Kaleela." Dimitar exhaled her name, and Olaf answered with a grin. "I want to see her."

Catching the tension in Dimitar's voice, Olaf said, "She's gonna be al'right."

"You saved her, you know. If not for you, it would've been too late... the guards, they would've been too—"

"But it wasn't," Olaf interrupted, giving Dimitar a half-hearted swipe upside the head. "I watched her, just like ya asked me to. And when she needed help, I knew what I had to do. Even if it meant not stayin' to see the sonofabitch done in. More's the pity."

Dimitar laughed out loud, cringing as his shoulder panged. Even with his arm complaining, the laughter felt pretty damn good. He dressed himself, slow and awkward with the sling holding his arm close to his body, and Olaf helped him manage the fresh jerkin over his torso. He reached for his armor tucked off to the side before realizing he didn't need it anymore. Strapping on his boots, Dimitar favored his bandaged ankle but was able to bear weight.

A healer entered the tent with a tray of light food, motioning for Dimitar to eat in a way that left no room for argument.

"Eat up, lad, and bring that strength back," Olaf said, eyeing the warm loaf, dried cuts of meat, and fresh apple next to a wooden cup filled with steaming coffee.

Dimitar forced himself to partake in the breakfast, and his energy returned. Stepping into the new day's sunlight, he noted it had rained at some point, surprised he'd slept through a storm. The air no longer held the pervasive stench of foulness, blood, and death; dampness settled the dusty air. A clean breeze rolled through, and lingering moisture caressed his skin.

Less than half of the elves remained around the encampment to the battlefield just beyond. Many soldiers returned to Quinthal to spread the news of victory and send back helpers. The rest stayed behind for the painstaking side of post-war: cleanup. Elves darted from tent to tent, loosening spikes from the ground and tucking the canvas into taut rolls. Excess food was wrapped in large leaves and packed onto wagons. Olaf shared that the remaining troops hoped to bring all the goods back to Quinthal in one trip, gathering and sorting gear.

Carried by the wind came the unmistakable notes of music. In the distance, he spotted an elf sitting with his legs crossed on a tall pillar of stone, a wooden instrument at his lips. The tune played through the air, off the stone boulders around the battlefield, and carried well into the horizon. Mournful and haunting, the notes sent a chill up Dimitar's spine. An entire group of elves searched the ground for their fallen comrades, kneeling beside each one and saying a silent prayer, lifting bodies out of the carnage. The music conveyed a true warrior's song: a funeral air.

Soon they arrived at an expansive tent marked by Quinthal's green and purple flags embellished with the sun-framed tree crest. Dimitar pulled back the flap of the private tent with caution, mindful of the stern warnings from the exiting healer to not agitate the resting princess. He expected to find Kaleela lying undisturbed on a bed, fragile and weakened from her ordeal.

Instead, she sat propped against the headboard by several pillows, a small meal picked through on a side table next to her. A healthy, cool flush colored her skin, and her movements were strong. On a chair next to her bedside sat Rialyn, her arm bandaged and immobile in a sling like his own. The two women spoke in elvish, connected in conversation.

"Hello, my lady."

Kaleela's eyes sparkled at him, and his heart gave a squeeze. She reached for him as he crossed to her bedside, pulling on his extended hand so that he sat beside her on the cot. She tugged him closer, then touched his bandaged arm, her fingers light and soothing as they traced upward to the bruises around his neck, noting every scar and wound. Her gaze searched his, and Dimitar smiled as he captured her hand, fingers entwining, bringing them to his lips.

Rialyn commented in elvish, and Kaleela shot her a scandalized look.

"Rialyn," Olaf greeted her, coming to stand behind Dimitar, "I'm sorry for ya and yer fallen brother. 'Tis a great sorrow, and I wish he wasn't taken from ya."

He saluted her and Dimitar did the same, placing a fist on his chest and bowing his head in respect.

Rialyn nodded at the two men, her eyes cool, her posture relaxed. "My people will bring our dead back to the Sun'Din. They, along with my brother, will be laid beneath memory trees in the sacred grove. He'll be remembered."

"I'll raise a toast to him m'self," Olaf said, adding in a grumble, "if I can find anything worth drinkin' 'round here."

To that, Rialyn reached into her vest and withdrew a flask.

"Oooh," Olaf said and made his way over to her side.

Dimitar turned to Kaleela. By the gods, he craved to be near her. He'd always yearn for her now.

"You look wonderful," he said truthfully. "How are you feeling?"

"I'm a little sleepy but other than that, good. The healers won't let me out of this bed, though. You should've seen their faces when I asked to get up and put my armor back on."

Dimitar laughed and squeezed her hand. Kaleela was thoughtful for a moment, then her voice lowered when she spoke.

"I don't remember much after... after I passed out. I drifted in and out, because I wondered where you were and also sensed my father nearby. Everything hurt. Your voice sounded as if from a distance, and I wanted so much to be with you. But it was like slipping into darkness, and I couldn't stop it from happening. All I felt then was scared, alone, fading." Kaleela paused, the corners of her mouth pulling down.

"Don't get caught up in the past." Dimitar brushed his lips over her knuckles again, and she blushed a rose pink.

"I remember this sudden jolt, and all at once I was filled with indescribable... well, life. That's the last I can recall until waking just a bit ago."

As she described the very events that unfolded before him, Dimitar again experienced all the accompanying emotions. He drew a deep breath and caressed her hair in solace, running his fingers through the silky strands.

"I can't tell you what might've happened if not for Willem and Olaf," he said. "Willem saved you with one of his spells. Whatever he did was a miracle; knocked him right off his feet," he added with a little smile. He cleared his throat, trying to shake the scratchiness. "Olaf, he saved you too, because he's the one who went to find Mage Willem before—"

Dimitar bit off the last of his words with a shake of his head, unwilling to finish the thought. Kaleela searched his face, then laid a hand on his cheek.

"And you"—she drew his gaze up to meet hers—"you saved me too. I can tell you've been hurt. Whatever you did, you were true to me, my father, and all our honor."

The truth and insight of her words struck Dimitar, and he closed his eyes and leaned into her touch.

Olaf hiccupped once, then came over to scoop Kaleela into a bear hug. Pulling apart, Olaf placed a large, wet kiss on both of her cheeks before once again drawing Kaleela into a tremendous embrace. She was left winded and flushed when Olaf stood back.

"I'm glad yer awake, Princess. For a while, I wasn't sure you'd make it." Olaf paused, the words hanging in his throat. "Thank you for savin' my life. Ya almost died for me, and I'll not forget it. Next time, don't be riskin' yer life for me."

Kaleela took hold of Olaf's arm. The simple gesture and warm touch quieted the large man.

"Hush, Olaf." She held his bandaged forearm with gentle hands. "We all made sacrifices."

"I'll not forget it," he said again.

"And to all of you..." Kaleela searched for the words as her voice caught. She placed her hand over her heart, a gesture of thanks. "Conrad has been avenged."

Rialyn extended the flask, and Olaf took it without even a glance, tossing back a swig. He offered a sip to Kaleela, who laughed and waved him away.

The flap at the tent entrance pushed aside as a guardswoman and healer entered. The guardswoman spoke first to Rialyn, giving a status report, and Rialyn stood to accompany her out. The healer spoke as well, and Rialyn translated for the men.

348

"She's requesting more rest for the princess." Rialyn gestured for them to take their leave. She raised one eyebrow as Kaleela began to object.

"Ohh... you're not asking, are you," Kaleela said.

Rialyn smiled back, pleased at this. On her way out, she turned to Olaf.

"Keep it." She threw him a wink and exited the tent.

Olaf slipped the flask into his pocket and sighed. "By the gods, I'm so in love."

The men left to the peal of Kaleela's laughter.

"I'll be back this afternoon," Dimitar promised.

"I hope so."

Pushing past the tent flap, Dimitar inhaled the air's freshness, made even sweeter by Kaleela's recovery. "Do you know where King Kahled is?"

Olaf pointed to the next tent over.

"Give me a minute."

Dimitar headed over and ducked inside. Kahled sat on a padded chair at a small table on the far side of the tent, his back to the entrance, engaged in written correspondence. Dimitar cleared his throat with a wince, the medicines starting to wear off.

"Your Majesty," Dimitar said, announcing his presence.

"Come in, lad." Kahled pointed to a chair a couple strides from his own.

He didn't yet look up as he finished scribing thought to paper, the quill's scratch the only sound in the tent. Dimitar found himself transported back to Blackburn's throne room at that moment, reminded of the day that started the entire journey with Kahled's singular request. How long ago it seemed, a time of innocence he'd never recapture.

He'd never miss it.

Kahled set aside his quill and turned to face him, and Dimitar inhaled sharply.

Kahled's face was battered and bruised, scrapes and cuts lining his forehead and chin. His nose appeared broken, not for the first time, and his shoulders hunched as if trying to keep weight off his injuries. Dimitar spotted thick bandaging under the layered clothing, from midsection to his shoulder. Kahled seemed aged beyond his years, the creases in his face more pronounced and his skin sun-worn. For a brief moment, Dimitar almost didn't know the man before him.

Kahled's eyes, though, normally dark and infinite, held warmth and compassion. The elder king extended a comforting smile, both sympathetic and tender, as he surveyed Dimitar.

"You're looking worse for wear," Kahled observed.

"I thought the same about you. Sire," Dimitar added, forgetting his place.

Kahled laughed heartily, flinching as he triggered aches anew in his body. "I received word from Blackburn." He gestured to the letters as he settled back into his seat. "The Corrupted didn't reach our borders, thank the gods, though damn them for trying. Stormgard was also unharmed. Arrowsfall and its cities to our east held the Corrupted back."

Kahled hesitated, his eyes growing haunted. "Because Blackburn's force is... reduced, Sir Talin kept the city walls closed, save for refugees from other towns, and held our defenses in the city. We couldn't send aid across the Green Lands. Our people were spared, but many weren't so lucky. There's much to rebuild across the land."

The weight of the world settled on the king's shoulders once more. *Would he ever be free from it?*

"My lord, how can I be of service to you?"

Kahled leaned forward in his chair and clasped his hands together, thinking. "I asked you to guard my daughter all those weeks ago. I picked you for a reason, Dimitar, and you've never failed me. Many men would've run for their lives and forgotten their duties. You stood your ground before monsters and worse, and I'm indebted to you for my daughter's life, as well as my own. I'm proud of you, Dimitar. More than you know."

Dimitar bowed his head to cover the flush of pride reddening his cheeks.

"The question is not what you can do further for me," Kahled said, "but what can I do for you?"

Dimitar blinked, caught off guard. He could ask for damn near anything in Kahled's power right now, and the king would grant it to him.

I know exactly what I want.

"I'd like for us to go home," he replied, and Kahled smiled.

62

DIMITAR

Dimitar paced the middle of the castle suite. The shutters of the closest window were thrown open, sunlight and warmth streaming in, early autumn's colors beginning to tint the trees. Voices talking and laughing in the courtyard provided a steady background hum, the mood around the castle upbeat. Refreshments filled a side table, and servants and squires bustled about in assistance. Lush, velvet-lined chairs curved in a semi-circle around an unused fireplace, but Dimitar couldn't sit. Despite the lavish surroundings—and in part because of them—his nerves ignited and wouldn't settle.

What happens after your life's wish comes true?

Adorned in Blackburn's full ceremonial regalia, he wore a dark gray tunic layered under the deep-blue knighthood uniform and topped with a dress of chainmail down to his thigh. A leather belt cinched his waist, and a scabbard belt hung on his hips. Blackburn's emblem of three entwined circles, sewed with silver thread shining in the day's light, graced the back of a ceremonial cloak draped across his upper chest and over his shoulders. Metal bracers encircled his forearms, and his black leather boots gleamed.

Olaf strode up, dressed in equal attire with his left sleeve pinned up mid-forearm. He came to a stop when they were toe to toe, breaking Dimitar's nervous pacing, and scowled down at his friend.

"Ach. They're lettin' anyone into the knighthood these days," Olaf said, without humor.

"Is that so?" Dimitar replied, deadpan.

"So t'would seem. And do ya know what I heard?" Without waiting for an answer, he went on. "I heard they're only wantin' the most disciplined, strongest, hardened bodies in the army." Olaf gave Dimitar a slow once-over, his eyes narrowing. "Unless they've dropped their standards."

Dimitar held Olaf's fearsome gaze. "You know what I heard?"

"What's that?"

A heartbeat passed between the two squared-off men.

"I heard they only let the prettiest eyes into the knighthood."

Olaf and Dimitar stared each other down a moment more. Olaf broke first, bending over in a long wheeze of laughter while Dimitar's shoulders shook with silent mirth.

"Lad, for the love o' the gods," Olaf said in between gasps, "ya can't be puttin' that thought in m'head, not when I hafta' go stand before King Kahled and Sir Talin and the lot, lookin' 'em dead in the eye. You've wrecked me, ya have."

Some of the nervousness eased from his body as Dimitar laughed along with his friend. A month had passed since they departed the battlefield up north. The elven medicines sped their healing and allowed them to journey back to Blackburn within the week. Coming back to a life and city that carried on as usual gave Dimitar an out-of-sorts feeling, but that faded each day as he adjusted.

His biggest ache was leaving Kaleela's side. She and Kahled immersed themselves in the kingdom's affairs, long delayed from their absences and in coordination with the surrounding cities and villages. Sir Talin and the other troop leaders swept up Dimitar and Olaf. The First Knight wanted all the details of their journey, then directed the two men to consult with troop leaders on the task of rebuilding their forces. Dimitar and Olaf were welcomed back without any castigation. The city received them as heroes.

A servant stepped around them to answer a knock at the suite door. Dimitar sensed who waited on the other side before the door even opened. Amidst all the activity, Dimitar had received word from one other on his way, and he counted down the hours until arrival that very day.

Ral stood in the doorway, his cloak latched with a silver brooch. He lowered his hood as Dimitar approached and wrapped him in a fierce hug.

"By the gods, it's good to see you," Dimitar said, happiness pinned like a medal upon his chest. Olaf joined them, clapping Ral on the shoulder then bringing him into his signature bear hug.

Ral motioned to their shining appearances. 'Look at the two of you.'

"Am I... am I *too* good lookin'?" Olaf asked, unsuccessfully smoothing back his hair.

'Always,' Ral signed.

Olaf roared with laughter as he stepped over to the refreshment table to pour Ral a drink.

"We have some time before the ceremony," Dimitar said. "Did Master Karn receive the letter from King Kahled?"

Ral nodded, taking the goblet from Olaf with thanks.

"Then you'll stay to catch up with us, and of course speak with Kahled," Dimitar said. "He has a room for you here in the castle. But... your message said nothing about while you were gone. Can you tell us what happened, with you and Master Karn?"

Ral took a drink, then set the cup aside as he motioned, 'I cannot.' At Dimitar's raised eyebrow, he continued, 'I'd tell you if I could, but I don't remember any of it.'

"Any o' what?" Olaf asked, frowning.

'We made it to the Eastern Mountains. I remember standing at the entrance and a bit of navigating through the tunnels, and then...' Ral held up his hands in a shrug.

"It's 'cause of that Karn, isn't it," Olaf grumbled as if personally offended.

'Master Karn,' Ral signed.

"Olaf's just being protective," Dimitar said with a wave toward the large man. "We were worried for you—all of us. I can tell you, though, Kahled received good tidings from the southern cities. He tells us the goblin army fell not long after the Corrupted. 'Tis strange to hear of it... a faction of Corruptors and goblins fought their way united until reaching the kingdom of Tildare, and then the reports say they turned on each other. Fighting one another at the gates over control of the city."

Ral nodded in agreement. 'The Lachans aided the southern cities along the Tempest. They stood with our kind against the goblin army.'

Olaf let out a low whistle. "Now that I'd like to hear about," he said, a gleam in his tactician's eye.

A sharp rap at the door interrupted further discussion. This time, Sir Talin himself entered the room with a small armed escort.

"Gentlemen. 'Tis time," he said in greeting. "The king awaits your presence."

Ral raised his hood, bowed to Dimitar and Olaf, and signed a quick message to them. 'No one deserves this ceremony more than you.'

Ral stepped aside as Sir Talin and his accompaniment ushered the men toward the open-aired hallway leading to the courtyard. Staff tended the grass and flowers throughout the summer, the plot flourishing and fresh. A number of chairs lined the walls to either side, the occupants on their feet and applauding the men, raising drinks in toast as they made their way through the crowd.

At the other side of the courtyard, marble steps ascended to a small terrace with carved railings. The pathway arrived at a pair of large, wooden doors leading to the main interior of Castle Blackburn. Opened wide, the doors stood above the courtyard, the entrance casting long shadows obscuring the chamber beyond. Dimitar's smile faltered as he gazed past the darkness. It wasn't so much that he walked toward the door as that the unlit entrance expanded to meet him, laden with his fate.

Passing through the entryway, the two men proceeded to a small antechamber and turned the last shadowed corner into the throne room. The vision greeting them transformed Dimitar's concern to serenity.

Hundreds of candles lined the main walkway to the thrones. Sir Talin led the procession, Blackburn's remaining knights and guardsmen flanking the aisle in rank formation. Sunlight flooded into the room through a picturesque window high in the chamber onto the two main thrones. Kahled presided, his face serious and kind. Kaleela sat beside him, a vision of beauty and strength. Even without the light shining on father and daughter, they illuminated the room with their grace and love. Although he kept his face solemn, Dimitar's heart softened.

Neither Dimitar nor Olaf ever recalled afterwards the walk between the entrance and thrones, where they then knelt before Kahled and Kaleela, heads bowed in respect. Recalling the words taught by Blackburn's royal council, the men broke the silence of the room.

"We come before you, Your Majesty, to ask for your guidance," they recited together.

In response, King Kahled rose from his throne. Two pages approached, each presenting a sword. King Kahled lifted the polished blades, turning back and lowering them to rest on the inside shoulder of the two kneeling men. His voice resonated through the hall as he began the ritual.

"To fight in life, not with brawn or recklessness, but with skill and thought—this is a knight's bravery."

Kahled raised the blades and placed them on the outside shoulder.

"To protect, not for glory or fame, but for love and decency—this is a knight's heart."

The swords rested again on the inside shoulder.

"To judge the enemy, not in terms of death or revenge, but with respect and appraisal—this is a knight's honor."

This time, Kahled turned the sword points to the ground and held them out.

"Rise, Dimitar and Olaf of Blackburn." Kaleela's voice carried just as powerfully in the hall as her father's. "Do you, Olaf, vow to uphold a knight's bravery, heart, and honor with wisdom and valor?"

Olaf placed his grip on the sword's handle. "By this blade, I vow it."

Kaleela turned to face Dimitar, meeting his gaze. Sparks flew through his body, his heart swallowed by his desire. His lips raised at the corners before returning to the seriousness the ritual proclaimed.

"And do you, Dimitar, vow to uphold a knight's bravery, heart, and honor with wisdom and valor?"

Dimitar took the sword. "By this blade, I vow it."

Kahled released his hold on the swords, finishing the transfer of knighthood. Dimitar and Olaf sheathed the blades into the empty scabbards hanging at their sides. Only when the handle landed with a small clink did Dimitar fully comprehend what they'd accomplished. Their childhood dreams had come true.

"Let us show the rest of the city its two newest guardians," Kahled proclaimed.

The hall filled with thunderous applause and cheers from the knights and guardsmen. Dimitar and Olaf bowed in service once more, then turned toward the doors. As customary, Kahled would lead them outside, followed by the new knights, and Kaleela completing the procession.

As they entered the dimly lit antechamber, Dimitar couldn't wait any longer. He faced Kaleela, taking her arm and pulling her aside until they were alone. She stepped toward him, clasping his forearm, and his breath caught in his throat.

Dressmakers fashioned Kaleela's gown to match the color of her eyes, a difficult task. At first glance, the tailors did a wondrous job. Now, as he gazed into her emerald eyes, nothing made by the hands of anyone but the gods could hope to contain such brilliance. Dimitar shifted closer, bringing his hands to her waist. The entire world vanished, leaving a vision of pure, flawless beauty caught between candlelight and sunlight. His heart spoke its promise.

"I've watched you almost my entire life, and our fate was sealed even before this journey. Your joy, your strength, your passion, are my vows. I would do anything for you, and all I wish is for you to be happy and safe. The path is clear before me when I'm with you. I love you."

The words relieved a pressure strapped around his chest. Emotions poured through his body like a released dam, his skin tingling. Kaleela's upturned face blossomed into a smile, and she wrapped her arms around his neck. Dimitar caressed his hands up from her waist, running them across the back of her smooth gown and through her silken hair. They both pulled at the same time, mouths and bodies drawn together with each other's unleashed passion.

Their lips met in perfect union, fiery warmth racing through his body. Dimitar cupped her face as his mouth melted over hers. Her lips parted under his, and he took the kiss deeper, eager. His hand swept down upon the curve of her neck, craving the softness of her exposed skin. Kaleela gasped at his touch, and Dimitar pulled back, trying to slow down, but she plunged her hands into his hair, just as reckless. He hungrily bent to her again, capturing her willing lips and exploring the taste and feel of her sweetness. A small sound escaped from her throat as his hands slid to her hips, shifting her closer before moving up her body. Nothing was ever as good, as right.

Finally, he was home.

Dimitar's love enveloped her, an unfailing shield, even as the kiss ended and became a warm embrace as they both caught their breaths.

"My love is yours," she said, her lips a caress against the side of his mouth.

With Kaleela's tender declaration, the entire world came rushing back to Dimitar. The candles, the weight of the new blade at his side, the sunlight peeking through the doorway, all seemed foreign and new to his eyes. Their kiss forever changed his world.

Before they rejoined the others, Kaleela paused and, with a sweet grin, smoothed aside the lock of hair on his forehead that still refused to stay in place. Dimitar lifted her hand to his lips, placing a kiss on top of her fingers. They continued to hold hands as they walked to where the men waited. Kahled and Olaf stood at the top of the stairs, their knowing smiles brighter than the sunlight shining behind them.

"To hells with custom," Kahled said as they lined up, not in a formal straight line but side by side: Olaf flanking Kaleela as she held Dimitar's hand, and Kahled next to them. They stepped out into the daylight, and the entire world exploded with applause and cheers. The courtyard now overflowed with Blackburn's people.

Ral stood at the base of the stairs and bowed low to the group as they descended. He glanced over Dimitar's and Kaleela's clasped hands, and Dimitar could've sworn the man winked under his hood. Ral stepped aside to let the troop pass, only to be pulled back by Olaf. The big man wrapped his arm around Ral's shoulder and drew him into the group.

The king, two knights, a half-elven princess, and a thief accepted the applause of a nation as they crossed the courtyard to the festival in the city beyond.

The End

ACKNOWLEDGEMENTS

This novel is the culmination of a decades-long endeavor through winding paths and remarkable sidequests. We'd be remiss if we didn't give our gratitude to those who helped along the way.

A number of friends and family read very early drafts, and we appreciate your telling us how great the story sounded then, even though it wasn't ready. Your enthusiasm helped us to keep going and tackle repeated improvements. Recent beta readers provided invaluable feedback and helped focus our revisions. A huge thanks to Shannon, Meagan, Vera, Mike, Becky, Ian, Bridgett, Keith, Clementine, Irma, Az, and the Elemental Authority for your thoughtful comments and suggestions. The story shines all the brighter because of your insights. Becky deserves a special thank you for steering us into the world of editing, which truly set off an elevation to this story.

Keith and Molly provided advice on blacksmithing and equine behavior, respectively. It should go without saying that all things accurate are due to their generous expertise, and any mistakes come from us.

We thank Claire Andrews for her guidance and support from the start of our publishing journey; her freely given advice helped ease us into the industry and steer our way. (Go buy her books.) We're also humbled by her and the authors who read and provided words of praise for *In the Name of Honor*: Kaitlin Corvus, Katie Abdou, C.W. Rose, Erica Rose Eberhart, and Kassidy Coursey. (Go buy their books.)

Courtney extends a heartfelt group hug to Christine, Erica, and Kassidy for the daily support, levity, and commiseration we share as we fulfill our publishing dreams together. There's not enough cheese and sin in the world to show how much she adores each of you.

We're very grateful to Shadow Spark Publishing and its authors for accepting us with such a warm welcome. We'd like to recognize our impeccable editors, Kaitlin Corvus and Ashley Anglin, for adding the extra polish to truly make our narrative sing. Our gratitude also goes to Azshure Raine for the gorgeous interior formatting that shaped our story into a real-life book.

Thank you to the artists who brought our cover and world map to life. David Gardias designed a cover that truly stands on its own, and Black Meadow VT added the horrific, perfect Corruptor art. Tiffany Munro created the map, turning our sketches into reality and bringing us that much closer into the world of Mirodaigne.

Writing is long hours living inside make-believe worlds, delving into the depths of lore, and pressing onward in the face of all obstacles. We cherish our friends and family who have championed us, and who gave us your excitement every step of the way. Thank you for sticking by us with your support and love.

Most of all, to our children, Muirin and Tor, we love you and your ability to extend understanding to Momma and Daddy when we needed time to write. We hope you enjoyed the extra screen time.

ABOUT THE AUTHORS

Megan Elizabeth Photography

Courtney grew up two doors down from the local library and crushed every summer reading challenge. She worked in libraries and bookstores before deviating into a higher education career by day and a burlesque dancer by night. She's published extensively in her local town newspaper. She holds a BA from Hamilton College and MSW from Boston University School of Social Work. Her own queerness and mother-loss influence the fantasy world created alongside her husband.

Owen Leavey Photography

Clarke read *The Hobbit* at 10 years old, and has lived in the world of fantasy ever since. When he's not escaping into video games and tabletop realms, he's working hard to improve healthcare. He holds a BA from Hamilton College. He earned a black belt in Shaolin Kung Fu, and has faced more than his fair share of war hammers to the head while weapons training.

Clarke and Courtney reside in Vermont with their two children.

Made in the USA
Middletown, DE
09 February 2025

70660503R00220